# In the Light of Silence

# In the Light of Silence

LINDA CARRILLO

RESOURCE *Publications* · Eugene, Oregon

IN THE LIGHT OF SILENCE

Resource Publications
An Imprint of Wipf and Stock Publishers
199 W. 8th Ave., Suite 3
Eugene, OR 97401

www.wipfandstock.com

PAPERBACK ISBN: 978-1-7252-6068-9
HARDCOVER ISBN: 978-1-7252-6066-5
EBOOK ISBN: 978-1-7252-6067-2

Manufactured in the U.S.A.   04/27/20

For my mother, who taught me to love books,
and
For my father, who taught me to love language.

Let all bitterness, wrath, anger, clamor, and evil speaking be put away from you, with all malice. And be kind to one another, tenderhearted, forgiving one another, even as God in Christ forgave you.

Ephesians 4:31–32

And if a stranger dwells with you in your land, you shall not mistreat him. The stranger who dwells among you shall be to you as one born among you, and you shall love him as yourself; for you were strangers in the land of Egypt: I *am* the LORD your God.

Leviticus 19:33–34

# Prologue

SECONDS OF TERROR.

Next, metal on metal, glass exploding, flesh rending from flesh, bones snapping, my head hitting the steering wheel with unearthly force.

Then nothing.

Silence.

They forced the women and children into huts, the men into the church, and committed the unspeakable, the unthinkable.

Fleeing the screams raised to a God who could not save them, Felipe collapsed to the ground when he could run no farther.

He lost consciousness.

Silence.

# Chapter 1

"No miracles. No guardian angels."

My hand, splinted on thin metal down to the fingertips, wavered over the keyboard and hunted again for the "N." The chaplain waited beside me, not prompting, and I resented her patience, resented the fact that she could have typed this message in mindless seconds. I longed for the day when my reconstructed jaw, now wired shut, would have healed well enough for me to speak.

"No visions. No holy messengers."

My hand jerked in an uncontrollable spasm, and my arm slid off the communication board clamped to the chair. With my arm back in place, I continued typing. When I punched the button to play back the words, the board's atonal voice repeated, "No belief in God."

The chaplain said, "But Kate, you survived the collision, and you're progressing better than anyone expected. Everyone said there was no earthly reason you should be alive right now."

Ah, but there were earthly reasons, and I had expected this argument from her. I searched for the keys, their locations slipping out of my memory as quickly as salamanders darting in and out of rocks. The chaplain had been visiting me a couple of times a week since I'd arrived at the rehab center. Sometimes we sat together in silence out in the courtyard. When she saw my light on at night, she'd slip in and read poetry to me, her voice too soft to awaken my roommate. The patterned cadences of the poems bloomed into a monstrous lie that order and reason existed, a lie I was willing to accept in exchange for the distraction. I pressed the button and the voice hovered between us, the vowels twining around each other. "Rescue squad, surgeons' skills. My body's strength. My parents. My hard work. My will, not God's."

"You really feel this way?"

My face contorted with the effort to find and press the keys, my shoulders hunching forward. The letters scrolled across the small screen facing me, and the voice answered with gratifying finality, the words a buoy bell's clanging. "Yes. Go save someone else."

Later at night, I navigated the wheelchair into the courtyard. Tipping against the wheelchair's brace for my head, I looked at the stars, the moon, the faint fretwork of tree branches against the sky. The idea occurred simply, encapsulated in a glistening bubble of certainty: I could reinvent myself. When I left the rehab center, I could go where no one knew me and present myself as a different person. I had always done what was expected, followed the rules, colored inside the lines. I showed up for appointments ten minutes early, turned in library books on time, and never tried to sneak the thirteenth item into the twelve-item-limit line. I played it safe. My life was as precise as a porcupine's quills.

Wheeling the chair in a slow, halting circle, I thought if I went far enough away, people would only know what I chose to tell them. I stopped the chair at this thought, my skin tingling on my fingertips: I didn't even have to tell anyone the truth.

Damn you, I cursed the drunk driver who'd crashed into me. May you have sleepless nights for the rest of your life

The city's lights arced from the road, a twinkling sweep of a fisherman's net cast far into the darkening twilight. It had been a long time since I'd felt such a frisson of anticipation, prompted by a delicious freedom from the rehab center and medical appointments, mixed with a sense of hopefulness. Weeks earlier, I'd rented a cabin in Drake's Springs, a rural town in the Shenandoah Valley of Virginia. A couple of hours from my apartment in Chantilly, near Washington, D.C., it was far enough away to give me the feeling of a fresh beginning.

The roads narrowed and became rougher. As the sun sank below the horizon, my eyes ached from trying to imagine the turns beyond the headlights, but I knew I was close to the cabin. Having been here once after answering the ad, I looked for my landmark. Yes, there was the bridge, and the first road to the right was what I wanted. The dirt lane carved through the woods for almost a quarter of a mile and ended in a clearing in front of the cabin.

Stopping the car, I sat in the silence. No one was making me do this, and I could go back, simply say I'd changed my mind. The problem, however, was that my mind had been changed for me. I sat suspended in this moment of decision. I could turn back. "Decide, Kate. Go in or go back." The cabin looked sturdy and quiet, as though it were waiting for my commitment. It calmed me. Go in, I told myself. Don't hesitate, no splinters of doubt. I grabbed what I would need for the night and headed for the door.

The cabin was uncluttered and furnished with basic pieces, old but well crafted. Drawn to the plainness of everything, I wondered if I could fashion a life like this house—pared down, scaled back, and focused on what was essential. Standing in the living room, I felt myself relax for the first time since leaving the city. Studying the room, trying to discern why it satisfied some yearning within me, I realized it contained only what was needed, no more and no less. I welcomed its simplicity, and its serenity made me feel cocooned, safe.

Perched on the fireplace's raised hearth, I called my parents and my boyfriend, David Shannon, to let them know I'd arrived. When I'd made my decision, my parents had protested the move, unsure if I were ready. It was David's reaction I hadn't expected, a tepid, "Whatever you think you need to do," as though he didn't care one way or the other. Last, I called my best friend, Diane Moravec, whom I'd known since first grade. "I'm here," I told her.

"Are you nervous? Scared? Excited?"

"Yes, yes, and yes."

"Kate, remember to get out of your own way."

Were there any blueprints for reinventing yourself, some sort of self-help guides at the bookstore? The enormity of what lay ahead expanded inside me and became water balloons of worry. How to begin and where and with what? I was a biochemist at the Neuroimmunology Research Institute in Fairfax, Virginia, or at least I had been. If I could no longer be a scientist, what could I become? Reconstruction. Was that in my power to create? These concerns were in addition to my official reason for being here: I'd been granted a year's sabbatical, delayed because of the accident. This significant gift of time to think deeply without interruptions needed to count.

After a simple dinner of soup and a salad, I felt refreshed. Eager to be organized from the beginning, I unpacked, set up my office, and created order in the cabin. Few things brought more peace to my soul than order.

At last, I filled the tub for a bubble bath. In the bathroom's mirror, I saw a younger version of my mother looking back at me: auburn hair and green eyes, a small, curved nose, and a slight frame. No single feature was more prominent than the other except for the scars from the accident. They arched over my scalp and snaked along the hairline of my forehead, under my chin, and down my neck. A crooked line extended from my left breast, down my side, and across the front of my body. One long scar angled from my left knee to the ankle. My arms would never fully extend, my fingers' strength and flexibility were compromised, my balance and coordination were poor, and my neck's mobility was reduced. It was quite the litany. What was the phrase? Battle scars? Won the battle but lost the war? Or was it lost the battle but won the war? No matter which expression was right, I didn't know which one applied to me. I thought of Humpty Dumpty with his jagged, eggshell cracks.

Slipping into the red bathtub, a monstrosity with knobby toes, I let the water lap my chin. Lifting my arms, I watched the water drip down and break the bubbles along my sides. Water. Birth and rebirth. Baptism. Reinvention. I could reinvent myself as an eccentric person like my Aunt Constanza, who was technically my great-aunt. Because my father had received a scholarship for post-graduate study, my parents had moved to Barcelona when I was two. We lived there for five years; later, while in high school, I returned to Barcelona as an exchange student and lived with former neighbors.

I had visited Aunt Constanza in Zaragoza when I was an exchange student. She, my father claimed, straddled the line between genius and lunacy. She'd recently returned from a trip to Greece where she'd traveled with a group of seven monks, telling me, "It's the safest way to travel, my dear, you should try it." Constanza was a believer in signs, omens, and visions; and after spending time with her in Spain, I realized all the stories about her in our family lore were true.

During my visit, she took me on a tour of her village and introduced me to people as flamboyant as she was, making me admit that in comparison, I existed on the sidelines, on a plane of dull safety. Although I didn't want to mirror her eccentricity, I admired Aunt Constanza for following her own spirit, for not being afraid, for reaching out for adventures without reservations. I had always been cautious, but the accident had made me fearful. I might be able to reconstruct my life, but could I reinvent my essential personality? "I don't want to be afraid all the time." I heaped the bubble bath foam into my hands and blew the bubbles off my palms. "I will not give him that."

Determined to make a good start, I spread out my cell culture log and my lab notebook and began outlining a conference presentation to be given after my sabbatical. When I read the first page of my notes, the technical language and the discussion of the experiment's design and resulting data seemed familiar, but it was like words half-heard in a noisy room. When language had begun to return after I emerged from the coma, I couldn't make sense of conjunctions, pronouns, and prepositions. Words like "above," "since," and "with" looked strange even in print to me. Arguing with my father, I'd insist, "They're not words, you're trying to trick me."

I talked myself through the notes, writing the introduction in short spurts. "Step by step. Take it apart, one small thing. Word by word. Sentence by sentence." I wrote a few sentences at a time then read them aloud. Completing two pages after an hour, I threw the notes across the room and ran out of the house, the door slamming behind me in a sharp clap of punctuation.

I leaned against a tree trunk and slid to the ground. "Ha! That attempt went well." Picking up a fallen leaf, I twirled it between my fingers and traced its veins, finally letting the breeze lift away the dry pieces. This first full day had dragged by, the hours ticking off in their own humid pace.

I recalled how inexorably time had passed at the rehab center. For weeks on end, my limbs had been stretched and manipulated every possible way for thousands of repetitions. I had struggled to button my shirts and zip my pants; to pull myself along the parallel bars until slipping on my own sweat; and, when my jaw healed, to reshape garbled sounds until they became recognizable words. I relearned how to hold a fork, write a check, make a bed, and set a table. Now, I was walking, speaking, and driving. I had been put back together as well as possible. Humpty Dumpty came to mind again.

Would I still be here at Thanksgiving, three months from now? I tugged leaves from a low branch and shredded them like daisy petals. I thought of Annie Sullivan, Helen Keller's teacher. She'd considered giving up to be a sin. I stood, announcing, "I will not give in, not to him. Not to words, either." I yelled toward the woods, "Do you hear me? I will not give in!"

Damn you. May you be reminded of what you've done to me every time you drive.

A number of residential streets surrounded Drake's Springs, but otherwise, most people lived out in the countryside. The official town consisted of four major streets, and so far, I'd seen three traffic lights. I parked the car and walked, cataloguing two banks, a number of churches, a drugstore, a general store, some restaurants, and a group of offices. Down a side street I saw a school and a sign for a community park.

Opening the screen door of Drake's Springs General Store and stepping inside, I let my eyes get used to the dim light. A lunch counter extended along one wall, and six rows of merchandise continued far back into the store. Grocery items stocked the first three rows; the remaining aisles contained household needs and a jumble of miscellaneous items. Obviously, there were no "big-box" stores in this town, and if you wanted something, this would be your sole option. Searching for something green and growing and hopeful for the house, I wandered around and looked for a garden section.

"Hello, be of help to you?" a woman behind the lunch counter called to me. She mopped the counter with one hand and refilled someone's coffee cup with the other. Through an opening behind her, I glimpsed someone cooking in the kitchen.

"Yes, do you have any seeds for herbs?"

"What kind?"

I hesitated, not knowing anything about herbs, thinking instead of dishes with spices in them. Were spices and herbs the same thing? Had I come in for something else? The woman continued to look at me, raising an eyebrow. Potato soup, I thought for no reason. Did potato soup have spices in it?

"Maybe basil or thyme?" she suggested. "They're easy to grow, and we've got a few packets of those." Her speech had the hallmarks of the mountain lilt I'd already heard in this region. She looked to be in her forties, with her dark brown hair streaked with gray and combed back from a widow's peak. Her face was lightly freckled, and she wore no makeup other than lipstick. She struck me as a woman who didn't care what others thought of her.

"I'm Maggie Mackenzie." She extended her hand to me over the counter. "You must be the scientist renting the Drury place."

"Katherine Solterra. Kate. And yes, I am. How did you know?"

"In a place small as this? What do you think we do for entertainment? Cup of coffee and some pie? On the house to welcome you." She reached beneath the counter and pulled out cups and saucers of heavy, white cafeteria china like we'd had at the rehab center.

"Thanks, I'd like that."

"Are you getting settled in all right? How's the Drury place working out for you?"

"It's a great place." Wonderful, I thought, except for words tangling together, warring for space and meaning and memory. Stop, I told myself. The coffee was restorative, the homemade apple pie a thing of wonder; I focused on the sound of her voice until the nattering in my mind receded.

"What kind of scientist are you? What do you do?"

"I'm a biochemist for a research institute, primarily studying therapies for multiple sclerosis. I'm on a sabbatical to do some intensive research and writing." I had practiced this response until I could say it fluently and feel a certain distance from it.

A man came in through the swinging doors leading to the kitchen. "This is my oldest, my son Charles. We run the store together. This is the scientist who's renting the Drury place, Kate Solterra."

"I go by Cooper," he said. He had his mother's wavy hair and freckles. His nose looked like it had been broken once, and his uncombed hair fell over his forehead. "Pleased to meet you, Kate. Welcome to Drake's Springs."

Chatting about the town, they filled me in on the area. When ready to leave, I chose packages of basil and thyme, and Maggie suggested I grow mint as well. She followed me out to the porch. Picking up one of the pots of marigolds from the railing, she thrust it at me. "Here," she offered. "It'll brighten up your windowsill until your herbs get started. If you need anything, come by, won't you? I'm usually in the store or upstairs. We have two apartments upstairs; my daughter, Abby, and I live in one and Cooper has the other." She didn't mention a husband, and I noticed she was not wearing a wedding band.

Listening to the tone of her voice, I had the feeling she was offering more than the marigold plant, but I wasn't sure I wanted to accept. Remaining somewhat anonymous would be less complicated; after all, I'd be here for less than a full year. "Thanks, Maggie." I glanced at the flowers and smiled. It had been far too long since I'd been given a token of friendship.

Opening the latest *Journal of Neuroimmunology*, I slogged through the article discussing the attempts to trick immature cells into producing myelin, the tissue protecting nerve cells that MS destroys. In a partnership with a group from Johns Hopkins University, my team was working on one aspect of this very issue.

After several hours of reading and notetaking, I needed a break. Lacing up my running shoes, I started stretching. I used to run with David several mornings a week. Although I was not a fan of running, he was, and I pretended to like it in order to spend the time with him. I knew it was good for me, however, and my orthopedic surgeon had advised me to start exercising to regain my strength and flexibility. I felt sluggish and stiff; it was time to start getting back in shape. Heading down my driveway, I gradually increased my speed as I turned onto the main road toward town. I wouldn't be able to walk all the way there yet, but it was a start. Breathing deeply, I loved the sharp scent of the pine trees. I caught a glimpse of a chipmunk on a rock. Had I ever seen one? Living here would connect me to nature in a way the city did not allow.

Veering off onto a spur leading past a few houses, I let my mind wander over the research I'd been reviewing. I missed being in the lab, missed the rhythms of running experiments, looking for changes in proteins, and measuring the interactions between the cell lines and various drugs. I hungered for the lab's orderliness with its shelves of labeled equipment. I even missed the slight humming of the incubator and the bubbling of the water bath that served as white noise and helped me to concentrate. Above all, I craved being immersed in complex problems, spending my days trying to inch the scientific world toward an answer to a mystery.

When I returned to the main road again, I circled back onto the spur. Although not much traffic passed me on the larger road, the side road had none, making it easier for me to focus. The third time down the spur, I saw a man waiting by his mailbox; he raised his hand in greeting. I slowed and came to a stop. He was in his sixties, I estimated, and dressed in worn jeans and a heavy plaid jacket.

"Good mornin', Missy. Are you lost or somethin'?"

"I guess it looks like I am, but no, I keep going back and forth because there's no traffic here."

"Not much traffic anywhere here, but you're from the city, I s'pect."

His speech, like Maggie's, had the musical cadence I'd begun to expect as part of the valley's dialect. I extended my hand to him. "I'm Kate Solterra. I guess I do scream 'city,' don't I?"

"Grady Mulroney. No, I reckon you're not a screamer," he assessed. "I've heard about you. Scientist, right? Wal now, I won't be a'keepin' you, but if you need anything, you call on us, you hear? My wife," he gestured toward a plain bungalow set off from the road, "Delia and me, we don't get out and about much; we're almost always around. I keep a lot of folks in wood for their fireplaces and woodstoves. Don't let those big outfits that put cards in your mailbox charge you too much. And I've got a snowplow, one a' those attachments for my truck, in case you get snowed in. Half-price discount for my reg'lar wood customers."

"I'll definitely keep you in mind, Grady, thank you. I've been wondering what I'd do for wood and plowing. Do you get much snow here?"

"Tolerable. Some years more'n others, of course. I think this year's goin' to be a big one for snow." He tipped the brim of his hat to me as I thanked him and started back to the main road.

Gaining more confidence in my driving, I explored the countryside every week, navigating switchbacks on the narrow, curvy roads and roaming from one small place to another. I was falling in love with these villages sheltered between the Blue Ridge and the Appalachian Mountains with their picturesque shops, vintage houses, country churches, and town squares.

Returning from the grocery store in the neighboring town of Bridge-water, I crested a rise and came upon a horse-drawn Mennonite buggy. I braked and slowed down. I'd seen them from a distance, but this was the first time I'd been directly behind one. Rolling down my window, I enjoyed the horse's steady, rhythmic clopping, an iconic sound of a bygone era, as it made its way along the winding road. The black buggy with the reflective triangle on the back turned into the Dayton Market, a long, rambling building set close to the road. Maggie had described it as having aisles of separate stalls for Mennonite vendors to sell items such as baked goods, quilts, cheese from local dairies, and crafts.

Deciding to check it out, I parked and entered the building. I drifted up and down the aisles, taking in the smells of roasting coffee and fresh breads and pastries. The building itself was utilitarian, but the stalls were full of interesting, practical, and decorative items. I stopped at a booth featuring quilts, wanting to have something unique to the area.

Examining them, I discovered that in addition to the patterns created by the colored fabrics, the stitching for the layers formed intricate designs, as well. The owner of the stall, a young Mennonite woman in a pastel-colored dress, white apron, and organdy cap, greeted me. "Are you interested in a particular one?" she asked.

"They are exquisite. It will be difficult to choose, but I'd love one." She helped me look through the selections until one in shades of purple and blue caught my attention. "This one is my favorite."

"The pattern is called 'Railroad Crossing,' and it was made here in the Shenandoah Valley."

"Did you make it?"

She gave a small nod, as though reluctant to claim such fine work and thereby boast, and quickly added, "Yes, along with my quilting group."

"I'm living here temporarily, but these colors will remind me of the mountains when I leave."

On the way back to the cabin, I found myself thinking of Occam's razor, the principle—often underpinning scientific investigations—that the simplest, most straightforward explanations were usually the best ones. There was an elegance, a purity, to what I'd seen at the Dayton Market: the handmade wooden toys, the jewel-toned jams in glass jars, the women's plain dresses all of the same style. I sensed that these items reflected the lives and values of the Old Order Mennonites. As a research scientist, I drew together disparate elements, but I employed a laser focus on them. Being here in the mountains, away from the lab and the frenetic pace of the city, I was broadening my outlook. What was it about the Dayton Market that resonated with me? The products and the people, as well, gave me the same feeling I'd experienced when moving into the cabin. It wasn't merely the simplicity; it was deeper than that. I perceived a combination of rightness, of a conscious decision to live a certain way, and of even small items chosen or made to reflect order and attention to detail. I sensed a collective determination to conform one's outward life to an inner compass.

# Chapter 2

## EL SALVADOR

"*Desaparecido.*"

Disappeared. Too long a word for what happened when a bullet exploded a skull, Emilio thought.

"*No.*"

"*Desaparecido.*" Emilio held the woman by the shoulders and leaned into her face. Her bones felt so frail he knew he could crush them with his hands, and startled by this image, Emilio stepped back, his shoulders tensing, his arms dropping. Thinking volume alone might compel her to act, he shouted at her, "*Debemos irnos.*" We must leave. His voice, quieter now, but emphatic, "*Debemos irnos.*"

He couldn't understand the old woman's refusal to leave. Was it because her son was not the person who'd disappeared? She is not my mother; I could leave without her, he thought, but with the idea barely formed, he knew he couldn't. Magdalena Suárez was family. Her only child, Graciela, had married his oldest brother, Tomás. He had known Magdalena all his life, had watched her hair become gray and thin, her smooth skin become wrinkled. He had known her from the old days of laughing, of dancing in the square, of hopeful tomorrows. Perhaps somewhere inside her, Magdalena remembered those times, guarded them like someone cupping a hand around a church candle's flame, and thus could not acknowledge the brutality of events since then. He understood that this was the only home she knew, a place to which she was tethered by memories, but he'd hoped the disappearance of his brother Felipe would make her realize they had to leave.

"I cannot leave everything I know," she pleaded, her eyes wide, grasping. "I cannot go away and be someone I'm not in a new place. *Toda mi vida ha sido aquí.*" All my life has been here.

"There is no life left here."

"My husband is buried here."

"Your husband was murdered here." The words slapped, and Magdalena, drawing in her breath, turned her head. He waited, but her face remained closed, refusing to permit him to probe further.

Emilio walked out of their wattle hut with its walls made of branches plastered with mud. When it rained, the water beating on the few ragged squares of tin interspersed over the plywood roof sounded like the sporadic artillery in the hills. He knelt on the ground. All he'd ever wanted was a piece of land of his own. He dreamed of waking before dawn, slipping outside, and watching the light spill over soil that he knew as intimately as a man would know a woman. He dreamed of planting and harvesting, of straight furrows, of a straight and simple life dictated by no more than the cycles of the earth, the rain, the sun. Alberto Delgado, Emilio's father and one of the few educated men in the village, had been a farmer, journalist, and part-time teacher before his land had been taken, before he, too, had disappeared. His father had spoken of the land with untamed poetry: "The land is linked to your soul, Emilio. There is strength in the soil; it has rhythms, it thunders and it whispers."

The land, Emilio thought. He knew that before the Spanish conquerors came in 1524, El Salvador had been called "Cuzcatlán"—"land of jewels and precious things." Now, it was a land of violence and perverted power. A mere fourteen families owned most of the land and controlled the coffee in this region, as well as the sugar cane and cotton in other areas. Worse, these families supported the civilian-military junta that passed for a government and committed unconscionable atrocities. After these families and the officials had suckered in the powerful United States, he held no hope for his country.

He'd tried to reach a refugee center in Honduras but turned back for Magdalena when he realized the government was forcing the refugees farther away from protection. Emilio closed his eyes against bursts of brutal images: National Guardsmen pursuing refugees to the river; the screams of women and children crowding the bridge leading to Honduras, only to be driven back by Honduran soldiers; and the dead left for packs of wild dogs and buzzards to devour. He forced himself to open his eyes and stop the images. No place in the country or the region was safe. He'd made it back home, but Felipe was gone.

Emilio scratched into the earth, the dirt forming small piles of the fertile, volcanic soil. He should not have dreamed of land, he told himself, rubbing the dirt between his fingers, the silt outlining the creases in his hands as though readying them for a palm reader. Dreams could be snatched away, like land, one's house, one's own father and brother. "Dreams are dangerous, dreams are for children," Felipe had insisted. However, Emilio had not wanted to listen, for what was left when even one's secret dreams were claimed and demolished?

Emilio, sitting with his back against a tree, pulled his knees up to his chin so his body would be out of the sun. Two nights ago, he'd awakened to the sound of running footsteps outside the hut. Someone whispered a message at the screened window, the quiet words a susurrus drumbeat of warning. He knew Felipe was in trouble before the friend recited the whole message, knew by the beating of his heart in his ears, the thrumming in his head. Felipe had gotten reckless, too outspoken in an organization for social and economic justice. Because of his youth, Felipe had thought he wouldn't be taken seriously, wouldn't be considered a threat. But he should have known any son of the writer Delgado would be labeled an anarchist, a magnet for concentric circles of enemies and admirers.

Emilio had not had time to mourn for his brother. Perhaps time was an excuse, for he had not wanted the anger to subside enough to allow grief. He wondered if Felipe had fought, knowing there would be no escape. Had he been brave? Growing up, he'd been the most daring of the brothers. Or had he been consumed with a fear that stopped the heart and the mind in a way no bullet could?

Emilio and Felipe had been inseparable, close in age, closer in spirit. They'd been altar boys in the church. They'd worked next to each other in the coffee fields, sweating through the planting seasons in the Santa Ana region and celebrating the harvests. Together, they'd watched their mother die, their own flesh and bones aching as they witnessed her back arching in agony while the cancer assaulted her. Together, they'd helped their father bury their mother. Siding with each other, they'd argued with Tomás when he'd decided to break from the family and go to the United States.

Last July, Emilio and Felipe had gone to a major fiesta; the excitement of the crowds, the fireworks, and the jubilation held at bay images of other crowds, of other bursts of light and commotion, these marking violent demonstrations and clashes with the government's forces. While at the fiesta, ignoring Tomás's advice, they'd joined the farmworkers' organization. Now there would be no more adventures, now there would be no special brother who understood him.

At dawn, Emilio slipped into the building that served as a church, school, and meeting place to light a candle for Felipe. The building was a source of pride for the village. Every week, the women scrubbed the floor and cleaned the windows. They tended the flowers in the courtyard's garden, pouring leftover dishwater around the spindly stems and murmuring blessings to the earth, which they patted with their rough, capable hands. They left offerings of food—rice dishes and *arepas*, a breakfast bread made with maize—on the young missionary teacher's desk. They were at once wary of her teaching, knowing they might lose their children to the larger world when they were old enough to leave, yet respectful of the mysteries she understood.

Emilio watched the candle flame's shadow on the wall making a parallel dance. He wasn't sure he believed in the practice of lighting a candle any longer, but he found comfort in the tradition, nonetheless. "I will not pray for your soul, brother," he said. "I refuse to believe you are dead. I pray for your safe return. Better, for a safe escape." The light around the flame made a perfect circle, and when he spoke to the flame, the halo quivered in response. "I will be leaving, Felipe, with Magdalena. You understand I can't wait for you? *Perdóname*." Forgive me.

Emilio wrote out the itinerary, sketched a map of the route they would take, and listed food and the amount of water needed. Would Magdalena be able to survive the trip? He was young and strong; every day he ran in the hills to build his endurance and to memorize the curve and sweep of the land he'd never see again. He ran past the woods where his father had taught him to hunt; past the fields where he and his brothers had worked; and past the cave where, on a pile of blankets, he had first made love to a girl, their cries echoing along the rock walls.

He would be able to move from his past, wrap the blades of his regrets. Magdalena, however, was over sixty years old with the frailty of having survived too many losses. He admitted to himself that without Magdalena he'd have a much better chance of escaping, of traversing the rivers, of eluding the border patrol officers. She didn't want to go, and he'd played with the temptation of allowing her to talk him into going alone. *Supervivencia*. Survival. Who would blame him, wanting his own survival? He sighed. Leaving Magdalena behind would be a betrayal of family honor. It would slice beyond words, an unhealable wound, a shame for future children. He pictured himself standing before Tomás and Graciela, unable to meet their eyes. He could not disgrace his murdered father's memory by abandoning Magdalena.

Emilio no longer had the certitude of the simple faith of his childhood, when as an altar boy he'd been part of the wonder and mystery of the Mass. Now, doubts frayed the frontier of his faith, threatening to deconstruct the core of his being. His family was all he had left to claim with any kind of confidence. *No hay otra opción*. No other choice. He could not let his father's death be in vain. In the newspaper he owned, his father had campaigned against the deportation of refugees farther away from the Salvadoran border, extending into Honduras. He'd cited the United States as the supplier of planes that dropped bombs of white phosphorous on rural civilian settlements. In a merciless exposé, he'd recounted the abuses in the camps and reported the beheading of Santana Chirino Amaya, who had been deported twice from the United States. For his outspokenness, his father had met a similar fate. Who would tell his father's story? He had to survive. *No hay otra opción*.

"What are these papers?" Magdalena asked Emilio, poking misshapen, arthritic fingers at the edges of the sheets. "Is it wise to send another letter to Graciela and Tomás?"

"No, no more letters," he told her, for mail was opened and read. He showed her the plans.

At one point, she closed her eyes and covered her ears. "You go. You go alone."

He reached for her hands, pulling them down and holding them. Bending his face close to hers, he looked at her eyes. They used to be fierce—he'd seen a single glance from her silence fools and trespassers—but now they were full of fear and dread.

"I can't go alone," he told her. "I can't leave you to die. To disappear. To be killed."

"The trip is too long, too hard. I cannot make it."

"You have to try. What will I tell your daughter?"

"The trip is too long, too hard. I will hold you back. *Los dos moriremos*." We will both die.

She spoke in absolutes; he knew she spoke the truth.

# Chapter 3

Taking a break from my research, I walked outside and gloried in the peace. Relishing the privacy of the yard, I stretched my arms up to the sky, my left one angling awkwardly, a stunted supplicant. I turned in widening circles with my head tilted back, my eyes open. I felt light and unencumbered.

Something rustled in the tall grass surrounding the shed. Moving the shed's door so I could see what was making the sound, I froze. It shot out of the grass so quickly, so completely, that I couldn't be sure it hadn't been in front of me for several moments. At first, I could not put a name to it. Snake. I tried to step back, tried to remember what the markings along its back meant and wondered if snakes could climb trees, if a noise would scare it. My mouth felt dry, papery, and my voice came out as a thin whisper. "No . . ." Flinging out my arms, I hit the shed's door. When I reached for the axe, the snake arched its back, somehow moving forward in a blur at the same time, ready to strike.

I lifted the axe. "Keep your eyes open, eyes open, don't miss it!" The blade sliced into the snake as I yelled "Eyes open" for the last time. Dropping the axe, I stumbled toward the cabin. My legs shook and felt weak, numb. Unable to cross the few yards to the house, I wrapped my arms around a tree.

A voice called to me, "Katherine Solterra?" In a few seconds, someone was holding my shoulders and supporting me. Instead of being startled, I felt an immediate sense of comfort. Without looking behind me, I sank back and allowed the person to hold me, my fright subsiding in increments.

"Did it strike you?"

"No, it didn't. I'm not hurt."

"That took courage," he spoke slowly. "It was poisonous."

I turned around to face him. He was an older man, perhaps in his early seventies, with skin browned and toughened by the sun, his mouth and dark brown eyes seeming less a part of his face than the wrinkles and sagging cheeks. He wore overalls and a plain cotton shirt with the sleeves rolled up to his elbows. Short strands of gray hair rimmed the stained baseball cap molded to his head, giving him a bemused appearance.

"Let's get you inside where you can sit." The man followed me into the cabin and brought me a glass of water. He didn't speak, letting me take my time to calm down.

"I'm sorry." I looked at him. "I've always been afraid of snakes; my uncle was bitten by one and almost died. Some scientist I am." I tried to smile.

"No need to apologize." He waited until I drank the water. "I'll take care of things," he said finally, and left.

While the man was gone, I scrubbed my face as though I could erase what I'd seen and changed my blouse, the material damp from sweat. When I returned to the living room, he was standing in the doorway. "Axe is in the shed, cleaned off. Snake is gone, too."

His speech was uncluttered, spare and direct, as if the fewer words he used, the more they would count. I found myself wanting to respond in kind, if only because it took less energy. "Thanks. Sit down. Please." I waved him to a chair. I noticed he walked with an odd gait, a very slight shuffle. "Kate Solterra," I introduced myself before remembering he'd called me by name. Maggie had told me everyone in town would have heard of my arrival within a week.

With his palm, he slid off his cap in one smooth motion. "Virgil Schoenfeld."

"Live nearby, Mr. Schoenfeld?"

"Virgil. On the ridge, mile or so."

"How did you know I needed help? Did I scream?"

"Yes. My wife Eleanor and I've been away, and I was coming to see if you'd had any problems with the cabin. I keep a check on the place for the Drurys." He stood and moved to the door, crossing the threshold. "You're all right now."

"Virgil." He turned, sliding the baseball cap into place. "Thank you."

"You did the hard part. Keep an eye out and wear boots when you're out in high grass or in the woods." He smiled and held up his hand as he left.

That night, I awoke with a shout. Letting go of the blanket twisted in my hands, I locked my arms around my knees and rocked back and forth. The nightmare wasn't about the snake but about the car accident, the car hurtling toward me, its normal size magnified many times. "No, no, no, no. Not now." Why did I persist in feeling that if I kept pushing the dream away, eventually I could obliterate it? Reluctant to turn off the light, I wrapped up in my robe and paced around the house.

At last, I settled on the sofa to watch the sunrise. Taking the cup of cocoa I'd made and pressing it to my chest, I let the steam warm my face. With it being this cold in September, I'd have to ask Grady to bring wood for the fireplace soon. The snake. "I killed a snake," I said aloud. Could I do it again if necessary? "Probably. Maybe. Of course. I did it once, didn't I?" Courage, Virgil had said. I smiled, swirling the cocoa in the cup. He'd said it had taken courage. "Pioneer woman." I raised my cup in benediction to the sun, now sealing the ridges in molten gold. Gaining security from the light, I set my empty cup on the floor, nestled into the sofa cushions, and slept dreamlessly.

I set out the ingredients I'd purchased at the grocery store in Bridgewater. Virgil had cut the grass and brush around the shed, and I wanted to thank him with a loaf of homemade bread. Lining up the collection of pans, measuring cups and spoons, flour, and yeast, I began to have misgivings. The cookbook's pictures and explanations looked much more complicated than they had a few days before. What about brownies from a box? A cake from the deli? "You're such a wimp." I'd never improve my cooking skills if I didn't challenge myself. Bread it was.

With each ingredient, I measured and checked and rechecked. By the time I read a direction in the book and picked up the measuring cup or spoons, I would forget the amount and have to reread it. "You're going to have to trust yourself and get on with it." Maybe this was what Diane had meant when she told me to "get out of my own way." While I was painstakingly methodical, living my life within the confines of the scientific realm, she was more daring and outgoing; she had always served as a balance for me. She joked that she was my interpreter, my guide to the modern world outside of science.

The kneaded dough should have been smooth and elastic, according to the directions, but mine had ragged-edged holes on the dough's surface. I had no idea what "elastic" meant in this case. Cradling the rounded mass in my palms, I started to lower the dough into a bowl when an image came to me. "Please," I whispered and was rewarded with a series of childhood memories, running stitches of images, smells, and sights: my grandmother Noni making bread, her wrists pressing into the dough; the metal kitchen table bending under her hands and sounding like faraway summer thunder; the dough rising underneath the linen towels like a small child's stomach rounding out her cotton shirt; and Noni showing me how to squeeze the dough through my fist to form rolls. I settled the dough on the kitchen

windowsill and covered it with a dish towel. I loved the expectant and sym-
bolic way it looked, and I was grateful for the memories it had elicited.

Resisting the urge to keep checking, I waited until moments before the
end of the minimum twenty-five minutes to open the oven door. The loaves'
tops were a dark brown, matching the cookbook's photograph, but the bread
hadn't risen much above the pans' edges. Perhaps they would rise in the last
five minutes. Going outside to escape the kitchen's heat, I marveled at the
lush and yielding quiet, and melting into it, I felt my breathing even out and
my muscles relax. Stretching out my arms, I flexed my fingers. I wondered
what to do with the rest of my afternoon. Since Virgil had cleared the brush
around the shed, I could rake the leaves in the backyard. It was too beautiful
a day to stay inside.

Nearing the back porch door, I could see, then smell, the smoke; the
smoke detectors began blaring, startling me. In my hurry to get inside, I
tripped on the steps and went down hard on my elbows. What could be on
fire? In the kitchen, there were no flames, but smoke puffed from the oven
door. I turned off the oven, opened the windows and doors, and waited for
the smoke to dissipate enough to silence the alarms. Of course. I'd been
baking bread to thank Virgil.

Damn you. May you choke on guilt for the rest of your life.

I opened the oven door when the timer rang, having stayed in the kitchen
this time. The loaves in the second batch were rounded, smooth, and light
brown. I grinned to myself as I drew the pans out of the oven. The recipe
advised waiting until the bread cooled before slicing it, but as soon as it could
be touched without burning my fingers, I cut a slice, slathered butter on it,
and went outside. Sitting on the grass in front of the cabin, I ate the bread, un-
ashamedly licking the butter running down my fingers. It was the best thing
I'd ever tasted. "I did it!" I shouted, leaning back to watch the sun streaming
like Maypole ribbons around and through the trees. It was not a prestigious
science award, not a generous federal grant for promising research, not a
breakthrough after years of rigorous clinical trials, but still: I'd claim this, too.

Virgil had said he lived a couple of miles away on the ridge, but every
rise looked like a ridge to me. Maggie could give me directions. I wrapped
the uncut loaf in a clean kitchen towel and laid it on the car's front seat.
On impulse, I returned to the house and wrapped up the other loaf as well,
wanting Maggie to have a taste.

A pickup truck and a bicycle were in the store's parking area. Cooper,
tilting his head when the door's hanging ribbon of bells sounded, saw me

and called out, "Hail the great snake slayer!" I reddened and tried to duck behind the display of snow shovels.

Cooper and another man joined me at the lunch counter, and Maggie came through the swinging doors. "We heard about you killing the rattlesnake," she said.

"Virgil told you?"

"He mentioned it when he came in to let us know to be on the lookout," Cooper said. "I want you to meet . . ."

"How prevalent are poisonous snakes around here?" I interrupted, trying to sound as casual as he did.

"Oh, it's not at all uncommon . . ."

Maggie punched his arm. "Shush, don't y'all go spoutin' mountain superstitions to scare her. Virgil wanted us to be careful, wear boots in the woods, and look where we're going. We tend to get careless, and it doesn't hurt to be reminded. It took nerve to do what you did."

Cooper motioned to the man beside him. "I'd like you to meet Paul Whittaker. Paul, the fearless Katherine Solterra."

Taller than Cooper, Paul had dark brown hair and deep-set, blue eyes. Had I seen him in town before now? I couldn't recall. He was about my age, I guessed, maybe a little older.

"I'm happy to meet you, Katherine Solterra." He looked down at me and shook my hand.

Maggie asked, "What are you holding? Something needing to be fixed?"

I placed the bread on the counter and uncovered it. The four of us stared at the cut loaf until I realized they were puzzled. I explained that this was the first bread I'd ever made. "To be honest, the initial two loaves came out flat and burned. This is the first edible bread I've made. I wanted to make it and take a loaf to Virgil to thank him for helping me the other day."

Maggie made fresh coffee and set butter and raspberry preserves on the counter. "This is wonderful bread. Light, not crumbly, good crust," she critiqued.

"Lucky beginning." Was that the right phrase? Beginning lucky? Starter's luck, lucky starter?

"You can make bread for us anytime." Cooper cut another slice for himself, and Paul reached for the knife.

"Cooper tells me you're a biochemist. No wonder you make terrific bread." He waved away the butter. "Can't improve on this."

"Believe me, my being a scientist had nothing to do with this bread."

"What do you do as a biochemist?" Paul asked.

"I work at a research institute; my department is trying to develop more effective drug therapies for multiple sclerosis. I'm on sabbatical now." Uncomfortable with being questioned about my work and the sabbatical, I turned to Maggie and asked if she would write down how to get to the Schoenfelds' place. She started giving me directions, but I stopped her. "Would you write them down for me, please? I'm terrible with directions."

"It's easy. From here," she pointed behind her, "make a left turn and go about two miles across the holler out of town; take the next left and go another mile or so up the mountain. Make a right over the bridge and the next left onto their drive."

I tried to repeat in my mind what she'd said but couldn't recall anything after "make a left turn." I felt my throat tighten. "Please, Maggie, write it down . . . do you have a pen? And will I know a 'holler' when I see it?"

"It means a valley, and it's one of the prettiest spots around. Two lefts, right, left. It's not tricky."

"Please write it down." I could hear the edge to my voice. "Then I'll have it later if I need it."

"Sure, no problem." She scribbled the directions on a napkin, and I left for the Schoenfelds' house.

Promptly answering my knock, Virgil swung open the door. "Welcome, Katherine Solterra, come in." He sounded almost as though he had expected me, and I wondered if Maggie had called him. I stepped inside to find an expansive room with enormous windows on two sides. Four banners depicting the mountains in different seasons hung from a loft, and woven hangings splashed color and texture over white walls. A mobile hung from the ceiling in the living room, and a sculpture filled a corner by the dining table. Everything—the furniture, the objects from various countries, the colors, the art, the house itself—had a sense of rightness. This was not an ordinary home.

"I apologize for not calling first."

"Nonsense; we're pleased you came." He looked up toward the loft. "Eleanor? Company."

A woman peered over the railing before coming down the stairs. With posture as erect and balanced as a dancer's, she moved with light grace. Her youthfulness surprised me; she seemed to be quite a bit younger than Virgil. Standing next to him, she offered her hand.

"This is Katherine Solterra. Kate, I'd like you to meet my wife, Eleanor."

"Welcome to our home and to Drake's Springs. I heard you've met one of our more notorious residents." Her voice was low and musical, her words spoken with precision.

"And survived to tell the tale with Virgil's help." I gave him the bread. "This is to thank you for coming to my aid and for clearing around the shed."

He unwrapped the bread and held it aloft, turning it in admiration. "No need for thanks, but I'm happy to have this beautiful bread."

Eleanor said, "I've never been able to bake bread."

"I haven't, either, until this morning, and I'm sure it was a fluke." Fluke? Something with whales? Why would I know that, much less remember it? I pulled my attention back to Eleanor.

"Will you stay and have lunch with us?" she asked. "I'll find something to put on this bread."

Although not hungry after eating the bread at home and half a slice at the store, I felt it would be rude to refuse. Virgil took me out to the sunroom, a curved glass enclosure filled with wicker furniture and baskets of plants. "What a remarkable home."

"Eleanor designed it, and friends helped to build it."

"Eleanor is an architect?"

"Artist."

That explained the wall hangings and the concert of colors and patterns knowledgeably chosen. Eleanor came out to the sunroom. "Virgil, lunch is on the serving cart; would you please bring it out?"

Virgil wheeled the cart next to the table. Eleanor had cut the bread and put sliced roasted chicken on one plate and tomatoes and lettuce on another. She set a bowl of potato salad in the center. "Ready?" he asked, and his wife nodded.

She turned to me when we were seated. "It is our custom to observe a few moments of silent grace. Would you like to join us?"

Virgil reached out and clasped one of my hands, while Eleanor held the other. A silent blessing? I bowed my head and closed my eyes. I heard the dry leaves riffling in the breeze and the call of a solitary bird; otherwise, the silence was sudden and encompassing, as though we had been slipped into water. Eleanor squeezed my hand and let it go, and a second later, Virgil pressed his fingers around mine. I raised my head and opened my eyes to find them both smiling at me.

Eleanor passed me the plate holding slices of my bread. "I hated to cut it," she said.

I told them about the impromptu coffee break at Maggie's store. "I've never lived in a small town, so I'm not used to a country store where the owners and the customers sit down and have bread and jam together."

Eleanor asked, "Have you settled in all right? We were sorry we were away and couldn't welcome you when you moved in."

"The cabin is perfect for my needs. I'm alone but don't feel as isolated as I sometimes do in the city, though maybe I will this winter when it's harder to move about."

"Virgil will have to teach you how to cross-country ski and use snowshoes."

"I know how to ski, but I've never tried snowshoes. I'm not the most coordinated person."

"No matter, I'll teach you how to get up, too," Virgil said.

"What do you do during the winter?" I asked him, but he turned to Eleanor, letting her answer.

"I have my weaving and art, and Virgil has his animal stations in the nature preserve and various other projects. This community is more active than it appears."

"Your work in the living room is stunning; I've never seen anything quite like those wall hangings. Virgil told me you're an artist and that you designed this house."

"With a lot of help from Virgil. He was an engineer, but we're both retired now. The planning of this house was the most fun, though we argued a lot." She described how they'd disagreed on where to put the deck. "I'd wanted to see the sunrise from the deck, and he wanted the sunset. We flipped a coin."

"I won." Virgil smiled at his wife.

After we ate our dessert of ginger cookies, Virgil stacked our plates on the cart. "Let me help you with these dishes before I go," I offered.

Eleanor shook her head. "No, the first time you're company . . ."

"Second time you're a friend . . ." Virgil continued.

"And fair game after that," they finished together, sharing the look of a couple long married. I felt a spiral of jealousy.

Eleanor said, "Let me give you our phone number, so in case you need something you'll have someone you can call."

"Thank you, I'd appreciate it. And when I get past appetizers and bread in my cookbook, I'll call you to come have a meal with me." I gave her my number and hoped I'd remembered it correctly.

"We're not fancy people; we like peanut butter and jelly sandwiches," Virgil said as we stood on the front porch. "Especially if you'll make the bread for them."

Returning to my cabin, I thought what an unusual couple they were, with Eleanor's warmth and animation, Virgil's quiet manner, and his way of glancing at his wife when he talked. His gentle courtliness, her artistry. And there was something I couldn't put a name to, something indefinable, like the unusual prayer before lunch.

# Chapter 4

THE BEGINNING OF OCTOBER marked my first month at the cabin, and the cloudless, azure sky prompted me to celebrate. With soup in a thermos and a map Eleanor had drawn, I headed to Virgil's nature preserve. I drove in case I became too tired to walk home. The past week had not been one of my better ones.

Two stone columns marked the preserve's entrance. Past the entrance was a rustic shelter with raised ledges for bedrolls, a fireplace, a stack of cut wood, and basic survival items. The shelter, Virgil had told me, was for travelers who'd been hiking the nearby Appalachian Trail and needed a safe place to stay overnight in bad weather. A rectangular box marked "Donations for Preserve Maintenance" hung on a wall above a wooden table that held a guest book and maps.

Leaving the shelter, I noticed a brass plaque by the door. "Drake's Springs Nature Preserve. In Memory of Elliott Morgan Schoenfeld, 1950–1969." Virgil and Eleanor's son? A nephew? So young—an accident, an illness? It was a sobering reminder to me that everyone had a sorrow to bear, although some hurts were more visible than others. I'd hated the rehab counseling sessions when we were told such things. The dangers of self-pity, and how to respond to the pity extended by others, had been major topics. But surely, of all of life's challenges, the loss of a child had to be the worst.

Hiking up the north trail, I arrived at an overhang to find a picnic table, a covered trash can, and a stone cooking pit. Everything looked old and used but cared for. Spreading out my lunch on the picnic table, I sat facing the view. It was as though my eyes could never look long enough at the mountains. When I first came to this area, I'd thought the mountains looked the same every day, but now I recognized the effect of the changing light on the forms and colors. Hadn't I thought about this idea of extra awareness in another context? I couldn't remember. When had it been?

"Drop it. Let it go." I knew I was afraid that if I kept letting the little things slide with no attempt at recovering them, the big things would disappear in the momentum. "One day," I addressed the mountains, "I'd like not to be reminded." Eating my lunch, I stilled my mind long enough to take in the peace and beauty of these mountains folding over one another like blankets covering curled up giants. At least for now, it was enough.

"Elliott Schoenfeld. Virgil and Eleanor's son?"

"Yes." Maggie picked up her dishcloth and started to wring it dry. "They called him by his middle name, Morgan."

"I went to the nature preserve and saw the plaque with his name in the shelter."

She drew the cloth around my coffee cup, cleaning out of habit the spotless counter. "They don't like to talk about their son much, even though it's been a long time now. Morgan died in Vietnam. If you're political on the subject, you'd best keep it to yourself around these parts, though I guess you were too young to have been affected much by it."

"There was controversy at the seminary where my father taught, but we didn't have to deal with it on a personal level. Was Morgan their only child?"

"Yes. There are deep wounds in this community from the war; it near to tore us apart." Maggie folded and refolded her dishcloth. She seemed reluctant to say more, and I didn't want to press her. When customers came in, I returned to my cabin, stopping to retrieve my mail from the box at the main road.

I opened my mother's note first. She asked if she and my father could stop by on their way home from my father's conference three weeks from now. She tended to write rather than call so I wouldn't have to remember oral information. We'd had too many instances of my garbled notetaking.

The next letter was from Matthew Novaleski, my director at the institute. "I know this is a beginning draft," I read, "but what about the results of the drug assays conducted by the Stanford lab? They need to be discussed in the manuscript. And several of your calculations are incorrect. I realize you're still threading your way back to where you were before, but this article needs work. Call me if you need further clarification."

I threw the letter and the edited draft onto the kitchen table. Threading my way back. Was that how he saw what I had to do? Humpty Dumpty follows Hansel and Gretel's breadcrumb trail. Or was I thinking of Jack and Jill? No, Jack "fell down and broke his crown." Maybe it was Jack. I couldn't figure out why people read fairy tales to children anyway; the stories were full of accidents and bad things such as boughs breaking, wolves with sharp teeth, and evil witches. What were we thinking? Wasn't the world on any given day scary enough?

The next letter was from my lawyer, containing the final details about the settlement. When it had been awarded, I could not walk, speak intelligibly, or take care of myself without assistance. It was one of the largest settlements ever awarded in my state, and there had been a good amount of publicity. Handled with reason and sensible investing, the settlement could last me the rest of my life. Although I'd made remarkable progress, I could not yet return to the kind of work for which I'd trained so long, what I'd always thought would be my life's work. And despite knowing I should rejoice in my progress, I continued to keep in motion the pendulum weights ticking off the unfairness of it all. I folded the lawyer's letter, placed it in a file, and went to bed, not caring it was early in the evening.

Cold and hungry, I awoke before dawn the next morning. I remembered having gone to bed without eating dinner. Why had I done that? After slipping rolls into the oven to warm, I grabbed a handful of raisins. Reading through the suggested menus in the back of a cookbook, I tried to plan what to serve my parents. They would be here on a Saturday morning and would leave sometime Sunday afternoon. One breakfast, two lunches, and one dinner. Perhaps Maggie, Abby, Cooper, and the Schoenfelds would come over for coffee and dessert Saturday night. And maybe Cooper's friend, Paul Whittaker? We'd seen each other in passing a few times. Wouldn't my parents see I was doing well if I could host a gathering for eight people? Had I ever done such a thing?

I pushed aside the cookbook and picked up Matthew's letter. I reread it, studied my manuscript, and checked the tables and figures. He had circled errors in transcriptions and formula derivations. Why hadn't David mentioned this? We didn't work on the same team, but it was a cross-departmental project. Since beginning my sabbatical, we'd called each other a couple of times a week, but the conversations had been quick and almost always about work. I fought to maintain my composure. "Concentrate on one small thing." Something nagged at me concerning David, but I couldn't place it, couldn't bring it to the surface.

As soon as I knew David would be in the office, I called the lab. When I heard his voice, his crisply enunciated words, I did not hold back. "Why didn't you tell me about my errors? Didn't you think I needed to know? Were you planning to tell me sometime, or were you going to keep covering for me?"

I could hear him sigh. We both tended to avoid arguments, anything messy or emotional. "I'm in the middle of something and right in the middle of the lab. I need twenty minutes. I'll go into my office and call you back."

I hung up and paced the floor, then stood in the doorway and watched the wind blow the leaves into a dancing circle. I had never thought numbers would betray me. When the phone rang, I answered right away. "What kind of mistakes did you find?" I asked him.

"A few reversals, wrong transcriptions, miscalculations, and incorrect use of formulas. Some discussions of procedures and findings didn't follow logically from the data, which may be more a problem with wording."

How could I have missed all these errors? I tried to piece things together. "Matthew saw the draft first?"

"I was away at a conference."

"Did he say anything to you?"

"He said maybe it was a rush job, and no, I didn't say anything to him."

"You had no right to withhold the information from me or to change things without my knowledge."

"I was trying to save your job, not to mention the research," he answered. "Don't make it so hard for someone to help."

"Don't put this back on me. You should have told me so I would know what was going on." He didn't answer, and for a moment I thought he would hang up on me.

"Send the next draft to me." He ended the conversation. Wanting to review the reports before getting too confused, I started writing down as much of our discussion as I could remember, realizing too late that I should have taken notes during the call.

Smelling smoke, I ran into the kitchen. Opening the oven door, I saw the two rolls, burned beyond saving. Pulling them out and turning off the oven, I looked down at them. I didn't remember putting them in. My mother was right: I could burn the place down. Why couldn't I acknowledge I needed to make it a routine to set the oven's timer every single time? I threw the rolls as hard as I could at the kitchen wall. They skittered across the floor, charred flakes dotting their path. Sliding down, I sat for a long time with my back against the oven, its warmth comforting. I reached above me and got the raisins, eating them one by one until I finished the rest of the box. I got to my feet. "So, you have a knack for burning bread. It's not a big deal. At least this time the smoke detectors didn't alarm. Don't give up. Don't you dare give up."

Damn you. May you have difficulty at work until the day you retire. May you burn every roll, every muffin, every piece of toast.

❖ ❖ ❖

I walked past the nature preserve and turned left onto a narrow road barely wider than a single lane. The walking stick Virgil had given me made a rustling sound as it angled through the fallen leaves, then a solid thud as it hit the road's surface. The road ended in a circular clearing in front of a white clapboard church with black double doors, leaded glass windows shaped like a bishop's miter, and simple black shutters. There was no steeple. It was an unpretentious country church. A sign to the right of the doors read, "Drake's Springs Friends Meeting. All Welcome," and it stated the time of the service. There was no sign on the main road, so how would anyone know a Quaker church was here?

I tried to see through the windows, but they were too high off the ground. Behind the clapboard structure, joined by a covered corridor, stood a newer brick building. A fenced playground and a grassless parking area took up the back. Returning to the church's front steps, I ate the apple I'd dropped into my jacket pocket.

I began shivering from sitting still in the cold, but I didn't want to return yet to the cabin. I tried the door, which opened easily, and pushed through an inner set of double doors to the sanctuary. Sitting on one of the wooden benches, I felt a settled silence, a sense of palpable calmness. Three rows of benches ran along the sides of the room, with two more at the front. A piano stood in one corner, and two posters hung on the pale gray walls. There were no candles or crosses, no stained glass, no carpet, no altar. It was hard to envision a plainer house of worship, though its austerity possessed a surprising beauty.

The bulletin I'd picked up in the vestibule had last Sunday's date on it. It contained news of potluck suppers and dates for discussion groups on spiritual friendships, war tax alternatives, and nuclear disarmament. There were drawings, poetry, and reminders of a workday to paint and clean the Meetinghouse. This building felt like a place apart, an oasis, and the irony that I would experience any kind of peace in a church did not escape me. I'd rejected my parents' church, then their religion, long ago. And any remaining belief I might have had died during the crash.

Warmed, I replaced the bulletin and left the building, making sure the doors closed securely. Halfway down the lane I looked back, almost as if to reassure myself it existed. It gave the appearance of having been here for a hundred years, and nothing would have looked more appropriate in this setting.

# Chapter 5

## EL SALVADOR

THE ARMY, SUSPECTING THAT members of a leftist group were meeting inside, bombed the church. Magdalena and Emilio, the first to arrive, halted in shock before the piles of rubble emitting smoke. With building parts blown across the village, with shards of the tin roof and doorframes piercing other buildings, they knew there was no need for urgency, though they worked feverishly, nonetheless. Others soon joined them, gasping at the sight and choking on the smoke. Pulling away first one piece of wreckage and then another, they cleared a path to what had been the church's doorway, cleared the inevitable path to the unfathomable.

Fingering her rosary, Magdalena stood with the other older women, the somber line of village matriarchs grasping for what they would say to their sons and daughters, the parents of the dead. She knew what they would find, everyone did, but her heart continued to hope her eyes were wrong. As the men lifted out the twenty-three bodies, they gingerly wrapped them in the blankets the women had brought from their homes. Magdalena thought, *Ni tan siquiera puedo llorar*; I cannot even cry. There was a point beyond sorrow and rage, after all. Twenty-two children and one adult dead in a church, and I cannot cry. Where was God in this church?

The mothers of the children fell to the smoking ground and exploded in keening screams. Weighed down by their failure to protect the children and unable to look at the women, the men lined up the misshapen bundles and stood with their arms by their sides and their heads down. The children were burned and damaged beyond recognition, and in mute, numbed assent, each family claimed the number of bodies to equal the number of children they'd lost. The village's self-appointed patriarch knelt before the body of the teacher, who had no family. "She will not be alone," he murmured. "We will be with her. She will not be alone." With infinite care, he and his wife wrapped her in a blanket, and Emilio helped them to take her to their home.

Magdalena retched from the stench of charred flesh, the sight of the dismembered children. We are now a ghost village of women and old men, she thought. Emilio is right that there is no life here. I have seen so many deaths I cannot cry. Not even for children.

She dreamed a vision of such purity she knew it could not be doubted. An angel spoke to her in cascading tones, sculpted in authority: "*Vaya a la iglesia, Magdalena.*" Go to the church.

She saw herself standing and answering the angel, "There is no church left; it was bombed. Couldn't you have stopped it?"

"The building is gone, not the church."

"But the children are gone. Why didn't you stop the bombing? Why did you let them die?" Magdalena cried out, taken aback by her own vehemence, her temerity in accusing an angel of God.

"*Vaya a la iglesia.*"

"Why? I can't do anything."

"I will tell you one more time: *Vaya a la iglesia.*"

She rose from the bed, slipped from the hut without wakening Emilio, and found herself at the remains of the church. The men had raked the rubble into piles, their very neatness an incongruous sight. Villagers had constructed a makeshift altar from the damaged boards. Using a smoldering ember, Magdalena lit one of the votives, then another candle from it, and all the others in turn. With balletic poise, she arranged the candles in a circle, a boundary of light for the burned area, a demarcation for evil. After sweeping a space with a piece of a doorframe, she sat in the middle of the circle, her nightgown caressing her ankles in the slight breeze. The candle flames straightened, announcing, "This far and no more."

"Angel of God, what do I do?" She was fully awake and knew with certainty the angel was nearby.

Minutes passed but she waited, patient and unafraid. The candle flames wavered, then steadied, though the breeze continued.

"Magdalena," said the voice in liquid compassion, a cream of knowing.

"*Sí.* Will you tell me what to do now?"

"You already know."

Silence, and Magdalena knew the angel had vanished. The candle flames grew until their saffron light suffused the entire area, cleansing the ground and reclaiming, consecrating the souls.

The Mass of the Resurrection for the children and the teacher was to be held three days after the bombing. Emilio went to the next village and hitched rides from there to the closest town where a priest resided. The priest would know how to get the news to the teacher's parents in the United States. She had been a missionary, impossibly young and full of hope and dangerous innocence. Hurling a rock at a tree, he thought only the privileged could afford such hope. If she had stuck to teaching the children, not adding special programs like the choir and the plays, they might be alive now. They'd been in the church after normal school hours rehearsing a choral program for the village when the bomb hit.

People he met along the way had heard the news, spread from house to house, village to village. We will be there, they said. We will not be quiet about this; fear this time will not silence us for they have murdered our children, and the world must hear our outrage. He saw their unblinking eyes, heard the resolute tone in their voices, felt the grief and anger in their hearts; but he knew that although they might come to the Mass, they would not speak out. Words turned into deaths with brutal swiftness.

The priest refused to come. "Too much risk. It will get out of control. Instead of a Mass for those who died it will turn into a political rally and more people will die."

"But you are a priest, you must come." Emilio could not believe the refusal. "Children have died and a Mass must be said."

"I do not want this responsibility. They assassinated my colleague, Rafael Palacios. And of course, Archbishop Romero. If something happens to me, my parish will be without a priest for perhaps a long time. Go to the next town. They have a younger priest who will be unafraid to conduct the Mass."

Emilio, after hitchhiking a ride with a farmer and his donkey cart, found Father Hannan, the priest from the United States. "Of course I will come. And yes, I will call the teacher's parents."

Father Hannan led Emilio from the church steps to a dark hallway, then into a dingy, windowless office that also served as his bedroom. Emilio watched as the priest checked his kit holding the bread and wine, the paten, the chalice, and the Sacramentary, the book of prayers. It is reduced to this, Emilio noted, a few pieces in a bag.

"There will be many people at the Mass?" Father Hannan asked.

"Not many people are left in the village. But people I met on the way said they would come. Word has spread from village to village, but I don't know. People are scared. Aren't you?" he asked the priest.

"No."

"You should be."

Father Hannan directed Emilio to sit on his bed while he began the process of trying to reach the missionary teacher's parents, calling first the young woman's diocese, next, her parish church, and finally, her home. Emilio couldn't follow much of the English that was spoken, but he had no difficulty recognizing the moment when the gravity of what the priest had to convey overwhelmed his limited experience. Father Hannan's English broke into long pauses after speaking a few words, his voice becoming strained, his fingers twisting the telephone cord as though that would cushion the news. When he finished his calls, they sat in silence until Emilio stood.

"Father, we must go. They are expecting us."

The priest picked up his bag and motioned toward the telephone. "Her parents don't understand how this could happen. They thought she'd be safe here, with the church."

"No one is safe here any longer."

When Father Hannan and Emilio arrived, the priest surveyed the village with one quick glance. Despite Emilio's doubts, people had come to attend the Mass. The children had been buried already, the haste a necessity in this heat with such primitive conditions. The teacher's body would soon be en route to the United States; her parents had wanted their daughter returned home, and a representative from the mission's office had volunteered to escort the coffin to New Jersey.

After announcing the Mass would begin at eight o'clock the next morning, Father Hannan said he would meet with the children's families, and later he would hear confessions, a request from some of those in attendance. It had been a long time since a priest had served this cluster of villages. At first he had felt uncomfortable in this community, but the people seemed not to see his blonde hair or to hear his rudimentary Spanish, reacting to him as a priest without connections to any country.

The villagers set up makeshift tents, communal cookpots, and campfires. The atmosphere remained somber, the grief over the loss of so many children underlaid with the sorrows of previous tragedies. Everyone had stories to tell. Going from group to group, the priest heard the story of the worker for the Green Cross, the Salvadoran equivalent of the American Red Cross, who was murdered in a public square, the fetus inside her mutilated.

More than one villager recounted the story of the man who was organizing factory workers for decent working conditions and reasonable wages. The death squad caught him at night, stripped and beat him, and dragged him behind a truck until he died. And they told of the Salvadoran battalion, trained in the United States, that attacked forty people—mostly women, the elderly, and children—in a shelter. He heard their fear of being sent to Honduran refugee camps such as El Tesoro, Mesa Grande, and La Virtud. The places where massacres had occurred in El Salvador formed a rumbling undertone: El Mozote, Sumpul River, Lempa River.

These individual stories needed to be publicized, Father Hannan realized, for who could relate to the number of over seventy thousand civilians killed so far? The number was too big, but everyone could be horrified by the account of the family who had been forced to watch while military men raped three of their daughters, then killed two of the girls, all because one daughter belonged to a student organization for peace. You couldn't have compassion for a number; people wouldn't protest a number, a statistic. He understood if this region had something valuable that the United States wanted, the policies would be different. But still, he hoped, if people knew these stories they would stop such barbarism.

"*Perdóneme, Padre, porque he pecado mucho . . .*" Bless me, Father, for I have sinned. He heard the ancient phrasing dozens of times, one confession latticed into another until they melded into one giant plea for forgiveness, no differences between the enumerated sins. After the last confession, Father Hannan approached each group, offering his condolences and measuring the tenor of the gathering. At last, standing alone by the makeshift altar encircled by candles burned to waxen craters, he felt like a true priest for the first time since his ordination. He perceived a connection with the priests of long ago and felt himself to be subsumed within this large and mysterious terrain.

When Emilio returned from his stint of guarding the village, he shook Magdalena awake. She jerked with a startled cry, and he lightly placed his hand over her mouth. "*Debemos irnos mañana.*" We must leave tomorrow, he told her. She assented without complaining, knowing he was right. Ever since the bombing they'd been preparing to leave, making lists and deciding what to take, how to leave, when to go.

"We will leave after Mass and join the people who are going back to their villages." Emilio made her look at him in the light of the one candle left burning. She glanced down but soon lifted her head and met his gaze. "You cannot tell anyone we are going. Do you understand?"

"Not Sofía?"

"No one."

"She is my best friend. We were in school together, we married the same year." She thought of all she and Sofía had shared.

"No one. It wouldn't be safe for her to know. You wouldn't want her to have to lie for you or to get hurt. Once we start we cannot turn around, do you understand? *No podemos volver nunca.*" We can never return.

Emilio left Magdalena to finish packing, and outside in the moonlight he dug into the earth with his knife, loosening the soil. Scraping together the only part of the land he'd ever own, he put the few scoops of dirt in a packet, his dreams reduced to a square of paper.

When Magdalena finished folding their clothes into tight bundles, she slipped outside, carefully skirted the bombed church, and cautiously made her way to the village's graveyard. She approached her husband's grave, marked by a wooden cross Emilio had carved. They'd buried her husband's broken body at night, rushing through the prayers themselves. Earlier that morning, two death squad members had pulled Agustín out of his bed and dragged him to the woods. The villagers had fled to the fields, to caves, but Magdalena had not been able to leave the hut. She had remained rooted to a dark corner by Agustín's screams as the soldiers tortured him for information. They would not believe his truths: He was not a member of the workers' union; he was not a supporter of the student organization; he was not a member of any leftist group; he was not involved in his relatives' activities. He had no information to give. When silence finally released Magdalena from the corner, she searched the woods with her breaths coming in painful gasps, her heartbeats thunderous blows inside her chest. An hour later, she found Agustín's body in a ditch at the village's edge. In an instant, her heart sealed.

She knew Emilio looked at her as an old woman, past feelings and desires. But she remembered the first time she'd seen Agustín at a dance. She'd been part of the inner circle and he was on the outside; he'd tracked her with his eyes while the circles revolved in opposite directions. When they were introduced by her aunt weeks later, he'd kissed her hand, and she had shivered with the electric acknowledgment of immediate passion. On the night of their wedding, she opened herself to him with an eagerness born not of experience, but of a wondrous knowing, nonetheless.

By the cross, Magdalena's hands swept over the blades of grass she'd finally coaxed into life. "If I don't go, Emilio won't either. I know I'm breaking my promise to you, but we will meet in the world of God and the angels, I am sure of it. *Quiero tu permiso, y tu bendición.*" I want your permission and your blessing. She bent her head until her ear pressed the grass, and after some moments, satisfied, she rose and made the sign of the cross. She walked away without glancing back.

# Chapter 6

I'd never tell David, but my early morning exercise edged toward being more a pleasure than drudgery. I had graduated from brisk walking to walking with intervals of light jogging. I could tell that my legs were stronger and my flexibility was improving. Not quite able to run yet, I nonetheless had made progress. The time spent exercising had become important, too, for me to mull over my research. The study I was reviewing now—following the steps of a particular cell's pathway, observing how and when it changed, and in what order—seemed a corollary to my current situation: one thing leading to another, one thing having an impact on something else. Whether it was proteins interacting with cells, or humans trying to navigate everyday challenges, this process captured for me the very essence of life. How do we all interact, how are we all connected, and what did it mean?

This morning, Grady was loading large pieces of hinged plywood into his truck. We had established a friendly rapport. He teased me and continued to call me "Missy." Maggie had told me that he struggled to remember people's names, so he called every woman or girl "Missy," and every male was "Bud" or "Buddy." I could relate to this, I thought, and admired his strategy.

"Morning, Grady." I peered into the truck's bed. "This certainly doesn't look like your usual firewood."

"Oh, no, Missy. These are the pieces of scenery I'm making for the traveling Shakespeare troupe in Staunton."

"You work for a theater?"

"Yes'm. I build these. They paint the scenery and decorations on them; I'm not much of a hand for paintin' anything other than the side of a barn." He winked at me and grinned.

The pieces were crafted with ingenuity and care. "I'm impressed, Grady." He beamed at me. "I'm here on official business, however. I'd like to order a load of wood from you." We agreed on the details, shaking hands to complete the deal.

The bright lights in the Bridgewater grocery store made my head hurt. I aimlessly pushed the cart up and down the aisles. Everything was too abundant, and I had difficulty making decisions, in part because none of the brand names sounded familiar to me. What kinds of cereal, coffee, milk, and bread did I usually buy?

After the accident, I had no idea which foods I liked and disliked, and I swore food such as eggplants and cantaloupes were not edible. During one phase of my recovery, when I kept arguing over every word with my father, he'd pushed his chair back with such force that it hit the dining room wall. He grabbed some food and a knife from the kitchen and returned, shouting at me, "This is an apple, Katherine." He rammed the knife through it. "Whether you believe it or not, that's the name of it, and this is what it looks like inside. This is called a cantaloupe." He chopped it open, the knife creasing the dining room table's surface, the juice magnifying the table's grain, the fresh, bright smell of it seeping into a consciousness of summer mornings on a concrete porch. "And these are grapes." He dumped them in front of me. "These are cornflakes." He tore open the box, and the rough flakes coursed over my arms onto the floor. "Things like these have names, and you can't argue about it. You're going to have to accept that what I tell you is the truth." He'd leaned closer to me and shouted, "Some things even you, *even you*, have to take on faith." My nightmares at that point had kept us awake for weeks at a time, and his face reflected his lack of sleep. He had stopped abruptly, aghast at his anger as his frustration drained away. I'd never told my father that names of foods could still sound strange to me.

After roaming the store's aisles for more than fifteen minutes, I felt uneasy because nothing looked like what I needed for my parents' visit. I finally remembered I had a list in my pocket. I relaxed when I saw I'd written down what to get, including brand names and the exact amounts of each item.

That night I checked my list: fresh linen on the bed, clean towels and soap in the bathroom, dry wood by the fireplace, floors vacuumed and polished, ingredients for apple cobbler measured out, and the table set for dinner. The cabin shimmered with order. I was ready.

My parents arrived at the cabin as I finished going through the house one last time. This was the house of a competent person, and my parents would have to agree I was doing well. Watching them get out of the car and size up the yard and the cabin, I focused first on my mother. When I pictured her, physical descriptions did not come to mind, but adjectives describing her personality did: capable, creative, intelligent, straightforward. My father, however, I visualized in physical terms: erect posture, lean build, well-defined features.

They seemed reassured by the look of the cabin and with my progress. While we ate a picnic lunch in the preserve and caught up on family news, I remembered our battles over my coming here to live alone. They continued to invent hypothetical situations, even in our recent conversations. Their fear threatened to claim me, and I worried about what would happen if the part of me that was scared, too, gave in. They needed to see I was coping and improving.

While my parents took a nap, I rechecked everything, wanting my small party to go well. Standing between the kitchen and the living room, I thought about the evening's logistics. The kitchen had limited counter space, and the dining area, actually part of the living room, was tiny. I could set the glasses, cups, and beverages on the kitchen counter; the apple cobbler and the bowls for it could be on the dining room table, of course; and the platter of grapes, cheese, and crackers could go in the living room on the . . . what was it called? How ludicrous, a simple piece of furniture I saw and used every day. I stared at it. "Stop. You're nervous about having company. Take your time." I tried using the memory techniques I'd learned in rehab to deal with aphasia. Describe it: brown, wooden, rectangular, four legs, put things on it, chairs . . . table. Table and chairs. It was an end table. No, they were at each end of the sofa. I knew it had another part of its name but couldn't remember it.

I made a quick call to Diane. "I need words. What do you call the kind of table that sits in front of a sofa? A sofa table doesn't sound right."

"A coffee table. Why do you need to know?"

"I'm having people over for dessert and coffee. My parents are here and I want to prove to them I'm doing well."

"You? A party?"

"Yes. And I'm beginning to get nervous. You know how my aphasia becomes more pronounced with stress."

"Kate. Take a chill pill."

"A what?"

"A chill pill. Relax." A high school English teacher, Diane frequently used her students' slang to tease me.

"I'm trying to. Thanks. How's your dad?" Diane's father had been diagnosed with Alzheimer's last year.

"We're losing him by inches. It's getting to the point where Mom can't take care of him at home any longer, and we all dread the day that is coming."

"I'm so sorry. Hug your mom and dad for me, will you? And one for you."

I ended the call and began naming everything I could see in the living room: fireplace, sofa, chairs, lamps, curtains, coffee table. Remembering earlier therapy exercises, I made a chart, drawing simple line pictures of as many objects as I could with their names next to their pictures. I taped it on the inside of a little-used kitchen cabinet. I realized the likelihood I would need one of these words was slim, and what did I think I would do? Ask someone to wait while I ran to the kitchen and looked at my chart? Still, it made me feel more confident.

After dinner, the Schoenfelds knocked on the door. Although I'd told people not to bring anything, Eleanor held a plastic jug filled with hot cider, while Virgil gave me a container. "Eleanor's cheese straws."

"His favorite," she announced. "He's sharing them with great reluctance and much prodding from me."

"Thank you, both of you. These are my parents, Rachel and Evan Solterra. Mom, Dad, I'd like you to meet Eleanor and Virgil Schoenfeld."

"We've been eager to meet you," my mother said. "Evan and I are delighted Kate has such good neighbors."

"We feel fortunate to have Kate close by, too," Eleanor replied.

I opened the door for the Mackenzies and Paul. I'd invited Paul last Saturday when we'd walked out of the store together with our newspapers. He'd responded without hesitation and seemed pleased to be included. I was glad to have enough people to make it a real occasion, something my parents would have to acknowledge as a sign of progress.

I blanked on names but everyone introduced themselves to my parents, and before long, Paul was popping corn in the fireplace, Abby had poured coffee and cider, and Virgil had distributed dishes of cobbler and ice cream. There was a lull but Virgil asked, "Who's doing what for Founder's Day? Has the planning committee met?"

"What's that?" I hadn't expected help from Virgil in keeping the conversation going. Virgil glanced at Paul, who answered.

"It commemorates the day John Drake and his large family and their friends decided they'd settle here and not push farther west. They founded the town. We have an old-fashioned celebration with canoe trips down the river, softball games, scavenger hunts in the preserve, hayrides, a potluck supper, and a big bonfire at the Meetinghouse to top it all off."

"The little white church near the preserve?" I asked.

Paul poured more popcorn into my bowl. "You know about that?"

"I found it while I was out walking."

"A Quaker church?" my father asked.

"Yes. That's right, you're a history professor at a seminary, aren't you?" Paul measured more popcorn kernels into the wire basket. I'd told Paul about my parents when I'd invited him to the gathering.

"Yes, and of course, I've studied about Friends."

"Is Founder's Day a Quaker event?" I asked.

Abby replied, "It's a community-wide event, but we help to organize it. It's not until the spring, but we're not known for our quick planning."

I'd met Abby when she'd been working at the general store during her fall break. She had a sense of assurance about her that I knew I hadn't possessed when I was her age. I wondered if everyone here was a Quaker; Abby had said "we." Virgil and Eleanor, with their silent grace? Paul, with his quiet manner?

As my guests were leaving, I saw Paul speak to my father, who checked his pocket calendar. Eleanor helped me carry glasses and cups into the kitchen. "It has been a pleasure to meet your parents. They're worried about you, though."

"My parents worry too much."

She laughed lightly, placing her hand on my arm. "That's what parents do, Kate. Your mother said you'd been seriously hurt."

I felt my throat tighten. That's what I'd meant to tell my mother when she'd awakened from her nap. I'd forgotten to tell her no one was to know. I felt annoyed with her, but more so with myself. It would have been simple enough to have written it down so I wouldn't forget to tell her.

"Virgil and I are up the ridge if you need us. You know you can call on us."

I took the glasses from her. "Yes, I do." I schooled the impatience from my voice and added, "Thank you, Eleanor."

After my guests left, my parents and I sat on the sofa and finished the last of the coffee. "I like your friends," my father told me.

"I do too," my mother said. "Eleanor and I talked about art and teaching. You didn't tell me she had taught art at a college."

"You also talked to her about me."

"Oh, Kate, it was one mother talking to another. You're up here all alone."

"I'm doing better than I have in a long time. I hadn't wanted anyone here to know."

"Why not? I didn't know you were planning on keeping it secret. It's nothing to be embarrassed about. I didn't go into details."

"I'm not embarrassed, but I don't want to be thought of as an accident victim. In fact, I don't want to be a victim of anything or anyone at all." I tried to lighten my tone. "Please don't worry about me. Can't you see I'm doing well here? But even if I don't progress any further than I have right now, it won't be what I'd hoped, but it will be all right." Hearing the words, I wanted to believe them, wanted the truth of the words soldered into fact, wanted them to expunge the worry I saw in my parents' faces.

My father straightened the living room while my mother took the dishes into the kitchen. I followed her with the last plate. "Leave those dishes and I'll wash them in the morning. It's late."

She had a peculiar expression on her face. "Mom, what's wrong?" Then I saw the cabinet door open, saw her pointing to my picture chart.

"Haven't you been saying everything's fine during our visit, Katherine? I guess you want this removed before any of your friends see it?" She ripped my chart from the cabinet door and slapped it on the counter. "You expect to live in this isolated place by yourself with no one knowing anything about you, yet you can't remember 'plate' and 'chair.' And you expect me to give you my blessing and let you do it."

"You can't keep me from doing this, and I'm not asking for your blessing. But I would like you to stop fighting me on it." I could feel my father's presence in the kitchen doorway, but he remained quiet. I saw her blinking back tears.

Feeling manipulated, I had a flash of anger. "Stop crying, Mom. This isn't worth crying over." I tried to link together words that would make sense. "If I let fear control my life, I am a victim. Sometimes it takes all my energy to keep my fears at bay, so I don't have the strength to guard against your concerns, too. One of the reasons I came here was to stop being a fearful person. The rehab center's chaplain was right about one thing: Not many people hurt so badly get a second chance. Considering most of the other people at the rehab center, I got off lucky. I try to remember them when I'm feeling sorry for myself. Making a chart of words is a small price. I must make my peace with this because I can't undo it, it's not going to go away, and it might not get any better. Drake's Springs feels like a place where I can figure this out."

My mother dried her face. "All right. I'll try to stop fighting, but don't expect me to stop worrying."

I gave her a hug. "I don't expect that, Mom. I understand that's a mother's sacred role, according to Dad."

After my parents had gone to my bedroom, I turned the sofa into my bed for the night. Overall, it had been a good evening. I hadn't even needed to look at the chart, but then, I'd not said much. I did resent my mother's talking to Eleanor about the accident and wondered how much she had told her. On my visits home, my parents would scrutinize my face to detect any pain I was trying to hide. The last time we saw each other before I came to the cabin, we had a cutting argument over my mother's request that I call to let her know I'd arrived safely. It was trivial, but it came after a month of arguing about my plans to come here. When I was ready to leave, my mother refused to say goodbye. My father explained, "You can't imagine what it's like to see your child hurt."

"But it's been a while now."

"There are some things time doesn't change. When the phone rings late at night or the doorbell rings unexpectedly, your mother is so nervous she shakes. Having your child nearly die cuts into you in a way I'm not sure ever completely heals. We were so full of fear, Katherine, that there was no room left inside for anything else. Don't be selfish, especially over something so small and reasonable. She'd want you to call even if there had never been an accident. Call her." I had called, but the conversation had been pulled taut with my lingering resentment and her anxiety.

In the morning, no one mentioned last night's argument, though I felt it wrapped around us like reeds ringing a lake, soundless sentinels to the lapping water. As my parents drove away, I felt relieved they had come and had seen for themselves that I was not living a tenuous life in the mountains. Reveling in the silence, I started to sit down at my desk to work but felt empty and unsettled. I decided to give myself the reward of more sleep and dreamed that my parents won the Quakers' sack race at Founder's Day.

The silence in the Meetinghouse, concentrated and expressive, assumed a physical presence. It limned the faces of the Quakers and tinged even the rectangles of light tiptoeing across the floorboards. As people entered, they added to the silence until the entire congregation sat bathed in a reverent quiet. I recognized the Hispanic family I'd seen one time at the Bridgewater grocery store.

What was everyone thinking? A baby cried briefly but no one seemed disturbed. A few weeks ago, I'd asked Paul about the service, what it was like and if I could come. Despite my lack of religious belief, I'd felt a baffling pull toward the Meetinghouse. "Of course," he'd told me. "It's called a 'Meeting for Worship,' and it's probably different from what you've experienced. It's so plain, however, that you can't go wrong, if that's concerning you. We always begin and end a service in silence. Sometimes several people speak if they feel so led, and anyone may speak, even children, newcomers, and people who aren't Quakers. The Meeting may be silent for the whole time.

About twenty minutes after beginning, the children leave for First Day School, the Quaker version of Sunday School. At the end of the service, called Rise of Meeting, whoever is presiding greets the people next to him or her. Everyone shakes hands, visitors introduce themselves, and people make announcements. Doesn't sound like much, the way I explain it. And because people always ask me this, wear whatever you'd like. If you wear jeans, you'll blend right in."

At the front of the room, I saw Paul resting against the back of the bench. He looked absorbed and unaware of others around him. I spotted the Schoenfelds on the bench nearest the piano. Virgil sat with his palms down on his knees with Eleanor leaning lightly against him. Along with Cooper and Abby Mackenzie, I recognized others I knew from sight, people who had been at the Mackenzies' store or in Bridgewater. I counted about fifty people.

Once the children left for First Day School, I closed my eyes and wondered what my father would think of this worship service. He had once asked me when I'd stopped believing in God. He had genuinely wanted to know if there had been a specific time when my faith had disintegrated. Trying to remember a time when I had truly believed, I couldn't. It wasn't so much that I resisted religious belief; I simply felt an echoing hollowness. During one of my father's visits to the rehab center, he'd asked me if I'd called out to God when the other car was going to hit me. "Did you, Katie? Knowing there was nothing you could do, what was your last thought?"

"I don't know," I had answered him, the communication board's voice sounding flat and emotionless when I'd wanted to scream at him to stop forcing me to remember; it was cruel to keep asking me. Filled with explosive terror, the instant had held no time for prayer.

A man who was speaking pulled my attention to the surface. He stood with his fingers curved over the bench in front of him. No one moved or even turned toward him. "I was out in the field one morning a few weeks ago, repairing my fences. I didn't hear anything but rather felt something behind me, and when I glanced around, I saw an albino doe. She was beautiful, almost supernatural. After we looked at each other for several seconds, she disappeared so silently I wondered for a moment if I had imagined her. Seeing her underscored for me the beauty of creation. Sitting here this morning, I thought of how we sometimes see human beings who are different as less than perfect. How would their lives change, how would *my* life change, if I saw them with their own beauty, as a welcome part of creation, like the doe?" The man sat down, and the silence sealed over the hole his words had made.

At the end of the hour, Josiah Kendall, whom I'd met on the Meeting-house steps, shook my hand. "We're glad you came." The person next to me, and those on the benches in front of and behind me, extended their hands in turn.

Everyone looked toward the bench facing the door. Paul stood and spoke. "Good morning. I'm Paul Whittaker, Clerk of the Meeting. I'd like to welcome everyone, especially our visitors and anyone who's been away for a while. If you will, please stand and tell us about yourselves."

He was Clerk of the Meeting? Was that like being a minister? Why hadn't he mentioned it when I asked him about coming? I waited a mo-ment before standing. "I'm Kate Solterra. I'm here in Drake's Springs on a sabbatical."

"We're happy to have you with us, Kate. Please sign the register if you'd like before leaving. Do we have any other guests or anyone who's returned after an absence?" No one stood. "Announcements?"

At the conclusion of the announcements, people stood and talked, the conversation sounding especially loud after the prolonged silences. I'd planned to slip out the door, but several Quakers came up to me, introduced themselves, and asked me about my work and sabbatical. Paul appeared at my side and drew me over to the side door. "Would you like to see the rest of the building?" He led me into a narrow back foyer. "We tend to mob visitors; you looked taken aback."

"I was. Thanks for rescuing me."

He took me upstairs to show me the library, the nursery, an office, and classrooms. We went downstairs to the kitchen and an all-purpose room. "This is where we have our Shared Meal, a potluck the second First Day of every month. The phrase 'First Day' is probably unfamiliar to you. Early Friends refused to use the pagan names of the months and days of the week; we continue the tradition, so First Day is Sunday, First Month is January, and so forth."

"You're the Clerk? A minister?"

"Not a minister. We don't have ministers, at least not in what's called an 'unprogrammed Meeting.'" He saw my confusion. "Friends hold to the 'priesthood of all believers' concept, in that you don't need an intermediary to come between the individual and God. Clerks do such things as help with the business of the Meeting and work with committees and special pro-grams. However, the 'programmed Meetings' do have pastors; their services would probably feel more familiar to you."

We went outside where people lingered in the side yard. Josiah stopped Paul and offered, "I'll close up if you'd like to go ahead." Paul and I walked down the lane leading away from the Meetinghouse.

"May I ask what you thought of Meeting?"

"The quiet made me restless at first, but eventually it surrounded me and felt comfortable. Comforting, even."

We approached the driveway to my cabin. "If I don't see you before you leave for Thanksgiving, have a great holiday and a safe journey to and from." He lightly touched my arm. "It was good to have you in Meeting."

# Chapter 7

## EL SALVADOR, GUATEMALA

LEADING THE PEOPLE THROUGH the solemn ritual, Father Hannan waited at intervals to allow for the interpreter's translation. He had felt the occasion was too significant to rely on his school-learned Spanish. "I have been thinking, this morning and when I first heard about the bombing, about the will of God. How can it be the will of God for twenty-three people to die such a cruel death, twenty-two children and one young, devout woman who had sacrificed an easy life to come here? We are God-loving people. If it is the will of God, our obligation is to accept. To grieve, yes. To hold their memories close, yes. But ultimately to accept the loss of twenty-three innocent lives."

Gathered under the awning, the people looked up at him with their faces as closed as stone, their eyes anchored in grief. Spreading out his arms, he continued. "What if we choose not to accept? This bombing was evil. Children and their teacher were killed in a church, a sacred place where, above all, they should have been safe. This was evil; how can it have anything but an evil source? How could this be the will of God?"

Father Hannan's voice rose, his questions a persistent rhythm trying to penetrate their sorrow. "Christ charges us to love our enemies, which, admittedly, seems an unbearable command in this tragedy. How do we find our way through the thicket of pain and forgive those who have in such a brutal manner torn loved ones from their families? Is there some way to forgive and not have it be a betrayal? Can we forgive them and still honor the lives that were lost here? Consider if we truly loved our enemies, we would stop them from committing atrocities—not by returning evil with evil, for that makes us equally guilty, but by showing them how to return to their essential humanity. What if the will of God is for us not to accept, but to resist? To say no more children will die from violence and evil? No more women, no more men, will be the victims of death squads? And not simply to state it, but to act on it by writing about it? By gathering and marching together, shouting with all our grief until the world listens? To tell the universe about El Mozote, and the massacres at Lempa River and Sumpul River? To stand up and say the source of this evil is not God, but the government of your country and the government of mine? If the will of God is for us to resist and put an end to this continuous slaughter, can we deny our obligation? Have these children and their teacher died in vain?" Father Hannan finished more quietly, spacing out his words: "If it is the will of God for us to renounce the killing of innocent people, the power of God will give us strength and will protect us." He spoke the names of the children and their teacher, saying something about each one. "We will remember," he ended.

The people wept for the lost futures lined up in front of them, the fresh graves an abomination. Emilio hoped the children had not had time to be afraid, that death had been as sudden as a spear of summer lightning. As they chanted the last prayer, Emilio thought about his father and about Felipe, whose grave would be unknown. Did this young priest realize he might not make it home because of what he had said here? Didn't he know about Archbishop Óscar Romero, who was killed while celebrating Mass? Resistance would be a noble cause, but would it make any difference whether he died in the resistance or was killed like the children, like Felipe, like their father, like Magdalena's husband? Did the people here have the strength left to defy the government? They had heard it all before, words like the North American priest's, words from outsiders who came, stayed a short while, then left.

Magdalena sought out her friend. "So many people," Sofía said. "I had not expected many people would come, so perhaps someone will do something."

"Maybe." She wanted to say more, standing there and holding her friend's hands for the last time. She tried to memorize what Sofía looked like, with her flashing dark eyes, the curve of her brows, her long, tapered fingers, in order to imprint her friend's features in her memory. Sometimes she couldn't remember her own husband's face and had to run and get her photograph of him.

"Sofía, at least we will always be friends, no matter what. *Siempre amigas*." Always friends. She thought back to when they'd first become close. It was on the morning Sofía had stolen down to the river to wash the first stains from her clothing; they'd shared shy looks, a mixture of embarrassment and pride at officially being women. From then on, their lives unfolded in a series of parallels. The two friends were courted and married within the same year. They experienced the anxiety and elation of childbirth and the wordless, inconsolable anguish of Magdalena's stillborn son. They grieved the loss of Sofía's husband through betrayal and the death of Magdalena's to the death squad. Through it all, they'd survived.

"Yes, we will forever be friends." Sofía gave Magdalena a hug and then left. Magdalena looked at her hands, her feet; this lie to her best friend, this sin of omission, had changed her in some irredeemable way, for some price had to be exacted.

Emilio and Magdalena joined a crowd headed toward the next town, which was much larger than their village. Emilio knew many of the men. "I have business there," he replied to their questions, and accounting for the old woman's presence, added, "My brother's mother-in-law is afraid to stay alone."

Watching the young man in the presence of other men, Magdalena measured Emilio for the trip ahead. She'd always seen him as a boy, someone who got into scrapes and who had a reputation among local girls for talking big. She had her doubts he could lead them all the way to her daughter, but she had no choice.

"Do you think there will be trouble tonight?" The men talked about the priest's message and about the rural cooperatives trying to organize the campesinos, the farmworkers. Finally, however, they were pulled by the sinews of the women's silence; an ocean had already formed between those who had lost children and those who had not. It would be an immovable divider for the rest of their lives.

Leaving the group, Emilio and Magdalena approached the house of Felipe's friend. Eduardo opened the door, looked behind them, and welcomed them inside. "You've decided. I was afraid you wouldn't go through with it, but the car is packed with your things and the maps." Emilio had brought additional food and clothes to Eduardo the previous week.

Changing her clothes behind a curtain partitioning the single-room house, Magdalena removed the black dress she'd worn to the Mass and put on her husband's shirt and overalls. He hadn't been much larger than she was, though she would need to roll up the pants legs. In the mirror that leaned against a wall, she noted something else she'd have to do. Unhooking the bib of the overalls and taking off the shirt, she wrapped the spare shirt around her breasts and secured it with the safety pins she'd brought to fix the overalls. She viewed herself in the mirror one last time. With her hair up and a hat on, she might pass for a man, at least from a distance.

When she rejoined the men, Eduardo advised her to cut her hair. "But I'll wear the hat; my hair has never been short, not since I was small." Pressing her palms along the sides of her head, she remembered how Agustín had brushed her hair, often as a prelude to making love to her, his hands smoothing the hair and continuing down her back.

"It might come loose from the clips. If it's short, it will be easier to take care of." Eduardo gave the scissors to Emilio.

"It will grow back," Emilio told her. She removed the clips, and he cut her hair. She tried not to glance down as the hair fell in light clumps to the floor, more remnants to leave behind.

When he'd finished, she again put her hands up to her head and held back a cry. "It feels so strange; my head feels smaller." She managed a smile for Emilio. "Maybe I will like it short. *Una mujer moderna.*" A modern woman.

Eduardo motioned them toward the door. "You must leave now."

"Thank you for what you have done," Emilio said.

"It was my pleasure to return a favor Felipe did for me." After checking up and down the street, he ushered them out the back door and into an alley. "*Tengan cuidado.*" Be careful. He helped Magdalena into the car, locking and shutting her door.

When she heard the click of the lock, she thought, we are leaving. I will never see my homeland again. I will never pray by my husband's grave again, and I will not be buried next to him. From this moment on, my life will be different.

Felipe's friend tapped on the window, signaling for Magdalena to roll it down. "*Vayan con Dios,*" he told them. "*Vayan con Dios.*" Go with God.

Drained from the driving, from the heat, from looking over their shoulders and worrying about every sound and movement, they spent much of their time in silence. Emilio gleaned food from untended fields, and Magdalena cobbled together what she could from their scant supplies. She pressed on him as much food as she could, slipping portions from her plate to his when he wasn't looking.

He caught her. "You must eat," he admonished.

"I'll be fine, but you must keep up your strength."

"And so must you. We'll have to give up the car later, travel on foot, and cross the river."

"We must be careful. I had a dream this morning. We were crossing the river and enormous sea creatures dragged us to the bottom. We couldn't breathe; they were choking us."

"You're scared about crossing the river, that's all."

"These creatures had the faces of the children from our village. This is a sign. We abandoned them, and now terrible things will happen to us. Is there another way to cross, a bridge or a ferry?"

"It was a nightmare, Magdalena, a bad dream. Do not invent worries."

They camped close to the Guatemalan border. Emilio let Magdalena sleep, assuring her he would wake her in a few hours for her turn to watch. She had fallen asleep almost as soon as she tucked one hand under her cheek. At some point on their trip, they'd switched roles, and Magdalena now looked to him to make the decisions. For even inconsequential matters, she deferred to his judgment, and he'd never been more scared.

Soon they'd be in Guatemala, not that it was a safer country. He knew thousands of people had fled from Guatemala to southern Mexico, forced from their homes because of yet another civil war. They drifted through a strange realm of refugees, living in a state of constant flux and uncertainty with too little hope for better times. At least three children died each day in the Honduran camp where Emilio had spent a wretched month; the refugees in Guatemalan camps struggled to survive with little water, one or two tortillas a day, and meager servings of rice or beans. Safety existed nowhere in this region of the world. Where was justice, with some living in abundance and security, while others existed from one meal to the next, surrounded by violence?

Emilio jerked himself into full awareness. Had Magdalena called to him? He turned his head. No. She slept with her hat under her head for a pillow. He sensed someone watching them, though, felt the air fluctuate with an evil charge. Glancing around, calculating the distance from where they were to the car, he regretted not sleeping inside it.

"Don't try." An armed soldier appeared next to him. "And don't worry about getting the car back to your friend, for he won't need it."

Emilio grabbed the tire iron he'd hidden underneath the blanket. He stood, raised his only weapon above his head, and hammered it onto the soldier's skull with one brutal blow. The sound of iron on bone through flesh and muscle resounded in his own skull and sickened him. The soldier slumped at his feet. Reaching down, Emilio removed the soldier's gun from its holster and, with shaking hands, pulled ammunition from the bandolier. Retrieving the tire iron, Emilio scrabbled for his blanket and the backpack. Magdalena stood, swaying unsteadily, trying not to look at the soldier's bloodied head but unable to resist staring. She wanted to go to him and try to stop the blood. She reached out, but Emilio yanked her arm and shoved her to the car. "¡*Rápido, rápido!*" Quickly!

Magdalena kept repeating, "*Dios te salve, María, llena eres de gracia; Dios te salve, María, llena eres de gracia.*" Hail Mary, full of grace; Hail Mary, full of grace. She was unable to think of the rest of the prayer. When the car roared from the scene, she looked back at the motionless form, the blood spreading shapes of giant amoebas across the dry ground.

"You killed him! You didn't have to kill him. Now you're a murderer like the rest of them."

"¡*Cállese!*" Emilio yelled at her to shut up. "He might not be dead. I hit him just once. He would have killed us or forced us to go back to be killed."

"Stop the car." Seeing the resolve in her face, he stopped with sudden force, the car's tires scattering rocks. She reached for the door handle.

"What are you doing?" He caught her arm, but she twisted away from his grasp and faced him.

"I want to get out. You go ahead; I'll find my own way. Or I won't go at all. I can't be part of murder. I want to be with my daughter, my family, but not at this price."

Emilio slammed his hands against the steering wheel. "He was going to kill us! We're fighting for our lives here! And all your praying and your faith cannot change what's happening to us."

Pulling her cross out from under her shirt, Magdalena slipped its chain over her head. She thrust the carved cross in his face and shouted, "This is all I have! My daughter left, Agustín was murdered, children have been killed, but I have my faith. It is the only thing I have, and it *must* be enough."

"Faith!" he spat out. "Faith may save you in heaven, if there is one, but it does you no good here, now. It's the biggest sham priests have to sell."

Magdalena returned her cross to its place around her neck, under her shirt. Surely, the shock of perhaps having killed someone was talking here, not Emilio. How could she entrust her life to a godless man?

"I did not want to hurt the man but had no other choice. They'll find him soon, and we will be hunted down. We are on their list. If you leave this car now you will die. You will not live even one more day." Without waiting for a response, he drove back onto the road and they continued, a silenced waterfall between them.

Neither Emilio nor Magdalena spoke of the soldier for several days, as though not talking about him would erase what had happened, would reverse the direction of the tire iron, would deaden the sound of metal crushing bone. She asked, "Do you think you killed him?"

"I don't know. I smashed the tire iron on his skull."

"Why couldn't you have hurt him just enough to let us get away? This is murder, Emilio."

"Self-defense. And there is never only one soldier. He knew Eduardo had given us the car, and my guess is he killed him. Others know about us now. We will be hunted down."

"Maybe you should have buried him."

"There was no time."

"This is a sinful thing."

"Don't you think I know that?" he shouted at her.

"You would do anything to get up north?"

"I'll do what I have to for our survival."

"*Por favor,*" she pleaded, "*no más asesinatos.*" Please, no more killings.

"I can't promise you."

"We will have to answer to God for this killing."

"Forgive me, Magdalena, but maybe God should keep us safe on this journey."

I had to admit it had been that way for months. When I'd moved back to my apartment, not yet able to work, I'd fought bouts of loneliness during the day. But when David would come over, I'd be even lonelier. He would immerse himself in work, read the paper, or watch sports on television. It hurt that he'd prefer doing those activities to spending time with me. I felt invisible. When I tried to get him to take time off, he'd snap, "I have too much work to do." I felt embarrassed to ask him to pay attention to me. No longer his colleague, I sensed he didn't find me interesting and saw me as less worthy. How had we gone from making marriage plans before the accident to being two stiff strangers? If we moved in together now and eventually married, I could see myself becoming his housekeeper, cook, and errand runner, but his wife in name only.

In fact, since I'd left the rehab center, we hadn't spent much time together at all, with practically no physical intimacy. When I was recovering, he claimed he was afraid he might hurt me; later, he pleaded fatigue from long hours at work. Our relationship had devolved into a quick kiss when he came to see me and another one when he left. I'd privately begun calling them "Obligatory Kiss Number One" and "Obligatory Kiss Number Two." I chastised myself: Why would I stay with someone who didn't want to touch me? Was I the bigger problem here, allowing myself to be treated with disregard? I suspected he was biding his time, waiting for me to be recovered enough so he wouldn't look like a heel for ending the relationship. But since we'd considered moving in together with the intention of marriage one day, shouldn't we fight for our relationship before conceding defeat?

"How did you come up with this result?" he asked.

"What?" His question brought me back to the moment. He repeated his question, not quite masking his impatience. I studied the figures and reread the passage, a lengthy discussion of the biochemical interactions of certain new drugs on multiple sclerosis. "I don't know. Isn't it supported in my tables?"

"No. This was the major discrepancy, but there are other minor ones."

I stared at the page then went over to the fireplace to sit on the wide hearth's edge. The warmth of the fire felt good on my back.

"Can you set up more comprehensive systems?"

"I thought I had with this." It was more than a matter of reversing a few numbers; there were breaks in my thought processing. David knew the facts related to my injuries, but he had little idea how these limitations played out in my life. To be fair, I hadn't shared the specifics of my day-to-day experiences with him, even hid as much as I could from him. I'd known on some level all along he wouldn't be able to cope with this reality, for he was ill at ease with any kind of weakness. He wouldn't want who I was now. I would never make enough progress in his eyes. I wanted to hold this against him, but who could say I wouldn't feel similarly if it had happened to him? It took patience to live with someone like me. The sadness of it all reshaped my anger into a canyon of hurt.

He placed his papers back in his briefcase. "What are you going to do?"

"Continue, for now. I have time before I need to give Matthew my decision."

It was late when David left. I remained near the fireplace and watched the fire die. The logs shifted, causing a cylinder of sparks. Since I was the one who'd insisted I didn't expect him to wait for me, I wasn't being fair to him. He didn't have to play the martyr. I wasn't the same person, and he should be able to break things off without feeling guilty. He could be honest about how he felt, though.

"So could you," I told myself. If I were honest, I'd admit that although I'd insisted he didn't have to wait for me, I didn't want to think he'd leave me. If I were honest, I'd face up to being afraid to let him go.

I tended the Thanksgiving meal while my parents and my aunt and uncle went to an ecumenical service downtown. Covering the table with my grandmother's white damask cloth, I then counted out the plates and distributed them. Setting down the last plate, I snatched it back up, annoyed with myself. I'd assumed David was going to come to Thanksgiving dinner as usual. I'd started giving him the specifics the other night after we'd finished working, and he'd stopped me. "I'm sorry, Kate. I made other plans some time ago because I didn't think you'd be home. I should have told you." Replaying the conversation in my mind, I wondered about his excuse. There was something about how he'd glanced away when I'd started talking about the dinner. And why did he think I wouldn't be with my family for Thanksgiving? Did he think I'd still be at the rehab center?

My anger hadn't been quenched by sadness after all. "What a fool I've been." I slapped down the forks at each place. "Thinking he'd stick by me. He probably was seeing another woman before I even got out of the rehab center." I banged knives and spoons down on the table and parceled them out. They clinked against the plates. Slamming one of my mother's ruby goblets onto the table, the crystal shattered, the fine shards blood-red droplets on the white linen and on the carpet.

I sank to the floor. My tears splashed down my face and onto the front of my silk blouse. "No matter how many tears I shed, how many things I smash, it doesn't make me feel any better." I waited, and the surrounding quiet reminded me of the Meeting. I can move forward from this moment, I decided. It is a choice I can make. I lifted my head and wiped my face. "Take a chill pill, Kate. Get out of your own way. I doubt David is thinking of you right now."

My legs felt heavy when I stood, then stooped again, to pick up the broken glass. I hoped I could get a replacement for the goblet. Studying the fragments as if their thinness contained the answers I needed, I thought of all I'd lost. Continuing to count the losses didn't change the number of them, however. Despite my anger and hurt, I still didn't want to lose David. I'd thought we had something that would grow and last. Would he go to counseling with me? After all, the drunk driver had affected him, as well. We should work to preserve our relationship, not allow the accident to claim it, too. Letting go of David felt like one more defeat, and how I hated to give up—even when I probably should.

Having a half hour before my parents and aunt and uncle were to return, I pulled aside the drapes and watched the rain falling. It was a dreary day. Thanksgiving. Giving thanks. Images of people at the rehab center flashed in my mind: people with crushed limbs, amputees, those with paralysis, stroke survivors, and those with massive brain trauma. It was difficult to see some patients as whole human beings, the damaged parts of their bodies seeming to enlarge and magnetically draw all the attention. Who could have imagined the human body could sustain such an array of assaults?

Once, when a woman who'd been severely burned came in to regain the flexibility of her arms and legs, I couldn't bear to look at her. Half of her face had been burned off, and knowing it could have happened to any of us, to me, I had to fight being sick to my stomach. No amount of gauze and tape hid the horror of it. Another patient caught me averting my eyes and pulled me aside. "Why are you looking away? You're one of us now." I'd recoiled, thinking straight away, I'll never be one of you. I don't want to be one of you. "How long are you going to pretend you don't see her? Until her burns heal? Until her scars fade? You're not going to be here that long." Ashamed, I'd forced myself to look at the burned woman. Concentrating on her remaining eye, I began to talk to her, even though she couldn't reply because of the burns around her mouth. She endured more pain than anyone I'd ever known, and I often wondered if she wished she hadn't survived. Swallowing hard and blinking to clear away the images, I ordered myself, "Count your blessings. Move on."

My parents came in with my mother's older sister, Maria, and my Uncle Simon. I had washed my face, redone my makeup, and changed my blouse. If anyone suspected something due to my reddened eyes, they made no comment.

My father stood to give his traditional blessing; this time, though, he added, "Last year our Kate spent Thanksgiving at the rehab center. Today we offer thanks to God for bringing her home to us. She has survived and even triumphed. We are not the same," he steadied his voice, "but we are blessed." My composure, too fragile to witness the looks on my parents' faces and to hear my father's tremulous voice, disintegrated once more, but this time, I smiled and rose to embrace my parents. My uncle made us laugh when he replaced the centerpiece with a box of tissues.

My father finished his prayer. "May our laughter sustain us; may this be a Thanksgiving of joy, of peace with what is and what is to come, and of happy memories. Amen."

# Chapter 9

Since the day after Thanksgiving was unusually warm, my mother and I spent the morning cleaning off the back porch. While I swept debris out of the porch and down the steps, she dumped dirt and old plants out of flowerpots. After stacking the empty pots, she took the broom from me. "Let's take a break. Come sit on the swing."

I knew this was a prelude to a discussion. During my growing-up years, the porch swing had been the site of "serious talks," and today, my mother did not disappoint. "I know you were upset with David for not letting you know earlier about Thanksgiving. How long do you think he knew about those other plans?"

I shrugged, and my mother gave me a rueful smile. "Why did you start dating him in the first place? I've never told you this, but from the beginning, I've thought you were wrong for each other."

"From the beginning? Why? Because of what you observed about him?"

"No, more from the way *you* behaved I expected—oh, not a giddy schoolgirl response, because you've never been the type—but the kind of happiness you exude when you're excited about a new relationship that could be serious. Joy. A bubbling over. I know you're a private person, but you hardly ever spoke about him. There was little joy. Why did you choose him? Why do you continue to see him?"

"We have a lot in common, Mom. We understand the same things, we're compatible, we share similar goals."

"That sounds as exciting as a grocery list."

"It's not as though men were lining up to take me out and get to know me. I rarely dated in high school and college, or grad school, for that matter."

"So you went out with him because no one else asked, and you didn't want to be alone?"

"When you put it that way, it sounds sad and desperate."

"Is it the truth?"

My mother's question sharpened the ache between my eyes and sliced open what I feared I'd always known. "It's time we got back on track." I saw her eyes cast down for a second or two. Now, feeling hurt and irritated, I asked, "What? Go ahead and say it."

"He's not going to get back on track. My initial doubts have been confirmed. The accident brought flaws to the surface, serious ones that would have caused problems in a marriage even if the accident hadn't happened."

"We all have flaws." I could feel myself getting defensive, despite what I'd forced myself to confront the previous day. "If you think we'd be making a terrible mistake if we stayed together, don't hide behind your reasoning that it's our decision, our mistake to make."

"Perhaps this is obvious to me because your father is my reference point. Whether it's bringing me flowers for no special reason, listening to me talk about what's on my heart, or thanking me for every meal I place before him, his favorite or not, he demonstrates that he thinks of me. He pays attention to me and makes me feel cherished and respected. He acknowledges even my minor accomplishments. It's not what he gives me to mark the occasion that is important; it's that he shows he's proud of me."

My mother was a librarian, and I had observed how Dad marked her milestones. He planted a rose bush when she was a panelist for a national conference, and after an arduous reorganization of her library, he took her out for a special dinner and dancing. When she received an award for her literacy work, he gave her lovely pearl earrings. But the daily acts of courtesy and thoughtfulness that they extended to each other were what had made an impression on me.

"Despite all our years of marriage, your father doesn't take me for granted. He's not perfect, of course; neither am I. However, I come first for him when it's possible, not his career or outside interests. I'm afraid David doesn't put you first, not in minor or major ways. I've noticed he makes time for the things he wants to do but shows little interest in your pursuits. You'll propose something, he'll make a face, and you drop it. He doesn't keep his promises to you. I'm not saying he must always bend for you, but when he consistently doesn't take your feelings and wishes into consideration, I'm concerned."

I recalled suggesting we set aside time each week to do something fun and not talk about work. He'd instantly said, "I can't commit to that." It was evident to me that he didn't feel the need to provide a reason or to explain. He expected to have the final say. It was early in our relationship, and unwilling to cross him, I'd never mentioned it again.

"He's impatient; he loses his temper easily," she continued.

I thought of how when I didn't understand something or didn't get it quickly enough, he'd grimace and say, "Never mind," brushing me off. But didn't we all behave that way at times? I know I did. Any number of my mannerisms and behaviors caused David to roll his eyes or sigh in exasperation. "I'll grant you he's intense, Mom. He forgets not everyone can operate at his level."

"Do you realize how often you make excuses for him?"

I didn't respond, aware she was right. I automatically guarded what I said to David to avoid an argument or a look of disapproval. I tried not to make comments that could be construed as criticism. It wasn't worth it to me to see his pained expression or hear him mutter things under his breath. It was easier, less hurtful, to back down. I swallowed so many words I could have been one of the balloons at the Macy's Thanksgiving Day Parade. My mother waited for me to process what she'd said. I finally asked, "And the major things?"

My mother looked out over the yard for a moment before facing me. "Are you sure you want to hear this?"

"Yes."

"Following the accident, he came to the hospital and waited with us while you were in surgery. He gave blood, and he stayed and made phone calls for us. After the first surgery, the team met with us, explaining that they couldn't offer much hope you'd survive. As our vigil continued all night and into the next day, David started finding reasons to leave the intensive care unit's waiting room. He left and brought us coffee and sandwiches. He left and brought back newspapers. He left and brought us dinner from our favorite Italian restaurant. Finally, he just left."

"Without saying anything?"

"No, he kept looking at his watch, and then he apologized, saying he had an important deadline. He said if we needed him, he'd make other arrangements, but he clearly was uncomfortable being there. And it was such a half-hearted offer that it was easier to tell him to go. I was furious he couldn't put you first when you needed him the most."

"Anyone would have found the situation unnerving. It's unfair to judge him for how he behaved under such stressful circumstances."

"It doesn't take a whole lot of skill to show up, to sit by a bed, or to hold a hand."

"There were many times I told him not to come."

"Was it because you didn't need or want him? Or was it because you knew he didn't want to be there? Were you afraid he'd hide behind the excuse that he didn't know what to do or say, and you couldn't bear the disappointment and hurt that he wouldn't try to make even a minimal effort?"

"He's not an unfeeling, uncaring person."

"No, he's not, and I don't mean to make him out to be. David is a brilliant man, and I have no doubt his scientific contributions have helped to improve many lives." She reached for my hand and made me look at her. "As have yours," she said. "His actions are telling, though; they define his character, the depth of his compassion, and his ability to think of others. When you remained in the coma, at first he would come every day and spend a few minutes with you before going on to work. Then he started coming by when your father and I were preparing to go home, saying that way, you'd still have someone with you. I found out from the nurses that he stayed with you only a couple of times before stopping. He led us to believe otherwise; that's a disturbing deception."

"I would have found it difficult, too, if I had been in his place."

"Your father and I found it *difficult*, but it wasn't about how we felt. Was David there each time you had to have surgery?"

"I didn't ask him to be."

"You shouldn't have to ask a person to be there for you during life's hard times." My mother's questions came rapidly, her voice becoming sharper and angrier until she was shouting. "Did you not ask because it was so hurtful to admit he wouldn't put your needs ahead of his own? How often did he see you at the rehab center? How many times did he come and work with you? Did he help you with your speech therapy? How many times did he come and take you out for a nice dinner? Does he ever ask you about us? Does he even call and ask you how your day is going? How often is he seeing you now?"

Her eyes darkened. "Kate, when someone you love is going through a fire, you go with them! You don't put your job first; you don't put yourself first. I pray this will be the toughest thing you'll ever have to overcome, but I can almost guarantee life holds more challenges for you. Will David be there for you as you get older? How he has treated you since the accident makes me fearful for your future. He is an honorable man; I know he'd make sure you received the care you might need. But will he *want* to take care of you if your eyesight dims and you walk slowly with a cane? Will he have patience with you if your hearing diminishes or you need to be in a nursing home? You deserve someone who, when you need it, puts you first. He treats you like a convenience. I raised you to have more self-respect than this. Tell me I didn't raise you to be the kind of woman who would settle for some self-centered man's crumbs!" She sat back in the swing and took a few deep breaths.

I was shaken by my mother's intensity. "Were you going to let me marry him without telling me how you felt before the accident?"

"It was your choice. And the signs I saw concerned me, but I wasn't alarmed. However, I knew I couldn't let you proceed now without at least telling you what your father and I witnessed after the accident. David may love you, Kate. But he doesn't love you enough. You deserve someone who loves you for who you are."

We sat in silence and swung back and forth, letting the words and emotions settle. My mother reached for my hands and drew me to her. I whispered, "You're right."

"Besides, he's a bit of a humorless prig at times, to boot," she finished.

Surprised, a laugh burst out of me.

The following week, I waited until the commuter traffic lessened before driving to the office. I met with Matthew and explained the difficulties I was having with the presentation. "Until I received the proofed report I didn't know the problems existed to that extent."

He nodded once, a confirmation he believed me. "In the future, send work to me; I'll check the accuracy."

"Matthew, that isn't right. You hardly have the time to do my work on top of yours."

"The reason this is necessary isn't right or fair, either." He removed his glasses and rubbed his eyes. His voice softened like water dampening the edge of paper. "It's not your fault. I'm not going to be judging you as a scientist against the quality of the work you submit. I'll be judging its accuracy. If it's not right, we'll correct it. You're the best person to pull together this research so that it can be as valuable to us as I feel certain it will be." He stood, concluding our meeting. "We can't afford to lose the work you did before you were hurt. I won't surrender that."

David stopped me as I was leaving Matthew's office. "Do you want to go out for dinner tonight?"

Thinking about my resolve to set things straight, to be honest with him, I accepted. I resisted asking about his Thanksgiving.

After dinner, David and I returned to my parents' house for coffee and dessert. They'd gone to a late dinner and a movie to give us the house to ourselves. After helping me to identify the stages at which I needed to recheck data, we devised a lengthier checklist to follow. I told him in general what Matthew and I had discussed. "You're off the hook as my editor. He'll give you the sections you'll need for the collaborative research."

Arranging the papers in order, I placed them in a file. Now is the time, I told myself, feeling a twinge of nervousness. "David, I don't know where we stand, and I need to know."

"I thought we agreed to put things on hold."

"But for how long? Are we going to pick up where we left off, or what?"

"Is that possible?"

We were both advancing and retreating, like the shadow from a candle's flickering light. As a child, I'd wanted to pass my fingers through a candle's flame, being almost irresistibly attracted to it, thinking that if done quickly enough, I wouldn't feel any pain. "You didn't come often to see me when I was in the hospital or the rehab center, and we barely see each other now. Why not?"

He started to speak but stopped, looking everywhere in the room but at me. "It's hard to see someone you care about hurt so badly. You couldn't talk, couldn't communicate. Sometimes you didn't even want me there. How do you think I felt?" He absentmindedly played with his coffee spoon, moving it in an arc on the table. "I guess you think those are weak excuses."

"Yes, I do. I don't want excuses; I want a reason. I can sympathize with it being difficult, but we were making plans to live together, to one day get married. Since then you've hardly touched me. Is there someone else?"

"Kate, stop."

"In all this time there hasn't been anyone else?"

"What are you getting at? Are you trying to break off this relationship?"

I realized he hadn't answered my question. "I'm trying to put my life back together. I don't know where or how we fit; breaking it off might be the easiest thing to do." I stopped, trying to remember what I'd wanted to say. "But there's nothing like having your life in jeopardy to put your priorities in order. I'm trying to speak more honestly, trying to do a better job of letting people know I care about and love them. You're an important part of my life. I know I'm not the same person I was before, and I'll never be that person again, but maybe you aren't the same, either. The truth is I couldn't count on you."

"Why didn't you bring this up before now?"

"Because I was ashamed. It hurt. It hurt to find this out about you. When I needed you, you weren't there."

"I'm here now," he said, his even tone making me more upset.

I felt the familiar buzzing in my head and tried to ward it off. When I looked at him, he appeared blurry, and for a second I couldn't recall his name. "Now is easy. I can talk to you. I don't have tubes sticking out of me. The scars are fading, and if we went to bed you might not be repulsed by them. I want a reason; I want to know how you felt. I thought what we had was important enough not to throw it away without fighting for it, without seeing if there wasn't something we could save and build on."

He stabbed his spoon at the table's surface, punctuating his words. "You want to know how I felt? The woman I loved was almost killed; she was torn into pieces and there was not one damn thing I could do about it. The woman I loved pushed me away, saying she didn't want to see me, wasn't ready for me to see her in pieces, didn't trust me to be able to cope with it. The woman I loved has been so consumed by anger and fear she *radiates* with it." He swept the spoon across the table and slammed down his hands. "The woman I loved didn't have any room left for me!" he shouted. In all our time together, David had never raised his voice to me. Strangely enough, it was a relief. It struck me, too, how selfish he sounded, and that he referred to me in the past tense.

He stood and moved to the opposite end of the living room. "And you want to know how I'm feeling now? I'm feeling trapped. I'm not proud of that, but it's the truth. What would it say about me if I walked away from you?"

"You already did. I'm asking why. Because I was no longer your equal? Did you ever consider me your equal? Or was I just close enough to keep you interested, but not so close I was threatening? Now I'm someone you wouldn't date, much less marry, right? I'm no longer on your level."

"You're not being fair. Or accurate."

"Fair?" I hissed. "You're right about that at least. Nothing about this has been fair. But when two people love each other, sometimes one person must carry more of the burden for a time. You didn't even try. You say I pushed you away? You should have pushed back; you gave up on me!" We stood apart, the living room and years between us. I wavered for a moment, then decided not to suggest counseling. "We still have to work together."

"I think we can do that." He sounded farther away than he was. "I will always care about you, Katherine. I will always love you. The accident didn't damage that." Crossing the room, he reached out to hug me.

Not wanting to break off our relationship with hurt feelings and angry words, I looked up at him and tried to find a way to honor what had been good during our relationship. I wanted to end this well. "I loved every drive through the countryside, every art museum, the chess games, all the concerts and movies," I began. "You thought I loved the coffee and doughnuts you brought me on Saturday mornings, and I did, but the fact that you went to the trouble to do something just for me was what pleased me more. I loved how you would reach out for me in the middle of the night and those late Sunday mornings in your big, comfy bed; I'll miss that. I didn't love falling out of the canoe or twisting my ankle playing softball with your buddies, but I appreciated that you wanted to share those experiences with me. You made me a better scientist by challenging me to tackle the hard questions. Thank you," I ended simply, "for choosing me."

When he left, I didn't hear the door close. I had been right. He'd been waiting for an excuse, for me to lose patience with him so he could say I ended it. One more loss, a necessary one. I had passed my fingers through the flame, and although there was a certain sense of relief, it still hurt. And despite the drunk driver not having anything to do with the core of the problem, I cursed him anyway.

Damn you. May you grow old and have no one to love you, no one to play board games with, no one to hold you when you're scared.

# Chapter 10

BACK IN DRAKE'S SPRINGS, as I started to get out of the car, it occurred to me that this felt like coming home. Someone had taped a note on the outside of the front door. "Kate, Welcome back! Join us for dinner when you return? Call us. Eleanor and Virgil."

After unpacking, I made gingerbread to take to the Schoenfelds and cleaned up the kitchen. These chores comforted me with their small rhythms. For someone whose work involved projects spanning months and years in which each milestone led to another target, I liked tasks with a definable beginning, middle, and end.

I called Diane and told her about David. "When is something going to go right? Does this have to fall apart, too?" She was uncharacteristically quiet for a few moments. "Diane, are you there?"

"Yes. I'm trying to figure out how to say this without upsetting you. Kate, most everyone has had a heartbreak, a relationship that fell apart."

"So just get over it?"

"Stop wallowing. From what you've been describing, you're carving out a lovely life in the mountains with this community of perfectly charming people, including some men who sound worthy of your time and effort and worthy of *you*. Suck it up, buttercup."

"Another current expression with which I'm not familiar? No promises, but I'll try." Even though her candor stung, I knew she was right. "How's your father? And your mom?"

"Mom wants to give Dad one last Christmas at home. We've been visiting potential memory care centers and nursing homes."

"Oh, Diane. No chill pill on earth for this, is there?"

"No. I also need to 'suck it up, buttercup,'" she said so softly I could hardly hear her.

Late in the afternoon I went to see Maggie. Since the store was empty of customers, we sat at the counter. "Anything exciting happen in my absence?"

"No, no big events."

"What constitutes a big event here?"

"Births and weddings and funerals. The occasional theft or fight. Accidents. Blizzards, hurricanes, and floods," she counted off on her fingers. "And newcomers. I reckon you're an event."

"Lumped with hurricanes and floods and thievery, I'm not sure how to take that." Maggie grinned at me. "Blizzards and floods I'd expect, but I didn't realize you'd get hurricanes often."

"Not as common as on the coast, but Hurricane Camille, one of the most powerful hurricanes ever recorded, was devastating. As a scientist, you'd be interested in the exhibits about it at the Nelson County Historical Society. I imagine you were a youngster when it happened."

"My parents and I weren't living in Virginia at the time, but my aunt and uncle were. I vaguely recall hearing them talk about it." Maggie asked about my Thanksgiving. I hesitated, divided between wanting to confide in her and wanting to deal with my hurt in private.

"Something wrong?"

"David and I broke off our relationship."

"I'm sorry. Had you been seeing him a long time?"

"Yes, we started dating toward the end of my fellowship, before we got jobs in different departments at the same research institute. At the time, we discussed whether or not that was wise, in case our relationship didn't work out, but the positions were too good to pass up, especially at the beginning of our careers. We'd been talking about marriage." I recalled what Diane had said about wallowing. Before Maggie could ask, I added, "It was one of those things, I guess. Something we didn't count on happened, and we couldn't get past it."

"I thought you looked a little sigogglin when you came in."

"A little what?"

"Old mountain word for out of balance. You must think I'm such a country hayseed for speaking like I do, but it's how I was raised. When we were living away from the mountains for a time, my children were so embarrassed they scoured every bit of twang and all the mountain expressions out of their speech. No longer living so far back in the hills, I've tamed my speech, too."

"I like the regional idioms and the accent, though. I want to hear I'm in a different place. I can understand Cooper and Abby wanting to fit in, especially when they were younger, but the dialect adds energy to your speech. I have a friend who loves language and expressions, and I can't wait to share 'sigogglin' with her."

Maggie poured us coffee. "I guess this wasn't a happy Thanksgiving for you. It will be memorable, but not for good reasons."

"Actually, that's not true." I thought of my family's dinner. "My Thanksgiving with my parents and my aunt and uncle was special. Memorable, even, for good reasons." I lifted my coffee cup and clinked it against hers. "Onward, Maggie."

She beamed at me. "That's the spirit. What is it you call yourself? Pioneer woman!"

After dinner, Virgil, Eleanor, and I sat around the fireplace. "Are you and Virgil what Paul called 'birthright' Friends? Do you mind my asking?"

"Not at all. Virgil was born into a Quaker family, but I'm what is termed a 'convinced' Friend. Virgil always says he's not sure of what I'm convinced."

"I come from a family of Rhode Island Quakers," Virgil told me.

"When did you join the Friends, Eleanor?"

"About a year before we married, which was right after the end of World War II. Because of the Quakers' peace testimony, Virgil was a conscientious objector and served in an ambulance unit in Europe. When I joined him, he was stationed in England to help with the relief work." Eleanor reached for Virgil's hand. "It was a terrible time, dealing with the aftermath of the war, trying to help so many people whose homes and families had been shattered. Yet, in an odd way, it was exhilarating." She smiled at Virgil. "We were newlyweds engaged in critical, life-sustaining work."

"You got married in England?"

"Yes, much to our families' disappointment."

"Did you have a Quaker wedding? What was it like?"

"Yes, and it was very plain, of course. I remember sitting with Virgil on the facing bench in front of the congregation, in a pure and open silence. Since we were far from home and our families couldn't attend, the villagers took us to heart."

"You don't have a minister, even for weddings? Does the Clerk marry you?"

"No. Those are sacred vows between God and the couple. It's recognized as legal, however. We haven't been living in sin all these years!" She lifted a framed certificate from a wall. "This is our wedding certificate. Everyone attending signed it, even the children. Because we were in the village temporarily, though, we had no idea who most of these people were."

Virgil said, "They were thrilled to have something to celebrate, and it was a joyful assembly. They had survived years of war and massive food shortages, yet they organized a ceremony, a reception, and even gifts out of their depleted possessions. They also arranged a short stay at a seaside inn for our honeymoon. It was a humbling display of heartfelt generosity, and such a meaningful way to start our marriage."

I read the certificate. In elegant calligraphy, it recorded Eleanor's and Virgil's names, their parents' names, the Meeting's location, and what they had vowed to each other, "promising, with Divine assistance, to be unto thee loving and faithful."

"I attended one service, but I confess I didn't understand the purpose for the silence. Couldn't people have stayed home and been quiet?"

"We're not often silent as individuals in this noisy world," Eleanor explained, "and a corporate silence must seem especially unusual to you. We gather to wait upon God, to listen to what Quakers call the 'Inner Light,' the presence of God inside each of us. Have I made it more confusing?"

"No, but . . ."

"I haven't made it any clearer, either."

"It's fascinating. Why is everything so plain? My parents' church and most of the ones I've ever been in have altars, stained glass windows, flowers. The Meetinghouse is simple, austere, even."

"The plainness goes back to the beginnings of Quakerism," Eleanor continued. "The early Quakers in the sixteen hundreds feared that the true meanings and purposes of worship were being lost. They felt people didn't need a formal, fancy church or an intermediary, such as a minister, to experience God."

I reread the marriage certificate. "I love the sound of the language used here. Do Quakers still say 'thee' and 'thy'?"

Eleanor said, "You'll hear them occasionally. Some older Friends use these archaic forms, called plain language, especially in their own homes, but it's no longer customary because the reason it was used no longer exists. At one time, the formal second-person pronouns of 'you' and 'your' were used to address one's superiors, and the familiar forms of 'thee' and 'thy' were used for everyone else. Quakers felt it wasn't proper because everyone was supposed to be equal; they used the familiar forms for all. Some Quakers were jailed for doing so, as well as for not removing their hats and for refusing to swear oaths in courts of law."

"My mother and father used plain speech," Virgil said, "so I grew up with it."

"The first time Virgil took me to his home, I felt like I'd stepped back in time. When his mother greeted me at the door and said, 'I'm so happy to meet thee,' I was enchanted! I'd been nervous, but her welcome put me at ease."

I checked my watch. "I must be enchanted, too, because I didn't realize how late it was. Thank you, it has been a lovely evening." As I drove away, I could see them framed in the yellow light of the doorway, Eleanor's head resting on Virgil's shoulder. I felt a pang of envy, wanting that kind of devotion.

Sitting in the same corner of the sanctuary as the last time, I watched Paul as he crossed the room and sat near the piano. Josiah caught my eye and smiled fleetingly, and the Hispanic family filed in with the Schoenfelds. An African American woman with a baby and a little girl sat next to me; the mother, positioning the baby on her lap, helped her toddler wriggle out of her coat. The baby opened and closed her hand in front of her face, engaged by the motion of her fingers.

The silence continued unbroken for twenty minutes. When the little girl left for First Day School, the baby crawled over the space and onto my lap. I gestured to her mother to let her know it was fine. The baby was beautiful with delicate, perfectly shaped features. I couldn't recall the last time I had held a baby, and her weight felt good in my arms. I rocked her, and her smile felt like a gift. After a few minutes, she went back to her mother.

When it was nearly noon, an older woman stood and began singing a hymn. The rest of the congregation joined in. As soon as everyone had stopped singing, the silence flowed back into the room. A few moments later, the woman next to me offered me her hand, and I realized the Meeting was over. "Hello. I'm Ruth Erickson. Thank you for holding Laurel, not that she gave you a choice."

"Kate Solterra. It was my joy. It's been a long time since I've held a baby."

When it was time for announcements, a man holding a sheaf of papers stood. "I'm Mark Gilberti, and I have the information about the 'Call for a Peaceful Resistance.' As most of you know, this refers to actions that those who sign would agree to take if the United States goes into another country. Actions might include writing to Congress, participating in an organized protest, or sending humanitarian aid. At present we're concerned about Central American nations, especially El Salvador. If you're interested in signing this pledge or would like more information, please see me at the Rise of Meeting."

Paul addressed the congregation next. "In light of this, the sense of the Warren Central Meeting of New Hampshire is to offer sanctuary to refugees fleeing political and religious persecution. They have asked for our prayerful support. And, one final announcement, you're all invited to the Shared Meal downstairs. Now don't sneak away because you didn't bring anything, for we have plenty. Everyone is invited as well to attend the Meeting for Business after lunch."

Ruth asked, "You're going to join us for lunch, aren't you?"

"I don't think so. I'm the lone visitor today."

"Did you know that the first time you come we consider you to be an attender? If you don't want to stay for the Meeting for Business, at least come have lunch with us."

"I wouldn't feel right, coming empty-handed."

"Don't deprive us of the opportunity to put the 'loaves and the fishes' to test. We always have leftovers."

"I thought Quakers didn't push."

"We don't. But we've been known to persuade with enthusiasm." She introduced me to her other daughter, Caroline, who had returned from First Day School and was tugging on her mother's jacket.

I followed Ruth downstairs, and we sat next to the man who had made the resistance pledge announcement. He had a neatly trimmed red beard and pale blue eyes. Ruth introduced us. "Kate's in Drake's Springs on a sabbatical."

"Nice to meet you, Kate. I remember you from a few Meetings ago."

Ruth and Mark discussed the Call for Resistance. "In some ways, the Quakers' involvement in today's sanctuary movement parallels the establishment of the Underground Railroad, in the sense that not all Friends support it, or at least not all wish to deal with it in the same manner. It's a controversial topic," Ruth said. She paused, as though weighing whether to say more. "Quakers saved members of my family on the Underground Railroad. We have records and journals the family has kept and handed down for generations. This is personal for me."

I decided not to stay after lunch. When leaving, I saw the papers Mark had spoken about and picked one up to read. The paper explained the situation in Central America and reviewed the government's role. Although I usually watched the news every day, I hadn't paid much attention to it lately. I had to admit that since the accident I'd been preoccupied with my own plight. The Middle East, South Africa, Central America . . . the list continued from the beginning of time, I supposed. What could be worth the loss of all those lives, multiplied by centuries? How could we be so advanced in areas like technology and medicine and not have made any strides in being able to live peacefully with each other? Folding the paper, I slid it into my coat pocket.

# Chapter 11

## MEXICO

EMILIO PULLED OFF THE road and pointed to an abandoned shack with its windows missing glass and its door hanging from one hinge as though the house had suffered a stroke. He and Magdalena circled it, making sure no one was inside. Magdalena protested, but he made her stay there while he took the car to someone he knew in the village.

After he left, she paced the uneven floorboards. She prayed, "Father in heaven, forgive me for my doubts. How can I put my trust and faith in this boy? I know. I know. I should remember we are both your children, and you will provide for our needs and keep us safe. But I humbly ask you, if we must cross the river, could we have a bridge? A ferry? Or shallow water?"

When she thought she heard a sound, she'd stop and listen. "This is madness," she muttered. "We cannot go on like this. With me along, he will die; we both will die. Without me he might make it, and he should have this chance." She straightened the few pieces of furniture and dusted the table, as though putting the room to rights would result in an order that would spill over into her life.

Every time she argued with Emilio, he'd have none of her talk about staying behind. But he's not here now, she reasoned. She knew where the village was, and if she left right away, she could find a hiding place and stay there until he gave up and moved on. She could leave a note telling him not to wait, for she would not be coming back. Since she would no longer be his responsibility, there'd be no shame or guilt if he continued without her.

The angel's voice, with its columns of swirled resonances, did not startle her. She had begun to expect it. "To leave him now would be to choose death," the angel warned her with forcefulness.

"To continue with him would be to choose death for both of us."

"You do not know that."

"Emilio's best chance is without me."

"Has it not occurred to you that he may need you as much as you need him?"

"Without me he'd be closer to safety. Maybe he wouldn't have had to kill the soldier. Where were *you* then? Why couldn't you have helped us?"

"You didn't ask, Magdalena."

"I had to *ask*? What kind of angel of God are you? *Es una locura continuar.*" This is madness, to continue.

"*Es una bendición continuar.*" This is holiness, to continue. The voice dissolved, leaving Magdalena alone in the darkened, desolate room. Crouching in a corner, her head down on her knees, she wept.

To keep her mind off the stabbing pains coming with every step, Magdalena sang songs and chanted prayers to herself. She made up songs and poems when her memory failed her. Next, she made up alphabet games, thinking of names beginning with each letter. She was aware of Emilio beside her in his own trance of exhaustion, but they rarely talked now, needing all their energy to put one foot in front of the other.

"Magdalena." When Emilio touched her arm, she drew back, startled. "We have to talk about how to cross the river."

"You think about it and tell me when we get ready to do it. I don't want to know now."

"Let me tell you how I think we'll do it."

"I don't want to know. You cannot tell me what I do not want to know." Turning away from him she prayed, "Holy Father, thank you for the blessing of Emilio. Please help him to continue if it is your will for me not to survive the crossing." Her petitions had become as much a part of this journey as the heat and the hunger. More conversational than prayerful, they bubbled up in a constant stream. "*Gracias, Padre,* thank you, Father, for lifting my feet over these boulders. Merciful Father in heaven, protect us from evil men who would harm us. *Padre nuestro, que estás en el cielo,* Our Father, who art in heaven . . . Father, thank you for this food; I know it is wrong to steal, please forgive us, we are starving. Dear Father, your land is great and far-reaching, but does it have to be so hot? *Amén. Amén.*"

At first, the angel looked the way Magdalena had expected with a beatific face, white robes, and golden, gossamer wings reaching above its head and extending below its elbows. Up to now, she hadn't seen the angel, only heard its voice. Curiously enough, she couldn't tell whether it was male or female, but a knowing compassion imbued its eyes. She was surprised it was Hispanic. Perplexed, she moved closer and scrutinized its features. Hovering a few inches above the ground, it was about her size. Strange, she thought, I expected an angel to be more imposing.

"*¿Es usted realmente un ángel?*" Are you really an angel?

"*Sí.*"

Magdalena felt a warmth spilling inside her, a softening of her bones. "May I touch you?"

"*No.*"

"Then you *aren't* real."

"I exist."

"Why are you here?"

"To carry you and Emilio across the river."

"I've asked God to find us a bridge or a ferry."

"I know. I am your bridge. I am your ferry."

Magdalena tried to circle around the angel, but it kept turning to face her. "I don't want to go across the river. I want to go home. Can't you arrange this?"

"You can't refuse a journey that was designed for you."

"Forgive me, *Ángel*, but it wasn't designed well. We're starving and exhausted. My feet are torn up. Sometimes we get rides, but never for far enough. We're having to steal food. And I think Emilio is lost, though he won't admit it."

"You're not lost. You can't be lost on a journey of the spirit."

"But my spirit doesn't want to go on this journey. This is cruel," she protested, but the angel was gone. Only light remained.

Arriving at the town before dark, Emilio and Magdalena found the church. The priest ushered them downstairs, helped Magdalena to a chair in the kitchen, and wordlessly assembled a basin of water, soap, and a first aid box. She moaned from the pain when he removed her shoes and cut and peeled away the bloodied socks. With practiced care, he washed her feet, coated them with a sweet-smelling ointment, and bandaged them. He brought her clean clothes, underwear, socks, and another pair of shoes. Holding the clothing in her lap, she looked down at the priest who was once more checking the bandages on her feet. She wondered how many refugees he had cared for in this basement kitchen. "¿*Cree usted en los ángeles*?" She asked if he believed in angels.

"I've never seen or heard an angel, but I've read about them, known people who've seen and heard them," he answered without looking at her, fearing a personal connection would make it impossible to continue. Dispassionate care felt like his lone salvation from the unremitting misery coursing through this kitchen.

"That's not what I asked you."

He shrugged, smiled. "These days it is hard to believe."

"I've seen and heard an angel." He tended to Magdalena's hands, their flesh torn from brambles and briars in the fields, the edges of the wounds puffy with infection. "You don't believe me? An angel has spoken to me, many times, and has appeared to me. I can describe it to you in detail. God sent an angel to get me across the river."

"I believe you." Bandaging her hands, the priest securely taped the gauze. However, she knew the young man did not believe her. It didn't matter. The angel was real, and she didn't need anyone else's belief to confirm it.

Drawing Emilio aside, the priest told him that he thought the old woman was dying and that she would not survive much longer on the road. She was not the first starved, frightened, and debilitated refugee to speak to him of angels.

# Chapter 12

THE LETTER, WRITTEN ON cream-colored stationery, felt heavy in my hands. I didn't recognize the address, but it had been forwarded to me from the institute. Opening it, I glanced down at the signature, not registering it at first. Once beginning the letter, however, I realized it was from the drunk driver who had hit me. My heart beat hard and fast, my vision blurred, and it was difficult to focus.

I finished the carefully worded, restrained letter. Grabbing the sides of the pages, I ripped the letter apart, wanting to cause more destruction than the elegant paper could give me. How dare he, after all this time, think he had the right to enter my life in any fashion? Until now, I'd been able to depersonalize him, not knowing what he looked like, his age, or where he lived; I thought of him in terms of "the drunk driver," not by his name. Now I knew more about him than I'd wanted to—his stationery, his address, his penmanship, his controlled sentence structure. Wanting to be able to think of him as an evil person, I didn't care how he felt. Most of all, I didn't want him praying for me.

Looking for a diversion, I decided to make a lunch and drive to the preserve. I could build a fire at one of the picnic shelters, focus on the mountains' serenity, and refuse to give this man any power to crash into my life again. After packing food in my backpack and making a thermos of coffee, I started out, unlocking the front door and reaching for the car keys on the nearby table. They weren't there. I felt in my coat pockets and checked the car's ignition, despite feeling even I wouldn't leave them in the car. Irritated, I began going through the house. "How hard is it to leave the keys in the same spot? Why can't I do at least that?"

The keys weren't anywhere I looked. When had I last gone out? I couldn't recall. "One small thing, Kate. Look here. Go to the next room. Have a system." I scanned the living room, the bedroom, and returned to the living room. As my frustration mounted, I couldn't remember what the key ring looked like, couldn't visualize the shape or the color. Realizing the keys could be anywhere, I began opening cabinets, the refrigerator, and even the linen closet. I tore through the rooms, looking under the pillows on the bed, under the sofa cushions, in the medicine cabinet, in desk drawers. Nothing.

"I hate this." I tossed a chair's pillow across the room. "I hate not remembering," I yelled. "Every day is a struggle. This is what you've done to me; how dare you write to me!" All the fury and the losses coalesced, cascading liquid turning into fire. I swept papers off the desk and picked up a stack of magazines, tossing them at the walls. I threw books, holding one and twisting it, tearing out and ripping the pages. Hurling a glass as hard as I could, it exploded into fragments when it hit the wall. Kicking the table by the door, I knocked it over then picked it up, smashing it back down until one of the legs broke and bounced across the floor. Grabbing a log, I slammed it along the hearth's edge until the wood split, chips of bark flying up into my face and sticking in my hair. I pulled on the curtains, the rod loosening and clattering down, the curtains covering me. I fought with the fabric, wanting to rip it, to tear it like the pages of the books, to damage it somehow. Tangled in the material, I tried to get up but fell. I beat on the floor and screamed until my throat hurt.

I suddenly was aware of someone pounding on the door and shouting my name. The door flung open, banging against the opposite wall. Paul ran in. "Kate, what's wrong? Are you hurt?" He unwound the curtains from me, helped me up, and led me to the sofa. "Are you hurt?" he repeated. When I didn't answer, he shouted, "Answer me! Who did this to you? Where's the phone, I'll call the police."

I pulled him down beside me. "Don't." I didn't know how I was going to explain this.

"I didn't see anyone out front. Did they go out the back?" He stood up. "Let me call for help."

"Don't."

"I have to."

"No."

"This has to be reported. Look at this place. Look at you. Where's your phone?"

"No." I reached out to stop him. "I did this."

"*You* did this?" He grew still, his eyes widening. "Why? I don't believe you."

"I can't talk yet." I closed my eyes; in my exhaustion and my shame, I couldn't move. I felt him touching my hands. They throbbed, and I realized I must have banged them down on the glass fragments without even feeling anything. Paul rushed to my bathroom, found my first aid kit, then dabbed my hands with an antiseptic. When he'd finished, he sat down and held me. I began to shiver, and he tucked an afghan around me and cradled my head against his chest.

The late afternoon shadows darkened the room. Paul stood, propped pillows behind me, and turned on the lamps. "I'll be back." I heard him moving about in the kitchen. He returned with a cold washcloth and a cup of steaming tea. I held the cloth to my face; my eyes felt swollen, and the coolness of the cloth was soothing. He gave me the cup. "Can you hold this?"

Without talking, Paul swept up the glass, replaced the curtain rod, and started picking up the books and magazines. When everything was in order, he sat down beside me. "I damaged your door getting in. It locks, but it's not as secure as I'd like. I'll fix it as soon as possible. You should have deadbolts, anyway, the back door as well. Now, you're not hurt, other than your hands? Are you sure I shouldn't call the police?"

"No. I told you the truth. I did this." I couldn't meet his eyes. "I can't explain this to you. Not yet."

"Would you like me to call your parents?"

Alarmed, I sat up. "No, promise me you won't call them!"

"I can call Will Cameron; he's a doctor from the Meeting. Or what about Maggie or Eleanor?"

"No. I'll be all right. You don't have to stay."

"You're not ready to be left alone yet. I won't make you tell me anything you don't want to, but I'm not leaving you right now. I'm going back into the kitchen and make us some dinner. Lean back and rest." He unlaced and removed my shoes, making me feel like a child. Pulling the afghan over me, I curled up on the sofa.

I must have fallen asleep immediately, because the next thing I knew he was setting a tray on the coffee table. "Comfort food," Paul told me. He'd heated up soup and made a salad and grilled cheese sandwiches.

"You're kind to do this, but I'm not hungry."

"I think you need to eat something." He offered me the bowl of soup. "I came by this afternoon to ask if you'd like a Christmas tree from my farm." Paul continued to talk, and although I couldn't keep track of what he was saying, I focused on the sound of his voice. It was melodious, a light spring rain of syllables. I hadn't realized I'd eaten the soup, the sandwich, and most of the salad until he took the dishes from me and went back into the kitchen. When he returned, he sat on the other end of the sofa.

"I don't want you to think I'm given to such hysterical behavior."

"I'm not asking for an explanation. You don't have to tell me."

"I know, but I need to." Staring at the flames of the fire he'd built, I began. "A while ago I was in a serious car accident, and I almost died. I'm still recovering, and it's why I'm on a sabbatical. The man who hit me was drunk; I got a letter from him today, telling me how much he grieves what he did. The letter made me so angry that I wanted to destroy everything in reach. I didn't know I could feel this kind of rage." I faced Paul. "I didn't want anyone here to know because I didn't want to be an accident victim anymore. I wanted to create a new life for myself and didn't want it complicated by people knowing about my past."

"I respect that. I won't tell anyone; you have my word."

I couldn't talk any longer and fell back asleep.

Waking up at dawn, I was perplexed to find myself on the sofa. The blanket from my bed was over me, and I was still wearing yesterday's clothes. I must have fallen asleep before I could go to bed. Feeling stiff and cold, I wrapped my robe over my clothes and went to the kitchen to get some food. My head hurt, so maybe eating something would help stop the pain.

I saw the note on the kitchen table. Had someone been here last night? Confused, I read, "Kate, I'm being called away on an urgent matter for the Meeting. You're sleeping so deeply I don't want to wake you. Don't worry, I'll keep my promise. Call me if you need anything. I'll hold thee in the Light, Paul." I'd heard the phrase "in the Light" at the Meetinghouse. But what did the rest of the message mean? What had he promised? What might I need? I noticed he'd written his phone number at the bottom of the page.

I sat on the sofa after pushing aside the curtains. The thin, gray light of morning began defining objects in the room. Something had happened here yesterday, but what? I took inventory. The table by the door was on its side with one of its legs next to it. One of the lamps had no bulb, its dented shade sitting on the floor. Torn books sat in a pile on the hearth. Had I gotten angry and trashed the room while Paul was here? Angry with him? That didn't make sense.

While I was finishing my breakfast, I began to feel much worse. All at once, dizziness overcame me, and I rushed to the bathroom and vomited. The pain in my head increased with astonishing speed, becoming a furred, visceral being inside me. "I'm in trouble. I need help." I lay down on the bathroom floor, the tile comforting in its coolness, its hard surface reassuring me I couldn't fall.

Shutting my eyes, I tried to control my breathing. Was this one of those meltdowns? The pain massed and fragmented inside me. I pushed my feet against the tub and arched my back. Wait. Wait. What was I supposed to remember in a crisis? Think. Calm. Breathe. Emergency folder. Crawling but keeping my head and neck as motionless as possible, I made it to the filing cabinet in the living room. The strength dissolved out of my fingers, but I pushed the latch down with the heel of my hand. The red folder marked "Emergency Information" was at the front. The first sheet had a series of pictures with captions instructing me not to drive but to call for help. The second sheet told me to take the red folder with me. It had Nina's name on it, a set of phone numbers, a hospital's address, and the instruction, "If given this, take Katherine Solterra to the nearest doctor or hospital. Contact Nina Grazio, MD."

Holding onto the folder, I crawled back to the kitchen and pulled the telephone down to the floor. If I called for a rescue squad, could I give directions to the cabin? I couldn't remember my address. Was that in the folder? I flipped through it, but nothing looked like directions or an address for where I was living. Call someone here, I thought. Paul. He'd been here last night, though I couldn't reconstruct why, and his number was on his note. I managed to reach the note I'd left on the kitchen table. He answered after the second ring.

"Paul," I whispered.

"Kate, how are you feeling?" The strength of his voice made me feel safe. All I needed to do was figure out what to say to get him over here. My grasp on words disintegrated into pinpricks of light.

"Kate? Are you all right?"

"No."

"I'm on my way. Don't move."

By the time Paul arrived, I couldn't sit up. I pointed at the folder. "My head hurts. I'm dizzy and in a lot of pain. Call Nina."

He checked through the folder. "The hospital in Harrisonburg is closer. Dr. Grazio is over an hour away."

"No, I need to see her."

After calling the doctor, he carried me to his car. Placing a blanket around me, he reclined the seat and buckled the seat belt. On the drive to the hospital, I kept my eyes shut. I couldn't remember what had happened yesterday. What if I had lost everything I'd gained and had to start over? No. I could not bear that.

Nina met us at the entrance to the emergency room. She started me on medication for the pain and left to talk with Paul. Afterward, she returned and examined me. "Do you remember what happened yesterday?"

"No."

"Your friend Paul Whittaker told me you received a letter. Do you recall it?"

"No."

"It was a letter from the drunk driver who hit you." She waited.

"No."

"Mr. Whittaker found you. You were screaming and beating your hands on the floor. You'd smashed furniture, thrown books, broken lamps. Does any of this sound familiar?"

I glanced away from her penetrating look. A poster on the wall caught my attention, and although I couldn't concentrate on the words, unable to make sense of them, the black writing against the cream background struck hard. The letter. The heavy cream-colored stationery. His apology. My rage.

I turned to Nina. "I remember now. Nina, I can't do this any longer."

"No, you can't. You got lucky this morning. You realized you couldn't function and got help. All kinds of dire things could have happened to you. I'm admitting you for observation; your friend said he could come get you at any time when you're released. I'm going to make changes to your medication, and we'll talk later about counseling." She held up her hand. "I know you've opposed it when I've suggested it, but I may make it a condition of your continuing in the head trauma program here."

"I had counseling at the beginning."

"I know. It helped you with your initial adjustment. But mood swings and bursts of anger and frustration are a function of the damage from the injury. They are going to happen. You need strategies to cope with them." When I started to protest, she shook her head and left.

Once I'd been moved to a room, I slept off and on for the rest of the day. At one point, I was aware of a hand holding mine, and despite not being able to swim up to the surface and waken fully, I felt my distress subside at last, ebbing into a soft lapping of water at a shoreline.

By the next morning, I felt significantly better. Bargaining with Nina over the counseling, I agreed that if the anger went out of control one more time, I'd start counseling sessions.

"You don't have to do this alone," she insisted.

"Yes, I do. I want the whole victory."

# Chapter 13

STANDING IN FRONT OF me, Paul was at the lane leading to the Meeting-house. It was Sunday, midmorning. Not thinking what day it was, I'd come out for a walk. "I'm torn between encouraging you to attend Meeting because sometimes it will uncannily speak to your condition, standing aside and letting you go on by yourself, or asking if I may accompany you," he said.

"How would anyone know what my condition is?"

"They wouldn't. It's an old Quaker expression, meaning you'll receive a message or a feeling in some form that will touch you deeply and directly."

We stood still. People I recognized passed us on their way to the Meetinghouse. What did I want more than anything else? I closed my eyes and felt myself sway a bit. Paul put his hand on my arm to steady me. Make a wish, I thought. Make a wish. I wanted to stop fighting, not in the sense of giving up, but of letting go. A surrender, a relinquishing. I wanted to stop crying, to stop being so angry. Peace. Stillness inside. Peace—the sound of the word itself full of yearning and solace. Opening my eyes, I turned with Paul falling in step beside me, shortening his long strides to match mine. We proceeded without speaking as though we had already entered the silence, and at the door he drew me close and lightly, carefully, embraced me.

The room was unusually full, but Paul and I found a place near the door. Previously, I'd had the bench almost to myself, but this morning six or seven people filled every bench. Was this a special Meeting? It wasn't the second Sunday of the month, their usual day for the Shared Meal and Meeting for Business.

The Schoenfelds and all three of the Mackenzies sat on the bench in front of us. It was the first time I'd seen Maggie in attendance. The silence became a restless one. What was going on? The Meeting lacked the tranquility I had felt before. I reviewed the day I'd received the letter and recalled my anger, the living room in a shambles, Paul's kindness. My thoughts drifted to my recent trip home and the discussions with David, Matthew, and Nina. Could I remain in my specialized field? No one would hire a biochemist who couldn't remember the most basic of science essentials, where she placed her keys, or the names of everyday objects. Would anyone hire me for anything, much less for a position in my field? What would I do if I couldn't be a research scientist? For months I'd pushed back these questions because I hadn't let myself think of a partial recovery. And what about the wish I made while in the middle of the road with Paul standing beside me? How do you find such stillness, such peace? Do you create it?

No one spoke until the Rise of Meeting. There were no new visitors, and after the announcements, Paul stood and moved to one side. "It is good to be among Friends this morning. We have a challenge before us that will require everyone's prayerful insight. Although the sense of the Meeting is not yet evident, we've been continuing to work on the sanctuary issue. The committee for Ministry and Worship and the committee for Peace and Social Concerns would like to call a special Meeting for Business today. Some of you who are here today are not members or long-time attenders; however, we encourage you to stay. We value your thoughts, and our decisions may affect the broader community. Young Friends volunteered to provide childcare, and the Hospitality Committee will be serving sandwiches so we can begin at once."

This was why the Meeting had been so full and the silence unsettled. Remaining on the bench, I planned to stay a few minutes after everyone went downstairs. Reluctant to go back to the cabin, I wanted to remain in this light-filled, tranquil room. Paul came over to me. "I meant what I said about new attenders."

"I know, but I've never been to a Meeting for Business, and I don't know anything about this issue. I hadn't even planned to come this morning."

"This Meeting for Business doesn't obligate anyone, not even Friends. I'm not trying to pressure you into attending; I simply want you to understand you're welcome to attend." Placing a hand under my chin, he lifted my head. "Are you all right?" Afraid his gentleness would dismantle my composure, I moved my head back and focused on the floor. "Look at me, Kate." His voice was as quiet as the first morning light. I forced myself to meet his gaze. "Are you all right?"

"Yes."

"You'll call me if you need anything?"

I nodded, and following the others, he left. I had no reason to stay, no reason to stand on the fringe of their concerns. How could my presence be of any help? I had no power to make decisions over my own life these days, and I didn't want to watch people make decisions about the lives of others.

Despite my qualms, I found myself going downstairs. Paul sat next to me. No one was speaking, so apparently they began Meetings for Business in silence as well. After several minutes, Paul spoke. "For those of you who are new attenders, Meetings for Business are essentially Meetings for Worship in which we work on the business of our lives, attempting to arrive at the will of God. We don't vote, but we strive to achieve unity or consensus on what is the truth. The unity we achieve gives important strength to our decisions. We invite you to join us in this process and to feel free to speak if you are so led." The restlessness I'd noticed during Meeting for Worship dissipated; it was as though everyone began breathing together.

Eleanor spoke after a short silence. "I'm Eleanor Schoenfeld from Ministry and Worship. Paul asked me to explain the situation, but first let's go around the room and introduce ourselves so new attenders can get to know us, and we can get to know them."

After the introductions Eleanor continued. "Several years ago, this Meeting sponsored Tomás Delgado, his wife, Graciela, and Miguel, Enrique, and Sara, their children. They suffered from political persecution in El Salvador. The Salvadoran Civil War began in 1980 and continues to rage on. The Delgados are hoping to become citizens one day and have been working toward that goal. Sara was born here. They came here a few years before the INS, the Immigration and Naturalization Service, began to apply more stringent regulations related to immigration and asylum.

"Tomás's brother Emilio and Graciela's mother, Magdalena Suárez, haven't been able to obtain visas to come here. The situation in El Salvador deteriorated rapidly after Tomás and his family left. A death squad murdered Magdalena's husband, Agustín, last year. The government of El Salvador targeted them because Emilio and Felipe, his other brother, organized the campesinos, the local farmers, in a union, giving them greater power to deal with government officials. Their father, Alberto Delgado, had helped to establish the union, and for that, he was killed. He was an influential newspaper editor and teacher in their region. In a letter sent to Tomás, Emilio writes that Felipe has disappeared, which usually means the person has been murdered; consequently, he is afraid for Magdalena's life and for his own. He writes that if they must leave, they will, but they'll try to wait until they hear from us. Tomás tells me their situation must be grave for Emilio to risk sharing so much information about their plans in a letter. It may have been opened. We have reason to believe they may be on their way out of El Salvador by now."

"Why was permission denied for them to get visas?" asked a man I didn't know.

Paul answered, "On the premise that they were seeking asylum for economic reasons. Visas based on economics have been banned indefinitely. In addition, the government stated they had no proof of persecution. Such reasoning on the United States government's part has been standard policy for a long time."

"What if Magdalena applied by herself?" Josiah asked. "Could the INS deny entrance on economic grounds to an older woman who wouldn't be seeking work?"

Graciela spoke, her voice hesitant. Tomás translated, but I understood what she said in Spanish. "'My mother would be afraid to come alone. She doesn't want to leave her homeland; she wouldn't come with us. The situation must be terrible. I think she is coming now only because she knows Emilio won't leave her, and she wants him to have a chance.'"

Ruth, the woman whose baby I'd held, wanted to know, "Do we treat this as an individual case, or do we try to deal with the larger issue of sanctuary? Can we do one without the other?"

"If we got arrested for helping Emilio and Magdalena," Sharon Cameron spoke, "what would happen to them, and would any action be taken against Graciela and Tomás and their children?"

Paul told her, "Emilio and Magdalena could be deported immediately. As far as Tomás and Graciela, I'm not sure, but they could be charged with harboring illegal aliens as well. That they aren't citizens yet worries me. They could be denied citizenship and deported, and reentering El Salvador carries its own risks. They couldn't return to their home and expect to survive long; in fact, it's possible their village no longer exists."

"Maybe this calls consensus into question. Are there times when it's not expedient? Or right?" Mark asked. He was the man who'd provided information on the resistance pledge.

"We're talking about understanding the will of God here," Virgil said in a sharp tone. "How could it *not* be expedient and right?"

"Let's stop for a moment," Paul intervened. "Anyone want another sandwich, more to drink?" A few people got up, but the rest of the group stayed silent until the others returned.

Mark continued. "I'd prefer to reach clarity on the issue before bringing Emilio and Magdalena here. But what if circumstances force us into a decision? Emilio and Magdalena seem to be in immediate danger. If something happens to them and we could have helped, but didn't, how will we reconcile that?"

"This isn't the first time we have been faced with offering sanctuary to asylum seekers," Josiah reminded the group. "During Vietnam, we acted before we achieved true consensus as to the will of God, with disastrous results." He nodded at Mark. "I think those of us involved in the previous situation understand the dangers of moving too quickly now."

"Our decisions during Vietnam divided this Meeting and this community," Eleanor said so softly I struggled to hear her. "The split took years to heal. Even now, we are not the same. Can we turn our backs on that experience and deny what we learned from it?"

Tomás leaned forward in his chair. "We are . . . desperate? Desperate, yes. But what we ask, it must be right. We know we ask something great of you." The Friends' insistence on examining all sides of an issue impressed me, but I began to understand that reaching consensus, what they called the "sense of the Meeting," could take a long time.

"There are other Meetings, other churches and agencies dealing with this as well," Abby said. "Couldn't we contact them and get advice? If we can't reach a decision, couldn't we at least contact another organization to help Emilio and Magdalena? Surely, the Yearly Meeting has a list of those agencies."

"For new attenders, the Quakers organize their Meetings in geographic units, with Monthly Meetings being grouped together with an overseeing Yearly Meeting. There's more to it, but this will suffice for now," Eleanor explained.

"Are Friends in agreement," Paul asked, "that if we decide not to offer sanctuary to Emilio and Magdalena, we will be responsible for finding a group that will?"

Cooper spoke for the first time. "Is it right for us to ask another group to assume such a responsibility and possibly incur penalties when we are not willing to do so? Tomás, Graciela, and their children are part of our Meeting."

Everyone settled into an uneasy quiet that lengthened, ribbons of silence stretching into thinness. At last Paul said, "It's obvious we have no clear sense of the Meeting, yet we recognize the urgency. While we hold this in the Light, we charge the Peace and Social Concerns Committee with contacting our Yearly Meeting and other Meetings and organizations dealing with this issue, as well as with finding answers to questions raised during this Meeting for Business. We will continue to search for the will of God for us in this matter."

Another long silence. Paul reached for my hand and for the hand of the woman on his other side, officially ending the Meeting for Business.

Paul escorted me home. We said little to each other on the way; he seemed preoccupied by the events, and I felt the fatigue of the past couple of days. At my door he said, "I'm glad you stayed." I stepped into my cabin. Although I knew it was wrong to feel this way, being able to concentrate on someone else's situation, much more desperate than my own, had brought a welcome respite. Maybe in order to find my way out of the labyrinth of anger, I needed to shed my skin.

I repaired my torn books and, with Cooper's help, the broken table. Running my finger down the table leg that had been broken, I could feel the lines of the breaks but could barely see them. What was the old expression about china? Was it, "Once broken, twice as strong with the mending"? As with the table leg, there had to be a way I could fit together the puzzle pieces of my life so I could accept the resulting picture.

I considered what made me the angriest, the most scared. Being uncertain about the future. Not being able to trust my own mind. Simple things being difficult. Having my life altered by a drunken stranger. The unfairness. Unfairness? Matthew had labeled it that, too, and so had I, many times. But was it unfair that he should run into me? As if anyone else deserved being hurt like this? Unfair because I'd tried to be a good person and to do what was right? Unfair because I had an important job that made a difference in people's lives, as though I should have some magical protection? However, I had been taught, and firmly believed, that all jobs were important; everyone's work had dignity and the capacity to improve our lives. This accident would have been unfair to anyone. I wasn't hit because of anything I'd done wrong. It had happened, and to me. I had been dealing with the bitterness, the physical pain, and the dread of what was ahead, but I had tried to contain the fury, afraid it would grow out of control like a jungle vine choking out air and light. Lining up the mended books, I thought of all the objects I'd thrown and tried to ruin. But no matter how many things I destroyed, the life of the man who hit me wouldn't be changed the way mine had. Vengeance might give me some measure of satisfaction, but it wouldn't heal me, and I doubted it would give me any peace.

Because a massive snowstorm followed by a layer of ice hit the East Coast three days before Christmas, I had to cancel my trip to Alexandria. Hours after the storm's initial power subsided, it began snowing again, a languorous snowfall this time. Thick flakes fell in slow motion, clumping on the evergreens until their weight started small avalanches, bending the branches closer to the ground. It was mesmerizing, and I watched from the window for a long time. Later that evening someone knocked on my door. I spilled the bowl of walnuts I was cracking, and the shells clattered across the wooden floor. "Kate?" a man called. "It's Josiah from Friends Meeting."

Skidding on one of the shells, I went to the door and opened it, the accumulated snow blowing in on my feet. "Good heavens, Josiah, you startled me. Are you all right? Do you need help? Please come in. I wasn't expecting anyone to be out in this snow."

"Everything is fine, not to worry. The rest of the group is on the main road because we didn't think we'd be able to turn around in your drive. Every year before Christmas, Friends gather on top of Virgil and Eleanor's mountain to build a bonfire and sing. We'd like to have you join us. We realized you weren't present when we announced this."

I hesitated. Here was a new tradition being presented to me. "Sounds like fun, and how thoughtful of you to think of me." I hurried to change into warmer clothes.

At the road, I understood what he'd said about not having room to turn around. A horse-drawn wagon was the lead in a procession of another, smaller wagon and two enormous sleighs, cherry red with silver runners and bells. The horses pawed at the snow. I saw all three of the Mackenzies, the Schoenfelds, Paul, and the Delgados, as well as other members of the Meeting. Abby pulled me up into one of the sleighs, with Josiah following me. The horses plowed up the hillside, leaving furrows of snow behind. I settled back underneath the blanket Josiah had tossed over me.

When we arrived at the top of the mountain, I saw a pavilion with picnic tables, and a fire pit was nearby. Someone had set up lawn chairs, and we distributed the blankets. The group began singing carols, one after another, their voices captured by the night. I listened, trying to come to precise terms with these Quakers. I wondered if they could maintain their convictions in a place other than Drake's Springs. None of them had countered my questions with chapters and verses or platitudes, for which I was grateful. They were not guilty of simplistic piety, and their beliefs stood isolated with an enviable strength. But when did an admirable stand on principle, however supreme, crumble under its own weight? And why did I have a disquieting feeling when I was around them? Did I shy away from their goodness out of disbelief it existed, or out of a fear that it did, and that I couldn't measure up to it? In my fierce desire to be independent, was I afraid to accept the kindnesses they wanted to offer me?

At the end of the caroling, Paul went with me from the main road to my cabin, dismissing my assertion that I didn't mind walking alone. As we got to my door, he said, "Tomorrow night we have a Meeting starting at eleven with a midnight breakfast afterward, hosted by the Camerons. Most Quakers don't celebrate Christmas elaborately like other Christians, but we do have singing of hymns and carols before Meeting and even a candle or two. If you'd rather not come to the Meeting, at least come for the breakfast. If you're at the Meetinghouse at midnight, you can ride over in one of the sleighs. You might as well join us because you know how persuasive we non-coercive Quakers can be."

"You're right. I'll give in now, graciously and gratefully. Thank you, I'd love to come."

I was startled for a second time this night when Paul leaned down and kissed my cheek. "Peace be with thee, Katherine Solterra." Peace. Hadn't that been my central wish?

# Chapter 14

## MEXICO

Worried that Magdalena would lack the energy to make the river crossing, Emilio stopped to camp in the late afternoons instead of early evenings. It amused him to watch Magdalena make camp. She'd set their few pans around the campfire in a particular order, arrange the dishes on a blanket as though they were on a table, and unroll the bedding in the same fashion each night. He knew she was trying to ritualize the chaos of their unsettled lives, though neither of them would mistake order for safety.

Emilio gave her the rest of his food. "I'm not hungry; you need to eat to keep strong. We cross the river soon, maybe tonight. Someone in the last village told me how we can get you across. He will bring us a raft."

"I didn't expect so many strangers would help. We are being blessed."

Magdalena dozed off, and when she woke up, it was dusk. Emilio stood over a tiny raft made of boards nailed together and logs bound with thick rope.

"On that? ¡*Dios mío!*" My God!

"It will be better for you than trying to swim. I'll swim near you and hold onto the raft. We'll cross together." He showed her loops of rope on one of the raft's sides. "You hold on to these. Don't let go unless the raft overturns."

"And if it does?"

"I'll help you get back on the raft. But it shouldn't overturn. All you'll have to do is hold on and stay down."

"I have thought about this on the trip." She gave him her photograph of Agustín and her rosary. "These are for Graciela if I don't survive the crossing. I wish I had something to give to my grandchildren. You will tell my daughter my last thoughts were of her." She reached up and patted him on the shoulder.

"You will be giving her these things yourself," he told her, but he placed them in the backpack. "We will leave right after it's dark."

"The border police?"

"Most crossings are later at night, so maybe earlier is a better time."

"And if they catch us?"

"We will try again."

"If they let us live." She knew this would be their last chance.

"*Tenga fé, Magdalena.*" Have faith. He smiled at her, not wanting her to detect his trepidation, to notice the trembling of his hands, to observe the alternating clenching and quivering of his jaw. He worried if he'd be strong enough to navigate the raft, strong enough to get her across the river, strong enough not to make a run for it on his own if they were caught. "Sleep while you can," he told her.

This time, the children in the nightmare were from the past: Graciela, a little girl caring for her doll; Tomás, Emilio, and Felipe, their eyes flashing in boyhood mischief; and the son who'd been stillborn, his translucent, pearlized skin stretched over tiny bones. How could it be? The features and limbs of the ghosts were elongated, their bodies bloated from being underwater. Their arms and legs twined around Magdalena, preventing her from rising to the water's surface, pushing her down, their faces apologetic.

"Magdalena, Emilio's right: *Tenga fé.*"

"I didn't ask for you."

The angel reached out and touched Magdalena's shoulder, but she could not feel it. So the angel isn't real, she thought. Betrayed. She'd put her trust in a mirage, after all.

"I am real. And your anguish summoned me."

"If you're real, why didn't you save the children from the bombing? Agustín? My infant son and the writer Delgado?"

"I did receive them."

"Is that why you're here now?"

"No. I came to tell you to send faith. And you must be truthful."

"Truthful?"

"What is it you say to yourself when you think of the children in the church, Agustín, Felipe?"

Magdalena felt water glide over her in a single sheet. "That God is not merciful."

"Do not be afraid of your doubts. Face them."

Magdalena felt herself being lifted up, the water shedding from her and becoming separate drops. *Redención.* Redemption.

They dissected the landscape, their eyes aching to see shapes in shadows, trying to make sense of the periphery. Helping Magdalena get on the raft, Emilio instructed, "Put the backpack under you. But if it falls into the water, don't try to go after it. It's not important. Remember, hold on and stay down. Stay as still as you can."

Hunched over the backpack, she held on while he started swimming a modified dog paddle. The raft swayed as he tried to control it. "This isn't working," he said.

"I could put my legs over the side and kick." She started to stretch out.

"Wait. Roll up the overalls and take off your shoes."

"Take off my shoes? No, please, let me leave them on."

"Don't argue. Get them off." He stuffed them into the backpack.

With her kicking and Emilio's paddling, the raft moved faster and in a straighter line. She tried not to think of what could bite her feet. "*Dios te salve, María, llena eres de gracia; Dios te salve, María, llena eres de gracia.*" Hail Mary, full of grace; Hail Mary, full of grace. She again couldn't think of the words to a prayer she'd said daily for most of her life. Oh, please, God, I can't remember the words. Does that mean it doesn't count? Hear my prayer: "*Dios te salve, María. Padre nuestro, que estás en el cielo, santificado sea tu nombre. Venga tu reino. Hágase tu voluntad en la tierra como en el cielo. En la tierra como en el cielo.*" Our Father, who art in heaven, hallowed be thy name. Thy kingdom come, thy will be done, on earth as it is in heaven. On earth as it is in heaven. What was next? The words wouldn't come. She started at the beginning, hoping momentum would carry her through, but she got no further.

"Be quiet. Your voice carries."

She hadn't realized she'd been praying aloud. "*Dios te salve, María, llena eres de gracia,*" she continued in a lower tone. Something brushed over her legs, and she clamped her teeth together to keep from screaming. River angel, you promised to carry us across safely, you promised to be our bridge, you promised we would not be lost. And I believed you.

Halfway across, Emilio panted out, "Stop. Got to rest." He stopped paddling and hung his arms over one of the logs.

"Look." She pointed down the river. "Lights."

"Searchlights."

"Are they looking for us?"

"No, they're just looking."

"What do we do if they come up here?"

"Go under the raft."

"Will they shoot us?"

"Warning shots, maybe. I don't think they'd shoot us," he said.

"But they'll send us back."

They began moving once more. Magdalena's legs scraped against the logs, hurting each time she kicked. When she heard Emilio's rasping breaths, though, she tried to kick harder. Were the lights closer? She couldn't tell. She thought of seeing Graciela, her beautiful daughter. When she tried to picture her grandchildren, she couldn't remember their faces. She couldn't remember her husband's face. Don't panic, she told herself. Kick. Kick. The lights swept closer. "Emilio," she warned him, pointing to them.

"Get in the water but don't let go of the raft." He threw the backpack's strap over his head. When she slid off, her sleeve caught on one of the logs. She ripped it free, and the water closed around her neck. "When I say 'Now,' take a big breath and go under."

"We'll lose the raft."

"I'll try to hold onto it."

"What if I need more air?"

"Come up with your head back, flat, enough to breathe. Immediately go back down. I'll be right here. I won't let anything happen to you. You can do this, Magdalena."

What was it the angel had said? Send faith. Earlier, she'd thought the angel's word choice was odd. How could she *send* faith? Please God, help us, please send your river angel to save us. She chanted quietly to herself, "*Sálvanos, ayúdanos, Padre piadoso.*" Save us, help us, merciful Father; save us, help us, merciful Father; save us. With her sense of alarm lessening, her breathing slowed to a normal rate. She felt composed, warm, enveloped.

"Now."

They slid under the water. Grasping hold of Magdalena, Emilio jammed the fingers of his free hand through a crack in the logs. The current was slow here, so maybe it was possible. The raft twisted and he felt a sharp pain.

Dear God, Magdalena thought as the fear returned. The children died by fire. We're going to die by water. She tried to quell her terror so that she could think, tried to ignore the heartbeats ripping around her chest. *Ayúdanos, Padre*, she thought to herself. Help us, Father. *Ayúdanos, sálvanos.* Help us, save us. *Dios te salve, María, llena eres de gracia, el Señor es contigo. Bendita tú eres entre todas las mujeres.* Hail Mary, full of grace, the Lord is with thee. Blessed art thou among women . . . she raced through the entire prayer. *Ruega por nosotros pecadores, ahora y en la hora de nuestra muerte.* Pray for us sinners now and at the hour of our death. *Padre piadoso, envío mi fé. Es todo lo que tengo.* Merciful Father, I send my faith. It is all I have.

Yanking her arm straight up, Emilio tried to pull her to the surface, struggling to keep his grip on her arm. She felt herself go limp, loosening from him, spiraling down; she closed her eyes and knew she was drowning. *Estoy lista, Señor.* I am ready, Lord. All at once, she felt her arms, her legs, and her feet being supported and lifted up with a powerful strength. She broke the water's surface to see Emilio's hand reaching out to her, over a foot away, his other hand still gripping the raft.

*Amén. Amén.*

# Chapter 15

Once they "centered down," as the Friends called the process of entering their worship, I expected to hear messages on Christmas themes. But the quiet increased until I felt engulfed in it. The children left, the silence opening enough to let them out, then closing in on itself again. No one spoke. Friends had explained the term, "gathered silence," to me as a sense of shared holiness, an awareness of God at that moment. Was this a gathered Meeting? Paul had told me the Quakers' form of worship had been essentially unchanged for more than three hundred years. Even some of the phraseology survived: "center down" and "way will open" and "speak to thy condition." What about these Quakers enabled them to exist in a culture that increasingly embraced technology and constant activity? What would it be like to possess such an enduring, steadfast faith? Nina had spoken of my having faith in myself. Could I somehow extract the strength from the Friends' kind of faith without taking its corollary of religious belief? Could it bring me peace? Could it safely dismantle the anger?

When someone broke the silence, I jumped. In the dim light, the voice was disembodied, and it took me a second or two to realize it was Virgil who spoke. "What is it that God calls us to do? That must be the imperative, above and alone. What is it that God calls us to do?" Silence, yet Virgil's question remained as though it were being repeated.

At a quarter past midnight, now Christmas, Friends shook hands. Paul rose. "Welcome, Friends. It is good to have so many here tonight. In the midst of celebrating the birth of the 'Prince of Peace,' it is fitting that we are dealing with sanctuary concerns. Committee members from Ministry and Worship as well as Peace and Social Concerns have asked if we could have another special Meeting for Business. We thought gathering later today, at two o'clock this afternoon, would give us time to reflect individually before we come together once more in corporate worship. Yes, it's Christmas, and

96

many of you have plans that will need to be honored; we understand. However, we have decided meeting today is warranted."

When he sat down, Sharon Cameron stood. "I'd like to invite everyone to the potluck breakfast at our home after the Rise of Meeting. If any visitors or recent attenders need directions, please let me know. We do have two sleighs outside."

Deciding not to go to the breakfast after all, I gave Eleanor my contribution to the meal. I thanked her and left, needing fresh air, needing to be alone. At home, wanting somehow to recreate the peace of the Meetinghouse in my living room, I collected all my candles and lit them. Looking around me, I realized that I'd come to love this cabin with its log construction and large windows, its simple furnishings and, most of all, its setting, ensconced in the woods.

I recalled what Virgil had said: "What is it that God calls us to do?" He had added it was the single imperative. Science had been my imperative, what I had been called to do, the passion of my life. What could I be called to do now? I couldn't imagine giving control over my life to something, some being, that couldn't be quantified, seen, or touched. "And yet, I envy their faith." Of course, the drunk driver had robbed me of the control I once had over my life. Would faith in God mean I'd still have no control? Ever?

Everyone settled around the tables in the fellowship room, and the customary silence, like a curtain swishing across a stage, opened the Meeting. I hadn't planned to come, yet without fully understanding why, I wanted to see how this would unfold.

Paul ended the silence and called for introductions. A woman I'd not seen before turned out to be an interpreter they had hired for Tomás and Graciela. Paul said, "Our primary purpose is to attempt to discern the will of God regarding the sanctuary movement in general and Drake's Springs Friends Meeting's specific response to it. We have a letter sent from a friend of Emilio's; it is signed with an illegible signature, and it's not dated. The postmark is unreadable, too." Paul motioned to Eleanor, who opened the letter along with a second sheet, the translation.

"'Dear Friends,'" she began, stopping to explain the person might be afraid to use Tomás's name, "'Hoping to find you safe and well. Your brother has had the good fortune of finding work. Unfortunately for us, this means he has had to move from the village, but a family member was able to go with him. He asked me to tell you he will contact you when he arrives at the new place. Everyone here sends you good wishes.'" She passed the letter to

Paul, who asked for a report from the committee convened at the previous Meeting for Business.

Mark Gilberti opened a folder. "Members have called Saguaro Avenue Friends Meeting in Arizona, Fellowship Methodist Church in South Carolina, and the Faith Partners for Central America, based in Minnesota. They caution us to apprise everyone of possible consequences. Arrangements are as varied as the people involved. We were told some church groups harbor refugees but do not transport them; other centers do whatever is needed."

Virgil asked, "And if the INS intervenes, the representatives are the ones charged?"

"The refugees are charged and deported, and yes, the representatives from the organizations are charged as well. Surprisingly, there hasn't been a shortage of volunteers to work in the sanctuary movement." He provided full responses to questions, clarifying terms and discussing the options. I didn't know anything about Mark's background and wondered if he was an attorney.

"What are the consequences?" someone asked.

"You can face up to five years in jail and a fine of two thousand dollars per refugee for each count. Thus, we could be facing ten years plus a fine of four thousand for harboring them."

"Do we have the financial resources for this?" one man asked the treasurer, a woman named Suzanne.

"We have savings of about five thousand in our legal defense fund, which wouldn't go far."

Sharon asked, "Isn't there some way we can do this legally?"

"Salvadorans aren't protected under Extended Voluntary Departure status; although the United Nations recognizes the refugee status of El Salvador and Guatemala, the United States government does not," Mark answered her. "And because the government's policy is that Central Americans are economic refugees, the recent Refugee Act, which requires us to grant asylum to anyone who has a well-grounded fear of persecution, does not apply. As far as doing this legally, the INS has denied all but some three hundred applications out of over thirteen thousand for political asylum from Salvadorans. Few visas are granted. For legal asylum, we'll need proof of direct oppression."

"But Magdalena's husband, Tomás and Emilio's father, and probably their brother, Felipe, have been murdered. Isn't that proof enough they have a 'well-grounded fear of persecution'?" Sharon protested.

"We don't have incontrovertible proof of who murdered them," Paul told her. "Death squads don't leave business cards. Thanks, Mark, to you and the committee for your work." He added Mark's notes to his own. "One more aspect we need to address. You can look at this in both a political and a religious light, as far as motivation goes. Are we using people to change policy, which would be counter to the Quaker principle of not using people as instruments, no matter how worthy the goal? Or are we bringing Emilio and Magdalena here to reunite them with their family members, who have become part of our community?"

Josiah reminded, "We need to consider the consequences that Emilio and Magdalena, as well as Graciela, Tomás, and their children, may suffer if we are indicted. Deported refugees have been detained by the police and later found tortured and left for dead. Have we fully communicated the consequences our actions may have? Do we have the right to be making these decisions in the first place? I'm worried we may be carried away by the urgency of the situation. We may do them more harm."

"Let's not lose sight of the simple fact that we know these two people's lives are in danger and they have appealed to us," Cooper said. "Can you turn your back on them?" He surprised me by addressing Josiah directly.

Paul started to step in, but Josiah answered, "There's nothing simple about this. No matter what we do, I think people are going to pay a high price, and there's a good chance it could be with their lives."

"This will call for an unwavering commitment," Eleanor said.

Josiah spoke in a measured tone. "I think it's best if I stand aside. I can't make that kind of commitment. I think we'd be using the refugees as instruments, and at the very least, I feel we don't know enough to do this in the best possible manner."

I had thought everyone had to agree, or the decision would be tabled. I hadn't known someone could abstain. Ruth reached across the table to touch Josiah's hand, but no one tried to change his mind.

"Josiah Kendall, I apologize," Cooper said formally. "I was out of line." Josiah gave him a nod.

Sharon said, "I agree that we don't know enough. No matter what we decide to do for the present, what about using the emergency problem-solving plan we learned from Rosemont Valley Friends last summer?"

"For those of you not at the retreat," Paul explained, "we learned this Meeting's method of dealing with complex issues. The adults and the older teenagers divide into groups, and each team focuses on one aspect of the issue. The time limit is usually two weeks or less. The groups research the problems as well as possible solutions, meeting frequently during the time limit for intensive work."

"Having everyone work on the issue instead of a single committee reduces the workload on any one member and educates everyone," Sharon said. "And in case you're wondering, the teenagers are included because it introduces them to the serious work of the Meeting and prepares them to be full adult members of the community." She smiled, adding, "They're also more adept at computer research methods."

Paul asked, "Are we in agreement as to committing our resources to the problem-solving plan?"

Silence. Wasn't anyone going to answer him? I knew Quakers traditionally did not vote, but how was Paul to know how they felt? I realized I knew almost nothing about these people's lives outside the context of the Meeting. I couldn't imagine a life where religious and spiritual matters were an important, even central, focus. Paul spoke again. "It seems to be the sense of the Meeting to institute the emergency problem-solving plan." He turned to Josiah. "We appreciate your discernment and your candor, and we will be mindful of your concerns."

He addressed the group. "We may need to continue this discussion after we receive additional information. Are Friends in agreement as to a delay?"

"They are on their way," Abby stated with emphasis.

For the first time in over an hour, there was a prolonged silence. Although I wasn't involved, the tension drew me into the whirl of questions and comments. Virgil leaned forward, placing his hands on the table. "Our faith requires that we attempt to do the will of God." He waited. "What is the will of God for our Meeting on this issue?"

I felt confused, not knowing if they'd decided now to reject the emergency problem-solving plan, or if this was about Emilio and Magdalena. Silence. Restless at first, a desperate grasping, a palpable searching. Several minutes went by before Paul said, "It seems to be the sense of the Meeting to defer for now a decision on the general issue of offering sanctuary to persecuted persons, but to go ahead with the problem-solving process. Is it the sense of the Meeting to offer sanctuary to Emilio Delgado and Magdalena Suárez?" He waited. No one spoke, and the silence expanded. The quiet silvered into a suspension of thought and feeling. I felt we were back in a Meeting for Worship, and then, realized we were. Impatient at first, I allowed the silence to close over me. Letting go of my own thoughts, I mentally withdrew from this place, this moment, and surrendered myself. The silence absorbed the small sounds of the clock ticking, a chair creaking, the coffeemaker sighing, until nothing remained but the feathered stillness. I couldn't tell how much time had elapsed when I sensed a sudden, definite change in the room; the back of my neck felt cold and my eyes opened in shock as I recognized the moment of decision, a silence of certainty. In a tone devoid of emotion or tension, Paul said, "It appears to be the sense of this Meeting to offer sanctuary to Emilio and Magdalena."

The Friends waited until the recorder drafted then read the minute that set forth the Meeting's decision to offer sanctuary to the two refugees. Following a short silence, Paul announced, "It appears to be the sense of this Meeting to approve the sanctuary minute in the case of Emilio Delgado and Magdalena Suárez."

The Meeting concluded, and Josiah and Ruth reached for my hands. Tomás and Graciela, looking drained from the proceedings, received the embraces of Friends. I noticed that Graciela had twisted her rosary around her fingers, pressing the beads into her skin until they left geometric imprints.

Slipping out the side door, I started home. Although I felt privileged to have witnessed this process, I knew I could never make such a decision based on what I believed was the will of God. I wasn't sure I'd attend a service again. I'd be busy enough with work and with continuing my recuperation; I didn't need more challenges. I stopped, knowing these were excuses. These Quakers conducted their lives in such a different way, with their actions emanating from their beliefs. I knew what they were proposing was controversial and radical. Having been raised in a church from a young age, I also knew it was exactly what God called us to do: We were to welcome the strangers in our midst and extend love to those in need, regardless of who they were. I was a nonbeliever; however, I stood on the precipice of their courage and faith, and my heart stirred.

"Merry Christmas." Diane said. "I called your parents and found out you've been snowed in."

"Merry Christmas." I told her about the sleigh ride up to the mountaintop and about the caroling.

"Mercy, this place doesn't sound real."

"I know. I wish you could come for a visit; you'd love it here." With my heart aching for my friend, I asked, "How was your holiday?"

"It was . . ." Diane started crying.

"What if I flew out to see you?" Diane's family had moved to Vermont after she started college. We managed to get together a couple of times a year when my work took me in her direction.

"Not yet, I think. I'll need you more later. Right now, I'm trying to focus on what is in front of me. We've decided on a memory care center nearby, and my father will move in after New Year's."

"The offer stands. You call me day or night, and I will come. Give your mom a hug from me, one for your dad, too. Did I ever tell you that when I was a little girl I loved your dad's lunch box?"

"Whatever for? I don't even remember what it looked like."

"It was one of those old metal lunch boxes men used to carry, especially construction workers. It had the curved top where the thermos fit." Diane's family had inherited a small farm, but her father also worked at a manufacturing plant. "My father always worked at a college and didn't carry his lunch. Your dad's lunch box somehow was a symbol to me of what a real working man would have."

She gave a small laugh. "I won't tell your dad you don't consider him to be a real working man."

While at Maggie's store, I'd found out that Paul and Virgil had gone to meet Emilio and Magdalena at the Mexican border near Laredo, Texas. I'd been surprised to learn Virgil was making the trip. Although he hadn't stood aside like Josiah, for some reason I'd thought he'd disagreed with the decision. When I asked Maggie about it, she'd said, "He may have disagreed on some aspects, but Virgil has a long history of involvement with social justice concerns; he's well known for it in the state, as well as across the nation and abroad in Quaker circles, for that matter. They would be aghast to hear this because Virgil and Eleanor are humble, private people, but it awes me to be in their midst."

Thinking Eleanor might not want to be alone, I invited her for dinner. I picked her up and brought her to the cabin. She updated me on the news. "Emilio contacted Tomás by telephone, but he wasn't sure exactly where they were. We've relayed word to Paul and Virgil, but it will be a miracle if they find each other."

"How long have you been working on this?"

"It must seem to you that we reached this decision quickly, but we've been discussing this issue for almost a year. As far as our Meeting's obligation, however, I believe the most difficult part is over. We made the decision, and I imagine they're on this side of the border by now. We've set our plan in motion, but the outcome is not in our hands."

She held my gaze, and I could see her strength. What had brought her to this point? What price had she paid? "I respect the Friends for their involvement with the sanctuary movement, but I'm not a risk taker."

"I'm not so sure. You're reinventing your life."

"I wouldn't have the boldness to do what your Meeting is doing." Thinking of my Aunt Constanza I added, "However, I'd like to be unafraid to take chances, unafraid to stand up for my convictions."

"For someone who's making a new life for herself, I think you have plenty of bravery. Anyway, it's not so much courage as faith. And to use an old Quaker phrase, to 'speak truth to power.'"

"Did the Meeting bring the Delgado family here?"

"No, one First Day they quite literally appeared on our doorstep with their visas, needing a community's support to get established. How they were able to get visas, and not the rest of the family, we don't know. We think they're reluctant to tell us too much. And how they found Drake's Springs is a mystery to us, too. My best guess is that it took God's intervention." She reached over and touched my cheek with the curved coolness of her hand. "Sort of the same way you came to us."

I felt Eleanor would have the answers I craved if I knew the right questions to ask. Instead, I asked, "Friends have alluded to a time when you weren't in agreement but made a decision anyway. What happened?" She hesitated. I regretted asking but couldn't figure out how to take it back. "I apologize if I'm intruding."

"It's all right It will help you to understand our responses to what is going on now. Our son and two of his boyhood friends who were not Quakers, Jacob and Scott, came to us, seeking sanctuary from the Vietnam draft. Ironically, we arrived one First Day to find them on the steps, like the Delgados. I can still see them: pale and frightened, but resolute. When it was over, Scott fled to Canada where he continues to live, estranged from his family. Jacob and Morgan went to Vietnam, where our son died.

"Separate outcomes, with their own regrets and heartaches. We weren't of one mind and couldn't achieve consensus as to the will of God for us and those young men. The protests in the country caused great turmoil, but I think unspoken, divisive forces within the Meeting were more than we could handle. In retrospect, I don't think we were honest enough with each other about what we were feeling and thinking. We are mindful that with this, we are being given a second chance." Eleanor looked as she often did in Meeting, as though she'd retreated to a place deep within herself.

I waited a few moments before asking, "How did you deal with such a terrible loss?"

Sipping her coffee, she placed her cup on the saucer, the brittle sound of china meeting china loud in the quiet. "There were chasms of emptiness. But do you know what I remember the most about those first months, and even years after Morgan's death? The anger. Overflowing anger at God, my country, the government, the Meeting, Virgil, the Vietnamese, Morgan, and myself. No one was exempt from it. I used to pray to be numb, which I thought would be easier to manage than the anger. I felt seared, skinless. I didn't know what to do with so much rage. I could throw it away from me in gobs, but I had an amazing capacity to manufacture more."

I felt tears welling in my eyes; she was describing how I felt, though I knew my situation could not compare to Eleanor and Virgil's loss of their son. "What did you do?"

"I changed. At last, I conceded my anger wasn't going to bring back Morgan. Unchecked, it threatened to break me. I finally noticed that every time I lashed out, Virgil was there, his arms outstretched to take my fury. Or someone from Meeting encircled me with compassion. Even Paul. He was a teenager, younger than Morgan and not a member then. But that dear boy wouldn't give up on me, no matter how many times I literally slammed the door in his face. At my most broken, I felt abandoned by God. But I came to understand that God had never abandoned me; Virgil and Paul and many others heeded God's call to intervene in my life. I, at last, reached out for their help. They saved me, Katherine. They saved my soul."

She looked into the fire. "To surrender that anger was one of the hardest things I've ever done, and yet on every anniversary of Morgan's death, I must admit I've not fully forgiven everyone involved, including myself—especially myself. I learned to be grateful, though, for the anger because I became more involved in peace concerns as a result. It made me less judgmental of others and more understanding of people's pain." Eleanor finished her coffee and faced me. "Something else I learned: Almost everyone has at least one or two people reaching out to her."

When I took Eleanor home, the house looked large and dark, almost foreboding. "Are you going to be all right here alone? Please come back and stay with me, or I'll stay here with you."

"Thank you, but no, I'll be fine. You can't imagine the number of people who've dropped by or called since Virgil's been gone."

I waited until she'd gotten in the door before driving away. The night was clear and cold, and wrapping up in a blanket, I sat on my front porch steps and looked at the stars. The images of the three scared boys and of the Salvadorans on the Meetinghouse steps stayed with me, as well as Eleanor's comment about my coming to Drake's Springs.

# Chapter 16

## TEXAS

ALTHOUGH EMILIO FELT ALMOST as afraid in Texas as he had been in Mexico, worried they would be caught and sent back, Magdalena laughed with elation. "*Norteamérica. ¡Los Estados Unidos.*" She grinned at him. "We are free, Emilio, we are safe."

"We're not citizens. We're not free or safe."

"But we won't face a death squad here. Soon we will be with Tomás, Graciela, and the grandchildren. You were right, telling me to have faith. You have been a good son of my heart." She took his face in her hands and kissed him on both cheeks. "*Gracias, hijo.*" Thank you, son.

Planning to leave at dawn to find the church in San Ygnacio, near Laredo, they spent that night in a park. Magdalena saw a few people settling onto benches with blankets and cardboard boxes around them. "Are they all refugees like us?" she asked. "Maybe they know where the refugee church is."

Emilio stopped her from approaching the man nearest them. He was filthy, his hair stringing around his face, his clothes torn and soiled; muttering to himself, he plucked at his shirt. "I don't think they are refugees. We have to be careful. Don't talk to anyone until we get to the church." He sighed and shook his head. Since crossing the river, Magdalena seemed unafraid of anyone or anything.

Curled up next to Magdalena on a bench, Emilio struggled to stay awake. His hand throbbed and he felt feverish; he knew he'd have to find the church soon. Despite his desire not to, though, he soon fell asleep to the even rhythm of Magdalena's breathing.

At dawn, Emilio woke to the racket of trucks passing by the park. He shook her awake. "Let's go. We must find the church today." Leaning over, he picked up their backpack and knew something was wrong. "We've been robbed!" He turned the backpack upside down to release the few remaining contents: a shirt, some underwear, a towel, a bar of soap. The rest of their clothing, their maps, and most of all, the little bit of American money, had been stolen.

Magdalena turned the backpack inside out, disbelieving him, thinking she would see the missing articles. "¡*La fotografía*! Agustín's photograph, why would they take an old picture of someone they don't know?" Emilio wanted to console her, but his arms, drained of energy and compassion, hung at his sides.

"I can't remember what he looked like without the picture! Why did they have to take Agustín?" Hearing her, other people in the park clustered around them. One woman handed her a tissue. "Agustín, Agustín," she wailed, squatting down and rocking back and forth on her heels.

He had never seen her like this and waved people away, afraid to attract attention. Helping her up, he murmured to her, "We have to leave." He led her to a gas station. Talking to her in soft tones, he took her to the door of the women's restroom. "Go wash up, you'll feel better. Remember, soon you'll see Graciela and the grandchildren. *Piense en ellos.*" Think of them.

In the restroom, Magdalena waited in line for the toilet. She kept her head down, her tears dampening the front of her shirt. Afterward, as she washed up, she ignored the stares of the other women as she soaped her face, her arms, and between her legs down to her feet. She felt as though she'd never be thoroughly clean again. She pressed wet paper towels over her face and ran her wet hands through her hair.

She stared at herself in the mirror. "Agustín," she breathed out in despondence. Why couldn't Emilio have placed the backpack with them on the bench? No, she scolded herself, you cannot blame him. You should have thought of that yourself. You will remember Agustín's face when you see Graciela and the grandchildren. She cupped her hands under the faucet, rinsed her mouth, and drank some water. Emilio was waiting. She knew he was bone-tired and in pain. Alone now in the restroom, she told herself, "I can't worry about a photograph because Emilio needs me. I will show him I can be strong. I will not give up because of a thief." She gave herself a firm nod in the mirror and rejoined Emilio.

❖ ❖ ❖

They moved as fast as possible, Emilio holding up Magdalena when she stumbled. Several cars slowed and drivers asked if they'd like a lift, but he smiled and said, "No, thank you."

"We could be there by now if we took a ride," she complained.

"No, they might guess who we are. They might be police in disguise."

At last, he pointed out the rooftops of a cluster of buildings. "I think this is the place; it's very small, so it shouldn't be hard to find the church. We'll get close and walk there at dusk. If it's not the right place, I'll get food and water and find out how much farther we have to go." He knew they'd have to find the refugee church soon, for neither one of them would survive much longer.

As the sun was setting, they walked into the town and found the church, its cross on top of the roof rising above the other low buildings. When Magdalena spotted it, she crossed herself and murmured a prayer. A priest greeted them when they entered the church. Magdalena managed to say, "*Gracias a Dios,*" before sinking to her knees. Thanks be to God. Emilio, reaching too late for the back of a pew, collapsed.

# Chapter 17

"It's done," Diane told me when I called after New Year's to check in with her about her father's move. "It went more smoothly than we could have hoped. The staff kept telling us that it's often harder on the family than the person needing the care."

"How's your mom?"

"She's taking it better than we thought she would. I think she's relieved but doesn't feel right in saying so."

"She's part of the original 'suck it up, buttercup' generation. And you?"

"I know it's what's best for him and my mother. How was your New Year's?"

I told her about my resolutions to have more fun and to try different things. "Keep me posted on those! I must say, you no longer sound like my cautious, methodical, predictable friend."

Finishing my work early in the evening, I decided to attend a program on El Salvador at the Meetinghouse. My ignorance about the Central American political situation was embarrassing, and I wanted to learn more. I decided to walk; the moonlight on the snow would be bright enough for me to see clearly on the return home, and I felt safer on foot than driving on ice and snow.

It felt strange to enter the Meetinghouse and hear people talking. Mark had set up a projector and focused a slide on the blank wall next to the piano. Facing the crowd, he called for attention. "All right, folks, I think we can get started. I'm Mark Gilberti, and most of you know I went to El Salvador last summer with a group called Congregations for Peace. We went to observe conditions, listen to the people's concerns, and see for ourselves what's going on. We also did mission work, helping with building repairs, construction projects, and medical care. For me, that was the most gratifying."

He flipped through slides showing green fields and mist rising from the bases of the mountains and volcanoes. "I wasn't prepared for what we saw and heard." He showed a picture of a little girl whose bright smile belied the desperate thinness of her arms and legs and her ragged dress. "This is Carolina. Her father was killed in an ambush when he was walking home from work. Her brothers, nine and eleven, now work in the coffee fields to support the family."

Another picture was of a woman leaning against a shack. Her eyes were vacant globes of hopelessness. "This woman's sons died from extreme heat and lack of water when they tried to cross the border in a crowded railroad car. The incident was highly publicized at the time."

Mark continued his litany of torn lives, orphaned children, and poverty. I felt a rush of shame for taking my life of abundance and safety as an entitlement. One picture depicted a group of children grinning and waving. "They love to ham it up for the camera, which we found to be reassuring in the midst of such conflict and poverty. They captivated us by their exuberance despite such chaos. It was humbling." The next slides of burned buildings and heaps of rubble were grim. "These slides illustrate the results of the depopulation policy."

A woman I'd seen before in the Meeting stopped Mark. "Before you go on to the next slide, would you please explain what you mean by that?"

"Sure. In order to take away civilian support for the guerrillas, the government employs 'scorched-earth' tactics to force the people away from the countryside. They've bombed and attacked certain key areas, resulting in displacements within the country of approximately five hundred thousand; over four hundred thousand refugees have left the country to date."

Mark switched to another slide. "These photos were taken from an airplane because we weren't allowed to be in the area. This is the outcome of 'Operation Phoenix,' when one morning in January 1986, mortar fire and bombing began on an area filled with civilians, followed by hundreds of soldiers being sent in."

He flashed through more slides. "Some accounts say the death squad killings of individuals have decreased, but when President Duarte took office in 1984, the depopulation campaigns—a euphemism for wholesale slaughter, actually—increased. Our government's role has been to ship aircraft to them and to have advisors from the United States train the Salvadoran military."

"You mean we're enabling the Salvadoran military to kill those people and burn them out of their homes?" asked the woman who had stopped Mark earlier. "I had no idea."

"Ostensibly, our actions are to promote democratic reforms, but the methods are more than questionable. And there's no need to apologize, so keep asking questions."

"I'm also here to get more information," a man spoke up. Unable to see him, I thought his voice sounded familiar but couldn't place it.

"I'm sorry, I don't know your name."

"My name's Jim. I can see the bombing of civilians is terrible. But aren't those on the other side guilty of appalling acts themselves?"

"Yes," Mark said, "and I don't deny it."

"Don't we, as a force for democracy, want to help a government that's trying to set up democratic reforms? We don't want a second Cuba down there or, God knows, another Vietnam."

"I think we can all agree it's right to help another government that is striving toward democracy. But do we accomplish it by sending planes that engage in bomb attacks against civilians and by not protesting human rights violations?"

With an edge of frustration, Jim responded, "We can't be expected to bring in every person who's having trouble at home, can we? Where do we draw the line?"

Why was he talking about immigration? Where had I heard that voice? The general store? Yes. A few weeks ago, two men had sat at the lunch counter and started talking about the Quakers. One of the men had complained, "These Quakers are bringing in illegal aliens who take jobs from Americans and do nothing but commit crimes. Hell, we've got people right here the Quakers could rescue if they wanted." Sitting next to him, a man dressed in a business suit had added in a high-pitched, strained voice, "The Quakers better be glad there are people loyal to this country who will do their fighting for them. They might get their comeuppance this time for their 'holier-than-thou' ways."

The first man who'd spoken had asked me if I were "that lady scientist." He smirked when I'd replied simply that I was a scientist. When they'd finished their meals, Maggie told them if they were going to talk like that, they'd need to take their business elsewhere. After they left, she'd turned to me and said, "It sometimes seems like the most intolerant people are the same ones who thump the Bible the loudest."

Surprised I remembered as much of the incident as I did, I keyed back into the discussion when Mark was responding to Jim. "These people have appealed to us. Most of them don't want to become United States citizens.

When it's safe to return, they want to go back home, back to their land. And international humanitarian laws, as well as our own Refugee Act of 1980, say these people have the right to a safe haven."

Listening to the statistics and watching the slides, I felt disbelief and sorrow. Had this information been on the news every night? Had I ignored it, thinking it was no concern of mine? Did I think because the conflict was far away, enmeshed in issues I didn't understand, that it didn't affect me? That I had the luxury of not paying attention? I'd recently been focused on my recuperation, but what about before the accident? Did I just not remember? The situation in El Salvador and other Central American countries had been going on for a long time.

Mark shut off the projector, and after answering a few more questions, he thanked everyone for coming. People began leaving. Two of the men ahead of me looked familiar. Had they been the ones at Maggie's store? When one of the men turned around and looked at me, I squinted, trying to see him in the dim light.

Mark tapped my shoulder. "It's good to see you."

"Thank you for doing this. I'm terribly uninformed. You know what is most memorable for me, the most haunting? The children. The slides of those children."

"I know. We wanted to bring them and their families back with us. But that's not the answer, either." While he packed up the projector and slides in a box, I helped Ruth and her husband, Adam, store the extra chairs. I'd met Adam a few weeks ago at Maggie's. "We'll finish closing up, you go ahead," Mark told me.

It was a cold night with few clouds, nothing diluting the light of the moon. A car pulled up beside me, and Sharon Cameron rolled down her window. "Kate, would you like a ride?"

"No, thanks. It's a beautiful night for walking."

"That it is." She waved and went on.

Unable to enjoy the ethereal beauty of the moonlight's glow, I couldn't shake the disturbing images I had seen in Mark's slides. When I was close to my lane, a car passed me, then slowed, turned into my lane, reversed, and came back in my direction. Someone must have forgotten something at the Meetinghouse. Slowing slightly, the car veered toward me. Was there something in the middle of the road it was trying to avoid? Did the driver think I wanted a ride? Heading toward me, the car sped up. The lights blinded me, and the realization that the car was going to hit me exploded into an isolated certainty. I couldn't move; my legs began to melt beneath me, and a scream ached in my throat.

Twisting, knowing somehow a ravine needed to be cleared, I jumped toward the woods. One foot touched the far side of the ditch, slipped, and lost hold. I reached out to break my fall, but as I tumbled to the bottom of the ravine with briars lashing my face, I was unable to catch hold of anything. I felt sharp pains in my right ankle and my left arm. What was the shouting I heard? Some quality about the voices sounded familiar, though I couldn't understand any of the words. I held my breath, trying to hear better. This could not be happening. This could not be real. The car was leaving, its lights grazing over the top of the ravine. I crouched down in the ditch with my heart beating so hard it made me feel sick. Blood ran into my eyes and stung. I couldn't decide whether to try to climb out or hide somewhere along the ravine until I was sure the car wasn't coming back. Home, I thought. Home.

Digging the fingers of my right hand into the hard ground, I crawled out of the ravine, falling back twice. I beat against the ravine's side in frustration. "Stop it," I ordered myself. "You can't fall apart. They might come back." Grunting, I pulled myself up to the road's edge and held my breath, as though not breathing would keep away the evil on the road. I focused on getting to my lane, trying to force myself across the expanse, suddenly dangerous. Virgil had said I had courage, so had Eleanor; I could get across this road. Maybe if I had courage, I could have faith. Courage for the left foot. Faith for the right. Was that my right foot? It hurt, so I tried touching just my toes to the ground. Courage. Faith. Courage. Faith. Courage. The middle of the road. Faith. Courage. I heard a car and turned. I knew this time I wouldn't be able to run. Not again, I thought. This could not be happening. No, don't panic. Think. Stay calm.

The car slowed and stopped. Someone called, "Kate?" through an open window. I stood in the light, knowing it was someone from Meeting, a Friend, but I could not move. Doors opened. "Kate?" I couldn't answer. First one person, then another, approached me.

"You can get out of the middle of the road now. I won't run over you, I promise," a man said. "You want a ride down to your house?"

When I didn't answer, they came closer. "Adam, something's wrong." A woman put her fingers under my chin and lifted my head. What was familiar about this gesture? "It's Ruth, Kate. Did you fall in the dark? Why didn't . . . Adam, there's blood all over her face and she's trembling. Can you walk?" she asked me. I nodded, and they guided me into the car.

In my cabin, they sat me at the kitchen table, and Ruth began to wash the blood and dirt from my face. "Are you hurt anywhere else?"

"I can't stop shaking. I'm cold."

Adam left the kitchen and returned with the afghan from the sofa. "Are you hurt anywhere else?" Ruth repeated.

"My ankle, my arm."

"Which ones?"

"I don't know." Left? Right? Courage? Faith? Ruth tried to take off my gloves and coat but stopped when I cried out.

"We'd better take you to the hospital," Adam decided.

"No."

"Something could be broken. You could be in shock."

"No. I won't go. No."

"Kate," Adam began, but Ruth stopped him.

"Don't upset her. At least let us take you to a doctor and let him decide. I don't know if you've met Will Cameron yet, but you've met his wife, Sharon, at the Meetinghouse."

My head hurt. Had I hit it when I fell? There was something important I was supposed to remember if I got hurt. Records, I recalled. "Ruth, my medical records, please get them. Living room. File cabinet, top drawer. In front."

In the car, Ruth buckled my seat belt and tucked the afghan over me. For some reason, these actions—being helped into a car, having the seat belt fastened for me, the afghan being arranged over me—felt oddly familiar, but I couldn't figure out why. "I couldn't stop it," I said, my teeth chattering.

Ruth leaned toward me. "Couldn't stop what?"

"The car."

"A car hit you?"

"I don't know."

"Answer me. Are you saying a car hit you?"

Her question confused me. Which car did she mean? "I couldn't stop it."

"Adam, we'd better take her straight to the hospital. I'll call Will when we get there."

At the hospital, I blocked out everything that was being done for me. It took too much energy to answer people's questions, so I stopped trying. Their voices sounded insubstantial, syllables of billowing chiffon floating around me. I'll surrender my body to you; do whatever needs to be done, I thought. Or don't do anything. I don't care. I give up. At last, I give up. Even Annie Sullivan might give up at this point. I don't have to participate in this. I cannot do this. I will not.

Shutting my eyes against the bright lights and the pain, I repeated the Quaker phrases I'd heard at the Meetinghouse: Way will open. Mind the Light. Way will open. Mind the Light. Breathe in—Way will open. Breathe out—Mind the Light. All at once, I felt warm and at peace. I stopped struggling, stopped trying to think, my fear enameling into tiny, polished capsules. The voices surrounding me retreated even further, my body light and forgiving.

Way will open.

Mind the Light.

Mind the Light.

# Chapter 18

A WOMAN'S FACE APPEARED over me. She looked like someone I knew. "It's Sharon, Kate. Sharon Cameron. How do you feel?"

"My arm hurts."

She touched my forehead and smoothed the blanket around my shoulders. "I know. Your wrist is broken. Adam and Ruth took you to the hospital, but Will brought you back here when they released you. You were adamant about not staying at the hospital any longer than necessary. You're welcome to stay with us as long as you'd like."

"My ankle?" Even my tongue felt heavy. When had it felt like that before?

"It's sprained, but not broken."

My tongue was sprained? That didn't make sense. No, she meant my ankle. "My words?"

"What about your words?"

"My words, are they clear?"

"Yes, I can understand you. You're probably feeling the effects of the pain medication. I'll call Will and tell him you're awake."

I kept sliding off into sleep, turning my head on the pillow. Each time I awakened, I registered more of the serene room, relieved I could put names to what I saw. Serenity. Was that what I'd wished for?

"Kate?" a man's voice called my name. Opening my eyes, I saw a man with silver-flecked black hair. "Good, you're awake. I'm Will Cameron, I'm a doctor." He focused a bright light into my eyes. "You're going to be fine. Your left wrist is broken, but it's a fairly uncomplicated break. You should heal quickly. Your right ankle is sprained and your right knee is swollen. With the broken wrist, I don't want you to use crutches; you'll have to use a wheelchair for a couple of days at least." I closed my eyes. He waited until

I reopened them. "Thanks for bringing your records; given your previous injuries, it was helpful for me to have them. I've spoken to Dr. Grazio."

"What about my head?"

"Did you hit it against something?"

"I don't know."

"Does it hurt?"

"Yes."

"They took x-rays and some scans as a precaution because of your history and because you had so many scratches and bruises on your face and neck. Everything looks fine right now, but it's something I'll keep an eye on. You may have hit your head during the fall, or it could hurt now because of the trauma to your body. As soon as you're able, you'll need to see Dr. Grazio. Sharon and I can take you, if you'd like."

He asked more questions and continued to examine me, his touch gentle and reassuring. "The police are here. I've put them off as long as I could, but they need to talk with you. Do you think you're up to it? I've explained to them that they can't question you for long."

"The police?" I struggled to sit up, and he rearranged the pillows behind me. For the drunk driver? The police?

"We called them because you told the Ericksons you were hit by a car."

Why would I have told Adam and Ruth about the drunk driver? Before I could sort it out, two uniformed officers entered the room. One officer pulled up a chair and greeted me in a soft voice. "We need to ask you some questions. Could you tell us what happened last night?"

Was it last night? The car. Stopped at the traffic light. No, no, still the wrong car. Staring at the officers, I shook my head.

"You were going back to your house from the Meetinghouse." Reading from his notes, the officer prompted me.

Finally. Yes, that car. Jumping into the ravine. I told them about walking home, and how the car had turned around.

"You say it veered deliberately toward you?"

"At first I thought something was in the road they were avoiding."

"An animal?"

"No, there was nothing." I tried to recall the scene.

"So the car veered and hit you. Was there ice? Did the driver lose control?"

"No. I mean, it veered in my direction, came near me, but didn't hit me because I jumped. If I hadn't, it would have hit me. But there wasn't any ice. The road from my lane to the Meetinghouse had been cleared and sanded. Had I known that, I would have driven."

"Can you describe the car? Did you get the license plate number?"

"No, it happened too fast. I had to turn and jump."

"Do you know of anyone who would want to hurt you?"

"No." I couldn't talk any longer. Will escorted the officers out, and for the rest of the day, I slept off and on. Sharon and Will took turns checking on me, urging me to eat something when I'd wake up. I didn't want food. In fact, I wished they'd go away and leave me alone.

When I woke later, Eleanor was in the rocking chair by the bed. She helped me to sit up. "How are you feeling?"

"Better. How did you find out?"

"There aren't many secrets in Drake's Springs. Cooper came by. The whole Meeting has been informed by now, I imagine." She fell silent and held my right hand with both of hers. Realizing she was praying, I allowed the quiet to wash over me.

"Katherine," she spoke after a time, "if thee will reach out, we will help."

"I know you mean this with great kindness."

"But?"

"But I don't want to count on anyone, or anything."

"Because others have let you down in the past? But most human beings need those connections, even with the risks, even with our failings. Don't take as long to learn that as I did."

"Just when I'd begun to feel safe, when I thought I'd made progress putting my life together, this happens. I thought I'd never feel that scared again." I tried to find a less awkward position for my arm. "I don't know how much my mother told you about what happened before I came here."

"Not much. You'd been in a car accident. Why don't you tell me about it?"

"It was a drunk driver." I found myself telling her about the past couple of years, the recuperation process, about my job, even about David. "I don't know what to do. Where can I go and be safe? How can I stop being so angry and hurt?"

Eleanor sat in silence. "You don't believe in God, do you?" she said at last.

"Is it so obvious?"

She settled back in the rocking chair. "You've alluded to it. Try to trust in the goodness around you, no matter how insignificant it may seem. It can come from God, whether or not you believe it does."

"That's your answer to how I can stop feeling this way? I'm sorry, I shouldn't complain. I've got a lot to be thankful for. My problems cannot compare to what you've lost."

"I don't think tragedies can be put on a comparative scale. I lost my son, needlessly. So did thousands and thousands of other parents on both sides of the conflict. And that's from one war alone. But I think you're miss-ing my point. Counting blessings is important, yes, but I think we need something more immediate, something more tangible."

"What do you mean?"

She drew back the curtains and raised the shades before answering. "After Morgan was killed, Virgil and I had a terrible argument, the kind where you get off track and bring up things better left unsaid, old hurts. Virgil wanted to go camping, but I couldn't bear the thought of doing some-thing Morgan had especially loved. It seemed like a betrayal. Virgil accused me of giving up, of choosing a sort of living death, of enshrining Morgan's memory. For my part, I accused him of not grieving, of forgetting Morgan, of forgiving too quickly." She gazed out the window. "It was awful, a crucible of pain and anger. After shouting for what seemed like hours, we spent the rest of the day not speaking to each other. And it wasn't one of those peace-ful Quaker silences, I assure you.

"Virgil decided to go camping by himself at dawn the following morn-ing. When I woke up, I found a thermos of coffee and a ceramic cup I'd made for Morgan on my bedside table. No note, just the thermos and cup. I saw them for what he intended, a gesture of love, of understanding, of tell-ing me he'd not abandon me. Striking all reminders of Morgan from my life was not going to erase my pain, but trusting in the goodnesses around me, no matter how minor, would move me forward. Virgil showed me that the small, sudden miracles are not random."

Eleanor reached out her hand, and I took it.

When the Camerons took me home, Eleanor and Mark met us there. I told the group my belief that two of the men at Mark's program had been in Maggie's store, criticizing the Quakers for offering sanctuary to refugees. I described how one of the men at the end of the program had turned and stared at me before leaving the building. "I couldn't see him clearly, but I got the distinct sense that he recognized me."

"I'd better call Maggie," Mark said, "and see if she knows who they are. If she does, I'll report it to the police."

"Perhaps you shouldn't do that. What would happen with Emilio and Magdalena? And I can't be sure." I glanced at Will. "I can't be sure I'm re-membering any of this correctly. Besides, just because the men at Maggie's made those comments doesn't mean they were the ones who ran me off the road."

"We have an obligation to report what we suspect," Mark said. "I don't think we'll have to be specific about Emilio and Magdalena."

After making his calls, he told us, "Maggie thinks the men in question might be from Harrisonburg. They haven't been in the store since that day, and she says they hadn't been in there frequently before. She said to call her if you need anything, and she'll be by later to bring you something to eat tonight."

At last everyone left, even Eleanor, though not until I promised to let her bring dinner. The long wait was beginning to tell on her, she told me, and she welcomed a diversion. Calling Maggie, I thanked her for her earlier offer but explained that Eleanor had insisted on coming and taking care of a meal.

"I'll keep it for you for tomorrow night. Put my number by your telephone and make sure your doors and windows are locked. Don't you want me to come and stay with you? Or I'll bring you over here."

"I'm fine. I'm not scared to be here by myself. I refuse to surrender that to them."

I napped until Eleanor returned. When she opened the freezer to get ice for our water, I couldn't believe what I saw. Dishes and wrapped packages, all neatly labeled, filled the freezer. "Those definitely weren't in my freezer before; what are they?"

"Friends knew it would be difficult for you to make meals with one hand. They gave me these while you were with the Camerons. They wanted you to know they're thinking of you and are concerned."

"At least they don't know it's difficult for me to make meals with two good hands." I tried to laugh. "This is a perfect example of your desire to have me trust in the small kindnesses. How wonderful of everyone." After dinner we sat by the fire and talked until I said, "I'll be all right. Why don't you go on home?"

"You'll call if you need anything, no matter the time? You have our number, right? I'm not sleeping much these nights, so don't worry about waking me." She made sure things I might need were in reach from the wheelchair before leaving.

During the night I awoke several times, unable to find a good position because of the cast. In the quiet, I imagined hearing noises outside. Despite my earlier bravado, I capitulated, turning on the front porch light, a lamp in the living room, and the light in the hallway. "I don't think this is what they mean by 'Mind the Light,'" I murmured, but it made me feel safer.

The next morning, someone knocked on the door. I tensed and wheeled the chair to look out the window, moving the curtain aside a fraction.

"¿*Señorita Solterra*?" Graciela called out to me.

I unlocked and opened the door. "Come in, *pase, por favor.*"

"¿*Habla español*?"

"*Solo un poco.* Only a little." She knocked snow from her boots and removed them before entering, setting them on the porch. From her pockets she produced slippers and put them on. "*Por favor, siéntese aquí.*" I motioned her to the chair closest to the hearth.

"No, I come to work."

"*¿Ha venido a trabajar? No entiendo por qué.* You have come to work? I don't understand why."

She replied in a stream of rapid Spanish, finishing in English, "We are sorry for what has happened. We feel a . . . *responsibilidad?*"

"This wasn't your fault. We don't even know for sure it had anything to do with the Meeting."

"*¿La verdad?*"

"*La verdad.*" The truth.

"Still, I can clean, no?" She stood and took off her coat, her luxurious, black hair tumbling free of the coat's hood.

"*No, por favor,*" but she was already in the kitchen, looking under the sink. I took the cleanser from her. "I'm all right, *estoy bien,* I can manage."

"*Sí, pero puedo limpiar.* Yes, but I can clean." Taking the cleanser from me, she motioned me back into the living room. I gave in and tried to read while she mopped the bathroom and kitchen floors, washed the dishes, and started a soup.

I convinced her to stay and have lunch with me. The steam from the soup warmed my face. "*Pronto, su madre estará aquí.* Soon, your mother will be here; I know you'll be excited to see her." We slipped back and forth between languages. I knew that many of my earlier memories were intact, but it surprised me how much Spanish I recalled.

"It is hard to believe she and Emilio are coming. *Los cuáqueros,* the Quakers, they are good to us, no?" Smiling for the first time that afternoon, her dark eyes, her whole face, became transformed; she was a true beauty, and I sensed an uncommon strength and determination in this young, petite woman.

"*Sí,* they are good to me, as well."

# Chapter 19

AT THE MEETINGHOUSE DOOR, Ruth greeted us, telling us that Paul, Virgil, and the refugees hadn't arrived yet. Coming in from the side door, Eleanor crossed the room and sat with me. I noticed no children or teenagers were present, which was unusual. The mood was not one of tense waiting as I'd expected, but one of confidence.

Eleanor looked unperturbed, her fingers clasped together and resting in her lap, her eyes closed. Still no one spoke. Were they going to hold Meeting until Paul and Virgil arrived, no matter how late? Moments later, though, the side door opened. They had come. Paul sat on the facing bench, and Virgil came and sat between Eleanor and me. Tomás, Graciela, Magdalena, and Emilio followed and sat together. No one moved, and most people showed no outward sign that they were aware of the arrival. If anything, the silence enlarged, erasing the fissures of doubt. Magdalena reached for her daughter's hand, and leaning against her, settled in to join the Meeting. She looked perfectly at home. Ten minutes passed. Sharon Cameron rose and sang, the others joining her, "Hallelujah, hallelujah," the one word eight times. A minute or two later, Virgil reached for my hand, and Meeting ended.

"Are you all right, Katherine? We have been worried." For some reason, his use of my full first name touched me. I simply nodded my head yes. When had he been told?

The silence of the long service broke with embraces and applause. Paul stood, looking weary and disheveled, and waited for people to settle down. "Friends, it is good to be home." His voice broke and he stopped, looking around the room until he saw me. "We had an incredible journey, and we felt your prayerful presence every part of the way. The Hospitality Committee informed me that the Young Friends have prepared refreshments. They invite us to come and share in this joyous occasion and to meet and welcome Magdalena and Emilio." He shook his head slightly and added in a lighter tone, "Homemade cake, people, and ice cream! Everyone come."

Cooper appeared at my side to help me down the stairs. I had graduated from the wheelchair to one crutch for support. The teenagers had put tablecloths, candles, and decorations on the tables and were serving cake and punch they had made. When Paul came over to me, I stopped him before he could speak. "I'm all right. How did you and Virgil find out?"

"Eleanor told us. I was afraid something like this might happen, though I didn't think so soon, or to someone who isn't a Quaker."

"We're not sure it was connected."

"Want to bet?" he said. "We'll talk later. But for now, Magdalena and Emilio asked to meet you."

Magdalena, still holding her daughter's hand, rose when we approached. She reached up and kissed me, first on one cheek, then the other. She pointed to my cast.

"*No se preocupe, por favor, estoy bien.*" I tried to reassure her. "Don't worry; I'm fine." She looked so frail that I couldn't imagine how she'd survived the journey. Tomás came over to us with his brother. "*Bienvenido,*" I welcomed Emilio.

Tomás interpreted for him. "He says he is sorry you were hurt because of them, and asks if he can be of service in any way to please call on him."

More help and I'd have to flee to the city for some peace. I explained in Spanish to Emilio that we didn't know who'd hurt me or why, but I thanked him for his offer of help. He bowed slightly, the formal gesture somehow fitting coming from him. When more Quakers came up to be introduced to the refugees, I found a corner where I could sit down. A teenager brought me cake and ice cream, but I didn't feel like eating. Will sat down beside me, balancing his plate on his knees. "How are you feeling?"

"Fine." I realized how abruptly I'd spoken. "I'm sorry. I don't mean to sound ungrateful, but I think I need a little time to myself."

"When someone we care about has been hurt, we want to reach out."

"I know, and people must think I'm rude, pushing them away."

"Somewhat puzzled, maybe. If you're cold and someone offers you a warm coat, you should accept it."

"Please don't take this the wrong way, but for the next couple of days, I don't want to see anyone. I'd like to be left alone." I stopped, knowing I sounded petulant. Standing up, I lost my balance, and reaching out to steady me, Will handed me the crutch. "Excuse me, I think I'll see if the Mackenzies are ready to go home. They brought me."

"Why don't I take you home? I'll ask Sharon to tell Maggie." Will spoke to his wife and then ushered me outside so we could avoid using the steps.

He drove away from the Meetinghouse, the car's lights outlining the trees. "Would you like to talk?" he asked.

"No. Thanks." I laughed. "Put on the warm coat, right?" At my door, he waited until I was inside. "Don't worry, I'll be fine."

"I'm not worried. Anyone who's gone through as much as you have must be tough. You're a survivor."

After Will left, I tried to go to sleep but found myself constantly lifting my head to listen, to look toward the windows. I knew it was irrational to blame the drunk driver for this, but if it were not for him, I wouldn't be here now. He'd made me find out how strong I could be, but he'd made me realize exactly how fragile I was, too.

Damn you. May you know what it's like to be afraid every day. May you always hear scary noises at night.

Will evidently passed the message along, because for the next couple of days, no one called or came by, not even Maggie or Eleanor. When I called my parents, I didn't tell them about getting hurt. I hedged about making a date for a trip home, hoping to stall until the cuts healed on my face and the cast was removed. There was no sense in upsetting them, for a fractured bone and a sprain would heal.

I worked hard, writing notes and reading research, and ate only when very hungry. I resisted going to sleep at night by taking short naps at intervals during the day. Listlessness yielded to a feeling of uneasiness, as though dozens of ceiling fans were whirling overhead. I knew this incident had brought the first accident, the first car, into focus again.

It was a Sunday morning before dawn, and I'd been on my way to check an ongoing experiment. I needed to feed the cells I was working with to ensure they were getting enough nutrients from the media, the liquid in which they lived. Trying to stop the memory, I placed my hands over my ears and closed my eyes. "No, no, no, not now," but the car kept coming. I was at a traffic light, the intersection deserted at that hour, and all at once, like the snake by the shed, the car was barreling toward me. So much clawing, encompassing fear in such a few seconds. I had screamed, "God, help me," so my father was right; then a horrendous crash, overpowered by my screams as flesh ripped, bones broke, muscles tore. Darkness and nothingness enveloped me with the blessings of no pain, no thoughts. Weeks later, though, my parents' voices marched into my consciousness and demanded, "Kate, wake up. It's Mom and Dad. Katie, wake up now," but I didn't recognize the voices that sounded annoyed with me. What had I done wrong?

And who was Kate? Voices I could not place, questions I could not answer, and words I did not know swirled around me in a vertiginous frenzy; my body became a tabernacle of pain.

How could God be called just and loving? And how could I put this behind me, make my peace with it, and go on? It was the question over which I kept tripping, as with a turned-up corner of a rug, each time thinking, "I need to fix this," then forgetting until stumbling again. I was working hard to be a different person; why couldn't I let go of the old Kate? Maybe I couldn't because I still didn't know what kind of person I wanted to become. There weren't any blueprints to roll out on the kitchen table, no precise white lines over cobalt blue to trace. Emilio and Magdalena had used "north" as their true constant, the magnetic compass needle steadying them, guiding them to the right path. I didn't know what the next step was for me, but at least I sensed I was ready to move forward once I figured out how. I finally pulled the sofa's afghan over me and slept where I was, tucked into the cushions.

I opened my eyes at first light. Not moving, I watched the sunlight bless the wooden floor. I remembered what I had thought about on New Year's Day, which I had spent alone. Getting up early, I had set up a circle of candles, determined not to mark the day with a sense of loss and anger. I had promised myself to stop giving the drunk driver power over my life, acknowledging it would require constant vigilance. Thinking of my Aunt Constanza, I had resolved to have more fun, to act on more impulses, and to try doing things out of character.

How I longed to defy the despair and the anger. Will had called me a survivor, but that sounded like someone barely managing. I needed to move past my life being centered on my limitations and my daily struggles. It would be a relief to focus on something or someone else. I was collapsing in on myself now; focusing outward might be my salvation. I felt tremulous but was glad to watch the sunrise. When the sun highlighted my feet and swept up my legs, its warmth a benediction on my face, I knew I had to claim more than survival. I wanted triumph. I desired joy.

# Chapter 20

NOT HAVING BEEN INSIDE Paul's house before, I tried to look around without seeming obvious. It was an old farmhouse with wooden flooring and thick oak beams that divided the ceilings. There were few adornments, but the effect was one of surety and of a sense of place and belonging. The house was Quaker plain. What kind of farm did he have? I couldn't remember, though I vaguely recalled having heard about his farm at some point. I wondered why he'd wanted to see me.

He came in with a tray of tea and slices of cinnamon bread. "Thanks for coming here. I'm expecting a neighbor to come by later to help me with some equipment and didn't want to miss him." He served me, then himself, and sat back in the chair across from me. "Eleanor told me you retreated and withdrew into silence. Maybe you're a Quaker and don't know it," he teased.

"No," I said, thinking about the past week. It wouldn't have been a Quaker silence with their unique form of inward-turning, inward-listening to their God within. I'd heard the phrases "Inner Light" and of keeping someone "in the Light," but I hadn't felt that kind of light within me. Did I yearn for it, though?

"The Meeting is concerned about you."

"They shouldn't be. My ankle doesn't hurt any longer, and the cast will be removed soon."

"I don't think you understand the depth of our concern. Yes, we've been worried about your physical well-being, now and in the future, should there be more acts of violence. But we also worry about the emotional effects. And they don't even know you were hurt before coming here, though I assume Will knows now."

"He does, but I don't want the other members to know anything."

"I would never betray your confidence, and neither would Will, of course. I'm mystified, though, because you don't seem upset about this.

The drunk driver didn't intend to hurt you, but these men the other night planned to hurt, or at least scare, you. I'd be angry and upset, but you don't seem to be either one."

I didn't answer him. Yes, I'd been frightened at first, with a fire flashing through me, suffocating all thought and reason. But I'd been reminded so forcefully of the car crash that this accident had faded in intensity, a cymbal's resonant clash fading to a hum. "We're not so worried about your ankle and wrist; it's your spirit," he said, his eyes searching mine.

At first, I wanted to dismiss what he said. Was one's spirit the inner shelter for faith? I had thought about faith that night while trying to cross the road. And when I'd asked Graciela how her mother had survived the trip, she'd responded, "My mother has much faith." When I'd wanted to know how her mother had gained her faith, what had sustained her, Graciela had given me a quizzical look, as though she found the question odd. "How does she gain her faith? Her faith . . . just is. Faith *is* my mother. Whatever happens, she believes God will take care of her. Maybe not so hard to have when it is the one thing left. She has no other choice."

Now, sitting in Paul's living room, I wondered if faith could be this simple. In a sense, I was like the refugees who were starting over, giving up what was familiar, and facing circumstances beyond their control. If faith were the critical leavening agent, though, I would never be able to start over and move on.

Paul broke the silence. "During the week and this past weekend, some vandalism occurred. There were 'Salvadorans Go Home' messages on posters around town, a bomb threat at the Meetinghouse, and crude messages left on our answering machine. It's possible the people who ran you off the road know you aren't a Friend. It's likely they believe you can identify them, which you can."

Could I identify them? Perhaps by their voices, but as time passed, my doubts increased. When the police had asked me about identifying marks, I'd recalled that one man had a tattoo, but I couldn't bring it into focus.

"The members of the committee for Ministry and Worship are worried. The entire Meeting is. We can't guarantee your safety."

"No one can guarantee anyone's safety. If the men know I'm not a Quaker, why would they want to hurt me?"

"We don't know. Perhaps they felt they could pressure us more effectively by hurting someone who's not a Friend. We think they might try to use you as a pawn, to force the INS to call for legal action against us. If you weren't here, they'd find some other way or someone else, but you are here, and we are afraid for your safety."

"Are you saying, or is the Meeting saying, I should leave?"

"We can't make that decision for you and wouldn't do so, even if we could. We are saying you should be aware of the risks involved."

Where would I go? My apartment in Chantilly was now sublet, and I didn't want to find another place for a few months. I wanted this time here to finish my work, to give my confidence a chance to grow . . . and there were those New Year's resolutions of mine. "I don't want to leave, to run off. When I leave it will be on my own terms."

He leaned forward. "They could have injured you more severely, even killed you. I don't think it was their intent, but it could have been the result. What if there's a next time? When messages and acts of intolerance appear regularly, others take it as permission to say and do things they wouldn't do otherwise. It emboldens them. It is how a climate of racism and bigotry begins to flourish. We're expecting more trouble. I think you should reconsider. It has nothing to do with how strong you are; sometimes it's counterproductive to stand on a principle."

"If you mean by principle what the Friends are doing, it's not about that for me. I might not get another chance like this. I need this time here. You don't understand how important it is to me."

"I understand how sick you were recently. You're still recuperating. Can you afford a major setback?"

"If something happens, I've been warned."

When Paul walked me to my car, he asked, "You'll be careful? You still have my telephone number, right? You'll call if you need help?"

"I'll call. But I think you Quakers are taking this much too seriously."

"Katherine Solterra," he began, but I interrupted him.

"Why do Quakers sometimes say both first and last names, or use my full first name?"

"A sign of respect, usually. Traditionally, Quakers didn't use titles of address like 'Mr.' and 'Mrs.' because they were used unequally based on social standing. But in this case," he grinned, "I was using your full name out of frustration at your stubbornness." He leaned over so his eyes were level with mine. "Katherine Solterra, I think you're not taking this seriously enough." His tone became firm. "Keep your doors locked, day and night. Don't open them unless you know who's there. Don't take chances. If you hear or see something unusual, let me know immediately."

"I guess I'd better not tell you about my New Year's resolutions." I drove away, leaving him to throw his arms up in the air.

Driving his truck into my clearing and turning around, Grady unloaded firewood in neat stacks near my porch. I went out to speak to him. "Grady? Thanks, but I didn't order any wood."

"I know, but I figured you were getting low." He reached into the truck and handed me a bag. "Delia made you muffins."

"Oh, how kind of her! Please thank her for me." I'd met Delia once at Maggie's. A shy woman with a natural grace, she'd welcomed me warmly. She and Maggie seemed to know each other very well, and I'd wondered if they were related.

"Missy, we were sorry to hear you got hurt." He gestured to my arm. "You be sure to call on us if'n you need to. Delia tucked our phone number in with the muffins." He touched my shoulder and leaned toward me slightly. "If I catch anybody trying to hurt you again, I'll jerk a knot in 'em so hard their eyes'll spin backwards." I would have laughed had he not been so emphatic. I guessed this answered the question whether or not he was a Quaker.

Graciela insisted on coming weekly to help me clean and to cook. I persuaded her to stay one afternoon and have tea with me in front of the fire. It occurred to me that despite the welcoming spirit of the Quaker community, she might be lonely for a friend her age who could communicate with her.

"*¿Cómo están sus hijos?*" I asked her about her children. I couldn't imagine having the responsibility for three children at her age, not to mention trying to care for the two older boys when they were in El Salvador. She turned her cup in her hands, and I saw tears in her eyes. "*¿Están teniendo problemas sus hijos?* Are your children having problems?" I thought if there were something wrong with one of the children, I would have heard about it.

"*No, señorita.*" I waited for her to look up at me. She brushed away the tears with her napkin. "It is the older ones at school. They don't know much English, and they come home with . . . frustradedness?"

"Frustration."

"Frustration," she repeated. "They are our hope. We left our country for our survival and for them to have a better life, a life without chaos. They must know English. They were good students before, but now, I am worried. They will be trapped between two languages, not knowing either one well enough. They want me to help them, but I can't. I know we should speak more English at home."

"Children usually learn a foreign language faster than adults, but it takes time."

"I know. But they're going backwards?"

"Falling behind?"

"Yes. This morning, Enrique cried, not wanting to go to school and be more confused. I am their mother. I must teach them how to start over, to make a new life. They must be strong, or they will not do well here. A good education is their best hope."

I knew private tutoring was out of the question, and she'd never accept money for it. Suddenly, I knew what I could do and hoped I could offer my help in a way that she, with her pride, could accept. I poured more tea in her cup and passed her the plate of cookies. "Graciela, I have a suggestion, something to help both of us. Your mother takes care of the baby during this time, doesn't she? I won't need assistance with cleaning and cooking much longer; the cast is coming off soon. But if you continued to come, I could teach you English, at least what the children need to learn, and you could help me review my Spanish." In her eyes, I could see she wasn't convinced. "It's important to me to regain the Spanish I've lost; it was my first language." I explained that my family had lived in Spain when I was young, and that I had returned to Spain as a high school student. "When I spend time with you I realize how much I miss it. As a native speaker, you would be the best teacher I could have."

"*¿No es caridad?*"

"No, this isn't charity; it's an even exchange. Is it a deal?"

"*Gracias, señorita.*"

"You must promise me one thing, Graciela."

"Anything."

"You must call me Kate."

"It's a deal," she pronounced, trying out the phrase. "It's a deal, Kate."

# Chapter 21

THE SCHOENFELDS INVITED ME to lunch, and after the silent prayer, Virgil said, "We've missed seeing you."

"I haven't been attending Meeting."

"Because of the people who ran you off the road?" Eleanor asked.

I laughed. "That would be enough of a reason, don't you think? Mostly, I've been working."

"What specifically are you researching?" Eleanor asked.

"In a layperson's terms, please," Virgil added.

I told them about my research, and despite Virgil's teasing comment, they asked perceptive, challenging questions. I experienced a sensation of what could only be expressed as homesickness, missing with a pang what felt like my native land. Science was simultaneously my passion, my anchor, my fulcrum.

Virgil went outside to refill the birdfeeders in the yard while Eleanor and I finished cleaning up from lunch. Eleanor took the dish towel from me. "I believe you have a snowshoe date with my husband. This really was one of your New Year's resolutions?"

"Yes, all in my campaign to try new activities and to have more fun. I've skied before but have never tried snowshoes."

"You want to try new things?" She raised her eyebrows. "I might be able to help with that. I'll get back to you."

In their backyard, Virgil strapped on the snowshoes, helped me up, and gave suggestions. "They'll be awkward at first, but you'll get used to them. There's not much skill involved." We headed toward the preserve. "You don't have to pick your feet up so high. Try swinging your legs in less of an arc," he advised.

We made it to the preserve's entrance and rested inside the shelter. While Virgil layered kindling in the stone fireplace, I brought logs from the bin. "Your arm," he cautioned, "be careful."

"It has healed. You know, something you told me when we first met helped me the night I got hurt. Remember when you told me it took courage to kill the snake? I thought if I could kill a snake, I could get across the road and make it to my cabin. Every other step I repeated the word, 'Courage.' It kept me from panicking."

"What about the between steps?"

"The between steps? 'Faith.' I thought if I had enough courage, maybe I could have faith. Not the kind of faith you and Eleanor and the other Quakers talk about, but faith in myself to get home safely. I do envy, though, the rock-certain kind of faith you and Eleanor have."

"It's rarely 'rock-certain.' It's more like entering a strange house late at night with no lights on, knowing there's a steep flight of stairs going down somewhere, but you keep walking." He poked at the fire. "One of Quakerism's basic beliefs is that within each of us lives a spark of divinity, whether you believe it's there or not. If I accept this premise, faith in God necessarily translates into faith in myself and others, bringing the intangible to a human level."

"What do you do if you can't see or feel the spark?"

"I act on it anyway. Fan it back to life by taking a step or two on my own. Like you, crossing the road. Courage. Faith."

"At the hospital, I blocked out everything that was happening and repeated to myself Quaker phrases I'd heard at Meeting, 'Way will open,' and 'Mind the Light,' over and over. I kept my eyes closed, stopped answering questions, and concentrated on listening to myself repeat those phrases."

"What happened?"

"It was like being in Meeting. The noises quieted and the pain lessened. I could feel people touching me, moving me, doing things to me, but I felt submerged in water, far removed from the emergency room. The scientist in me knows at least part of this feeling was due to the pain medication beginning to take effect, but I've never felt anything similar. I don't guess there was anything magical in my repeating those phrases, but while saying them, I felt safer, comforted. When I'd stop, the noises and the pain would begin to intrude. I'd start saying them again, and back I'd go to that safe place."

"It sounds like you felt a divine presence within you."

"But I don't believe in the existence of God; does that shock you?"

"Of course not. No thinking person I've known, including myself, has been without doubt. Something can exist without our believing it can." He spoke hesitantly, as though words were being handed to him. I waited.

"Science continuously shows us new discoveries, facts in the world, which we didn't believe existed because we didn't have the knowledge of them. Science and spiritual beliefs are not mutually exclusive; they can enlighten each other and coexist quite spectacularly, making our vision sharper, our hearts larger." He stopped and rearranged the logs in the fire. "Your doubts are a gift. You're like those early Quakers who were called 'Seekers,' or 'Seekers of the Truth.' We get complacent. Someone like you comes along, asking questions, and we begin to search more ourselves."

We watched the flames illuminate the stones of the fireplace. "How did you make the decision to go on the trip with Paul?"

"I asked, either in a Meeting for Worship or in a Meeting for Business, 'What is it that God calls us to do?' In the following silence, and I think you understand Quaker silences are not about the absence of sound, I listened to that of God within me. I didn't hear words or any kind of message in a conventionally recognizable form, no lightning bolts, but I felt a distinct answer. It wasn't a gradual knowing, which I've experienced before, but a knowing that arrived in an instant, as though it had been waiting inside me all along, waiting for me to ask about it. I have learned to trust that knowing, which Quakers call a 'leading.'"

"What was the knowing?"

"That *I* was the answer. Before, I hadn't felt a strong connection to the sanctuary movement; in fact, I'd tried to turn away from it because it brought back painful memories of Morgan. But I went with Paul because two people's lives were in danger, and I believed if I didn't listen to and obey the leading, they would die."

"Is it at once as simple and as terrible as that?"

"I think so."

I watched him extinguish the fire and take extra measures to be sure it was safe to leave. "Virgil, I don't think God will ever whisper to me."

"The question is not whether he's talking to you, Kate. He is. Are you listening? Are you talking to him? He may not be whispering; you might be one he shouts at. Trust that inner voice. You don't have to understand or explain it. Trust it. Lean on it, push on it, act on it."

I returned to the Meeting. I didn't know why, but I decided I didn't need to invent reasons or excuses. My thoughts drifted to my parents. Would they harbor refugees or do anything illegal in order to obey a moral law? Did I believe in what the Quakers were doing? I had no religious belief, but what about moral law? Wasn't this a case of preserving life? If only someone had stopped the drunk driver. Maybe someone had an opportunity but lacked the integrity to do the right thing. I would never know and didn't want to. The Friends had their faith to give them the strength to act on their beliefs, but what did I have?

A woman's voice snagged my attention. She spoke at length about her mother. "I feel small in the face of her illness; it is so much bigger than the two of us together. But she tells me things we'd otherwise not share. How my father courted her, bringing her daisies and ice cream; how she felt when I was born and when I graduated from school; what she dreams for her grandchildren; what worries her. She is teaching me that listening, genuinely wanting to hear what another person has to say, is a significant gift. It has made me reconsider the listening we do in a Meeting for Worship. I'm learning I've been too afraid to speak the truth. In the past, why did I refrain from telling her I love her? That she gives me strength, and I admire and respect her? Why don't I tell others how much I love them and care about them? She has shown me I must live without fear of what others might say or think, and I should love deeply and abundantly." She looked around the sanctuary. "And so, I start with you. I love you and care about you. I treasure this community."

I repeated her words until I could fish out the notebook and pen I carried with me. "Live without being afraid. Love deeply and abundantly," I wrote. The woman's message made me think of Graciela. I'd asked Graciela how she'd been able to start over, how she went about the process of managing in a new country with a different culture and language. She had been bringing me lists of topics, math concepts, and vocabulary words her children were learning. She'd replied, "I didn't have a choice. And since I had no choice, I wanted to do it the best way I could. Tomás and I are the children's examples. Mourning what we lost wouldn't help us now. I am many times afraid," she'd admitted.

"How do you move past the fear?" I'd asked her.

"I ask God to take care of it. And I make myself do one small thing. I tell myself to go wash the dishes or vacuum the floor. If I think of it all—new country, new language, the dangers for those back home—it is too much. I would hide under the bed and not come out. I tell myself, 'Today. All you have to do is your best today.' It is a mother's job to be brave for her children."

Courage, I thought now. Maybe it was more a matter of attitude than action, and of surrendering what had been lost. If Graciela could do this, could I? I did recognize her "one small thing" strategy as one I often employed.

The remainder of the Meeting was silent, and at the conclusion of the service, Virgil stood and introduced himself as a member of the committee for Ministry and Worship. He invited everyone to the Shared Meal and

Meeting for Business. This time I'd come prepared for the meal. Lunch was noisy with animated conversations all around me. It occurred to me I was beginning to feel like a part of the group. I'd never considered myself to be a "joiner," but being included here gave me a lovely sense of belonging.

We cleared the tables after lunch and prepared for the Meeting for Business. Did I want to be part of this? I hesitated at the door until I caught Paul's eye. I sat down between Maggie and Abby, and everyone settled into silent waiting. They dealt with the routine business, and afterward, much of the discussion centered on the sanctuary issue. Tension and urgency had marked the decision-making process, but achieving consensus enabled them to work without dissension or distraction.

"Did you drive here?" Paul stopped me as I was getting ready to leave.

"No. It doesn't make sense to drive when I live so close."

"Get someone to take you home. I have a committee meeting or I'd take you."

"Don't be silly, it's daylight. I'm always walking to town and to the preserve." My daily exercising had paid off; I was stronger and had more stamina than when I moved here. I didn't want to stop now.

"Don't argue, please," he said with uncharacteristic brusqueness. "Get a ride home with someone and start driving to places, even ones close by. Don't take chances."

"All right." I wondered if there had been another incident.

"One more thing. Virgil and I will be meeting with Emilio and Magdalena about their request for asylum. You know more Spanish than any of us; would you be willing to help?"

"I'll be happy to try. However, if the discussion gets too technical with legal terms, the Meeting should provide a certified legal interpreter."

"Of course. We'll see how it goes. We're planning to go tomorrow. Now," Paul gently turned me around to face the fellowship hall, "I see any number of helpful, neighborly, and kindhearted Friends who would be pleased to give you a ride home."

# Chapter 22

## GUATEMALA, MEXICO

Felipe stopped trying to keep track of the days, for only the direction remained important. Every morning at dawn, he made sure the sun rose on his right; by early evening, he made sure it set on his left, as though the laws of nature were going to betray him. Lying in a ditch while waiting for soldiers to pass, he imagined his body to be changed, the size of his organs now reflecting their role in his survival. His mental image of himself mirrored grotesquely oversized ears, bulging eyes, and enormous feet; he became a caricature of a man.

He had thought that living a fugitive's life would be second nature after so many weeks. Part of his body adjusted with his feet jumping into ditches before his mind registered a sound, his hand knowing when to clutch the gun before his eyes detected dull metal through the trees. But his mind and his will conjoined and refused to adapt. The fear became a tangible force, something physical now, too, with the constriction of his throat, the thudding of his heart, and a taste that could not be swallowed away. "*Desaparecido*"—disappeared, presumed to be dead—was the wrong label for him, for he was too much alive.

On the perimeter of a village, Felipe waited for darkness. The waiting gave him time to catalogue the memories slipping farther away with each mile, silent marbles rolling off a cliff. He ached with the desire for dozens of ordinary things: Magdalena's *pupusas*, tortillas stuffed with melted cheese and vegetables; her floured hands patting his cheeks; the smells of ink and oil from his father's ancient press; and kicking the soccer ball until his legs grew numb. He closed his eyes to focus on the new, extraordinary memory of Pilar's skin between, around, and over his, her daring when it came to breaking boundaries.

Darkness saturated the village, and at last he stood from his hiding place, his legs unable to straighten fully. Running in a half-crouch, he scuttled across the village's main square and reached the safety of yet another shadow.

Reserving what he needed for bus tickets, Felipe bought paper, envelopes, a couple of stamps, and food. After borrowing a pen from the woman who ran the store, he sat outside at the building's far end. He composed the letter with caution, wanting to say just enough to let his brother know he was alive and planned to be at the border soon. "*Querido Hermano,*" Dear Brother, he wrote, "*Estoy muy bien, y espero que vos estés, también. Vendré para una visita pronto. Te llamaré. F.*" I am very well, and I hope that you are, too. I will come for a visit soon. I will call you.

He held the envelope. What if Tomás and Graciela had moved? What if no one could meet him at the border? He would keep traveling, he decided. Crossing the border didn't change keeping the morning sun on the right, the afternoon sun on the left. Caressing the pen, he wished he didn't have to return it, for he'd not had enough money to buy one for himself. If Emilio dreamed of land, he, like his father, dreamed of words, of sentences swelling into paragraphs and looming onto pages. He shifted the pen from hand to hand. His father had died for words, for lines on paper. Felipe gripped the pen more firmly. For his father not to have died in vain, for the mere letters instead of the ideas they formed, he must get to the United States.

When he arrived at a Mexican town across the Guatemalan border, Felipe mailed the letter, thinking perhaps no one would notice it was being sent to someone in the United States with so many other letters going out. He slipped it through the mail slot and allowed himself a silver bead of hope.

Felipe waited in a long line to buy a bus ticket. The first day, they sold out with half the line remaining. The second day, the sign on the office window stated no buses ran through town that day. The third day, he ran to the window half an hour before it was supposed to open, but the bus had come the hour before; he waited in line to get a schedule, but the ticket officer told him the buses came too erratically for any kind of printed schedule. "When it comes, it stops. Be here tomorrow."

"Can I purchase my ticket for tomorrow now?" Felipe asked.

"No, the tickets must be bought the day the bus comes."

On the fourth morning, arriving at the ticket window two hours before it was to open, Felipe waited in line, bought a ticket, and finally, the bus lurched and smoked into the square. Finding a newspaper, he kept it in front of his face, peering over it when someone boarded the bus. Mexico, he told himself. I'm almost safe. Now it's a matter of time, of the bus not breaking down, of no one noticing, of not getting caught. He tried to make himself part of the cracked leather seat, tried to make himself less noticeable, even though he told himself Mexican buses were not like Salvadoran buses.

The one time he took a Salvadoran bus, soldiers at an army roadblock stopped it. A soldier marched a *subversivo*, a guerrilla who had surrendered, down the aisle of the bus to identify former comrades. When the man hesitated, the soldier thrust his gun at the man's head. The *subversivo* pointed at a man who was thrown off the bus. Felipe had thought he wouldn't hear anything above the rushing sound in his head, but he'd heard the single gunshot before the bus was allowed to drive away. At the next stop, he'd gotten off the bus and had hidden in the woods until nightfall. Quivering from fright, he'd tried not to think about how the man had felt in the moments before the bullet pierced his body. No, Mexican buses were not like Salvadoran buses, but he kept the newspaper in front of his sweating face, and he kept watching.

After the final stop on the bus route and six more days of walking, Felipe reached his next destination. He moved through the streets without glancing behind him, as though he belonged, as though he were not a hunted man. Tomás had given him the name and address of someone, but he was afraid the man might have moved on, gone north himself. Could he be trusted? Trust in this place, in these times, was like oiled fingers picking up glass.

He found the house, an adobe with a recessed doorway. Vicente ushered him in. "You were not followed?" he asked, peering around Felipe.

"I don't think so." Felipe thought how strange it felt to be talking, his voice sounding like something being rubbed on a metal grater.

"Here are papers for the border. With luck, you'll get across." Vicente put food in front of him. "Eat. You still have far to go." He busied himself wrapping up more food and putting it in a sack for Felipe.

Felipe hesitated, his fingers clutching the table's edge, his stomach quailing. "I have no money to pay you."

"Tomás sent money long ago; eat, and later you must sleep."

Felipe knew if Tomás had sent money long ago, it had to be spent long ago, too; but he began eating, his gratefulness to Vicente the solitary thing restraining him from shoving the food into his mouth. "Have you heard anything from Emilio or Magdalena?"

"No." Vicente stopped wrapping food and sat across from Felipe. "But I must tell you, I heard their village was bombed. People were killed, many at one time, children, mostly."

Felipe closed his eyes, as though sealing them could protect him against the world's madness, could somehow change what was inevitable. "They could still be alive," Vicente told him. "If I hear anything else I will send word to Tomás."

"I should go back, try to find them," Felipe said, knowing his words held little resolve.

"*Nunca lo lograrás. Tu nombre está en la lista.*" You'll never make it. Your name is on the list.

*Absolución.* Absolution, Felipe thought, carried an unimaginable price.

Vicente showed him to a cot in a back hallway. Even though this would be the first safe sleep he'd had in weeks, he couldn't shake off his sense of foreboding. He knew he couldn't go back, but what if his fear kept him from going forward? He'd always thought there was no measure to his determination; he'd had faith it would be there when he needed it. Now his faith crumbled, a chimera comprised of a fragile filament, a single strand stretched over the abyss. Surely it could not bear the weight of one more step.

# Chapter 23

PAUL CALLED AND ASKED if he could come see me. Working at my desk, I watched him as he swept snow from my car and picked up logs from the woodpile. I held the door open for him while he stamped the snow off his shoes. "Aren't you going to clean off the porch, too?" I teased him. After placing one of the logs in my fireplace, he got right to the point. "One of the police officers who took your statement stopped me when I was coming out of the county courthouse yesterday. We know each other. They've found the men who forced you off the road; the men admitted they were at the program and at the general store. The driver said he remembers coming around a curve and swerving to avoid hitting an animal, but both men insisted there was no one on the road."

"My word against theirs."

"They can say you thought they were going to hit you and therefore jumped off the road. You haven't recalled what they were shouting?"

"No. I believe the voices matched those of the men at Maggie's, though I'm not completely sure about it. I do recall the tone."

"What about it?"

"They were jeering. A window had to have been rolled down for me to hear anything. Why have a window open when it's cold unless they wanted someone to hear them? They weren't jeering at an animal on the road."

"They could easily make up some excuse. All the proof, of course, would be up to you, and intent is difficult to prove. Are you going to press charges?"

"It doesn't sound like I'd have much of a chance, and I don't have the stomach for it. I know I would resent having to deal with it during my sabbatical. If I did press charges, though, it might prevent them from hurting someone else. If I don't try to stop them and they hurt another person, I'll feel partially responsible."

"You can't blame yourself for their actions."

"But I can blame myself for *my* actions, or lack of them. On the other hand, if I pressed charges, wouldn't it bring more publicity to what the Meeting is doing? Perhaps they realize this. I have an unsettling feeling we're falling right into their plans. I wouldn't want to cause problems for the Friends or for the Delgados."

"You can't think of it like this. You have to do what you think is right."

"It's all rather blurred now, except for the alarm I felt twice that night."

"Twice?"

"I didn't recognize Adam and Ruth's car and thought the men had returned. The fear I felt is a mere sliver compared to the refugees' experiences; I'm not making a comparison, but do you think Emilio, Magdalena, and the rest of the Delgado family had to undergo intense, consuming fear every day in their homeland?"

"Yes, and this is difficult for us as citizens of the United States to imagine."

"How did they live with it? How do people cope with such constant fear?"

"I don't know. Some fight back, some leave."

"But people like Magdalena, who can't fight back?"

"I guess you have to have faith you'll survive, that life won't always be so precarious. You hope the next day will be better."

"I could not survive on faith alone."

"You could if it were the only thing you had." He stood and picked up his coat and gloves. "I have work needing to be done, and I've interrupted yours. I meant what I said about being careful and not walking around by yourself."

"I'll be careful, I promise."

"Please keep all your doors in the house locked, when you're here as well as when you're not. The car doors, too." We stood together on the porch, my yard looking luminous in its snowy beauty. "You won't reconsider leaving Drake's Springs?"

I looked up at him. "I'll admit to being scared, but I'm not going to give in to this fear or to these people. I refuse to give them such power." I had given these same reasons to Diane the last time we'd talked. She'd offered to have me stay with her for as long as I'd like. I was tempted, knowing I'd be safe; however, I also knew how stressed she was because of her father's illness.

After Paul left, I made an appointment with my lawyer, wanting advice before making the decision about pressing charges. I thought about what the men had told the police officer. Given my previous experience, was it possible I'd assumed the car was going to hit me? But I didn't imagine those jeering voices.

❖ ❖ ❖

During one of our lessons, I asked Graciela about her childhood and her family. "Before all the trouble began, we had many happy times. We worked hard, yes; I worked in the coffee fields starting as a child until Miguel was born. Gathering at the end of the day, we would sing and play instruments. We went to the dances and festivals. We brought dishes to share after church, and oh, we laughed. How we laughed, at simple things."

"Did you go to school in the village?"

"When we had a teacher, we went to school. Tomás and Emilio's father, Don Alberto, was my teacher for a couple of years, our best teacher. He showed us how to love learning and how an education could bring the world to our tiny village. He made us promise when we had children, we would make sure they got an education for a better life." Graciela added, "I made that promise when I was a child, but after Don Alberto was murdered, I vowed as a mother I would honor my promise."

When Graciela got ready to leave, we went outside and watched the waning storm. "I somehow cannot believe snow." Holding out her hand, she examined the flakes on her dark glove. "To come out of the sky and make everything sparkle. You asked me one time how I started over, made a new life for myself. You find joy in the good things, the small things that make you happy. Don Alberto also taught me, '*Aférrate a la alegría. La risa te dará el valor de vivir.*' Hold on to joy, he'd tell us. Laughter will give you courage to live. At first, when the disappearances and the raids began, I thought he was a foolish old man to keep telling us that. My children have seen violence no one should see; it darkens the soul. I worry they have been marked forever. The horrors, I will not describe. But Alberto Delgado was right. If you give in to the fear and the violence, you lose your life even before anyone takes it. He taught us to celebrate what we can, when we can. He taught me to be grateful and to move forward."

Alberto Delgado had taught Graciela, I thought, and she was teaching me—about so much more than Spanish. We watched the snow in silence for a few more minutes. Because Paul had made me promise not to walk anywhere by myself, I insisted on driving Graciela home. The refugees certainly would be a bigger target than I was. Although Paul must have given the same warning to the Salvadoran family, Graciela had walked to my cabin since Tomás needed the one car they had in order to get to his job in Harrisonburg. I told her that from now on, I'd be picking her up for our lessons. She protested at first, but I saw a look of relief. "I love snow!" I heard Graciela shout as she hurried across the yard to her front door. Watching her, I thought about Don Alberto's lessons. If people could find reasons to celebrate amid chaos and violence, I should be able to do it within the confines of my safe, privileged life.

"Load 'em up and move 'em out," Abby addressed us.

"What do you think we are?" Ruth asked. "Cattle? Sheep?"

Sharon countered, "Where do you think we are? Texas?"

"I'm more concerned where we're headed," I called out from the back of the van.

I'd received an invitation in my door last week, asking me to come on a "Mystery Adventure." Maggie had explained it was a tradition for the community's women, mostly those with ties to the Quaker Meeting. Every other month one group member planned an event, but none of the other women knew what was involved until they reached their destination.

"I'm not replying until I know more specifics," I'd told her.

"Where's that pioneer spunk of yours? Wouldn't your Aunt Constanza have signed up for this without a question?"

"My aunt would have led the pack." But I'd agreed, and now I was in a van with Abby driving. It was Eleanor's trip, though, so I wasn't too anxious.

We stopped in front of a brick house in Harrisonburg, a city a few miles north of Drake's Springs. The house was nondescript except for the multicolored lights outlining the garage and dangling from the tree limbs around it. Eleanor pointed to the garage. "That's where we're going, ladies!"

Abby said, "All right, I'll guess first." She caught my eye in the rearview mirror. "This is part of the tradition, Kate. We each take a guess as to what the event is. Based on some of our previous excursions with Eleanor, I'm guessing we're getting a lesson in engine repair."

Engine repair? I was thinking it would be more along the lines of a high tea, a chamber ensemble, perhaps, or a pottery class.

Graciela called out, "The tango!" The others chimed in with guesses of soap-making, yoga, a dog obedience exhibition, a rock-climbing wall, and scherenschnitte, the German and Swiss art of paper cutting which I'd seen at the Dayton Market. My guess was a clock-making class, since someone else guessed pottery.

"Graciela's closest," answered Eleanor. She faced all of us with a sly grin. "Belly dancing!"

"No!" Maggie laughed. "Please tell me you're kidding."

"Nope. Leave your inhibitions in the van, ladies."

I groaned. How was I going to manage with my rigid body and limited ranges of motion? I didn't want to be a poor sport, however, so I trooped after the others. "It's always the quiet ones you have to watch out for, isn't it?" Maggie said to me.

Eleanor introduced us to the studio's owner, Riya. A striking Indian woman, tall and willowy, she moved with a dancer's confidence. Her dress was a vivid teal and copper, and shiny coins and beads circled her waist. Welcoming us, Riya invited us to sit on luxurious pillows lining the room's perimeter. She sank to the floor in one fluid motion and sat on a pillow in front of us.

Soft music played. I took in the room's décor of ornate drapes and photographs of exotic places. In a wall niche, incense burned, the scent making me feel heavy and languid. "Some say," she began, "that belly dancing is the oldest known dance. Myth and mystery surround it, as well as misperceptions. For example, experts think it was a dance performed for other women, not as a way to entertain or seduce men. It may have been part of fertility rites or marriage ceremonies. Some claim this dance form served a practical function because the moves strengthen the pelvic and abdominal muscles to help in pregnancy and childbirth."

Riya stood and gave Eleanor a basket of diaphanous scarves in colors so gorgeous they seemed to radiate. I chose an emerald one. "I see belly dancing as a means for women to access their personal power, to tap into what is authentically feminine. I think we've been misled to believe that in order to be successful, we have to be more masculine in our approach."

She chose a scarf from the basket and wrapped it around herself, motioning for us to do the same. I considered her words. In the scientific field, men still outnumbered women, and I'd known some women who had adopted a decidedly blunt speech and manner in an effort to be heard and accepted.

"Belly dancing is a spiritual art form, as well. We acknowledge the natural elements and bless those about whom we care." Riya turned up the music and began dancing, slowly at first, then increasing the pace until she was a symphony of color and sound from the coins sewn onto her colorful skirt and the bracelets lining her arms. Entranced, I let the music spill over me until I realized she'd decreased her speed and come to a stop, smiling at each of us. Not wanting to spoil the moment, we clapped lightly. Riya held her hands together and bowed. "Now, it is your turn."

"I hoped there wouldn't be an audience participation portion," I said in an undertone to Maggie. "And for the record, I so underestimated Eleanor; I didn't know about her mischievous streak." Maggie grinned in response and pushed me to the front.

Riya led us through basic movements of hip circles, head slides, shoulder drops, and shimmying. "I can't shimmy," I protested to Maggie.

She watched me for a second and then burst out laughing. "That's because you have no hips!"

"What do you mean?" I looked in the mirror at myself and over at her reflection. We both started laughing until our faces were red and we were out of breath. "So I don't have any hips."

"You can have some of mine," she offered, setting us off once more. "I swear, I feel dumber than a coal bucket, but it's fun, isn't it? So exotic!"

"Coal bucket, Maggie?"

"My grandpa worked in the mines. He used to say that all the time."

Riya ignored our antics. She moved from person to person, suggesting more graceful arm positions and encouraging us to relax and worry less about correctness. By the time she got to me, I'd gotten myself back in control. Riya stood before me for a few moments, observing me. Resting her hands lightly on my shoulders, she said under the music, "You've been injured, no?" I tensed with the thought she might try to straighten my arms. She waited until I nodded. Her eyes met mine for a few seconds. "Relax, Kate. Forgive yourself for what you cannot do. Give thanks for what you can." She stopped, and a smile lit her face before she added, "And dance on!"

When I realized everyone was absorbed with her own dancing, I stopped worrying about what I looked like, lowered my head, and gave myself up to the music and the motions. It hurt to move too fast, my limbs jerking awkwardly, so I danced as slowly and as fluidly as I could. When the music stopped and I looked up, I realized the women had encircled me. Eleanor came forward as my face blushed. "Oh, Kate! I wish you could have seen yourself. You were beautiful."

# Chapter 24

DAVID WAS DUE TO arrive at my cabin in a few minutes. We would spend the morning working, and afterward, he was joining Paul, Abby, Cooper, Ruth, and Adam for skiing in the afternoon. My ankle and wrist had healed, but I was skittish about falling and knew I wouldn't be able to keep up with everyone else.

Watching out the living room window, I felt uneasy. This first meeting since we'd broken up was going to be awkward. Except for Maggie, no one knew about our long-time relationship; I'd simply spoken of him as a work colleague.

Right on time, David drove into the clearing. Pulling his duffle bag out of the car, he headed to the cabin. Even dressed in ski clothes, he looked sharp and polished. I opened the door. "Come in! Welcome!" Inwardly wincing at my overly cheerful tone, I could swear I saw him smirk.

Stamping snow from his boots, he entered the cabin and gave me a hug. He took in the log walls and the fireplace constructed with stacked stones. "This is . . . cozy," he said.

"You mean small?"

"I wasn't intending that as a put-down, Kate."

This short visit might be longer than I'd anticipated. "Let's start over. Welcome, I'm glad you're here. Thanks for making the effort to come here to work with me."

He rewarded me with a genuine smile this time. "Of course. And your cabin is warm and inviting." He reached out to run his hand along the walls. "I've never been in a log cabin before; the workmanship is impressive."

I showed him around the cabin. In the bathroom, he gestured to the pillows and bed linens stacked on the hamper. "No guest room, I take it, so the sofa for me?"

"Yes."

"What have you told your new friends?"

I detected a bit of an edge but let it slide. "Maggie knows we broke up, but she won't be here with this group. I told the rest of them that you're a work colleague."

After showing him the cabin and getting us both some coffee, we spread out our materials and got to work. We fell into the familiar rhythm of dissecting passages, discussing relevant research, and proposing different approaches. It felt so comfortable that I caught myself thinking a few times that maybe we could have smoothed things out. No, I thought, don't look back. No regrets.

We'd cleared away our papers and had finished lunch when the group arrived for skiing. After a flurry of introductions and transferring David's skis to Adam and Ruth's car, they got ready to leave. Ruth followed me into the kitchen with their contribution to our potluck dinner. "You've been holding out on us," she said.

"Holding out what?"

"David. How involved are you?"

"We're not. I told you we're work colleagues, that's all."

"Not buying it."

I held back a sigh. So much for that plan. "We broke up recently, Ruth. It's still awkward; let's not make it more so."

She nodded. "Got it. I'm sorry; I must have thought I was back in seventh grade."

I groaned. "That was the worst, wasn't it? By the way, I'm pleased Adam could join us; it will give me the chance to get to know him better." Working as a sales representative for a pharmaceutical company, he spent a lot of time traveling.

"He's been looking forward to this. His job takes a toll on all of us. When the children are older, we may have to rethink the situation because he's missing out on too much as it is." She gave me directions for the casserole they'd brought before she joined the others and left for the ski resort.

Passing the time tending the various dishes and setting the table, I enjoyed the peace of my cabin. I made a few research notes to mention to David later. Discussing work projects with him had given me more confidence than I'd felt for some time, and as the morning had progressed, we'd moved past the initial awkwardness.

Returning at dusk, the group entered the cabin in good spirits and filled me in on the day's highlights. "Tell me the rest after we're seated. Dinner is ready; find a place to sit, everyone."

Paul said, "Let me help you," and followed me into the kitchen. "Smells great in here."

"That's because I didn't make any of it! I did make my cheesecake for dessert."

With my prerogative as the hostess, I suggested we have a Quaker grace, explaining briefly to David that it was a few moments of silence. After the noise of getting the meal on the table and setting up extra chairs, the sudden quiet gave me a different dimension to the practice. As soon as the blessing concluded, however, lively chatter started immediately.

Abby said, "You didn't tell us David is an expert skier."

I smiled at him. "Whatever David does, he does well."

"She's not telling you the legion of things I don't do well," David told them. "Actually, I was surprised at what great skiing you have here. Good thing, since there's not much else going on in the area." The comment made me cringe.

"There's more around here than you might imagine," Cooper said. "True, not so much right in Drake's Springs, but in Staunton, for example, you have the new Frontier Culture Museum and the Shenandoah Shakespeare Express, a traveling troupe. James Madison University is in Harrisonburg."

"If you like history," Abby added, "there's Woodrow Wilson's house and presidential library. And we have a large Mennonite community; you'll see their horses and buggies. Their farms are beautiful. There are three elderly Mennonite sisters who make quilts that have been sold to New York museums for thousands of dollars each. They make them for their international relief projects."

"Since you've been impressed with what we have on the mountaintops," Adam added, "you should explore the caves we have around here. Kate has said she'll try spelunking."

David laughed. "Do you all work for the tourist bureau? And Kate? Getting dirty? You don't understand. She doesn't even like to make sandcastles at the beach. She'll walk a mile to circumvent a mud puddle." He continued with other examples, making me sound like a persnickety woman. He didn't catch on to the glances people were exchanging, though, and the moment became awkward.

Ruth stopped him. "We all have our foibles."

"We wish our children had Kate's penchant for cleanliness and order," Adam redirected the conversation. "Last week, our toddler discovered paint and used the bedroom walls as her canvas."

Paul complimented me on my dessert. "Kate, that was the best cheesecake I've ever had. You could start your own business making this alone."

"Thank you. It's not hard to make, but it takes time. It's a recipe that makes people think I can cook."

The next morning, I set David straight before he left. "These are my friends, and, for now, this is my community. It's true that Drake's Springs may not have much in the way of big-city amenities, but there are fine people here. This community is strong and vibrant. Last night, you embarrassed me, going on and on about my quirks, not to mention disparaging the area these people call home. I realize you were trying to fit in; I understand what that's like, but you hurt my feelings, and you were disrespectful to my other guests."

"I meant no offense." He turned toward the door, then faced me again. "So, is this the new Kate?"

"Yes."

His single nod was at once an acknowledgment and a dismissal. Closing the door, I felt emboldened, standing up to him the way I had, but I felt uncomfortable, too. This new persona of mine was going to take getting used to.

My mother had given me knitting needles, an instruction book, and skeins of wool. I'd mentioned wanting to learn how to knit, and she'd remembered. Now that my wrist had healed, I asked Maggie to teach me the basics. With the store closed, we went upstairs to her apartment. Large and rambling, the space had windows slung along the front wall and the same wooden floors as downstairs in the store. Maggie had decorated the apartment in blue and white with touches of yellow. It was as inviting and warm as Maggie herself. She cast on the stitches and demonstrated how to knit and purl. "You're putting the needle in the wrong direction. You're purling on this side, remember? Wrap the yarn counterclockwise."

"I am."

"You're going clockwise."

I described a circle in the air. "You're right. Don't worry, I'll catch on. I've got lots of yarn."

She laughed, "Honey, you might need your own band of sheep. Are you making this scarf for the handsome young man who came to see you?"

"David? I told you we'd broken it off."

"I thought since he was here the other day . . ."

"He came to discuss a project from work and to go skiing."

"Must be hard, mixing work and personal."

Changing the subject, I held up the knitting. "I hadn't thought of giving this to anybody. It's going to be too full of mistakes to claim it, much less give it away as a present."

"When we give of ourselves, it doesn't have to be perfect."

"How did you get to be so wise?"

She formed a skein of wool into a ball. "I had wisdom beaten into me." Startled by her tone, knowing without doubt that she was being literal, I dropped my knitting onto my lap. "I don't want you putting me on some pedestal as 'Wisdom Queen.'"

"You don't have to tell me anything," I said, knowing I didn't want to hear what she was going to tell me.

"I think maybe there's something in my story you need to hear." When she handed me a skein of wool to wind into another ball, I was relieved to have somewhere else to focus other than on her face.

"Charlie and I were teenagers, both of us from hardworking hill families. I'm ashamed of how ignorant I was. It's an old story, Kate. I got pregnant, and at that time and place, you got married. I knew from the beginning something was wrong, could feel it in the spaces between my bones, could feel it tingling along my scalp. Like so many women, I saw the warning signals but ignored them, starved for attention and thirsty for affection, for someone who thought I was special.

"Without much self-respect or self-confidence, I was a victim ready for picking. My father wasn't an abusive man, but there wasn't much love in my home. My mother gave in to my father to keep the peace. At that time, there wasn't the openness we have today, and like I said, I was ignorant, though that doesn't excuse his behavior. When Charlie yelled at me and made demands, I tried to placate him. He started drinking more heavily, missing work. Then he began striking me when I refused him, when dinner wasn't ready on time, when the children were sick and crying. He always tied it in with something I'd done, something he felt I should be responsible for. When you're being beaten, you slide right quick to thinking it's your fault, and then even further, to thinking somehow you must have deserved it." She unraveled a knot in the yarn.

"People question abused women, asking why you're allowing yourself to be treated that way. You begin to hear in their voices the implied accusation that if you don't leave, then you deserve what you get. Somehow, it seems like they never ask the man, 'Why are you beating her?' A lot of abused women don't have any money or a solid education with job skills to make it easier to break away. But it runs deeper because educated women with money are abused, too. And there are always the threats, that if you leave he'll come after you and it will be worse, or he'll hurt the children. This kind of violence steals the spirit from inside you and leaves you hollow, like a sucked-out egg with nothing sustaining left."

Picturing Maggie as a young woman cowering in a corner made my throat ache. "What did you do?"

"It took his hitting Cooper to make me angry enough and strong enough to leave. A broken jaw, broken arms, and years of bruises, cuts, black eyes, and lies weren't enough, but when he hurt my son, I took my anger and turned it into the strength I needed to pick up my children and leave. We lived on scraps and handouts, church charity, and what money I could earn from cleaning houses, yard work, odd jobs—anything where I could take my children with me until they were old enough to be in school.

"I heard a few years ago that Charlie had died of alcoholism. And yes, I had tried to go through the judicial system, but we're not committed yet in this country to stopping abuse." Letting go of the yarn, she stopped for a moment, looking out the window.

"For years, I fed my anger with every quarter and dollar I scrabbled for, with every time my children needed or wanted something, with every humiliation. I'd look in the mirror and would feel disgust for the bitter, joyless woman I'd become. Somehow I knew that although anger had kept me going while raising my family, it was time to let it go. It had outlived its usefulness, but I couldn't seem to figure out a different way of being. But at last, when I looked at my reflection the morning Abby went off to college, I didn't feel disgust, but a little bit of honest pride. I saw a strong, capable woman.

"I've made a good life for us, and I'm indebted to the kindness of many people here. If it sounds like I've told my story before, it's because I have. I volunteer at a women's shelter in another town, and I try to pass along what I've learned and what I've been given."

She took my hands in hers, letting the balls of yarn drop and roll across the floor. "I guess I told you this because I see you struggling. I don't know why and don't need to. But I want to tell you to honor the struggle and to remember you're a person of value, not because you're a respected scientist, but simply because you are Katherine Solterra. The who of you, not the what of you, is what's important." She picked up the yarn and gave it to me. "Keep knitting. I can think of some others who'd like a hand-knitted scarf."

"You're incorrigible."

"I know. It's part of my charm."

"Maggie? Did you get your spirit back?"

Her face softened. "Yes. I gave it back to myself."

# Chapter 25

GOING TO MY MAILBOX, I noticed tire tracks. Studying them more closely, I realized they were fresh imprints of tracks larger than those my car would make. No one had driven to the cabin since Paul had come; perhaps someone had headed down my lane to back up and turn around, or had made a wrong turn? Where the tracks stopped was the halfway point of my lane, and before this curve, you couldn't see the cabin at all. Suspicions bubbled up, and I decided to tell Paul. We'd been invited to have dinner with the Delgados, so I could tell him then. Not wanting to drive over the tracks, I got my coat and started to walk to their home. Paul could bring me back. It wasn't too cold yet, and the fresh air felt rejuvenating after a long day of writing and researching.

I read my mail on the way. A note from Matthew confirmed the arrival of the last set of reports. He wrote that for the most part the writing was clear and precise, but there were mistakes in formulas and calculations, despite my checking against the original data. At least the data, compiled before the accident, could be trusted, and these mistakes could be remedied. He asked if I could meet with him in a week or two to discuss my presentation at a major healthcare conference. Folding his letter, I thought I might as well give him my formal resignation at that time, effective for the end of May.

With the sun beginning to set as I neared Paul's house, I decided not to walk any farther. Leaning over the top fence rail for a few minutes to watch the sky, I thought about my decision to resign. It hadn't been made in this moment, of course. It had been a gradual understanding, of light sheening over water, of bright hues effervescing out of the dark. I was leaving the institute. A few weeks ago, Matthew had called me to relay the latest results of an ongoing clinical trial. "It doesn't look promising. I doubt we'll move into phase three," he'd reported. We'd thought that this drug might provide a breakthrough in preventing at least some immunological factors from damaging the central nervous system. We worked with people with MS who followed our trials, and the work of other companies and research centers, and for them, it was more than disappointing—it meant the crushing of hope. Every scientist knew, though, that a failure could drive science forward just as much as a success. Knowing what didn't work could lead to the discovery of what would; failures informed and refined the process.

I considered this paradigm for my own situation. I would never view the accident as a "blessing in disguise"; however, its reshaping of my life was a fact I had to accept. I had been defeated, at least relating to my work as a scientist at the institute, and probably as a scientist at all. It was hard to breathe around the alloy of anger and sadness pressing against my ribs, but I forced myself to remember it was merely one defeat. And frankly, I needed to leave the place where David worked. "Onward, pioneer woman," I said aloud. I recalled Riya's wisdom and announced it to the darkening sky, as well: "Forgive yourself for what you cannot do. Give thanks for what you can." I executed a twirl in the middle of Paul's lane. "And dance on," I whispered.

When I knocked at Paul's kitchen entrance, I noticed the flutter of a curtain at one of the windows before he opened the door. "Come in, it's a little early. Let me take your coat. I thought you were meeting me there." He looked behind me. "Where's your car?"

"I walked."

"In the dark? I asked you to drive everywhere, especially at night." I could tell he was irritated with me.

"It recently got dark, which is why I came here instead of continuing." I told him about the tire tracks. "I didn't want to drive over them in case you wanted to see them."

He motioned for me to sit at the kitchen table. "Those tracks are probably mine. Or Cooper's or Virgil's or Emilio's, or any of more than a couple of dozen or so men and occasionally a few women. It was Tomás's idea. He and Emilio planned to do it themselves, but with all of us it's no problem." I must have looked confused because he added, "We wanted to make sure you weren't hurt again."

"You mean the Meeting is guarding me?"

"We prefer the phrase, 'watching over.'"

"You decided to do this without asking me?"

"Would you have agreed had we come to you first?"

I looked down at the table, its scrubbed surface unadorned but polished with time and care. Would pride have won out over fear? "I don't know."

"We were afraid you wouldn't. If one of the Friends had been hurt, we'd do this, of course, but it's even more worrisome to us that someone who isn't a member has been hurt because of our actions. Are you angry?"

"No, I understand, and I'm touched people care. Maybe if I'd known I wouldn't have spent so many sleepless nights. But you needn't stand watch any longer. After being questioned by the police, they won't try anything else. No one came down the lane, right?"

"No, but I'm sure by the second or third night we were there, word had gotten around, like word will get around if we stop. This is a small community. And those men may not be the only ones causing trouble. It wouldn't take much investigating for someone to discover you're the sole non-Quaker attender we have at present, either, if they're trying to intimidate us into stopping our plans."

"I can't have you continue this. I'll be here until the end of May, too long to have you 'watch over me,' as you put it. Did this come out of generalized worry, or are there specific concerns?"

He hesitated, as though gauging how much to tell me. "We've had more threats at the Meetinghouse, and some have referred to you. We've turned them over to the police. The men who ran you off the road have been questioned again, but so far, there's nothing to link them with the threats."

"Having been identified, though, I can't imagine they'd be brazen enough to harass me at home. Do you think I'm in danger?" I thought of how Paul had moved aside the curtain and peered out before opening the door to me.

"I don't know. I don't want to scare you, but I do want you to be more cautious than you have been. Please think about leaving here."

"I'm not giving in to threats. And I wish you'd reconsider having the Meeting watch over me."

After buttoning his jacket, he helped me into my coat. "I don't think anything you could say will convince Emilio and Tomás. You may be operating from the perspective of an independent North American woman, but you're dealing with Latin American men, which brings another whole dimension to the concept of pride. Moreover, how often do men today get to play the knights in shining armor? Don't spoil it for us. There are always three groups of two each night, so we can divide the time. We're getting to know each other better and are having a grand time swapping stories. We say things to each other in the dark, small spaces of our cars that we wouldn't share in daylight. Think of it this way: You're giving us the opportunity to develop male friendships that do not involve a football, basketball, baseball, or hockey puck. We even discuss how to improve our relationships with the people in our lives, so you're doing a real community service."

"I . . . I am absolutely nonplussed."

"Lucky me, but I imagine that doesn't happen often."

At the door of their home, Tomás greeted us and took my wrap. After all the handshakes, a courtly bow from Emilio, and an enthusiastic hug from Magdalena, they led us into the living room. No longer shy around me, Graciela rushed over, chattering in a mixture of Spanish and English about teaching the children to make snow angels. Emilio and Tomás had refurbished a sled someone had given them, and even Magdalena had taken turns on it. "I sit myself down, Emilio give me push, and whee!" She giggled, her face radiant with her pleasure. I was gratified to see she no longer looked gaunt; she'd gained weight, and her eyes no longer reflected fear.

In the dining room, colorful pottery and a basket of fruit in the center of the table's plain white cloth set the stage for this special occasion, and I felt privileged to be included. Tomás said, "We'd like to say grace like Friends." We joined hands, Paul on my left, Magdalena, her hand slipping into mine, on my right.

After we sat down, Tomás remained standing and raised his glass. "*A nuestros honrados huéspedes, que ayudaron a reunir a nuestra familia.* To our honored guests, who helped bring our family together." I wondered why he thought I'd been of any help. Maybe he'd gotten that impression when we met with them about the legal proceedings, for which I'd provided as much translation as I could. Nina hadn't been surprised when Spanish, my first language as a child, emerged as more intact than my English after the accident, but it amazed me when the words came out as fluently as they did. With Graciela's tutoring, I was remembering even more, sometimes thinking of the Spanish word first when I couldn't recall the English.

"This is food like we eat in El Salvador," Graciela said. "*Tamales salvadoreños* are tamales with chicken." Explaining the other Salvadoran dishes to us, she pointed out the ones that might be too spicy. "For those you eat small bites, no?"

Yes, I assured her and was glad to see she'd set a water pitcher on the table. Magdalena's head bobbed from person to person as though checking to be sure we were all there. She would hold a dish for me to serve myself, then she would take the spoon from me and place more on my plate.

After dinner Tomás brought out his guitar, the finish worn and scarred. He and his brother taught us the words to the folk song they'd sung at the Meetinghouse the night Emilio and Magdalena arrived. The children joined in and showed us a dance; Miguel, the most gregarious of the children, pulled me up to enlarge their circle. I kept getting left and right mixed up but discovered I could manage if I hesitated a split second and watched the person next to me.

It had been a special evening, I told them when we got ready to leave. Magdalena beamed when Paul leaned down to kiss her cheek. She called him her son. "And you," she drew me to her, "*mi hija*, my daughter." She kissed me on both cheeks, drew the collar of my coat up around my neck, and patted my shoulders.

Tomás walked out to the car with us. "Tomás, I know you and the others have been watching my cabin at night. I appreciate it, and I don't think I've ever felt so cared for. But you must stop. There is no need now, and you can't continue until I leave, which will be the end of May."

"The others may stop if they want, but Emilio and I will not." The finality of his tone left no room for argument.

We left and Paul drove slowly along the winding country road and down my lane. He opened my car door and escorted me to the cabin, taking the keys from me and unlocking the front door. Smiling at his old-fashioned courtesy, I told him, "It was the right thing to do, reuniting this family."

"I think so, too."

"Do you feel the Meeting has a chance to keep them together?"

"I don't know. It's no longer in our control, although I guess it never was." He gave me the keys. "Rest well, Kate."

I met with my lawyer, Andrew Plover. I told him what had been happening, beginning with the Friends' decision to offer sanctuary, and ending with a concern from Amy, my department's secretary. She'd let me know someone had called the institute, allegedly about writing an article on women in high-level science positions. Eventually, however, the caller began asking pointed questions about me. Amy hadn't given him any information, but she'd said, "The more he talked, the less I believed him."

Andrew explained, "He's most likely an investigator. They must be worried enough to try to discredit you as a reliable witness. You could press charges, but I'm afraid their strategy will be to bring up the injuries you sustained in the accident."

"How did he make the connection to the institute? I don't think anyone in Drake's Springs knows the name of it."

"Routine checks to find out about you. You did know your accident was featured in a series on drunk driving, right?"

"Yes, my parents and I gave permission."

"As a prominent business leader who was a candidate at the time for lieutenant governor, the driver was the subject of unprecedented publicity."

"It's unfair that they can turn this to their advantage, and I can't stop them."

"You could, but would you want to deal with what would ensue? Now, if they persist, I'd change my mind. One more thing. As your lawyer and as your friend, are you sure you know what you're getting into with these Quakers and this sanctuary business?"

"I'm not directly involved, don't worry. I don't have their kind of nerve. Or faith."

"Do they know you don't?"

"They wouldn't want me doing anything against my principles. I've never known any people quite like them." I told him about the Quakers who camped out in my drive every night.

"That's impressive. As for the other matter, given the circumstances, I don't see any way around it. You admit to having doubts. I don't think this is worth what they'd put you through."

"How do people do things like this and live with their consciences afterward?"

"They don't have a moral conscience."

Rising before dawn the next morning, I ate my breakfast on the back porch, not caring it was cold. I watched the night diffuse into the first colors of the day. When the sun was up and I'd finished eating, I wrapped up in blankets and dozed until the brightness and warmth of the full sun woke me. Cabin fever, I thought. I wanted warm days, spring flowers, dogwood trees in bloom, and quick rain showers that left the smell of washed earth in the air; I wanted to go camping in the preserve, on top of a mountain, and read all night long by a lantern or a fire. Startled, I said out loud, "Camping? Where did that idea come from?"

# Chapter 26

I SLIPPED MY LETTER onto Matthew's desk. "Here is my resignation, effective the end of May, after the research presentation and a few loose ends."

"Ah, Kate." He sighed. "Are you sure?"

"Yes. I'd rather this didn't become general knowledge yet. It's going to be difficult enough as it is. Other than David, no one else is aware I'm planning to resign. I'll tell my colleagues on my team first."

"You don't think you'll improve?"

"It's not likely, not to the degree I'd need to continue here. And even if I did, I need a fresh beginning."

"Future plans?"

"I don't know yet. I'll send the presentation's preliminary draft in three or four weeks." I started to leave, glad I'd been able to maintain a business-like tone. I reached over to shake his hand, but he came around his desk.

"I'm sorry. You fought so hard."

"But lost."

He gave my shoulders a slight shake. "Don't ever think you did."

The emotion in his voice caused me to blink back tears, after all. When I left the building, however, I felt relief, confirming the rightness of my decision. I could stop demanding the impossible from myself. Spending the weekend with my parents, I told them about my resignation. They did not question my decision, oddly enough; despite their earlier attempts to encourage me to keep trying, they seemed relieved as well. With the release of this burden, we all shifted, clicking into new slots with the struggle acknowledged, the defeat cauterized. This part, at least, was over.

Damn you. May you lose your job, may you lose your identity, may your spirit always be vexed.

When I looked up from my feet, I could tell it was a breathtaking place with tiers of ancient rock layers, the egg-like beginnings of stalagmites, striated walls, and the primordial sound of water dripping in the distance. Spaghetti strands of white tree roots snaked down from the cave's ceiling. From the moment I'd slid down the muddy decline into this cave, however, I realized this adventure was a mistake, and it grew progressively worse. We crawled through tunnels and scrambled up steep slopes and over boulders. After David made fun of me in front of the others, I'd been determined to go caving. I felt like a fool for letting my offended pride overrule my common sense. Aunt Constanza and New Year's resolutions notwithstanding, if I'd known it would be like this, I never would have come.

And now, straddling the pools of water in a tunnel, I couldn't figure out how to crawl, how to alternate my arms and legs. After moving my right hand forward, followed by my right knee, I inched my left hand and left knee forward. It didn't feel quite right, and when I cleared the tunnel and stood, the others looked at me curiously.

Cooper led us through a narrow corridor to a cliff's edge and jumped down to a triangular shelf. "I'm right here; I won't let you fall."

Looking down, I felt unnerved. "I can't do this."

"Sure you can." He measured a length with his arms. "It's not even three feet."

"And if I miss the ledge? There's what? A thirty-foot drop off the side?"

"I'm not going to let you fall. You need to trust me."

"It's not a matter of trusting you."

Paul moved next to me. "Cooper?" he called down. "Let's have the others go first." He led me away from the rest of the group.

"I can't do this. I'm sorry, but I've gotten spooked. I'm afraid of falling and getting hurt." My voice tightened. "It's such a narrow, slippery ledge to land on. I don't have an accurate perception for these things, and my balance isn't the greatest. If I'd known it was going to be like this, I wouldn't have come."

"We're not going to force you to do anything you're not ready to do. You did fine scaling the overhang, and because you tried it, so did Ruth." He kept his eyes on mine. "It has nothing to do with being brave or proving yourself. You don't have to prove yourself to us. If you'd like, I'll be happy to take you back outside. We'll return the way we came."

"You say that as though it's a comforting thought." I could hear Diane telling me, "Suck it up, buttercup." I pictured Aunt Constanza. "All right. I'll try it."

By this time, the others had jumped and were shouting their encouragement to me. Ruth called out, "It's not as treacherous as it looks."

Paul whispered to me, "Anyone who can kill a rattlesnake, jump across a ravine, and create a new life for herself has more resolve than all the rest of us combined. You don't have to do this."

Returning to the edge, I looked down and tried to judge the distance in the dim light. Cooper stood by with his arms out to catch me. The rock formations blurred, but I thought of the others waiting for me. They had jumped, and it had been no big deal. Looking down the crevice running along the ledge made me feel unbalanced, though, and I pulled back. "I'm sorry. I can't do it. You go ahead and I'll wait here."

Paul leaned over the ledge. "Cooper? You take the others on through. We're going back."

I kept my eyes on the rocks in front of me as Paul led me back to the cave's entrance. Grateful for the fresh air, the sun, and the firm ground, I felt my legs give way. Sliding down beside the boulder marking the cave's entrance, I took off the heavy miner's helmet and handed it to him. "I feel like such a wimp."

"You shouldn't. One of the most important rules of caving is that you respect your limitations."

"I have enough limitations; I don't want to give up and add more. It wasn't such a big jump."

"It was if you weren't secure about doing it, and it was a precarious landing spot. You're the only one who knows what you can and cannot do. You made the right decision. Trust yourself."

He uncapped my canteen of water and gave it to me. The cool water calmed me. I leaned back against the boulder, its edges sharp on my shoulder blades. "I feel ridiculous now." I tried to laugh. "I guess if I'm going to try new things, I'll have to be willing to make a fool of myself and be embarrassed."

"Welcome to the human condition."

Maggie picked up one of the pictures Cooper had taken. "I can't believe you did this, but I'm right proud of you."

"I didn't get all the way through the cave," I admitted. "I got nervous trying to jump down to a ledge, and Paul had to take me back out. I'm glad I tried it, but I'll never do it again. By the way, Maggie, here's proof: I'm covered in mud."

"I did say I'd pay good money to see that, but we didn't set a specific amount. How about lunch on the house?" We ate our soup and sandwiches while Cooper waited on customers. "What's next on your quest to become a different person?"

"I'm going camping."

"Camping? I swan, it's getting so I don't know what you'll do next. I didn't know you were the outdoorsy type."

"Outdoorsy? No, believe me, I'm not."

"Why camping? And alone? Your Aunt Constanza has a powerful hold on you."

The idea of camping had come to me that morning while I was on my porch. If I stripped away even the walls and ceilings, perhaps the answers I craved could march in and find me. If I surrounded myself with the ancient classical elements of fire, air, earth, and water, perhaps I could find my way back to myself, the self beyond the scientist, the "who of me, not the what of me" like Maggie had said.

I realized she was waiting for an answer. "The weather's good, I've never been camping, much less by myself, and it should be lovely. How many reasons do I need?"

"Three, apparently."

After lunch, Cooper showed me his camping gear. "Why don't I go and set the tent up for you? It's cantankerous at times. All you have to do is tell me when and where."

"That would be cheating. Show me the basics and I'll manage." He demonstrated how to pitch the tent and discussed what kind of site would be best, what type of wood to gather for the fire, and what supplies I'd need. "I'm not going to explore the Arctic. This is your basic Girl Scout-level campout. A few tidy knots, a companionable fire, a snug little tent."

"'Companionable fire! Snug little tent!'" he mimicked. "Oh yes, I forgot, the great snake slayer, ravine jumper, and cave explorer can take care of herself."

"Yes, I can. And pass the word along to the knights and ladies in armor to take some time off. No one will know where I am. And don't get any ideas about camping out near me because there's no telling what I'll do if I hear strange rustlings in the woods. I'm taking my axe. And you can stop laughing at me."

He held up his hands in a show of surrender. "I'd never laugh at a woman who has her own axe."

"One more thing. When I come back, I'd like you to teach me how to change a tire and jump-start my car. It's past time I learned how to do those things for myself. Like your mother says, 'Every tub must stand on its own bottom.'"

❖ ❖ ❖

"Belly dancing? Caving? And next, camping?" Diane began laughing and continued until she was gasping for air. "Kate, I honestly don't know if I'll recognize you the next time I see you."

"You're the one who said to 'get out of my own way,' and 'take a chill pill,' right?"

"Yes, but I didn't think you'd turn into a completely different person. I'm so proud of you. I wish I were there. You sound like you're having such fun."

"I am. I'm beginning to realize what a narrow life I'd been leading. I even went out with a group from the Quaker Meeting; they go out for dinner every month or so. We went to this bar for dinner and to play pool." I couldn't keep from giggling.

"You didn't! You didn't tell them, did you?"

"No!" I began laughing as hard as Diane had at the start of our call. Part of my therapy at the rehab center involved playing pool to strengthen my eye-hand coordination and to improve my arms' range of motion. Along with some knowledge of geometry and physics, I turned out to have an intuitive talent for it.

"How much did you win?"

"Quakers traditionally don't gamble, but I am now in demand as a team member."

"Cool beans, my friend."

# Chapter 27

Felipe had begun to dream of death—not of how he would die, for he knew that would be brutal beyond imagining, but of what death would feel like. He imagined no more hunger or pain, a relaxing of muscles, quieting of nerves, suspension of heartbeats and lung breaths, stilling of thoughts, but above and through all: utter and immaculate peace.

He saw the army officer too late. Maybe it is a mirage, he thought, like the tree with food dangling from every leaf, its bark exuding sweet, cool water in droplets as large as plums.

The mirage spoke, "You are wise not to run."

"I have no need to run. I have not done anything wrong."

"You will find it will not be good to lie."

"I have papers to identify myself." He pulled out the documents Vicente had given him, but the officer lunged and snatched the papers, folding them and putting them in his pocket.

"There is a big reward for your return to El Salvador. Your American friends, they will stop looking for you." He tore Felipe's jacket when he searched him and took his gun.

Felipe's arm, stiff with fear and anger, swung out, hitting the officer in the face. Kicking him to the ground, the officer pointed his gun at Felipe's head. Felipe choked and prayed into the dirt, "*Dios*." God.

"It is better if you are returned alive to El Salvador, but it is not a requirement." The officer kicked him hard in the side and ordered him to get up, "*¡Levántate!*"

Felipe knew if he didn't obey, he'd be beaten to death or shot, right here, now, in the dirt, in the middle of the road. It would be over, peace would be his to claim, and he realized the choice was his, too. He felt a flicker of frustration and resentment. Why, God, do I have to make the choice? Please take this from me. He rose to his feet but fell back down in the dirt.

Struggling to regain consciousness, Felipe nonetheless welcomed the times when his mind and body skimmed below the surface of the dark waters. There, insensate of pain and fear and hunger, tempted beyond reason to remain in this tenebrous state, he dreamed of abundant gardens, of colors and sounds of astonishing clarity, of embraces from his father, his mother, his brothers.

In sequences spiraling out like slow-motion streamers, Felipe and his family danced with their friends, the music joyous, the laughter loud and fearless; in the following scene, he helped with the harvest, the baskets of coffee beans heavy in his arms, the smell of the earth acrid and affirming; next, he held a baby, its small weight a blessing in his arms, its features so achingly beautiful he felt tears in his eyes; last, he slowly kissed a woman, her skin sliding under his fingers like warm liquid, her shape and his transforming into shimmering vessels, pouring one into another and back again.

Let me stay, let me stay.

Felipe awakened fully and felt a shock to be alive. He didn't dare consider whether he was relieved or disappointed. He was in the officer's car, though he had no memory of getting in it. He eyed the officer. Wait, he told himself. He will make a mistake. He dreams of the reward, and my gun and his gun make him falsely brave. Wait.

The officer, driving recklessly, drank from a bottle he held between his knees. They traveled over the same route Felipe had walked, and he thought in despair that not only would he have to escape, but he'd also have to get one of the guns and the car. He would not survive the journey a second time.

Having rested in the car, he was more alert. He willed his mind to focus, to be ready if his chance came. He thought of his plea to God while he was lying in the dirt, though it was Tomás, Emilio, Graciela, and Magdalena who still believed in God, who sustained an impossible belief despite the murder of his father, of Magdalena's husband, of tens of thousands of others. Believing in a God who allowed such torture was hypocrisy turned on end, and yet, he admitted, he had called out to God, and he could not deny the curl of comfort he had breathed in at that moment.

The car swerved to the side of the road and dropped into the ditch. When they'd rolled to a stop, the officer tossed the empty bottle through the window and got out to survey the damage. He hauled Felipe from the car and untied his hands. "Help me push the car back up on the road."

Felipe's chance came after they'd gotten the car out of the ditch. The fight was swift and severe, but Felipe, his fear massing into strength, overpowered the drunken officer. He did not take the time to drag the man to the side. He took the two guns, his documents, and what money and ammunition he could find. The officer would regain consciousness soon and would alert others. Even with the car, Felipe knew he would not escape far. Pointing the gun at the man's head, the desperation unraveled from him, his hands lowered, and the sharp sound in his head swelled until his skull vibrated.

# Chapter 28

THE SILENCE IN THE Meeting was restless at first, as though people couldn't get settled. A man struggled to his feet, setting aside a cane and grasping onto the bench in front of him. "I held a new life yesterday, my first great-grandchild. She is tiny and fragile, and I was almost afraid to hold her. I've been thinking about the kind of world she's coming into. But it seemed such a miracle to hold her that I was encouraged."

After the children left, another man rose. "Martin's great-grandchild makes me think of the new people we've brought into this Meeting, enlarging our circle and enriching our lives. As we consider bringing another into the circle, let us be mindful that these lives are miracles, too."

Minutes later, Abby spoke. "Our recent actions have forced me to ask more questions of myself and of what I believe. Sometimes I don't like the answers I get, but more often lately, I don't get any answers. I've never thought so much about faith and seeking truth, taking risks and accepting consequences." Opening my notebook, I wrote down what I could remember from what she had said.

After the service ended and the regular announcements were given, Paul rose and said, "I have joyful news some of you apparently—thank you, Quaker grapevine—have heard. Tomás received a letter from his other brother, Felipe. While in El Salvador, Emilio had received word that his brother had 'disappeared,' but he is alive, somewhere in Mexico near Guatemala, or we believe he was there when the letter was sent. This afternoon at two o'clock you're invited to join us in discussing how we might help Felipe."

How could they risk another trip? Where did they draw the line between adherence to a principle and their responsibility to follow the law? I felt my energy for this situation seep out of me. Threading my way through clusters of Friends talking in the room's center, I found the Schoenfelds and told them of my plan to go camping.

"Let me draw you a map to a good campsite." Pulling a sheet of scrap paper from her purse, Eleanor sketched a route from the preserve's entrance to the mountain's camping areas. "The road should be clear enough for you to drive all the way up. If not, there's a shed here," she drew a star on the map, "and inside you'll find a wagon used to move supplies. But don't choose a site where the car will be too far away." She drew more symbols. "I suggest these sites because you'll have a nearby bathroom and shower. Nothing fancy, but it serves the purpose." She folded the paper and gave it to me. "Have a good time!"

"What, no words of wisdom?" I teased.

"You can take care of yourself."

Eleanor left through the side door, but Virgil invited me to sit next to him on what Friends called the "facing bench." Surprised by how different the room looked from this angle, I waited for him to speak, thinking he would be the one to give me camping tips. He paused for a few moments before speaking. "We've been watching you struggle. Why are you trying to reinvent your life in secret? It would be a privilege to be part of such an endeavor."

I wondered how much he knew about me but decided it didn't matter. "Virgil, I am never going to be the same."

"You're creating a new life for yourself after being injured by another person's decision to hurt you. Not many people do that."

"I nearly died." My words echoed in the empty room.

"But you decided to live. Why? And what are you going to do about it?"

He left, and I was alone on the facing bench. I could hear the faint laughter of the children playing in the education building. Taking out my notebook and pen again, I wrote down something he'd said before it escaped me. I'd think about it later, on the mountain. After writing, I sat still for a few minutes in the buoyant, lighthearted, almost teasing silence. What was it trying to tell me?

After unpacking the car, I looked at the jumble of equipment on the ground and became flustered. I couldn't remember the name of the main piece of canvas. What had Cooper told me? How was it all put together? What were those aluminum pieces called? Stop, I ordered myself. Sitting on the rock wall bordering the clearing, I calmed my thoughts as though I were in Meeting, centering down. I waited. Visualizing what it had looked like when Cooper had erected it, I got up and began fitting the pieces together. When I got stuck, I returned to the wall and waited. "Tent," the word emerged, enabling me to make sense of the square of material and the stakes. Until you lose your facility with language, I mused, you don't fully understand how language drives thought.

At last the tent, listing to one side, was up, and barring strong winds, it should hold. "So there, Cooper Mackenzie, one snug tent on its own." Like me, I thought. If I could at least attempt caving, I could do this, too. Finding the stream, I secured my cooler in it with a rope looped around a low-hanging tree branch. I was set. Sitting on the wall and eating my dinner, I felt complete and whole, a silver bowl of contentment.

The sky's colors faded to the pale luster of translucent china before darkening to streaks of ink. Too tired to read, I doused the fire, crawled into the tent, and zipped the screen, leaving the tent flaps open. Staring at the brocaded darkness, I missed the security of the fire. I placed the flashlight by my head and waited for my eyes to adjust to the dimness. Something hushed the rhythmic chorus of the insects, and I found myself listening attentively until they continued. Being alone outside at night was almost as different an environment for me as being in a cave. I settled into the broad sweep of silence and, through the screen, watched the clouds drift and close over the moon. All at once, I couldn't shake the feeling that hands were poised around the tent, seconds from grabbing me. Telling myself I was being irrational did nothing to allay my anxiety. One, two, three, breathe. There's nothing out here. No one around me. Hearing something to one side of the tent, though, I closed my eyes in order to concentrate better. No. No. Stop. You're all right. Calm down.

Making guttural sounds, I tore out of the sleeping bag and managed to unzip the screen. I needed to get to the car. Where was it? I spun in a circle and stumbled, falling to the ground. I couldn't remember where the car was parked, just that I couldn't park right at the site. Retrieving the flashlight from the tent, I squinted to see beyond its beam, but it illuminated only nearby trees and bushes. Was there a path? Had a path led from the car to the clearing? I couldn't recall. I started to move away from the tent but halted, realizing how easily I could get lost if I couldn't find the car.

"Stop. Think." My head hurt, and I shook from the cold. From my crate of supplies, I found my rehab notebook and flipped to the section on problem solving. "What is your problem and why is it a problem?" I worked my way through the steps in the notebook: I can't find the car. I'm too scared to stay in the tent. It's dark and I could get lost. I won't be able to find my way back here.

Continuing down the list of questions, I read, "If you don't have something you need, can you think of a substitute?" If I still had the fire going I could use it as my reference point, but I didn't have more wood nearby. If I went out of view of the campsite, I needed something to lead me back here. Finally, I saw a solution. String. Cooper had tossed a ball of string in the supply crate. Fastening one end to a tent stake, I bundled up the sleeping bag, made sure I had the car keys in my pocket, and held the flashlight in front of me. After four tries, I found the car. I crawled onto the back seat and relocked the door. Feeling sick to my stomach, I folded into a tight ball with the sleeping bag over me.

Damn you. May you have panic attacks every day. May you always get lost on your camping trips.

"Mind the Light," I chanted. "Way will open. Mind the Light." I found myself thinking of Felipe making his way through the dark, past the tangle of arms reaching out to grab him. At last, exhaustion overtook me and I slept, waking to the strong light of late morning.

From the car, I could see the campsite through the trees. Everything looked so innocuous that I felt ashamed of last night's nerves. Anyone stumbling upon the campsite would have thought I'd been abducted, for my rehab notebook and supplies from the crate lay scattered across the area, string wound around the trees in a giant cat's cradle, and one side of the tent drooped to the ground.

Sitting on the wall after breakfast, I tried to decide what to do. Below me in the valley, flowering trees, like tatting on an antique linen tablecloth, made a lacy overlay against the evergreens. Taking in the panorama, I could almost believe in a supreme and divine Creator because of the infinite variety, the fragility of some life forms and the strength of others, and the miraculous continuity of countless species. I spoke to the mountains, wishing I had their strength. "I'm sick of feeling weak, of feeling sorry for myself. I want to be strong and resilient. I know I keep saying things like this, but how do I make it happen?"

What had given the Salvadoran refugees the strength to flee their homeland? What was giving Felipe strength now? He had no choice, I realized. He continued, or he would be murdered. Even though my situation in no way could be compared to Felipe's, I didn't have a choice, either, I admitted. The alternative to this quest to reconstruct my life was to give up, to surrender. Was faith sustaining Felipe, the way it had for Graciela and Magdalena? Could faith be acquired by taking a series of risks like caving and camping alone, each time gaining confidence by acting on the unknown? Virgil said that when he couldn't feel the spark of divinity inside him, he would act as if he could and take a step on his own. Could faith be gained by a conscious effort, like practicing scales on the piano? Did I want faith? What kind of faith? Faith in myself, in my abilities, now reduced, rearranged? Faith to re-construct my life? Religious faith? I didn't think I could manufacture a belief in God. I found myself listening to the landscape, thirsting for the veined leaves and the mountain ridges to reveal their secrets. I recalled being in the hospital and in the rehab center, telling myself I had to get through the next hour, until lunch, until I went to sleep, the next day. I would try to stay at the campsite another night. I heard Graciela's voice, "When I'm scared, I make myself do one small thing."

I spent the day reading and hiking, though I remained straight on one of the paths. In the afternoon I napped in the sun, dreaming of a man who was running and panting in desperate breaths. When I woke, I knew the man had been Felipe.

Wrapped in my sleeping bag by the fire that night, I watched the flames' brilliance spear the dark. A framed poster in the Meetinghouse quoted Quaker founder George Fox's words enjoining Friends to respond to that of God in every individual. Was God in the drunken man who crashed into me? In the men who ran me off the road? In those who bombed the villages in El Salvador? And if so, what did it mean? What about the spark of divinity Virgil claimed was inside me? Did I have to acknowledge the presence of God in the drunken man who nearly killed me, who changed my life, before I could find God in myself? Or was it the other way around? First, of course, I'd have to believe in the existence of God. The religious terminology and concepts daunted me, forming a serpentine maze with no discernible entrance, leaving me on the outside, bereft. Would I be able to reconstruct my life without some kind of faith?

I tried to mute the torrent of questions. Another thought surfaced, though. I can't face what I can't name. I turned the idea around. Did I refuse to name what I didn't want to face? I never thought of the man who hit me in terms of his name, and I refused to picture what he looked like. I had visualized the car hitting me but had never given the driver a face. I'd cursed him almost daily, but I didn't want to think about how his life must have changed. I didn't want to know if he could sleep at night, if he had nightmares, or despite what he'd written in his letter, if he felt remorse for what he'd done to me. If I had this knowledge, I would begin to see him as a person. I would have to claim my anger, my bitterness, and a hatred I feared as much as I wanted to keep.

I couldn't face what I refused to name. What was it Virgil had said to me? Pulling out my notebook, I read, "Another person's decision to hurt you." He was right. It had been no accident. The man decided to get in his car after he'd been drinking. He'd chosen to drink and to hurt. And very likely, there had been someone around who could have stopped him but made the decision not to, or at the very least, someone at an earlier time who had not intervened in his life.

I cannot face what I will not name, I repeated. I had called it a loss of thought-processing skills, memory impairment, memory loss—a host of euphemisms—but I'd never called it the harshest phrase of all to me: brain damage. What I had prized the most and had built my life on had been torn from me. Maybe if I named it I could move beyond it.

Virgil had mentioned another decision, and I read from my notebook, "You decided to live. Why? And what are you going to do about it?" I left the fire's safe sphere of light and sat on the rock wall. I spoke into the quiet of the night, "I don't want to be merely a survivor. That's the first stage. I can't change what happened, but I don't have to be trapped in it. I want more than mere survival; I want to have a joyful, productive life. I know I keep thinking this, but how do I make it happen?" This question was becoming my refrain.

This night I was able to fall asleep in the tent. Hours later, however, I woke up with my heart beating fast, my breathing uneven and rapid. Felipe, I thought. Was he hurt? Had he been captured? I must have had another dream about him, though I couldn't recall anything. Unlike Aunt Constanza, I didn't believe in dreams as omens, but the thoughts and images of Felipe being in danger peppered the night. When I tried to fall back asleep, I couldn't. I was awake enough to be uneasy, and every small sound outside the tent startled me. Was this what it was like for Felipe, I wondered, the sensation of powerful hands ready to grab and twist until bones broke? Once again picking up the sleeping bag and flashlight, I followed the string to the car, where I'd tied the other end to the door handle. Burrowed inside the sleeping bag on the back seat, I thought, hold on, Felipe, hold on.

Having returned to the cabin in the late afternoon, I went to bed right after eating dinner. I rejoiced in the warm, soft bed with the convenience of instant light on the nearby table and fell asleep almost immediately.

With the blast of the gunshot, the man staggered back. I heard his screams, witnessed the agony in his open mouth, his eyes. I saw the blood spreading over the front of his shirt. Sitting bolt upright, I kicked off the blanket and tried to stand but, tangled in the sheets, fell to the floor. Someone had shot into the cabin; the sound reverberated, ricocheting around the walls. Afraid of being visible from the windows, I crawled into the living room. Everything looked peaceful and undisturbed. My protectors certainly would have heard the gunshot, but then I realized I hadn't thought to let anyone know I'd returned from my camping trip. They weren't guarding the cabin. I pulled myself up to the corner of the living room's picture window. Peering underneath the curtain, I saw no one outside. Breathing so hard that my chest hurt, I slumped down to the floor.

I was so confused. I'd heard a deafening gunshot and I'd seen blood, seen a man get shot. Suddenly I knew with certainty: Felipe. Felipe was in danger. He'd been hurt or killed. Again, I reminded myself that I didn't believe in dreams as harbingers of truth. Unable to go back to sleep, I repeated, "Way will open. Mind the Light," until I calmed down. What was happening to me? Courage, Kate. "Faith," I whispered as the sun rose.

The man, his skin hanging in strips from his body, ran up and down the hills, his heartbeat matching the pounding of his feet on the ground. The strips of flesh began tearing away from him until only a red shadow, a penumbra of a human form, remained.

He flailed in the cold, dark water, the waves engulfing, pouring into his mouth. Hands with claws for fingers grasped him, pulling him below the surface.

Flashes of light punctuated the screams, a crescendo of terror.

# Chapter 29

I DECIDED TO GO talk to Paul, but I couldn't figure out how to get the car moving. I could put the key in the ignition and turn it, but I didn't know what to do next. I'd stopped sleeping at night, trying to get by with naps during the daytime, but the lack of sleep had taken a toll. Worn out, in pain, and unable to think well enough to manage basic tasks, I had to do something, anything, to stop the nightmares. Despite what he'd told me about not walking by myself, I started toward Paul's farm. Turning into his drive, it occurred to me I could have called him and asked him to come to me.

"Kate?" Paul opened the door and looked at me. "Come in. You look like you're ill. What's wrong?"

"I haven't been sleeping well. Could we talk?"

He led me into his living room. After moving stacks of papers and books, he sat me down on the sofa. "Have you eaten anything today? How about a cup of tea?" I nodded and he left the room, returning a few minutes later with the tea as well as cheese and crackers.

I started telling him about the nightmares. "They've been horrific, the worst I've ever experienced. I'm afraid to go to sleep at night. I can't function."

"Did you have nightmares when Magdalena and Emilio were fleeing?"

"No."

"Maybe you're having them about Felipe because you've gotten to know the family. You and Graciela have been spending a lot of time together."

"This is going to sound absurd and utterly, undeniably crazy, especially coming from me. I don't even know how to express it. I've gone for days now trying to deny it."

"Take your time. Are you cold?" I nodded, and he handed me a quilt. Putting a couple of logs in the fireplace, he started a fire.

I tried to marshal my thoughts in order to express myself as plainly as possible. "I think I'm being told to try to help Felipe."

"You certainly are getting the impression that he's in terrible danger."

"Nothing like this has ever happened to me. I guess you know I'm not a religious or spiritual person; I haven't been hearing the voice of God up on the mountain or in my cabin. There have been no holy messengers or heavenly angels. But I keep having the nightmares, and I think about Felipe during the day. It's as though his situation is pressing down on me, and it's all around me. Virgil told me that he had a 'knowing' about rescuing Magdalena and Emilio. What if I am being called to help Felipe, and I don't pay attention?" I waited and looked at Paul, gauging his reaction. "You must think I'm crazy," I repeated.

"Your interpretation of why you're having the nightmares may or may not be accurate," he said after a long pause, "but I don't think you're crazy. If you think you might be called to help Felipe, what are you thinking of doing?"

"I've spent days running from this answer, but it haunts me. After all, how can I think God might be calling me to do this if I don't believe in God?"

"That's an easy answer: God believes in you."

"I can't fathom that." He waited, and we entered an extended silence. I could hear hissing sounds from the burning wood. "If the Meeting decides to bring Felipe here, I want to help."

"You're sick from lack of sleep. Why don't you rest, and afterward, we'll talk about it more." Seeing my expression, he added, "I believe what you're telling me. But I'm worried about the condition you're in now. You've got to get some sleep. Have you been taking your medication?"

"Yes, but I'm afraid to go to sleep."

"Why don't you try to rest here? Maybe you won't have the nightmares if someone else is with you. When you wake up, we can have dinner and talk."

Too tired to argue, I stretched out on his sofa and, as he had predicted, slept soundly for hours. Joining him in the kitchen later for dinner, I watched as he put the meal together. Paul was a precise cook, washing dishes as he went along and putting away ingredients after he'd used them. At the table, he reached for my hand for the silent Quaker grace.

After dinner, Paul stirred up the fire and settled in the chair opposite me. "Why do you want to help rescue Felipe? Because you feel you're being given some sort of sign, a message?"

"It begins there, I guess. I've thought about Felipe ever since you received word he is still alive. It's as though there's some connection between us. As a scientist, I don't believe in signs or premonitions. I know this isn't rational. In a much smaller way, I'm like the refugees; I'm having to change my life and start over because of the accident." Although Paul knew a drunk driver had hurt me, I'd never told him the most significant injury had been to my brain. I didn't want to tell him now, though I was confident he wouldn't treat me any differently.

"I don't understand how going down to the border to pick up Felipe connects to what you're saying about yourself. Am I missing something? It's a terribly big risk, for him and for anyone going down there to rescue him."

"Isn't faith connected to taking risks?"

"There are other ways to search for and strengthen faith. We try to be careful about not using people as instruments to achieve ends, no matter how worthy the goal. It's a central, critical tenet for us. Would you be going down there for the right reason or for some personal search?"

"Why bring faith into it? Why not say I want to do this because I believe bringing him here is the right thing to do?"

"You're the one who keeps bringing faith into it. Be honest with yourself."

"I'm trying to be. Why did you go down to rescue Magdalena and Emilio?"

"Their lives were in danger. The Quakers' peace testimony. The belief in individual divinity. Their relatives are part of our community," he enumerated. "Yes, I believe our government is wrong with its policies, but I am involved because particular individuals appealed to me for help. I did not choose for Graciela and Tomás to show up on the Meetinghouse steps. But when they did, I had no choice; knowing their lives were in danger, as well as their relatives' lives, I could not turn away. I don't understand it all, but I trust it is part of God's overall plan."

"As I understand it, one of the most basic Quaker beliefs is that there is something of God in everyone."

"Yes."

"Even if I don't believe in God, what if these nightmares, my continually thinking of Felipe, are God's way of whispering to me? What if it is, and I ignore it? It's arrogant of me to think there's something only I can do for him, but what if that is the truth?"

He leaned forward. "Maybe you do have what Quakers call a 'leading,' an inner feeling compelling you to divinely guided action. You can be a spiritual person without being formally, conventionally religious. But I'm not sure it should be acted on in this way."

"My first reaction is to doubt I could have something like this without knowing it."

"Your second reaction?"

"To be open to the possibility."

Paul started to speak but stopped, searching for the right words. "I want to frame this so you will understand me. Quakerism can be appealing and attractive to those who don't come from a formal religious context. Its lack of a formal creed, its focus on social justice, its lack of trappings, and the quaint phraseology can be misleading. Quakerism is not a free-form, anything-goes type of faith. It is the Religious Society of Friends, after all, and there are deeply held written and unwritten rules and customs. Some people, especially those under duress, are intrigued by the unique form of worship, to the signs of love and acceptance. I know I was drawn to Friends at a time when I was in turmoil."

"I'm not sure I understand what you're trying to tell me."

"Probably because I'm not sure of what I want to tell you, or how. I should speak plainly: The Meeting is not a panacea for what is troubling you."

"I understand no one else can solve my problems."

"That's not quite what I meant."

We lapsed back into silence. Finally, Paul said, "We will follow what we discern to be the will of God; I doubt Friends would ever consider someone who's not a member or a long-time attender, but as Clerk, I am compelled to lay your concern before the Meeting."

# Chapter 30

"KATE, PAUL TELLS US you'd like to help bring Felipe here," Ruth stated.

Ruth and the Camerons were members of the committee for Ministry and Worship, and they'd asked me to meet with them at Will and Sharon's home. "You don't think it's a good idea."

"This committee doesn't make that decision," Will answered. "We'd like to know why rescuing Felipe is important to you. We'll ask you questions that perhaps you haven't considered yet, and if we can, answer those you still have."

Sharon explained, "The three of us are technically your clearness committee assigned from Ministry and Worship. The clearness process helps members and attenders with decisions, issues, or major changes. We're here to support you in making this decision, not to judge you or the decision you make. A committee met with Paul and Virgil before they left for the Mexican border."

Will added, "You should know that the details we discuss are confidential. At the end of this process, we'll report a recommendation back to Ministry and Worship. We'd like to help you approach this decision with truth and clarity, to ascertain if it is the will of God."

But I don't believe in God, I reflected. Did that automatically rule me out? Did I feel I was being chosen to do this because of the nightmares and the unrelenting way thoughts of Felipe kept intruding in my life? Could the nightmares simply be a signal for me to relay a sense of urgency? Realizing we were in silence, I let this idea settle into the quiet. Was I latching onto this as an escape from the realities confronting me? Was I using . . . what was his name? The familiar trepidation rose within me. I couldn't fall apart now, for they'd never let me go. Felipe. Had they asked a question?

"I am a scientist," I began. "I believe in facts and in things we can prove. But it was like what Virgil had said to me: a knowing. I didn't understand him before, but I do now." I told them about the nightmares, about how I'd be reaching for the orange juice in the refrigerator or putting on my shoes, and I'd think, "Felipe. Felipe," his name a chanted heartbeat. I added, "I've tried to deny for weeks now that these nightmares were more than some kind of sympathetic reaction to his plight."

The committee members asked and answered questions for over two hours. It was a systematic, thought-provoking, comprehensive examination. Sharon brought our meeting to a close. "Those nightmares," she asked, "what do you think they are? Simple and direct, bottom line?"

"I think I'm being told to help the Meeting rescue Felipe. I'm being asked to do this."

The water sheared along my skin; my hair floated behind me in buoyant strands as I became almost completely submerged. The man, his expression trusting, stretched forth his arms. The water around him turned pink, dark rose, vivid red. His mouth widened into a perfect, soundless circle before he slipped beneath the surface. Waves closed over him, and I was left alone in the bloody vastness.

Screaming Felipe's name, I jolted awake from my nap on the sofa. Falling back on the pillows, I shuddered from the fright. Why was this happening to *me*? How could I save Felipe when I couldn't save myself?

The clearness committee met in my cabin this time. After a short silence, Sharon said, "We wanted to focus first on the legal ramifications. You've attended Meetings for Business on the sanctuary issue, so you're aware of the penalties for involvement. What if you're arrested and convicted? Do you believe strongly enough in this issue to go to jail for it?"

Ruth asked, "What about the consequences to your personal life? And your professional life?"

"Have you discussed this with your family?" Will asked. "How would they react if you were arrested and charged?"

I didn't try to answer their questions immediately but retreated into the silence. Feeling as though I were being lowered into a shaft of light, I thought how helpful it was to have quiet as an option. "I feel a connection with the refugees," I stated after a few moments. "I cannot begin to imagine what they have endured, but I have experienced a situation of starting over, of reconstructing my life. I have felt pain and great fear. It's this experience that gives me the connection, a slice of understanding. Maybe the nightmares are a coincidence. But what if they aren't? What if they are a sign and I ignore it? I know the risks and am willing to take them, to accept the consequences," I finished. Was I? The question flashed in my mind. Had I given the consequences much consideration at all?

Will asked, "Why would you take such a risk?"

"Several reasons, I suppose." I tried to gather my thoughts. "You act on your beliefs. This is an opportunity for me to make a difference for some-one." As soon as I said this, I recognized how self-centered I sounded.

"This is not about you, and furthermore, there are dozens of ways to make a difference without taking such risks," Sharon said. "Work in a soup kitchen. Visit people in a nursing home, volunteer to work with children in need. Why this?"

"Why not this?" I realized I now sounded defensive. "I have the re-sources to go. I know some Spanish and can communicate. I have the time and few outside responsibilities. What's wrong with my going?"

"Perhaps nothing," Ruth answered, "but is it right for you to go? Is it right for the Meeting and, most of all, for Felipe?"

"Paul explained to me it's highly unlikely you'll consider a non-Quaker or attender."

"Yes, but members don't have the inside edge on truth and the will of God," Sharon replied. "We would ask a long-time member or attender these same questions. We would express the same concerns."

"If you have a genuine leading, we would be wise to pay attention to it," Ruth said.

"What draws you to this family?" Will asked. "What about these rela-tive strangers has taken hold of you to the point you're considering such a risk?"

Didn't he already ask this? Did I have any answers to these questions? Was I using Felipe as a means to an end, a violation of Quaker beliefs? But what about those nightmares? I kept returning to them. I stopped question-ing myself and allowed the silence to lead. At last I replied, "They have had everything stripped away from them—their loved ones, their homes, their security—and yet they have faith. They have hope. They even have joy. That is what draws me to them."

I stood in the middle of a desert with my feet sinking in the scorching sand. Looking down, I saw I had no hands. I woke up screaming.

❖ ❖ ❖

Before the Meeting for Business, Will came over to me and drew me aside. "I need to express my concern as a physician. I've read your records. I don't know how your injuries play out in your daily life, but you'd be going to isolated areas where medical care might be hard to come by. To preserve your confidentiality, I can't say anything, of course, but I do admit I'm feeling conflicted about that. I want you to consider your condition, as well as the other people who would be with you. It's a rigorous trip, and they'll need to be able to count on you."

"You don't think I should go because of my medical history?"

"As a doctor, I would say this isn't the best trip for you to make at this time. I think your history needs to be a big factor in your decision, but you're the only one who can determine how much weight to give it. If you do go, be sure to take plenty of any prescription medications and take a copy of your medical records. If your condition is precarious in any way, don't go. Be honest about this, Kate. We will all regret it if you aren't."

The Meeting for Business got underway after lunch. After the opening silence, Paul called on Eleanor. After adjusting her glasses, she read a statement about making business decisions that emanated from an understanding of God's will. In my nervousness, I had trouble focusing on the words but forced myself to give them greater attention.

Next, Eleanor read a series of questions that instructed Friends to exercise patience and to wait until a clear sense of the Meeting had been achieved. One question encouraged Friends to weigh the consequences of their actions, as well as the possible outcomes of any lack of action. The silences between the questions gave weight to the words, and my tension grew. How could anyone conduct business like this?

Paul spoke, "Thank you, Eleanor. The first item on the agenda is a request from Katherine Solterra, an attender, to go on the trip to pick up Felipe. A clearness committee from Ministry and Worship met with her on several occasions, and they recommended we consider her request. Since I already have been cleared to go on the trip, I think it prudent for me to step aside as Clerk for this discussion. I have asked Eleanor if she will preside."

Did his stepping aside as Clerk mean he officially opposed my going? I felt members looking at me, and I began to worry. Had someone asked a question? No, the silence continued. Eleanor's last words concerning consequences of inaction echoed in my mind. Someone had failed to act to save me. The drunk driver had been at a bar all night. Someone had known. Someone had known and let it happen. He had been drinking all night. Someone had known. Someone let it happen, I kept repeating.

Will summarized what we'd discussed during the clearness meetings. When he stopped speaking, I realized I hadn't heard a word. Was I supposed to say something now? Why was I here? Breathe. Mind the Light.

"Kate? Don't be nervous. This isn't an inquisition," Will reassured me. "I asked if you could tell us about your feelings of connection to the Delgados, why you feel led to help them."

"I know it's unlikely you would consider a nonmember or a new attender for this trip."

"True," Virgil responded. "But that doesn't mean we're taking you less seriously. Thinking about what Eleanor read, I want to be mindful to set aside my preconceived ideas and listen for divine guidance."

"When you came to my talk about my Congregations for Peace trip," Mark Gilberti spoke, "you admitted you didn't know anything about the sanctuary movement or Central American political issues. This trip involves a significant commitment. I'm concerned that your lack of knowledge could be detrimental. This isn't a situation for a dilettante looking for adventure."

There was an awkward pause. Ruth asked, "It was after Mark's talk that you were run off the road and hurt. Did your interest begin then?"

At last, I thought, a question I could answer. I explained how Graciela and I were teaching each other our native languages and how the family had welcomed and watched over me.

"This trip will require more than feelings of friendship," Suzanne countered. I knew she had an official role, but I couldn't remember what it was. "If the Meeting is going to assume responsibility for you and for what happens, it needs to be sure you'll see this promise through. You're not a permanent resident here. We don't know if you have some kind of hidden agenda. For all we know, you could be working for the INS."

Virgil came to my defense. "Kate is exactly what she's told us, a research scientist on a sabbatical. She didn't search us out; for weeks she didn't even know we existed. She was hurt because of our actions. We tore into her life, not the other way around."

I sipped more of my water. I'd known there would be resistance, but I hadn't thought I'd be accused of anything. More members questioned me. I answered them as comprehensively as I could. "Kate?" Eleanor patted my hand and smiled at me. "We haven't let you tell us about your leading. I understand it has been an unsettling experience for you."

I was aware that my answer would be critical. How could I explain it to them when I didn't understand it myself? "I was camping when it first happened. I'd never been camping before. I panicked and finished the night in the car. I started thinking about Felipe, about how frightened he must be, about what it must feel like to be hunted down. I wondered what was giving him the strength to make this journey, what had sustained the Salvadoran refugees." I reminded myself not to get sidetracked, to stay on point.

"The second night I was camping, I was able to stay in the tent for a longer time. I woke up after having a nightmare about Felipe. Although I couldn't remember the specifics of the dream, I knew he was in danger. When I returned home, I began having more nightmares. One nightmare was so real I thought someone had shot into the cabin. I heard the gunfire and the echoes from the blast, I saw his agony and heard his screams."

Focus. Work your way through this, step by step, I thought, trying to keep my composure. I was glad no one from the Delgado family was present. "I started having many nightmares, almost every night, and it's gotten to the point I'm afraid to go to sleep. I've been trying to take naps during the day, but the nightmares have begun happening then, too. Sometimes Felipe is being tortured, sometimes he's drowning, other times he's running and I can hear his breathing. In one of my recent dreams, I was in a desert, sinking into the sand, and when I looked down, I had no hands, powerless to help.

"As a scientist, I don't believe in signs and omens, but I'm being haunted by these nightmares. I can't stop thinking about Felipe. What if this is a leading and I ignore it? Believe me, getting involved in this is not typical for me. I won't get into details, but I know what happens when someone should get involved but makes the decision not to. It must seem to you that I'm the least likely person here to be experiencing this. But these nightmares, this connection to Felipe, must be happening to me for a reason. Virgil told me once that instead of whispering to me, God perhaps would shout at me. How can I pretend this isn't happening? What if I am being chosen to help Felipe and I refuse? I know it doesn't make sense, but please," I finished, "let me go."

# Chapter 31

IN MARATHON SESSIONS, WE'D practiced Spanish with Emilio, Tomás, and Graciela, and members of the Meeting had spent hours on the telephone setting up arrangements. Now, folding the maps and shutting the Spanish books, Paul looked at me across my kitchen table. "We've run out of time," he said. "Are you ready for this ultimate road trip of approximately sixteen hundred miles?"

"I think so, although I might have been better off not knowing the mileage. I'm not going to attend the special Meeting tonight; I'd better stay here and get a good night's sleep."

"It's not mandatory." Paul placed his books and the maps in his back-pack. He hesitated, then told me, "You need to be sure about this. It's not too late to back out if you want. Stand in the Light, Kate."

After he left, trying to suppress the doubts that dried my tongue and fluttered in my stomach, I checked the contents of my suitcase and travel bag against the lengthy list I'd made, and for the fourth or fifth or eighteenth time, checked to be sure I had my medications, medical records, and rehab notebook.

The Meeting was to begin at seven. At a few minutes after seven, I knew I had to attend. I hesitated before the closed side door, for they didn't like a service to be interrupted unless it was during the time the children left for First Day School. Pushing open the door, I slid soundlessly onto the end of a nearby bench and surrendered to the silence. Half an hour later, no one had spoken. I recognized the suspension I'd felt when they had decided to rescue Emilio and Magdalena. With a velvety silence, it was a gathered Meeting.

My questions and doubts cascaded in a staccato rhythm. Was this right? Could I do this? Was I going because I felt led to oppose this injustice? Or was I going for my own purposes? Was it right to hurt my parents, to cause them worry, to do something they so vehemently opposed? A few weeks ago, they'd come to attend the Founder's Day activities. After the last event, Paul told me Tomás had received a phone call informing him that Felipe would be at the border soon. When I'd told my parents, they'd been stunned, and we'd argued long into the night.

"We nearly lost you once," my mother had said. "When you almost died in the accident, I didn't think I would survive. But that was something beyond your control. How can you place yourself in danger after what you've been through? You have no business going on a trip like this."

My father, familiar with the sanctuary issue, had grasped immediately that Felipe was an illegal alien. He'd shouted, "Is this how we've raised you, to break the law?"

I'd struggled to explain to them why I was going. I told them about the nightmares and about my connection to Felipe as a refugee. My mother had countered, "This isn't the answer, Katherine. We know you've been working to rebuild your life, and we respect what you're doing. But getting mixed up with this illegal sanctuary movement is not going to give you back anything you've lost."

"I don't expect it to; nothing will do that." I fought the buzzing that edged along my skull.

My mother had screamed, her voice raw, "This is a stupid, stupid thing to do, absolutely insane! Don't expect us to support you in any way on this."

"How could you do this to us, after all that has happened?" my father yelled, giving up all pretense of control.

"I'm going, no matter what you say or think. I'm going." We had stared at each other, the kitchen clock sounding loud. My mother had begun crying, and my father had led her out of the kitchen. His arm encircled her as if to ward off the impact of my words, making me an outcast.

They'd left early the next morning, refusing breakfast after deciding not to attend the Meeting. I regretted I couldn't explain my decision better. I knew it wasn't rational, and I agreed with most of the points they'd made. However, I knew I'd caused a break that would be long in the mending.

Diane had been as shocked as my parents. She'd told me, "I don't know what to say. I don't even know what to think. To take such a risk seems so unlike you."

"I know. I wish I could talk to you in person. Fill me in about you, though. How is it?"

"My father sometimes doesn't know who we are. And I am exhausted from the emotional upheaval. I feel I owe you an apology. I've been hard on you at times, expecting you to haul yourself out of those dark holes and get on with things, accept what's happened, and move on. I get it now."

"My friend, you owe me nothing. My heart aches for you."

Opening my eyes, I saw the Meetinghouse was full. Even those who had resisted my going on the trip were there. I knew Suzanne, Will, and Mark had stood aside, saying they could not reconcile my going. I recalled the long silence following my plea to go on the trip during the Meeting for Business. It was uneasy at first, but by steady degrees it settled into a satisfying quiet. At last, Eleanor spoke, with a formality matching the solemnity of the decision: "It appears to be the sense of the Meeting that Katherine Solterra should accompany Paul Whittaker on the trip to rescue Felipe Delgado. Godspeed."

I sensed the slight hum of people beginning to stir. People around me extended their hands, and the service concluded ten minutes after eight. Paul stood. He'd been sitting on the other side of the room where I hadn't been able to see him, though I knew he was present. "Friends, our journey will be strengthened by the power of this worship."

I found myself surrounded by more than a dozen people. Even those I didn't know wished me well, told me to have a safe trip, and to remember they'd hold Paul, Felipe, and me "in the Light," that cherished Quaker phrase. As I drove away, the Meetinghouse looked stalwart, unyielding, firmly in its place.

It was a brilliant morning, the sun ribboning through the trees with a clear and splendid light. Hearing a car, I went outside and saw that the Schoenfelds had followed Paul. I had hoped we could leave without more goodbyes. While Paul put my suitcase in the trunk, Virgil drew me aside. "It's not too late to change your mind. Say the word and I'll get in the car. Eleanor and I have discussed this."

I knew he meant what he said, but I shook my head. "Thanks, Virgil, but no. I'll be fine." I embraced him, startled by how frail he felt.

"Thee has a courageous spirit, Katherine Solterra. Trust it."

Eleanor dug into the sagging pockets of her sweater and brought out her hands full of change. "For the tolls. We raided our piggy bank this morning."

"Only you, Eleanor," Paul said, "would have the foresight! I hope this wasn't your mad money to go to Atlantic City," he teased her. She hugged us, and we got in the car. Standing on my porch steps, they waved until we were past the curve, and I felt a surge of affection for them. Glancing at Paul, I knew he hadn't wanted me to come, though he'd stopped short of standing aside when the Meeting gave its approval. I hoped the entire trip wouldn't be marked by the tension I felt between us now.

Until we got closer to the border, we'd be traveling mostly on interstate highways. It was a tedious, mind-numbing way to get from one place to another. On a break, Paul reviewed our route, spreading out the maps and lists of directions on the car's hood. I watched as he went from one to the other, tracing road lines and making notations. We were headed for Clarksville, Tennessee. Right after I'd been given clearance to join him, I'd talked to Maggie about it. "I trust Paul," I'd told her. "I know I'll be safe with him, but I still feel uneasy. He's against my going."

She'd given an unexpected answer. "Paul is a truly good and kind man. He respects you, and even though he hasn't known you long, he cares for you; you must have felt something. He's smitten, Kate." She had laughed at my expression.

"That's not possible."

"Of course it is. Sometimes it isn't logical and rational. My granny would say, 'Truth will stand when the world's on fire.' You're going to have to stop thinking like a scientist on this one."

That night, like all those to come, we stayed at the home of those participating in the sanctuary movement. Northrup Elkins and his wife, Elizabeth, met us at their door. For some reason, I hadn't expected them to be about my parents' ages. Stiff and aching from sitting in the car for almost eight and a half hours, I stumbled on the threshold, and Paul reached out to keep me from falling. After a tense day, I felt reassured by his touch.

The Elkinses were Methodists. They were warm, welcoming, and genuine. During dinner, they told us how they'd gotten involved in the sanctuary movement after a mission trip to build housing. Elizabeth admitted, "I don't understand the politics. And I know that what we're doing is illegal. I've never broken the law in my life, so this scares me. I've never even had a parking ticket! But we were both brought up in the church, and we can't turn the asylum seekers away. All throughout the Bible, we are commanded to welcome the stranger, to extend hospitality, and to care for the sojourner."

Northrup added, "These people aren't looking for jobs here; they're looking for life. It's easy to stop thinking about them when you turn off the evening news, but once you go down there, the pictures in your mind can't be turned off."

I was grateful when Elizabeth showed me to the guest room and at last I was alone. In a daze from being tired and in pain, I curled up on the bed. I couldn't be in trouble the very first night. Reaching down and getting my medication out of the suitcase, I checked the medication list against the bottle and took a pill for the pain. Swallowing it without water, I waited for it to take effect. Pressing my hands against my forehead and trying to breathe slowly, I knew I was supposed to do something before going to bed, but I couldn't think what it was and fell asleep. I woke up later, realizing I was still dressed and had left the light on.

Needing to go to the bathroom, I panicked. I couldn't remember where Elizabeth had told me it was. What if I opened the wrong door? None of the doors in the hall were open, and all the lights were out. I couldn't even figure out how to get to the living room and the kitchen. Standing at each door I waited and listened but couldn't hear anything. I went back to my room. I'd have to find a bathroom soon. Opening my suitcase, I pulled out my therapy notebook. It had a whole section on "Staying in Strange Places." I'd tagged it with a bright blue bookmark. "It is easy to become confused when staying in a strange place," I read slowly, trying to understand each word. "You won't realize how many coping strategies you have in place at your own home until you travel." This wasn't helping. I already knew I could get confused in strange places.

The checklist looked more promising. "First, look around where you are." Swaying from dizziness and leaning against the wall, I opened the louvered doors near the bedside table. It was a closet with boxes neatly arranged on the floor and a few hangers. Opening the other door in the room, I turned on the light and discovered the bathroom. This is where she had said it was. I felt like a fool. The therapy notebook was right about traveling, though, and I was going to need a whole new set of strategies.

Damn you, I whispered. May you get confused by the simplest of actions, may you not be able to find what you need when you need it.

When we left the Elkinses the next morning, Paul commented, "We'll have a couple more days like today, but then it will probably get tougher. Everything will become more pressured. Not everyone views sanctuary as purely as the Elkinses do. Some might expect us to do things that I, as a Friend, would find unacceptable. Last time we had several offers of guns for our protection. And we were counseled to employ such tactics as switching license plates on the car and using different vehicles."

"But if it would mean getting the refugees into the country, preventing a greater evil?"

"Why not do it? But where do we draw the line?" he asked.

"We're already doing something illegal. We've crossed the line. If we're able to achieve a higher moral law by using such tactics . . . what we're breaking is already so big."

"That adhering to the small points seems ridiculous, right?"

"Yes." I checked out the side window for the exit sign we needed.

"I don't know. But it's important to me to do this as cleanly as possible. Like Elizabeth said last night, breaking the law doesn't come lightly. Opposing my country's government strikes something deep inside. It's much more than knowing I might end up in prison. It calls into question everything I believe, what I've been taught and studied. But we have every reason to believe if we don't get Felipe into this country, if we are not obedient to what we feel is the will of God, he will be murdered."

Leaving the toll road, we stopped at a country church that had picnic tables under shade trees. Searching in the cooler for the lunches Eleanor and Virgil had given us, I found two packages wrapped in blue striped paper, one with Paul's name on it, the other with mine. "What are these?"

"I don't know, I haven't seen them before."

They were blank journal books, gifts from the Schoenfelds. On the inside cover of mine, they had written, "Kate, May the inner journey of your spirit bring you joy. We hold thee in the Light, Eleanor and Virgil."

"What a good idea." Paul opened his and fanned the pages. "And how like Eleanor and Virgil to think of it. I'd mentioned to Virgil I regretted not keeping a record of at least my impressions on our trip together, and he remembered."

After lunch I began driving. The quiet between us felt more and more strained, and I searched for something to ask him. "Have you always been a farmer?"

"What brought that on?"

"It seems an unlikely occupation for you."

"Actually, I'm a lawyer, as well as a farmer."

I stared at him. "Why have you kept it a secret? Do you still practice? I thought you were a full-time farmer."

"I haven't kept being a lawyer a secret. I practiced for six years at a large firm after law school, but I discovered I wasn't cut out for it. I now have a private practice. It's not a full-time endeavor, so I'm a part-time lawyer and a mostly full-time farmer. I inherited the land unexpectedly."

"Law seems an unlikely occupation for you, too."

"I'm afraid to ask what you think *would* be likely. I grew up with the law because my father was a lawyer. He taught me there are certain values one doesn't compromise. He was what they call a 'Virginia gentleman,' a formidable man. He believed in values such as duty, integrity, and that one so important to the generation of which he was a part, honor."

He added, "I don't mean to sound flippant. When I was a teenager, my father represented Morgan Schoenfeld, Eleanor and Virgil's son. You may have heard that he was one of the young men seeking sanctuary from the

Meeting during Vietnam. It had been a torturous time with conflict in the country, the Meeting, and my own family. That was my father's last case."

I slowed down as we neared a tollbooth, and Paul handed me some of Eleanor's change. "What happened?"

"All three cases went badly from the beginning. They were the topic in the press and around town. My dad and I began attending Quaker Meeting, though my mother didn't come. He wanted to understand Morgan's motivation and the Friends' peace testimony. But he continued attending because the silent worship spoke to something within him. Although my mother belonged to a Methodist church, he'd previously not been a churchgoer. His feeling at home in a Quaker Meeting was such a surprise. I'd never known him to be a man comfortable with silence, for he reveled in debates and legal arguments, in storytelling and long conversations. He was eloquent and loved language, even the sounds of words. He used to recite poetry to us. But even though I was just a teenager at the time, I saw a difference in him when he entered the Meetinghouse; the muscles of his face relaxed, and he turned inward. He would put on the silence like a jacket, buttoning up each layer."

I had turned off the toll road, parking in the side lot of a closed business, but Paul seemed not to have noticed. He stared out the window. "All three of the boys were denied conscientious objector status. The Friends had been supportive of my father and our whole family during the court proceedings, and when the case was lost, they continued their support. They wanted my father to know they didn't blame him for the outcome, and that he shouldn't blame himself. Scott went to Canada, and Morgan and Jacob were sent to Vietnam. Morgan wasn't there long before being killed. My father was devastated—we all were. He'd gotten close to Morgan, something he didn't do with clients. At the time, I was young enough to feel jealous and shut out, but old enough to understand how critical their rapport was.

"A couple of weeks after Morgan's funeral, Virgil came to see my father. They took a walk and talked for hours." Paul stopped, and I waited for him to continue. "Three months later, my father died of a heart attack. All during the case he'd had problems with his heart, but we didn't know. And although Virgil has never said so, I have a feeling my father told him he was ill, and during that long talk, I think Virgil reassured my father we'd be looked after, cared for, and cared about." Paul rubbed his face with his hands and drank some water. "I miss him, Kate. The sound of his voice, the way he looked at my mother. His wise counsel. His knowledge of the law. I wish I could talk to him about this."

"What would he think?"

"He'd support my defending the Delgado family in court, but as far as participating in the sanctuary movement, I imagine he would have disagreed with my breaking the immigration laws. There are many reasons why it's best to work through available channels to change the laws, and I'll continue trying to do that. For now, I'm acting on an individual situation. I feel I am being called to save someone's life. I hope my father would have respected me for trying to be obedient to the will of God."

"What happens if you're convicted of felony charges?"

"I could be disbarred, for one thing. Your next question is why am I doing this, why not let someone else make this trip? And, by the way, you do realize I could be asking you these same questions? To answer you, there are some practical reasons. My being a lawyer might be useful, and I've been there before, I know the way. I'm not married with a family to be concerned about. And there are some impractical reasons."

"Such as?"

"An inexplicable need once in a while to tilt at windmills."

# Chapter 32

An unforgiving vault of heat and mugginess clamped over us. I drove the remaining hours to Shreveport, Louisiana, and when I swung into the driveway of the green-shuttered, low-lying house where we were spending the night, Paul noticed someone peeking from one side of a parted curtain.

"Cloak and dagger stuff," I commented, though I remembered when Paul had moved aside the curtains before opening the door to me that time.

"Not what we want to promote."

A boy dressed in khaki shorts and a bright purple shirt trotted out of the carport, motioning for me to drive around to the back of the house. "But there's no driveway."

"Do what he wants."

I saw numerous bicycles and lawn chairs strewn about the side yard. We got out of the car and introduced ourselves to the boy, who looked to be about thirteen. "Come on in, I'm Nick." Because they had drawn the curtains, my eyes had to adjust in order to see the Seale family with Harry and Melanie, the parents, and their older teenagers, Eric and Marty.

"Any trouble getting here?" Harry asked. He was taller than Paul, his sun-bleached hair a strong contrast to his tanned face.

"No, your directions were perfect," Paul told him, shaking his hand.

"Y'all come sit down and have something cold to drink," Melanie invited, her speech as sweet and Southern as the iced tea she gave me. "You look done in." She drew me into the kitchen where they had tacked burlap over the windows.

"Dad said we could be guards, and we're going to take turns so you'll feel safe here," Nick, the youngest of the three boys, told us.

"That's not necessary. We're not advertising what we're doing, but we're not going to skulk around, either." Paul added, "There's no need to cover the windows unless you'd feel more at ease."

"Don't you worry," Harry said. "We got it all worked out, and it's no inconvenience."

I wondered what this family expected to happen. What had they been told? Or maybe I was the one who didn't know what was going on.

"Planning to keep guard with those?" Paul pointed to two guns on the kitchen counter. Rags and a bottle of cleaning fluid were next to them.

"I guess you don't approve," Harry said, "being Quakers and all. But it might come down to where we need them. You can do what you want, but I've got to protect my family, you two, and whoever you're bringing back. We've had some tricky situations at the border. You don't know anything about the person you're bringing here, either. Some of them are desperate, after what they've experienced. I wouldn't ask you to do something against your religion. By the same right, you can't keep me from doing what I think might be necessary."

We were at an impasse, and I was curious to see if Paul would suggest we leave. I was dizzy and suspected the heat and humidity were the issue. Hoping the dizziness would recede if I lowered my head, I bent over and retied my shoes.

Harry continued. "I admire you Quakers, your beliefs and working for peace, but I want to know what would've happened if people like my father hadn't been around after Pearl Harbor. I was in Vietnam, myself."

I imagined this was an argument Quakers often heard. The boys drifted out of the room, but Nick returned momentarily and leaned against the wall. Melanie and I sat at the high kitchen counter and drank our iced tea. If the decision were up to me, I'd leave. The closed curtains in the daytime made me feel as though we were underground, and I felt I couldn't get my bearings. Harry asked Paul if he'd been in Vietnam.

"No. I wasn't old enough at the time."

"But if we went to war, you wouldn't go?"

"I'd have no objection to serving in some sort of relief or medical care capacity, but no, I wouldn't fight." They carried on with their discussion while Melanie asked me questions about our trip.

Finally, Harry gave a short laugh and slapped the kitchen counter. "We're not going to see eye to eye. I guess you won't be stopping here on your way back, but at least stay the night."

I didn't say anything, determined that Paul wouldn't have to make concessions for me. Paul answered, "We'd like to stay, thank you."

With everyone careful not to offend, I was glad when dinner was over. As soon as I could, I excused myself and went into the den. Melanie had pulled out and made up the sofa bed for me, leaving fresh towels on the coffee table. Under the pretext of getting something out of the car, I walked through the house and returned to the den, surreptitiously making a map. I was set. It felt good to slip between the cool sheets, and although I tried to relax, I couldn't get comfortable. The room was stifling, and I realized the air conditioning unit in the den wasn't on. I turned it on and fell asleep despite the loud humming.

Waking up in the middle of the night, I struggled to breathe; the air conditioner had stopped working. I opened the other window, but although the night had cooled some, the mugginess was oppressive. With my flashlight on my map, I tiptoed down the hall to the bathroom for water. Calm down, I told myself. You'll be fine. It's the weather. Maybe Paul could get the air conditioner to work. After all, the man knew how to fix tractors. Using my flashlight and map again, I found my way to the living room and woke him up.

"Kate? What's wrong?"

"The air conditioner stopped working, and it's hard to breathe. Can you see if you can fix it?"

He couldn't get the air conditioner to work, either. "Let's switch places; you stay in the living room where it's cool. I'll be fine in the den."

I wanted to protest but knew I couldn't run the risk of having more trouble. Paul stayed with me in the living room until my breathing improved. "I'm fine now, thanks. Let's try to get more sleep."

He left for the den, switching off the overhead light on his way. I heard a slapping sound and immediately the light came back on. When I raised my head, I saw Nick holding a gun with unsteady hands.

"Easy, son, put the gun down. It's Paul and Kate."

The boy looked down at the weapon as though noticing it for the first time. "I'm s-sorry," he stammered. He blinked quickly, his face draining of color. "Oh, God, what if I'd shot you?" He slumped down in a chair. Taking the gun from the boy, Paul slipped on the safety and unloaded it, placing it on a table with the gun's barrel pointing away from us. For a Quaker, I noticed, he seemed to know his way around a gun.

"I heard some noises and thought someone had broken in, you know, to stop you. Eric and Marty said I couldn't handle one of the watches, that I'd be too scared or I'd fall asleep. When I heard a noise . . . what's going on?"

Paul explained about the air conditioner. Nick, shaken and embarrassed, kept apologizing. "Nick, we can talk about this in the morning." The boy started to retrieve the gun, but Paul stopped him. "I'd prefer that you leave the gun with me, please."

It took a long time for me to fall asleep, and when I woke, it was later than we'd planned to leave. By the time I was dressed, the boys had gone to school. Melanie gave me a glass of orange juice and a plate of scrambled eggs and bacon. "We're so sorry about last night. The den is an addition to the house and doesn't have central air. We'll need to get the unit repaired or replace it right away. Why didn't you say something?" She poured coffee in my cup.

I sat down with my breakfast. "Thanks. This looks wonderful. The air conditioner was working at the beginning, but by the time I realized it had quit, it was too late. Anyway, I'm all right now."

"We were discussing the idea that you should stay here with us, and Paul can pick you up on his way back," Harry said.

Was this Paul's idea? "My breathing is fine this morning."

"The humidity is lower and it's cooler; it probably won't stay like that," Paul told me. I could see his face tighten.

Melanie stood and put her dishes in the sink. "We'll leave you two to decide this. Harry and I need to get to work. You're welcome to stay, Kate. It would be no problem at all, and we'd feel better if you didn't try to go on. But if you decide to go, please be careful."

Harry seemed more subdued this morning, the hard lines of his bluster blurred. He coughed, started to say something, stopped, and at last said, "I'd like to say a prayer for you before you go, if it's all right."

"Of course." Paul put down his coffee cup and bowed his head.

"Heavenly Father, we humbly ask your blessing on Kate, Paul, and Felipe. Please keep them safe and help them, Lord, to do your work. Please help Kate to breathe easily and to be able to adapt to the humidity so she can continue to be part of your great mission. May they be guided on the route and not have any issues with the car. We ask you to keep them from harm as they travel, and give them wisdom and traveling mercies every step of the way. In Jesus's name, we pray, Amen."

The Seales left for work. Paul laughed. "Oh, Kate. If you could see your face right now."

"I've never been . . ." I held up my hands, at a loss for words.

"Prayed over by a Baptist?"

"And so specifically. I'm not making fun of him. He was genuine."

"Fervent, even."

"Yes."

Paul grinned. "Makes the Quakers seem downright dull by comparison." He helped me to clear the table. "Considering your situation, you're under no obligation to continue, and I want you to think about staying here. You could fly back. Maybe you should call Will and talk to him."

"I won't hold you back, if that's what you're worried about."

"I'm worried about you. It scared me to see you gasping for air last night. What if we get into an isolated area on the border and you can't breathe well?"

"I'm not going to stay here with this family of gun-toting children or fly back home. It's the humidity. It will be drier where we're going, but if I have more problems, if I can't keep up, I'll go back. I won't put Felipe in jeopardy, but I'm not going to be undone by the weather."

"You might be undone by your own stubbornness," he responded in a clipped tone.

While I washed the rest of the breakfast dishes and left a note thanking the Seales, Paul loaded the car. Usually, he packed carefully, storing everything in the same spots each time. This morning he shoved boxes into the trunk and tossed the suitcases on top of them. Our destination was a Catholic mission center in Corpus Christi, Texas, seven hours from here. We'd lost more than two hours already, and although it was my turn to drive, he wouldn't let me. "Get some rest."

Unable to sleep, though, I stared out the window. No wonder Paul was out of patience with me. Until the accident, I'd led a simple, uncomplicated life. Since living in Drake's Springs, however, my history included a temper tantrum that landed me in the emergency room, a broken bone from being run off the road, debilitating nightmares, and difficulty breathing. I couldn't blame Paul—I was a liability.

As we went farther, the land became dusty and dry, devoid of reference points, of anything to draw the eye and entice a longer look. Unlike the landscape of the Shenandoah Valley, with its serene mountains folding over each other in the distance, rounded hills of purple and blue, this land—no grass, few trees, and its thirsty, cracked ground—made me feel anchorless.

Unsure I wanted to know, I asked, "Did Harry say anything to Nick about the gun?"

"He advised him to hit the light switch first before he aims. Poor kid, he kept apologizing to me all last night and this morning. He camped outside the living room, listening to see if you were breathing all right."

"I'm not a helpless female who has to be protected. It unnerves me to be scrutinized."

"I wouldn't be so quick to interpret kindness as condescension. And I'm not sure you can stand on the line that draws the circle, be a person apart and a person included at the same time."

"I can if I'm the one who draws it," I shot back.

Paul turned the wheel, and the car's tires bit into the gravel with a sickening sound. He parked, wrenched out of the car, and stood in front of it. Picking up a handful of gravel, he threw the rocks one by one down the road, where they caromed off the asphalt. When he came over to me, I was reluctant to face him.

"We've got to resolve this because too much depends on us. We can't be tangled in a fight we haven't declared."

I nodded, hoping if we talked this out, the tension would dissolve.

"Here it is from my side. I think the Meeting's wrong. I think they've attached some sort of mystical aura to your nightmares and to what happened to you on that mountain ridge. I don't doubt your experiences, but I do question connecting them to your wish to come on this trip. I'm angry with myself for going along with it, for not protesting their decision more than I did, especially since I knew about your injuries. I was irresponsible. I should have stopped them from allowing you to come. Ethically, Will couldn't have done that, but I could—and should have." He shook his head. "I ignored what Eleanor read about the consequences of a lack of action." He stooped down beside the opened car door. "And I think you haven't been honest with me. About what, I don't know, but I'm not going to force it from you. Maybe you think it won't make a difference, but Felipe's life might depend on our adherence to the truth."

I knew what he said was right. In attempting to become a different person, had the essential truths of who I was slipped away unguarded, like coins into water? And were the new truths formed around my mountain persona flawed because of my evasions and omissions, the lies tiny chisels chipping away at the internal rock, threatening collapse? I could not face what I would not name. I had no answer for him. His expression changed, an almost imperceptible closing down, and he let out his breath slowly. He got back in the car and we continued, the strain between us a vibrating wire.

"Do you need directions to the Mission?"

"I remember the way. We should be there about five or so." He pointed to the dashboard's clock. "Strange, I hadn't noticed this before. I guess I always look at my watch instead, but I forgot to put it on this morning. I set the clock for the central time zone when we were in Tennessee, but I hadn't realized it was still on standard time. Would you please reset it? I think you hold the button down on the left. The minutes look close enough."

I stared at the clock. What was he talking about? "The clock is wrong?"

"It never got set to daylight saving time. This is Josiah's car, but since his wife's illness, he doesn't use it much. It's old and doesn't have many fancy features, but I borrowed it because it's so large; we'd never have gotten all this stuff in my car or yours. Press the button on the left for the hour."

"What hour?"

"You know, 'Spring forward and fall back'? Go forward, since I already have it in the correct time zone."

Spring forward to what? Daylight saving time? How do you save daylight? I felt a cold fluttering down my spine. Think, I told myself. Pay attention to what he's saying, figure it out. "What time should it be?" I had to ask.

"An hour ahead," he emphasized, spacing out his words.

I stared at the clock. An hour ahead. Ahead what? A head? To what?

Paul steered the car off the road and stopped it in the sparse shade of a straggly tree.

"You're acting as if you don't know what I'm talking about." He reached over, punched the button, and held it until the time was correct. "Is any medication you're taking making you groggy?" He offered me the perfect out, but I felt defeated, beyond caring, beyond the ability to keep up this charade. I'd fooled myself into thinking I'd made more progress than I had.

I dreaded telling him the truth. I brought into focus what Maggie had told me about him. At the time, I'd pushed it away, telling myself she'd meant he cared for me in a sort of spiritual sense, an all-enveloping Quaker sort of love toward one's neighbor. I hadn't wanted to consider she'd meant something else. After all, we hardly knew each other. But what woman wouldn't love Paul? He was intelligent, compassionate, and considerate. That he was good-looking hadn't escaped my notice, either. This was a man I cared about, and I knew I needed to stop lying to him and to myself. He was right about needing to be honest. Getting out of the car, I leaned against the tree and slid down to the ground.

He knelt on the ground in front of me. "What is it?" With all traces of his earlier impatience gone, his soft voice tore at my composure, serrating the edges.

I raised my head. "I don't know what you're talking about. Those phrases don't mean anything to me, 'standard time' and 'daylight saving time.' How can you save daylight? When you say, 'spring forward,' I don't know what you mean. An hour ahead of what? Fall back to what? Standard for whom? It's confusing. I can't make sense out of what you're saying."

"At our next opportunity, we'll call Will. I sure wish my phone worked around here."

"It's not the medicine."

"You're not making sense; maybe you're having some kind of reaction."

Turning my head, I looked out over the empty field. Such a desolate land, the perfect metaphor for how I felt right now. I'd been naive to think I could pull this off. I should have listened to my parents.

"I told you I'd been hurt by a drunk driver. I sustained a severe head injury that left me with permanent brain damage." I heard Paul draw in his breath, but I pressed on. "I relearned how to speak, walk, and drive a car; how to do simple, ordinary things like get dressed, make a bed, make coffee, and write my name. Although I've made a great deal of progress, it's far from being over. I doubt it ever will be. I will always struggle to remember names of objects, where I put things, what I'm doing; it's a daily challenge with my short-term memory. When you and the others came for coffee and dessert and to meet my parents, I made a picture chart of the furniture because I couldn't think of the phrase 'coffee table.' I came to Drake's Springs to continue recovering and to make some decisions. I can't be a scientist any longer, at least not in my current position. I've resigned my job, effective the end of May. At least now there are weeks, even months, at a time when I do well.

"I didn't want people to know about my condition because I didn't want to be viewed as a victim. On some level, I thought if no one knew, I could pretend it hadn't happened, and I could become a different person. I have to face the fact, however, that although I might succeed in becoming a different person, I'll still be someone with brain damage." At last, I faced him but couldn't read his expression.

"This is one of those times when there are no adequate words." He closed his eyes for a moment before standing and going back to the car. He returned with water bottles from the cooler. Pouring water on a bandanna, I wiped my face and pressed the cloth to my eyes. They were irritated from the dust and the heat; the cloth's wet coolness felt delicious.

"When we get to the mission center, I'm going to call the Meeting and make arrangements for you to go back."

"Because of what I told you? That's not fair."

"It's not a matter of fairness."

"You didn't want me to come in the first place, and now this is a convenient reason for you to send me back."

"It's not for convenience. There's more at stake here than the two of us."

"Why did you let me come? I thought in Quaker Meetings if someone objected and consensus couldn't be reached, a decision would be postponed."

"It's not quite that simple. I didn't serve as Clerk, but I didn't stand aside, either. The committee members saw something I didn't, and I decided it was important to honor and trust the process, and to trust them."

"What did they see?"

"Something not even you see yet, an unassailable spirit. But it doesn't change my mind about your returning to Drake's Springs."

"I don't want to go back."

"I need to be able to count on you. When Virgil and I were here, there were times when we had to split up and look for Emilio and Magdalena separately. How can I leave you alone to do something like that? You couldn't reset the clock. You've had trouble breathing. I can't look for Felipe and look after you as well."

"You don't need to look after me, and you don't need to patronize me."

His words came out in pizzicato bursts. "Don't misunderstand me. I'm sorry for what's happened to you. It doesn't change how I feel about you, but it's an extra consideration now. We can't jeopardize Felipe's safety because you came looking for answers, for solutions to your problems. And I can't risk your safety, either. I can't believe Will allowed the Meeting to make this decision, even with patient confidentiality. He was privy to more specific information than I had. If they had known, they wouldn't have let you come."

"Sometimes medical reports don't translate well into specific, day-to-day realities. Don't blame him. I didn't explain to him what it's like for me."

"You cannot be down here if you can't think clearly. I don't say this to hurt you, but because we have to be honest." Picking up a stone and flinging it across the field, his anger surfaced as quickly as the dust where the stone landed. "What the hell did you think you were going to do down here? Did you come along to play Quaker, to search for peace to silence the demons in your own life? I'll tell you something, Katherine, that peace over the years has been bought with blood. We've put Felipe's life on the line, and if we lose him because you can't remember simple words, you'll have an insight into that drunk driver's soul you *never* counted on."

I imagined his words scoring my flesh, and spreading my hands on the ground to steady myself, I half expected to see them bleeding. Picking up the bottles of water, he started back to the car. I waited for the echoes of what he'd said to recede, to stop thumping against the inside of my chest. I wished that rather than being in the car's close confines, Paul and I could be at opposite ends of a freight train, with tons of metal and iron and deafening clamor separating his anger and my confusion. Maybe he was right. Maybe I should go back to Drake's Springs, pack up, and go home.

I stumbled over to the car. He'd started it and had turned up the air conditioning. Reclining the seat, I put my head back, closed my eyes, and let him drive the rest of the way to the mission. He'd been right about another thing, too; the tension increased as we got closer to the border. The silence between us was like pellets of dry ice.

# Chapter 33

THE STEEPLE OF THE Santa Teresa Mission in Corpus Christi rose above the walled enclosure. Well-weeded flowerbeds, primly edged with bricks, marked the iron entrance gate. The setting sun coated the bricks with pale pink, giving the church a fairy-tale appearance.

A Franciscan friar, dressed in a brown habit tied with a knotted cord, greeted us at the main door, its wooden front adorned with an ornately carved cross. With his red beard and blue eyes, he looked like he'd be more at home somewhere in New England rather than in Texas. "I was getting worried about you. Welcome back!" He greeted Paul and smiled down at me.

"Kate, Father Michael O'Meara; he is the director here. Father Michael, this is Katherine Solterra."

The friar shook my hand. "Welcome to Santa Teresa Mission."

"We got a late start this morning, and the trip here took longer than expected," Paul explained. "I tried to call you but couldn't get through."

We followed the friar through the door, down a corridor, and into a spacious kitchen with gleaming appliances. A Mexican woman, dressed in a simple habit, set dishes on a long table.

"Sister Guadalupe, you remember Paul Whittaker, and this is Katherine Solterra. They've completed a long trip."

"You'll be hungry, no? One of my favorite things is to feed hungry people." Sister Guadalupe, Sister Guadalupe, Sister Guadalupe, I repeated to myself. Names quickly evaporated when I was this tired.

After days of elaborate meals prepared by our hosts, the beef stew and homemade wheat bread were the epitome of simple perfection. Finished with serving us, the sister left the kitchen. The emotions of the day curled around my ankles. My legs felt weighted with fatigue, and I hoped the food would revive me. Paul and Father Michael discussed the details of what would be happening. Aching as though I had the flu, I wanted to crawl into bed and escape the day's concerns. We finished dinner, and the sister, appearing as quietly as she had previously disappeared, showed me to my room. With the long skirts of her habit skimming the stone floors, she seemed to float. I hadn't thought any sisters still wore the long habits.

"I'll never remember my way back," I said, hoping she would give me easy directions. "I should have saved my bread and dropped crumbs."

"It's easy to get lost in an unfamiliar place. You will rest better if you don't have even small worries." She pulled a pen and a notebook from a pocket in the folds of her skirt. "I'll draw you a map." Humming to herself, she sketched a layout, labeled it, and gave it to me. I was so grateful I wanted to hug her.

The room was plain, but a woven rug, a vase of flowers by the bed, and delicate lace edging on the pillowcases and bedspread saved the room from austerity. On the bedside table were a reading lamp and a Bible. I felt more at ease than I had since leaving Drake's Springs. The uncluttered room possessed a welcoming air of privacy, a suspension of sound and movement that touched something familiar in me, though I couldn't place it. I basked in the peacefulness of the space and felt my tension recede. This room was lovely and light, cool and spare, and I fell asleep before I could plan how to convince Paul to let me continue on the trip.

I woke up before dawn with an unexpected feeling of happiness. I felt tempted to stay in this magical cocoon of a room but knew I had to find Paul. I met Father Michael in one of the corridors. "Good morning. You're up early; did you not sleep well?" he asked.

I hesitated. Phrases beginning with "did you not" confused me because I never knew whether to answer yes or no. "I slept unusually well, Father, thank you."

"I'm glad, for you needed the rest. Let's go eat breakfast. Sister Guada-lupe makes the best pancakes, bar none."

Sister Guadalupe told us Paul had eaten earlier. She didn't say where he was, and I didn't ask. Since our discussion under the tree yesterday, we'd not talked except for a few necessary words. Although I didn't regret my decision to tell him the truth, his silence was like the fog that often covered the mountains in the mornings; it changed the shape of familiar objects, the timbre of voices, and the sound of footsteps. I couldn't see or hear what was coming next, and the untethered feeling made me uneasy.

The sisters went about their chores, acknowledging my presence with-out intruding. After doing my laundry and repacking my suitcase with the clean clothes, I added to the journal the Schoenfelds had given me. Eleanor and Virgil seemed far away and long ago, as though I'd imagined them. By three o'clock, I paced in the courtyard and waited for word about Felipe.

Father Michael had said Felipe or a volunteer might call at any time. At four thirty, I slipped into the chapel, its coolness gliding across my skin. Shadows divided the interior into angles, and as if waiting for me to speak, statues of saints peered from alcoves. Obliging, I said to one carved face, "*No tengo nada que decirle. No quedan secretos.* I have nothing to tell you. No secrets left." After all, I had told my secret to Paul, and although the earth did not shake, the trees did not uproot, we were changed.

The next day we continued to wait. Paul kept to himself for most of the day, and the discord intensified between us, a prairie of disapproval and distrust. Tired of being cooped up within the mission's enclosure and having no other chores to do, I decided to take a walk. I'd go in a straight line, turn around, and come back the same way.

Outside the courtyard's gate, I looked up and down the street, trying to choose a direction. Arbitrarily turning left, I began walking, swinging my arms to loosen the tightness. The sun felt good on my arms and legs, and I began to relax. Although everyone had been attentive and, at the same time, respectful of my privacy, I relished being out on my own for a time, away from the inscribed patterns and customs of the mission, away from the sisters' watchful eyes, away from Paul.

It was not long before the tidy brick homes and buildings surrounding the mission gave way to unpainted wooden structures, held together more by hope and habit than from nails and solid beams. Skidding on the disintegrating sidewalk, I almost lost my balance. I looked up to see people loitering in doorways and children playing in the dirt yards dotted with cast-off appliances and furniture. They viewed me with suspicion, making me feel self-conscious. A barricade circled a missing section of sidewalk. Stepping into the street, I saw a store and decided to get a cold drink.

Inside the store I found a drink and paid for it, speaking in Spanish to the proprietor. Feeling more confident for having had a small adventure, I turned to head back toward the mission. I started speaking to the children and stopped once to listen to music blaring from a house painted with color-ful graffiti. Statues of saints protected an overgrown garden in the front yard.

Something about the graffiti house bothered me, but I didn't know why. I completed another block before I figured it out: I hadn't seen the house before, and even I would have remembered it. It could have been on the other side of the street, I reasoned, and since I'd kept looking down at the sidewalk to avoid tripping on the uneven concrete, I might not have seen it. Quickening my pace, I glanced from side to side to see if anything looked familiar. Some of the houses were little more than wooden huts. I stopped at a street corner. I realized I should be passing the brick houses near the mission's neighborhood by now. What had happened? How could I have gotten lost? I'd been careful not to stray onto any side streets. I'd stayed in a straight line. When I turned around, though, was it possible I'd made a quarter turn instead of a half? Did the store have more than one exit? When I went into the store for my drink, had I gotten confused? That must have been what happened. All I needed to do was turn around and walk until I reached the store.

Half an hour later, though, I hadn't found the store. Hot, thirsty again, and with my legs aching, I sat down on the curb. Soon it would be dark. When I didn't show up for dinner, Paul would set out looking for me. I wouldn't have any excuses left, and he would force me to go home. Considering that perhaps I hadn't gone quite far enough to find the store, I started jogging, ignoring the pains in my legs. How incapable could I be? Paul was right that I had no business coming here. I couldn't even go on a simple outing without getting lost.

I didn't notice the end of the sidewalk and pitched from the curb onto the street, skidding over the gravel with my arms spread out. The force of the fall practically knocked the wind out of me, and although I could hear cars rumbling nearby, I couldn't manage to get up. Lying in the mud and gravel, I felt humiliated. In the background, I heard voices and screen doors opening and banging closed; I soon felt a hand on my shoulder.

"*Señorita, señorita.*" Someone asked if I needed an ambulance. I struggled to my feet and replied in Spanish that no, I was not hurt.

Before I could protest, someone else guided me into a house and settled me onto a sagging sofa. An older woman bathed my face and arms with a cool cloth. It felt refreshing, and I let her continue. With what energy I had left draining from me, I limply submitted to her ministrations. She dotted my arms and legs with something that stung briefly, all the while looking up at me, smiling, and speaking in Spanish. Another woman gave me a glass of water and a mug of spicy, hot soup.

I explained in Spanish that I had gotten lost. I stopped, realizing I needn't have run off in different directions. All I had to do was stop someone and ask for directions back to the . . . where was I staying? What was the name of it? Where was it? The women hugged me as though I were a child, and I let them take care of me; these were wise and caring women, and they were not going to let me go until I was more stable. "Take the warm coat," I heard Will saying. I let out my breath in a shudder and managed to smile back at them. When they asked where I was staying, I told them I couldn't remember the name. Proffering more soup between their questions, they asked if it were a hotel downtown, if I were with a tourist group. "*No,*" I explained, "*un lugar católico,*" a place with sisters and a friar. Someone exclaimed, "¡*La Misión de Santa Teresa!*"

"¡*Misión de Santa Teresa!*" I repeated and asked if they could write out directions. One woman called out a name over her shoulder. The others laughed and said of course, that was the best thing to do.

After a flurry of motherly pats from the women, they led me back outside to meet the patriarch of the group, a monument of a man with a wild thatch of white hair. With a flourish, he presented an ancient motor scooter with a sidecar. Helping me in, he handed me a leather helmet even older than the scooter. The women waved from the house's porch, and we took off, the scooter smoking and sputtering. On the ride to the mission, the man flung his arms out to show me various sights and roared gleefully at whatever he was shouting. I began laughing, as well, caught up in his mood, now seeing the humor in the situation.

At the mission's gate, he helped me out of the sidecar as Paul and Father Michael emerged from the courtyard. Kissing me on both cheeks, the man presented me to them as though we were at a formal dance. Whirling around, he took off before they could say anything to him or before I could thank him.

"I'd like to speak to Kate alone, please, Father."

Father Michael went back into the inner courtyard. Paul looked at me, taking in the scrapes and torn clothing from my fall. "Are you all right?"

"Yes."

"Where have you been? Why didn't you notify someone you were going out? What did you think you were doing?" He motioned to my cuts. "What happened?"

"I fell."

He paused for a long moment. "Get your things. We received word an hour ago that we need to go pick up Felipe ourselves. He's in the area between Monclova and Castaños in Mexico; he may have gone by now. But first we have to get to Laredo."

Rushing to my room, I scooped up the few items on the bedside table and threw them into the suitcase. Back outside, Father Michael and Sister Guadalupe said a hurried goodbye, the friar blessing us with his hands on our shoulders. I was reluctant to get in the car, realizing the silence between us now had an extra layer.

I thought about my walk while Paul drove. Why hadn't it occurred to me to stop and ask someone for directions? My Spanish was more than adequate for that. With shame, I admitted to myself I'd been wary of the people because the area was so poor.

He interrupted my thoughts. "I need to know where you are every moment."

"I hadn't planned to be gone long."

"It doesn't matter. You should have written a note, at least."

"I know." I didn't want to tell him I'd planned to leave a note, but between thinking about the note and writing it, I'd forgotten about it. And I didn't want to tell him how I'd gotten lost or about the family who had to take care of me because I'd gotten rattled. Thinking about the family, though, made me smile. They had a sort of aggressive, madcap solicitousness about them with the hot soup being poured down my throat, the antiseptic for my cuts being dabbed from different directions, the women's kind concern, the zany motor scooter ride, and the man's ebullience. They restored my perspective and allowed me to regain my equilibrium. I was grateful to them. Eleanor, you win again. Small kindnesses abound.

# Chapter 34

## MEXICO

As if warning devices could sense my guilt, I half expected lights to flash and alarms to sound when we crossed into Mexico from Laredo. On our way to Monclova, we stopped at a gas station to check the map. Paul had been directed to look for a run-down house about a half mile off the main road. Once we made a wrong decision about an unmarked fork in the road, and after five miles, Paul turned around, nearly dropping the rear wheel off the shoulder. He drove back to the fork. "I guess Harry Seale was right to pray for help with the directions," he murmured.

Outside the city limits of Monclova, I saw a shack, nearly obscured by brush and vines, set far off the road. I pointed to it. "Is that it?"

"Yes, I think so. I don't know how you spotted it." He drove behind the abandoned structure with its rotting and broken boards.

"How will we know it's Felipe?"

"He looks like his brothers. Haven't I told you this before? And he has a scar on his right cheek from a childhood accident or something."

Inside, we found a bed with a couple of filthy blankets and a table with two chairs. A rusty, lopsided stove and a sink comprised the kitchen, and an outhouse listed to one side in the backyard. "When was he supposed to get here?"

"At about dawn. He could be lost or feel it's not safe right now to move, or he may have come and gone already."

"If he comes, will we wait here until dark before going back to the mission?"

"Depends on what Felipe tells us. I don't know if we'll be going back there."

Paul kept his answers short. His frustration with me created a distance as exact as paper between us. Since our argument, we'd continued to move and speak cautiously, formality providing safety. It felt like a hole in a knitted sweater, though, with the temptation of pulling on the one strand that would unravel the entire garment. At least our arguing had felt more honest than this extreme courtesy, each careful to remain on the line being etched on the glass in front of us.

After dinner we agreed on a schedule to stand watch. When it was my turn to sleep, I settled under the blanket, too tired to care how dirty it was or how grubby I felt. Falling asleep immediately, I was startled awake in what seemed like moments. Paul shook my shoulders, lifting me until I was propped against the wall.

"You were having a nightmare, and you were screaming." Tucking his jacket behind my back for a pillow, he draped another blanket over me. It had amazed us how cold it could feel here at night. "Tell me about it."

I felt flattened. I watched while he opened bottles of water and rummaged for a package of cookies.

He sat at the foot of the bed. "Tell me."

"No." I was afraid he'd again argue I should go home, and that if I told him, it would make the nightmare stay in my mind.

He repeated, "Tell me, Kate."

His eyes held mine until I found myself answering. "The car keeps coming and coming, and I know it's not going to stop. His car is enormous, the size of a city building, but mine is like a plastic toy car. The driver laughs maniacally; everyone around me watches and points at me, but no one does anything to help me. In fact, they cheer him on. What's odd is that there's no sound, no crash, but I keep waiting for it, knowing it's going to happen and will be horrendous." I stopped.

"Is there more?"

"This time those men from Maggie's store are in the car with the driver. Their faces look misshapen and distorted, their features not human exactly, but not caricatures, either." I swallowed hard. "They all turn at one time, their mouths gaping. I'm dismembered, arms and legs on opposite sides of the road. My head is on top of his car."

"No," he whispered and closed his eyes.

"I don't know how to make my peace with this. I'm sick to death of constantly ending up in tears. Every time I vow to move on, to get past it, something happens and I slide back down."

We lapsed into a familiar quiet. I felt unable to move, exhausted beyond caring. Aware of a dull pain in my legs and an aching in my face, I heard Will's advice: "If you're cold and someone offers you a warm coat, you should take it." It shouldn't be this difficult, I thought. I asked, "Would you hold me?" With his arms around me I felt warmer and supremely safe.

He asked, "What is your life like now? I'd like to understand how your life has changed."

Once more, my first thought was if I told him, he'd send me back. But my next thought was to tell him the truth. Wanting to melt into the warmth of being held, I let out a long sigh and began. "I've told you that I had to relearn ordinary tasks. What I knew as a biochemist, what I gained through study and research, is of course much more complicated to relearn. Right now, I can't keep the isolated pieces of information in my mind long enough to grasp the whole scope of it; even if one day I manage to regain the factual knowledge, will I have the cognitive ability to use those facts, to solve problems on a high level? I'm beginning to have evidence it's not ever going to happen, no matter how long I study and work at it. College, grad school, and my postdoc work took me almost fourteen straight years. I can't see myself going through that again, even if I could."

"You'll always be a scientist, Kate. It's how you walk in the world, who you are."

"I'd like to think that is true. I will so miss that life." I swallowed away the ache in my throat. "There are weeks when everything clicks along well. But it's the irritating, daily frustrations that wear on me. I get numbers reversed and make a lot of wrong phone calls. I used to be a punctual person, even early for appointments, but now I'm always running late because I look two and three times to see if the iron and the stove are off, if the doors are locked. I'll glance at the stove, turn around, and have to look back. I write a check, review it, put it in an envelope, and take it back out to see if it's signed. When the envelope is sealed, I can't remember if I signed the check, or even if I put it in the envelope."

"Everyone does some of those things."

"Yes, and they sound trivial and irrelevant even to me when I list them out loud like this. But I do them all day long, every day. I open a kitchen cabinet and stand before it, unable to figure out why I opened it. Sometimes, the topic we're discussing will escape me, no matter how long we've been talking about it. I'll forget people's names the instant they're told to me, and sometimes I can't recall the names of people I've known for a long time. I've blanked out on your name. By dinnertime, I won't remember what was for lunch, or even if I ate lunch. I could give you dozens of examples.

"After I came out of the coma, some information and memories came back in large chunks. Sometimes seeing a particular object or hearing a name will unlock a small treasure chest of memories. Other times, a memory darts under the surface, and while I'm aware there's something there, I can't reel it in, and it disappears."

I rested my head on Paul's shoulder, and he stroked my hair. "This is part of my life now, and I've developed coping strategies. Although I may still have the intelligence intact to relearn my field, I can't remember what I need to know, and my attention span is much shorter, as well. I need to be able to focus for hours, for weeks and months and years, even, on detailed problems. It's not a set routine, like making a bed or preparing dinner. It involves a high degree of judgment. The drunk driver stole that from me, and although I've improved, it doesn't look like I'll ever function the way I used to. I am fundamentally different."

"I would find what he did almost impossible to forgive."

"It is unforgivable! I will *never* forgive him for what he did." Feeling my throat tighten, I sat up, pulling away from Paul. "I suppose you think I'm being harsh."

"I'm not denying you have the right to feel angry and hurt."

"But that I should forgive him? What's the expression, 'Forgive and forget'? I think I have the 'forget' part well covered. My anger at him has helped me survive."

"Then it has served its purpose. I'd be afraid if you don't find a way to forgive him, he'll always hold you hostage; you will never heal. Likewise, if he doesn't forgive himself, he will never fully recover. He'll be in danger of committing another destructive act."

"Forgive himself? He shouldn't be able to. I don't understand what purpose my forgiving him would serve. Make me a better person? I don't buy into the theory that there was a reason this happened to me. If this was God-designed, God is cruel."

"I don't believe God planned this for you. Maybe it's easier to blame God than to admit a human being would make such a terrible mistake."

"It wasn't a mistake. He made a *choice* to get drunk; he made a *choice*, a decision, to drink and then drive, and he'd done it many times before hurting me. More than one judge made the choice to let him off with meaningless warnings and small fines. He kept making decisions to drink and drive," I repeated. "I would never put a person in such danger."

"No? What about Felipe's life?" he asked in a calm, gentle tone.

"How dare you try to make that connection again!" I stood and moved to the other side of the room, wanting greater distance between us. Without the blanket and Paul's warmth, though, I shivered.

"Sometimes others pay dearly for the terrible mistakes and wrong decisions we make. The only option we have for redemption is to forgive others and to forgive ourselves."

"Don't preach to me about forgiveness!" My voice sounded raw in the mostly empty shelter.

He leaned toward me but did not stand up from the bed. "Is it possible that you won't be able to move on, to make your peace with this, if you don't forgive him? What would happen if you could forgive the drunk driver? What would it mean?"

In the liquid spaces between my pain and confusion, these were important questions for me to answer, and despite how it felt to me, Paul was not being heartless. Sitting down on the floor, I rested my head on a chair's seat, wrapping my fingers around one of the rungs.

"Don't confuse forgiving with condoning; what he did was wrong, whether you forgive him or not. What would you have to give up if you forgave him?"

I sifted through the possibilities. "My anger. I'd have to admit I could make such a disastrous decision. The drunk driver would become a human being, not some monster who intentionally wanted to endanger my life and change it forever." Flaking old paint off the chair rung, I ran my finger across the smooth, light wood. I wished I could strip away as easily the ball of hatred and anger pulsating like a second heart inside me. Why would anyone want to keep such a thing? It might have sustained me these past few years, functioning as a catalyst to prevent me from giving up, but what price would I pay in continuing to harbor it? Eleanor, and Maggie as well, had said something about reaching a time to let anger go, but if forgiveness were required to be the shepherd, I wasn't sure I could manage it. If forgiveness and condoning were not the same thing, could I separate the man from his actions? Could I see him as a fallible human being instead of a malevolent person who had set out to harm me? I forced myself to make the connection with Felipe; if I caused Felipe harm, would I be able to forgive myself, even if others forgave me?

I heard Paul ask, "Which do you want to shape your new life, anger or forgiveness?" Every sound and object in the room telescoped inward.

"That's not a choice I can make."

"But it is, and it's no one's choice but yours."

"It's not that simple."

"Putting it into practice, no, but the choosing between the two is."

"I don't think I can forgive him. I know how to be angry at him, but I don't know how to forgive him."

"If you choose forgiveness with a sincere and open heart, I guarantee the rest will follow on its own. Way *will* open."

Minutes passed as the silence swallowed the sounds around us and became an enveloping, undeniable, crystalline presence. I watched as Paul came across the room to me, his footsteps sounding far away. He uncurled my fingers, aching now from gripping the chair rung. He picked me up, carefully put me on the bed, and with his eyes on mine, we wordlessly questioned each other. Remembering when I'd tried to come up with a central wish for my life, I wanted to speak plainly and honestly. Into the silence, I answered his unspoken question. "Yes. Not here and not now, but yes."

Paul extinguished our camping lantern and lay down beside me. He encircled my face with his hands and kissed my eyelids, my mouth, the hollow of my neck. He repeated my words, "Yes. Not here and not now, but yes."

# Chapter 35

## MEXICO

AFTER WASHING UP AND changing clothes, I joined Paul outside. The circumstances between us had altered once again, but standing next to him, gazing across the flat field, I felt no awkwardness. By unspoken agreement, we did not discuss last night's commitment, but it settled securely inside me, a touchstone of peace and delight.

By midmorning, Paul was worried. "There's a village between here and Castaños. I'll go there to telephone Father Michael and see if he's heard anything."

"What if Felipe comes while we're gone?"

"You're staying here. I'm afraid if he comes and no one is here, he'll think we didn't wait for him. I don't think he can make it all the way to Corpus Christi. You need to be the one to stay because your Spanish is better than mine."

After he left, I checked the road every couple of minutes. The heat made me drowsy, and afraid that I would go to sleep, I paced and sang and read aloud from one of the paperbacks I'd brought. Hearing a car outside, I looked at my watch. Paul wasn't kidding when he promised he'd hurry. It had been a little less than half an hour. He shouldn't be back for another twenty minutes or so, unless the village wasn't as far away as he'd thought.

But it was not Paul's car turning onto the lane from the main road. Hide, I thought. It was too late to leave through the door. I'd be in plain view and couldn't run fast on the rocky ground without losing my balance and falling. Scrambling under the bed, I pulled the blankets down over the side, leaving a slit to peer through. Could it be Felipe? Would he have a car?

When the man stood in the doorway, I couldn't tell if he looked like Tomás and Emilio, and I couldn't see a scar on his face. Wasn't that what Paul had said? A scar? He was not in uniform, though, which I took as a good sign. Could he be the volunteer? No, someone had mentioned the volunteer was a woman. Or was it a woman who had done the calling?

Crossing the floor, the man bent over to look under the bed, and seeing me, he jumped back. Forcing myself to appear calm, I crawled out and tried to move around him so I could escape. Breathe. Courage. Faith. Breathe. Maybe he left the keys in the car. Breathe.

"*Buenas tardes. ¿Está aquí sola?*" Good afternoon. Are you here by yourself?

Obviously, he could tell no one else was here with me. The man waited, as unsure as I was. He glanced at the table where two coffee cups rested on one of our maps. Not taking my eyes from the man, I folded up the map on which our route was marked with a red pen.

"*¿Dónde está su compañero?*" Where is your companion?

"*Él llegará muy pronto,*" I answered, hoping Paul indeed would return soon.

He stepped toward me, ducking his head to look out the window. I sidled around the table, trying to get around him to be closer to the door. What was the children's song about the mulberry bush? Focus. Pay attention. I asked him his name.

"*Me llamo Guillermo Alacena.*" He checked his watch. "*¿Conoce usted a Paul Whittaker?*" Do you know Paul Whittaker?

Guillermo Alacena. Guillermo Alacena. I wouldn't remember his name. What did it sound like? Alacena. Alabama, Alabama. Should I tell him yes? This was getting to be almost more amusing than frightening.

He gave a short, exasperated sigh. "*¿Es usted una cuáquera?*" Are you a Quaker?

I didn't want to fall into a trap, but he must know where Felipe was if he knew Paul's name and thought we were Quakers.

"*No tengo más tiempo. Escuche, no se preocupe.*" He held out his hands to gesture reassurance, telling me he didn't have time and not to worry. "*¿Quiere encontrar a Felipe, no?*"

"*Sí.*" Of course I wanted to find Felipe.

We smiled at each other in relief. He started giving me directions to find Felipe. "*¿A la izquierda, luego a la derecha?*" To the left, then to the right? I questioned him about the turns. Leaning toward me, he added more directions. When he finished, he thanked me, ran from the room, and got in the car. It was so covered with dust and mud I couldn't even tell what color it was as he raced away.

At least now we'd be able to find Felipe and leave this place. I repacked the food box and straightened the room. Hearing another car, I jumped up and stood to one side of the window. It was Paul this time. "A man was here. You just missed him. He told me where we can find Felipe."

"When? How long ago?"

"Less than ten minutes, maybe five. His name is Alabama."

"What?"

"Alabama."

"He has the name of an American state?"

No, of course not. That was the strategy I'd used to try to remember his real name. "It was something close."

"All right. It's probably not important. Where's Felipe? Are we supposed to go pick him up?"

"Yes, he gave me directions."

"Where are they? Let's look at them with the map." I glanced up at him, dread billowing inside me, and shook my head. "You didn't write them down? Did he give you the name of a town, a church, some kind of meeting place?"

"No, I didn't think to write them down. He was speaking fast, and he didn't speak English."

"Felipe's life is at stake and you didn't write down the directions? When you know you don't remember things?" Paul shouted. "Damn it, Kate, anyone with half a brain would write down the directions!"

We faced each other, stunned.

"Oh, no, Kate." He reached out for me, but holding up my hand, I backed away. I felt dark swirls of pain in my stomach. Afraid to say anything, I went out and got in the car, leaving him to pack the few remaining items.

At the main road he asked, "Did you see which way he turned?" I had watched, I recalled, but couldn't figure out quickly enough whether he'd gone left or right, and I couldn't visualize anything. Paul turned onto the dusty road. "We'll go away from town. If it has been just a few minutes, I would have passed him, and I didn't see anybody."

He finally turned on the radio, and a woman with an elegant, cultured voice read from a Spanish novel. Gripping a thermos between my knees, I unscrewed the cap and poured out water. I let the sips stay in my mouth, savoring the coolness of the water, wishing for a way to slake the tension and hurt between us.

After the program, he switched off the radio, and the silence grew, pressing against the windows with a dangerous weight. "I am so very sorry," he said.

"I know. So am I. You're right, of course, I should have written down the directions." I realized, though, even doing so immediately would have been too great a delay; I would have forgotten the details by the time I'd gotten paper and a pen. Knowing I was at one of those watershed moments, I made a decision. Reaching out to Paul, I smiled as brightly as I could. "Your choice of words left a lot to be desired, though."

Paul stared at me. He smiled then, too, and gave a small laugh. "Good for you, Katherine Solterra. Well done." He let out a long breath. "And thank you."

# Chapter 36

## MEXICO

WHEN PAUL CONTACTED HIM, Father Michael directed us to another mission church on the edge of Castaños, where two people said Felipe was "*desaparecido.*" Disappeared. My muscles contracted, my breath seized, my fingertips tingled. Disappeared. After accepting fresh fruit and more water, we left the ancient adobe church. We decided to return to the shack for the night. Looking back at the church, I reflected on the people who had established these mission churches long ago in this isolated, forsaken place. Had they heard God's voice as an insistent, constant whispering or as one single, shattering roar?

I'd been driving for less than an hour when I saw a single beam of light in front of us. A car with a light out? No, a person with a flashlight and others standing by the road. Slowing down, I woke Paul.

"Time for me to drive already?"

"Someone's up ahead. Should I turn back?"

On the other side of the road, a car's headlights turned on, blinding us. A man wearing a uniform headed toward us. "Paul, he's got a gun."

"Is your door locked? The back door? Roll down your window a fraction, don't put the car in park, don't switch off the engine," he ordered.

I thought of the American missionaries who had been murdered. But we were in Mexico, not El Salvador. Virgil's voice floated before me: "Courage. Faith." I inhaled the memory of his calm confidence, telling myself to stay composed.

"*Buenas noches, señora, señor.*" The man informed us that the road ahead was closed, even though we'd driven over it less than two hours ago and nothing had been wrong, no sign of construction. While he talked, he flashed his light in our faces and onto the car's back seat.

He started speaking in English. "You are Americans, no?" While he gave directions for the detour, I tried to memorize his features: his crooked nose, the triangular shape of his face, his protruding ears. He wore no name-tag on his uniform, which seemed to be a mismatched outfit. Paul asked why the road was closed. Why was he stalling? We could take the detour, though I hoped Paul had been listening and had the directions straight.

"This is a night crew to fix the road, in bad shape, you see. Best time to fix is at night, because we don't wish to inconvenience even one traveler." The man started to circle the car. "We talk on your side, no?"

Paul leaned toward my window. "It's not a bother; stay where you are."

I tried to remain as still as possible, sipping in air between my teeth. The men on the road had moved to the side and were talking, no longer interested in our conversation.

"We are tourists." Paul held up one of our maps. "I'm afraid we might get lost on the detour. We're tired and want to get back to the place where we're staying, so we won't mind if we have to wait a minute or two for any of your crews, or if the road is rough."

"It is not possible. Machines block the road and I have orders. I'd get into trouble . . . and so would you. Now, please follow the directions."

Paul tapped my knee. After nodding to the guard, he whispered to me, "Go," and pointed straight ahead instead of toward the road the man had in-dicated. Sliding my foot from the brake to the accelerator, I pressed the pedal all the way down as fast as I dared. The guard jumped back as the car picked up speed. Gunshots ruptured the night and I screamed, ducking my head.

"Keep going!"

"What if they follow us?"

"We'll have enough of a head start," he answered a few seconds later. "Keep your eyes on the road and don't slow down."

"What if there's machinery on the road?"

"Drive off it. There are no shoulders or ditches, just hard, flat land."

Not wanting to know how fast we were going, I didn't dare look at the speedometer. Even though my seat belt was fastened, I bounced around, and a few times my head grazed the car's roof. Please, I thought, I can't survive another crash.

At last Paul spoke, "Slow down."

"What?"

"Slow down. Stop."

I coasted, braked, and stopped in the middle of the road. My hands hurt from holding the steering wheel so tightly. Getting out and running around the front of the car, Paul helped me out and hustled me around to the passenger side.

He drove quickly, but not dangerously fast. We didn't see one piece of machinery or another car on the road; eventually, we arrived back at the dilapidated house. When I crossed the threshold with Paul behind me, a man rose from the bed, checking behind him as though hoping for another door.

"Felipe!" Paul greeted him, and the two men embraced. He introduced me and told Felipe about the guard who had stopped us.

Felipe's eyes widened. "*Debemos irnos inmediatamente. Por favor, ahora. Inmediatamente.*" We must leave immediately. Please, now. Motioning to the car, he pulled on Paul's arm. "*No tenemos más tiempo.*" We don't have more time. He appealed to me. "*Por favor, señorita.*"

We got into the car, with Paul driving and Felipe in the back, slouching down with his head below the level of the window. I kept peering behind us, convinced we were being followed by more than dust.

Hoping to get as close as possible to the border by dawn, Paul drove as fast as the conditions allowed. No other cars were on the route. "Are you all right?" he asked. Felipe was already asleep.

"Yes."

"I'm getting sleepy. Could we talk for a while?"

"You want me to drive?"

Paul laughed and touched my arm, briefly clasping my hand. "Don't you think you've driven enough for one night? Is that how the rehab instructor taught you to drive?"

"He'd be shocked."

"He'd be proud."

"It took me months to get up my nerve to go faster than twenty-five miles an hour and drive on an interstate highway. I guess it's true that you can do anything if you're scared enough. Where are we going next?"

"After we cross the border at Laredo, we'll continue to the mission. We need at least a day's break, and Felipe is in bad shape. He's been beaten, and, from the looks of him, he's suffering from starvation."

"How are we going to get him across the border?"

"I don't know, but we'd better not try to take him through ourselves. I'm sure by now the officials and bounty hunters alike have a description of us. I'll call Father Michael when I can."

"What happened back there?"

"The mock detour? My guess is they thought Felipe was on that road, and they wanted to prevent us from finding him before they did. He's definitely a hunted man. Or they'd planned to ambush us on a less traveled route."

I turned to check on Felipe. "I'm afraid to find out what he's been through to get this far."

"I know how you feel. Has this satisfied your desire for adventure?"

"Adventures don't have to include high-speed escapes and guards with guns, though who knows what I might try next."

On the outskirts of a town, Paul pulled over to call Father Michael. Felipe did not wake up, didn't even move. Paul returned and gave me the details. "Here's the plan. We head northwest past the next village, about twenty miles. We wait there, and another one of the volunteers will pick up Felipe and get him across the border. We cross at Laredo where the officials will see we have no one with us, and we'll pick him up on the other side. We'll go on to the mission." He didn't miss the look on my face. "I know. More deception. I'll do battle with my conscience later."

"'Doing battle' is a strange expression for a Quaker to use." He shrugged but didn't reply.

When Paul started the engine, Felipe woke, looking startled at first until he realized where he was. I asked him about his trip and translated for Paul when I saw he didn't understand some of what Felipe said. "'I mostly traveled at night from dark until dawn. If someone came, I jumped into the ditches or brush and hid. Picked fruit from trees and vegetables from gardens at night. In towns, I went through the garbage, but nobody throws out much these days.'" Felipe waited for me to finish translating. He resumed, speaking slowly enough for me to keep up. "'Some of the trip I made by bus. When waiting for you, I stayed in an abandoned mine for four days. It was not safe to go into town in the daytime. I was weak. I waited but got scared and tried to find the shack. Then you came in.'"

"No one followed you at any time?" Paul asked. I knew he was thinking about the guard who had stopped us.

"Yes, when I left the abandoned mine," he said in English.

"You were able to keep them from following you?"

"Keep them from following? I wasn't lost." Felipe indicated he didn't understand the phrasing, though I suspected he did.

"Tell us what happened, it's all right," Paul prompted.

Felipe averted his eyes. "*No es importante.*"

Paul insisted. "Perhaps. Tell us. It might be important."

"'On the road, a guard stopped me, an officer,'" I translated. "'He said there was a reward for taking me back to El Salvador, and my American friends would stop looking for me. He knew Emilio had been helped. He beat me and put me in his car. I was scared he would find you and hurt you, too. I was afraid he'd kill me, not for the money, he'd get paid for returning me dead or alive, but just for the killing. And if he didn't, I'd be murdered in El Salvador anyway.'" I finished translating, and Felipe nodded he was done.

Paul gave him a description of the guard who had stopped us. "No, I don't think the same," Felipe said in English.

"Are you sure? It's all right to talk to us."

He returned to speaking in Spanish, and I continued the translation. "'We fought. I knew I would be killed in El Salvador if we got there. This was my one chance, and I had come so far. I shot him. I don't know if I killed him because I did not take the time to find out. I did not want to know. From a distance, I shot at his leg, hoping it wouldn't end his life but would slow him down from getting someone on my trail. If he died from his wound, it will be on my conscience forever; I will have to answer for it. But I am not ashamed that I wanted to survive.'"

Paul was silent, his inner struggle evident in his eyes.

"Will you leave me here now?" Felipe asked.

"Leave you here?" Paul echoed him.

I translated when Felipe switched back to Spanish. "'I know it is against your beliefs to kill or use guns, even for those who are your enemies. Killing is against my religion, too; I did not hurt him out of revenge or anger, but for my own life. If you must, you can leave me here.'" Before anyone could answer him, however, Felipe slipped back into sleep, a half-eaten apple falling from his hand as he drew his legs up on the car's seat.

Paul said, "The Meeting didn't consider this possibility. He may have killed a man, not only to save his own life, but also to protect us."

"If he hadn't, he would have been killed."

"It might make the equation true, but it doesn't mitigate the consequences. That's the crux of breaking a sacred law. It doesn't end with the initial break; there's always a domino effect. We have a lot to answer for, too. We're now transporting someone who may have killed another person, but of course we're not going to leave him here."

Finding the side road we were supposed to take, we followed it between the fields on each side. Pulling off the road, we ate our lunch. Although he was less desperate for food, Felipe couldn't relax and jumped at even slight noises. Our journey felt interminable with the days dragged out by the driving, the stultifying heat, and the fear. How had I lulled myself into thinking this would merely be a matter of picking someone up, an extended carpool? I heard Virgil's voice: "Trust that divine spark."

After lunch, Felipe drew a soiled, crumpled piece of paper from his pocket. "I carry this list of names with me always," he told us. "They were murdered for speaking out against the government, for advocating for land reform, for championing the rights of the poor." He recited the names and told us who they were: "Monseñor Óscar Romero, archbishop of San Salvador. Rutilio Grande. Alfonso Navarro. Ernesto Barrera. Octavio Ortiz. Alirio Macías. Rafael Palacios. They were all Catholic priests serving under Romero. Maryknoll sisters Ita Ford and Maura Clarke. Dorothy Kazel, an Ursuline sister. And Jean Donovan, a missionary."

He refolded the paper and asked me to translate. "'Can you believe there are posters encouraging people to be patriots and kill a priest? Octavio Ortiz was holding a religious instruction class when an army tank and the National Police arrived. They said he and his students were subversives. And the women, all from the United States, were trying to do God's work.'" Felipe looked first at Paul then at me, as though he couldn't decide whether to tell us something. Leaning closer to us, he began breathing more rapidly.

"'I must tell you my story. If I don't get across the border, my story must go with you. I was in El Mozote, a village in El Salvador. I'd been looking for work, trying to escape being forced into a refugee camp, trying to get back to my village. Soldiers came, the Atlacatl Battalion. They seized people from their homes and herded women and children and old men, all of us, onto an open plain. Everyone was screaming and running, the children were ter-rified. The few men tried to fight back. I have dents in my head, and now I don't think the way I did before.'"

I felt sick to my stomach, but I couldn't stop him.

"'They forced the men into the church, and in the chaos, I slipped un-der the altar. It was covered with a cloth, such a simple thing, but it saved me.'" Felipe stopped. Tears ran down his face, and he wiped them with the back of his hand.

"What happened?" Paul prompted him.

"'They machine-gunned all the men and decapitated them. They lined up the women and killed them. They burned and shot the children. Out of about, I don't know, hundreds and hundreds of people at El Mozote, I may be one of a handful of survivors, one of the few witnesses.'"

We sat in stunned silence. I tried not to imagine the children's terror, the screams, the machine-gun fire. He took out the list of the assassinated religious workers. "'These were good men and women; they tried to help us. If something happens to me, would you remember them for me? Read their names occasionally. Light a candle for them, if that is your tradition. They deserve to be remembered.'"

I took the paper from him and put it in my pocket. "Yes," I promised him. "We will remember."

# Chapter 37

## MEXICO, TEXAS

CAMPING OUT IN A grove several miles from the main road, we waited for the volunteer. Wrapped in blankets, I sat between the two men as we centered down into Meeting after a brief explanation for Felipe. The silence out in the deserted field was eerie. I listened for sounds of cars or footsteps. Every time the idea surfaced that Felipe wouldn't make the crossing, I pushed it back. The magnitude of what we were doing clamped over me, a giant bell jar sealing out all the arguments, the rhetoric, and the politics, leaving behind one frightened, young man whose life was in our care.

We rose at the same time. Paul filled canteens with water and gave them to Felipe, and I handed him a folded blanket and as much food as he could carry in case something happened. We moved in the slow motion of our reluctance to part from this relative safety. We'd become a strange family of three. It was a pure belonging, I felt, like purple crocuses pushing up through snow, an announcement of color and shape and life uncomplicated by years of secret desires and hidden hurts.

At last we heard a car. Paul ran to the field's edge. "It's the volunteer," he called, motioning us forward. Felipe and I hurried to join them. The volunteer, a man in his thirties, conferred with Paul on where and when we could pick up Felipe. "We will see you tomorrow," Paul told him.

Felipe waved as they pulled away. He looked forlorn, his face pressed like a child's against the car window. What must it be like to be handed from one stranger to another, a single bucket in a brigade, entrusting one's life to the unknown?

Long before daybreak, we retraced our route to the border. Because Paul thought the authorities would expect us to come at night, we wanted to go through right after the daylight shift came to work. Arriving at the customs center at dawn, we found an all-night diner. In the restroom, I tried to clean up, grateful for plentiful, mercifully hot water. I changed my clothes and pulled back my hair.

Joining Paul at the table, I asked, "Are you sure eating here is advisable?"

"If we were trying to smuggle someone across, would we stop to have a leisurely breakfast at the diner right next to the border checkpoint?"

Sipping our coffee, we waited for time to pass. When the waitress refilled our cups, I noticed a man reading a newspaper at a corner table. I thought he looked familiar but couldn't place him. I knew, though, that my imagination was working overtime. "It's almost light outside. Can't we go yet?"

"Let's wait a bit." He summoned the waitress over to our table. Ordering apple turnovers and orange juice, Paul paid the waitress after she set down the dishes. Taking off his jacket, he leaned back in the booth and flipped through a magazine we'd brought in with us. I understood what he was doing, but I couldn't appear so relaxed. My fingers drummed the table's edge and my foot swung back and forth, hitting Paul's shin.

"Sorry."

"These are good, aren't they? My grandmother used to make the best pastries and pies in the county, with prizes from the state fair to prove it. She ran the family's farm in Oklahoma after my grandfather died." He continued talking about his family, but I didn't even try to follow his comments. I realized he had dropped a "Calm down, would you?" in the middle of his story.

I saw the waitress serving the man in the corner. Other people started to enter the diner, greeting the waitress by name and picking up a morning paper from the rack as they entered. Most of them wore customs uniforms.

"When I say 'Now,' I want you to get up and head for the door, but not too fast. I'll follow you."

"But . . . all right."

"Now."

Walking to the door, I felt as though I had a revolving red light on my head, and once outside, I didn't look behind me. Starting the car, Paul backed it out and drove to the customs checkpoint. "The man in the corner, reading the newspaper? Maybe I'm paranoid, but I think he was watching us. He came to the door when we left."

"I thought he looked familiar. Is he following us now?" I asked.

He checked in the rearview mirror. "Not that I can see, but it's time we crossed the border anyway. Don't answer any questions unless they're addressed to you, and don't give extra information. Relax. Try not to look worried or nervous."

"What if they ask about Felipe?"

"Do you know where he is right now?"

"No."

"Good. Neither do I."

"What if they ask if we know a Felipe Delgado?"

"Let's not try to think of every scenario, Kate."

We drove up to the booth. There were several cars in the next lane and one car in front of us. When it was our turn, the customs official approached us, and Paul rolled down the window. "Good morning, sir."

"Good morning," Paul returned the greeting.

Checking the car's back seat, the customs official asked routine questions about what we were bringing back. No fruits or vegetables, I thought, only an illegal immigrant.

"Will you open the trunk, sir?"

"Certainly." Paul got out, opened the trunk, and made a remark to the official, who responded and smiled. I wondered if it were the usual procedure to check trunks. Paul returned and put the car in gear. The official waved us on with a cheerful, "Welcome back to the States."

"I never thought the Texas wilderness could look so beautiful," I commented, my shoulders relaxing at last.

"It makes a difference, doesn't it, coming home."

"I feel so much safer. Couldn't we have planned to pick up Felipe now? It's a long time until dark."

"It won't be until almost dark that Felipe gets here. The volunteer didn't want to try to get him across until right before dusk. We can be patient. We can't afford to ruin it at this stage."

"I guess the man wasn't watching us, though now I'm beginning to look over my shoulder as much as Felipe does."

"Not a pleasant feeling, is it?"

"It underscores that what we're doing is illegal. And the fact that we think what we're doing is right doesn't make me feel better. So many people have been involved with helping this one person. The logistics of it all, and to multiply it by the hundreds of those involved across the country is hard for me to imagine."

Paul explained, "Not all refugees are as difficult to bring into this country. Even as young as he is, Felipe apparently has been a controversial and highly visible man, and he comes from a politically involved family. What he told us about El Mozote alone puts him in grave danger."

"Do you think his family knew about El Mozote and didn't tell the Meeting?"

"It's possible they didn't. I don't know where they were when it happened."

We found a library to pass some time in an air-conditioned place, and in the afternoon, we ate lunch in the shade of the lone tree on the library's grounds. Later, I tried to catch up on my journal writing while Paul read magazines in the library's reading room. Unable to sit still, though, I started pacing between the bookshelves. I stared out the windows. I hadn't expected to appreciate the landscape that seemed exotic to me. I noticed an ocotillo, a plant that Paul had explained was technically a shrub, not a cactus. The ocotillos were flowering now, with bright red blossoms at the ends of the slender, spiny stems, which swayed like ballet dancers' arms reaching heavenward. Although I missed the loveliness of the Shenandoah Valley, this region—with the flashes of color, the plants' sculptural quality against the unobstructed grandeur of the sky, and the huge swaths of open land—possessed a beauty all its own and answered a heretofore unrecognized longing within me.

At last, it was time to head toward the meeting place. We drove west, and the sun's harsh glare made us squint to see the road. After we drove for a couple of hours, Paul pulled off the main highway and veered onto a side road marked by a blue sign. "Might as well have dinner. I don't want to get there too early and have to find a place to wait."

"How long will it take us to get back to Drake's Springs?"

"It depends on how much Felipe can withstand. The sooner we get there, though, the better."

"What if the INS officials are there when we arrive?"

"For me, that's a 'cross that bridge if I have to' deal."

We entered the roadside café and shared the area's local paper while waiting for our meals. "I love small-town newspapers," Paul told me. "When I was growing up, I couldn't wait to move to the city. I enjoyed city life, but when I left the law firm, I was ready to move back to the country. It has the sense of community I want."

"Did you inherit the farm when you left the law firm?"

"No, I inherited the farm when I was much younger. When I left the city and returned to Drake's Springs, I made the farm my home for the first time."

"What do you grow on your farm? I don't have the slightest idea."

"You've seen my apple orchard, and I grow Christmas trees."

"Christmas trees?"

"Sure. Where did you think the ones in those city lots came from?"

"From some vague forest in the Pacific Northwest or in Canada."

"Christmas trees are somewhat odd for a Friend to grow, for the Quakers historically didn't have them. Most families probably do now. Growing trees seemed like it would be a straightforward occupation, peaceful and uncomplicated. Nothing ever is, I suppose, but it's been close."

"How long have you been a Friend?"

"I officially joined almost ten years ago."

"Sometimes the Meeting seems too good to be true, as though you're separated from others."

"That's an often-levied charge, but this Meeting, at least, has had its challenges. We've dealt with divisive issues, causing some members and attenders to transfer to other Meetings or churches. It's ironic that we're seen as separate. Quakers dropped plain dress and speech more than a century ago, partly in an effort not to be seen as set apart and above others." Noting the time, he added, "Perfect. Would you mind driving? I could use a break. I'll drive after we pick him up."

I drove for a few miles down an isolated, twisting road when Paul suddenly pointed to a church, its steeple and the cross above the door shimmering in the twilight. "Stop here a moment. This is our first landmark. Keep an eye out. He's supposed to be somewhere between here and an abandoned bus station about a mile away. Let's open our windows a little so we can hear better." I slowed down and inched the car forward. Peering through the thick mass of vines and brush, we surveyed the sides of the road, looking hard for any kind of movement. Paul asked me to switch on the high-beam lights for a few seconds.

"Did you see him?" I asked.

"No, but that was our signal. Let's drive to the station."

With boards nailed over the collapsed window frames and half of the platform sagging to the ground, the abandoned bus terminal was barely erect. "Maybe we should go inside, or perhaps he was inside the church, hiding," I suggested.

"It's risky for us to be prowling around. I don't have a good feeling about this at all."

I wished he hadn't admitted it. After turning on the high-beam lights, I strained to listen. My eyes ached from trying to see shadows and figures in the dark.

"Please, God," Paul said, "help us. We can't lose him now."

I drove behind the building, and he got out. "Wait here. If you see or hear anything, tap the horn."

"I'm not going to stay here."

"Lock the doors. You'll be all right."

"I told you I'm not going to stay here." Without the noise of the running car, though, I felt more vulnerable than before. Climbing up the platform, we skirted the broken floorboards. The back door was missing. Inside the building, cobwebs draped from the backs of benches to the seats' edges, and wooden chairs with iron frames clustered against a wall. A grille covered the ticket office window, but nothing else remained to indicate this had been a bus station. We checked around, opening the doors to what had been restrooms.

"Felipe?" Paul called softly.

I pointed to the dust-covered floor in the main room. "Ours are the only footprints."

"You're right, let's go back to the church." We paused at the station's doorway, trying to discern any shadows before hurrying to the car.

"I'll drive now," Paul said. "If he's not at the church, we'll continue up the road, find a place to wait, and come back in half an hour. I don't want to keep going back and forth. If we can't find him, we'd better call Father Michael."

Driving around the back of the church, he parked where the car couldn't be seen from the road. The sign next to the front door listed times for Mass. Unlocked, the church appeared to be well maintained; its uncarpeted sanctuary was in order with the hymnals stacked neatly, red cushions for kneeling spaced out under the pews, and music books on the piano. Proceeding down the aisle, we investigated each row and opened the doors, even the confessional. A door marked "Office" was the single one locked. I thought I heard a sound and turned, my finger to my lips to warn Paul. Where was it coming from? Above? No, the church had no choir loft or second story. A tree branch scraping against one of the windows? Possibly. Whatever, I didn't hear it again.

Paul raised an eyebrow, but I shook my head. Back in the car, I told him, "I thought I heard something, but I guess it was a branch hitting against one of the windows. The wind is increasing."

Choosing a dirt lane that ran between two fallow fields, Paul turned the car around so that it was facing out. We rolled down the windows so that we could hear. "Something's not right. Could we hold Meeting?" he asked.

Chilled by the wind, I shivered. Paul reached for the blanket, spread it over us, and put his arm around my shoulders. The old church reminded me of the one we'd attended when I was a little girl. I tried to shape the memory before it vanished. We'd moved right before a bell was to be installed in the steeple. The congregation's children had helped to raise money for the bell. Because I was so disappointed when we had to leave before it arrived, my father took me up in the tower and allowed me to have a last look at the town.

Why was it I could remember unimportant things from my past? I hadn't thought about my childhood church in decades, so why now? I retraced my thoughts: the church bell, the tower, the wind moving the leaves. "The bell tower," I interrupted the silence. "I didn't think of it at the time because there was no loft, but the church has a bell tower. The sound I heard was coming from overhead." I grabbed Paul's arm. "Someone was up there."

"Felipe would have come down."

"Not unless he could see the car. And we weren't there long."

"It's been nearly half an hour; let's go."

When we drove around to the back, the churchyard looked the same. "See? There's a grating. He probably couldn't see the car through the slats."

"You stay this time. Keep the car running and keep the doors locked until you see me coming out."

He ran up the back steps and entered the church. "Hurry up," I whispered, twisting around to check behind the car. Paul appeared in the doorway, but no one was with him. We headed back toward the bus station.

"The tower was empty, but I saw footprints in the entry and up the stairs in the tower. I think you're right."

"But was it Felipe?"

"I hope so. I hope he's out here waiting for us."

"Why didn't the volunteer take him to one specific place and stay with him?"

"I don't know."

"Maybe we should choose a place and stay put, let him find us," I suggested. "We could be missing each other by going back and forth."

"I don't see how, with a single road. Of course, he could be going through the woods, or maybe he's afraid to come out of hiding."

Entering the bus station through the back doorway, Paul checked under the benches again and called Felipe's name. Moving cautiously, I was walking toward the restrooms when I heard a loud grunt as Paul fell to the floor. All at once, before turning around, I knew someone else was in the room and was attacking Paul. Running toward them, I saw two figures wrestling on the floor. The other man pinned Paul down and started beating him. I heard muffled, choking sounds, and I saw Paul struggling to break loose. It was not a fight simply to gain control; I immediately understood the man was intent on killing Paul, and despite the dim light, I caught the glint of a gun

Not until I lifted the chair above my head did I realize I'd grabbed it on my way toward them. Jumping up, I brought it down with as much force as I could, knowing I'd have only one chance. The man howled and rolled away. Reaching for Paul's arm, I yanked him to his feet and guided him out of the bus station to the car. He pulled the keys out of his pocket and I grabbed them, unlocking the passenger door. Paul dropped onto the front seat. I slammed the door and ran to the driver's side. With my hands now shaking so badly I couldn't fit the key in the lock, I banged on the window. He opened the door and inserted the key in the ignition for me.

I'd gotten the car started when the man appeared in the back doorway. Paul shouted, "Head down!" and a second later there were gunshots. The car slid and the tires screeched as I rounded the curve, out of range. Midway to the church I flashed the bright lights, and without warning, someone stepped into the arc of the headlights. Braking hard, I screamed as my body flew forward and my head struck the steering wheel, Paul's arm reaching out too late.

A man ran up to the car on the passenger side. Paul reached behind him to unlock the back door but then shouted, "No! It's not him! Go, go!" I accelerated as fast as I could without losing control of the car.

"Can you reach your seat belt? Hand it to me; I'll buckle you in." He helped hold the steering wheel while I reached up to grab the metal buckle, then fastened it for me and put on his own. Paul slumped down in the seat. Minutes later he said, "Stop. Find a place to pull over."

"Felipe? Aren't we going back for him?" Paul looked at me, his face stained with blood, his left eye already nearly swollen shut. I felt dizzy, my voice sounding thin and far away. "What about Felipe? We can't leave him back there."

He stumbled out of the car, and I saw him lean over and throw up. When he came back, I gave him a thermos of water and a towel. I'd pulled out the first aid box, and after he sponged the blood off his face and rinsed his mouth, I bandaged the cut on his forehead. "We can't give up on him now."

"You don't understand, you don't know." He began shivering, and I wrapped a blanket around him. "When the man on the road came up to the car, I saw something . . . someone . . . huddled in the ditch."

"Maybe it wasn't Felipe. Maybe he's still alive. We have to go back."

He shook his head. "Don't make me tell you. Please. Besides, they know. They'll assume he told us about El Mozote. We're as hunted now as Felipe was. If we go back, they'll kill us. I'm sure of it. We've got to get out of here now. We've stayed too long as it is. Can you drive?"

"Yes." I started the car and gripped the wheel. I can do this, I told myself. "I need directions. Do I stay on this road?" He checked a map and wrote out the rest of the route, giving it to me.

"How's your head?"

"Fine," I said, then caught his look. "Don't worry. I'm tougher than you think."

"You don't need to convince me. But shouldn't we find a doctor for you? A hospital, given the circumstances?"

"Given the circumstances, I know the difference between life-threatening head trauma and a hard knock on the head. Trust me."

Only after we were many turns and miles away from the bus station did I begin to feel safer. Stopping at a gas station to fill up the car, I soaked paper towels in cold water and pressed them to my forehead. I studied myself in the mirror. My forehead was bruised, my hair was dirty and uncombed, even my facial features looked blurred and shapeless. "This was not what I had in mind when I wished for a joyful life," I told my reflection. When I came out, Paul was talking on the telephone. I washed the mud splatters off the car windows and cleaned out the clutter of wrappers and paper cups.

He joined me. "I've advised Father Michael we're on our way. We should be there in about three more hours."

He started to get in the driver's seat, but I stopped him. "Don't even think of driving. You're in no shape." He acquiesced and stretched out on the back seat without arguing, which worried me. The next time I checked on him in the rearview mirror, he was asleep.

# Chapter 38

ALERTED THAT WE HAD entered the mission's grounds, Father Michael met us at the courtyard's back gate. He assessed the situation in a glance. "I'll call our doctor."

We sat at the table in the kitchen's alcove, but as Paul started to explain what had happened since we'd left the mission, I excused myself. "My head is fine; I just need to sleep. Paul is the one who needs to see a doctor."

Crossing the guest room's threshold, I stood still to let the simplicity of the room settle around me, warming me like a shawl draped over cold shoulders. In the shower, I scrubbed off the grime of traveling and wished I could scrub away as easily the anguish and weariness trembling along my breastbone. My headache receded, allowing me to sleep until early evening. In my nightmare this time, menacing shadows pushed Felipe from the church's bell tower; with his arms and legs flailing, he catapulted toward the ground. Jerking awake, I heard the bells of the mission chiming the hour.

I hadn't let myself believe until now that Felipe was dead. I recalled his tears when he'd described the massacre at El Mozote. Thinking of my tears of frustration, of anger, of self-pity, I felt ashamed and humbled. Yes, my situation was unfortunate; it was serious. But I had lived and made progress. I ticked off more blessings. I had access to some of the best medical care in the world and plenty of money for it. I lived in a democratic country that was not ravaged by widespread violence and poverty. I had a future. Although I knew I'd still be beset by anxiety and frustrations would continue to abound, I felt something reposition inside me, and I understood that the time for crying over my situation had ended at last.

Unfolding the sheet of paper Felipe had given me, I read aloud the names, pausing after each one and adding one name: "Monseñor Óscar Romero. Rutilio Grande. Alfonso Navarro. Ernesto Barrera. Octavio Ortiz.

Alirio Macías. Rafael Palacios. Ita Ford. Maura Clarke. Dorothy Kazel. Jean Donovan. Felipe Delgado."

An older woman stood outside the gazebo. Like Sister Guadalupe, she wore a traditional habit and a cross on a thin chain. "Good afternoon," she greeted me. "May I join you?"

"Of course, please do." I stood as she entered the gazebo.

"I am Mother Clare, the Mother Superior here."

"Katherine Solterra." Had she been at the mission when we were here before? I couldn't recall seeing her. She was elegant and patrician, the fine bones of her face highlighted by the sun.

"Are you all right?" She sat down, the skirt of her habit falling into graceful folds to the floor.

I started to comment I was fine, but assuming she knew the whole story, I admitted, "No. Felipe is dead. Paul was right: I shouldn't have come. He might have been able to save Felipe if someone else had been with him."

"Perhaps."

"This is not something I can ever make right."

Mother Clare remained silent.

"I don't know how to make my peace with this."

Still, she waited.

Closing my eyes, I fell silent as well. The leaves of the trees in the courtyard moved in the breeze, a whispery counterpoint to the agitation in my mind. When she did speak, her measured words corralled my thoughts. "You're assuming a great deal of responsibility. You did not make the decision to come by yourself. You did not make Felipe's or the murderers' decisions. You do have a responsibility for whatever your part may be, but it is arrogant to claim responsibility for the actions of others, or for what is the province of God. There aren't any easy answers here."

She looked as though she'd never done anything wrong in her life, although I was beginning to understand these religious women were not as sequestered as I'd believed. I tried to guess how long she'd been in her order. She had an open, ageless face with sparkling, alert eyes. "Is it difficult, Mother Clare, for you to participate in the sanctuary movement?"

"I believe it is the will of God to do everything in my power to save people's lives," she answered readily. "For me, the will of God transcends political beliefs, government policies, and legal systems."

"That's the most concise, confident statement I've heard on the issue."

"I've had a long time to think about the issue in particular and God's will in general."

"How do you know it is God's will?"

"Because life is sacred, and his will is to preserve what is good and right."

"So," I began but stopped, not having the energy to pursue it.

"And so you wonder why he didn't protect Felipe?" she finished for me.

"Yes."

"The principle of God's will is usually simple and straightforward enough, I think. It's our acting on it that isn't. I don't know, Katherine. I don't know why the evil in this case was so much more powerful than your goodness and Paul's, your fortitude and Felipe's. I personally don't believe this was God's plan to have this happen. Someone, several people, made a choice to murder Felipe. But I cannot believe it was God's plan to have Felipe dead in a ditch by the roadside, although some people on both sides might claim it was."

"I shouldn't have come."

"This would have happened whether you'd come or not. It has nothing to do with you."

I wanted to believe her. I wanted to be able to look Paul in the eye again. I wanted to have the meeting with the man in the shack again, to write down his directions, to remember his name, to see where his car had gone. I wanted that Sunday morning, the day of my accident, back. I would have left my apartment five minutes earlier or five minutes later. Felipe. The drunk driver. It all seemed capricious and unfair. She started to rise but sat back down when I spoke. "Mother Clare."

The late afternoon sun shadowed her face, softening angles and lines. "You may ask me anything, Katherine."

"What does forgiveness mean to you?"

Folding her hands in her lap, she turned inward like the Quakers in Meeting. "I could give you a standard theological answer, but I sense you are searching for something else, although I'm not sure I can couch it in other terms." She faced me. "But you did ask what it means to me. I think forgiveness is one way we can engage in holiness. It is a sacred act that elevates and sustains us and the recipients."

"How do you forgive the unforgivable, such as what happened to Felipe?" Such as what happened to me, I automatically thought.

"You can't, if your definition is a strict one. But if you widen your definition, if even despicable acts can be separated from the essential humanity of the person who committed them, you can respond to the person, not to the acts. I believe a Quaker would say you respond to what is of God in that person." She reached out to me. "If you are unforgiving toward another, you are being unforgiving toward yourself. You are being unforgiving toward

God. Without forgiveness, the spirit dies. It does not thrive on anger and hatred, bitterness and resentment. I'm not saying it's easy to forgive, Katherine, far from it, but it is as critical as water."

On our return through the garden, she named the flowers I admired. When we got to the kitchen door, Paul met us in the entryway. "How are you feeling?" I asked him.

"Better. Sore, but I'll mend. We'll be leaving tomorrow morning, so Sister Guadalupe planned an early dinner."

"I'm not hungry. I think I'll get more rest." Turning toward Mother Clare, I told her, "Thank you. What you said was important to me." I walked down the corridor, craving to be in that secluded room. I was ready for bed when someone knocked on the door. Putting on my robe, I hoped we weren't leaving for some reason. Instead, it was Sister Guadalupe. She carried a tray with hot chocolate and a bud vase with one of the flowers Mother Clare had named for me. There were chunks of cheese, crackers, and apple slices arranged on a plate.

"Could I get you something more to eat? I know you said you didn't want dinner."

"No, thank you, Sister. This is what I needed, though I didn't realize it." I knew Mother Clare had requested this, and I felt warmed by the gesture. Fluffing up the pillows, I got in bed. While sipping the chocolate, I wrote down what Mother Clare had said about forgiveness. I wanted to be able to discuss it with Paul at some point. This thought held a soul-satisfying talisman of joy: I had someone with whom to share my heart.

The sun woke me the next morning at almost nine. I felt strong and rested but couldn't figure out why someone hadn't awakened me so we could get an early start. Since I knew Paul wanted to cover as much distance as quickly as possible, I got dressed and left my room. Bordering the inner courtyard, the mission's colonnade glistened in the strong light.

I found Paul in the garden's gazebo. "Good morning," he greeted me.

"Good morning. Why didn't you wake me?"

"Father Michael suggested we stay at least a day or two longer to give my eye more time to heal. We'll be safe here. You can't drive as much as you have been doing for the past couple of days. I know it hasn't been easy for you. Did you sleep?"

"Yes. Sometimes exhaustion can be a good thing." I sat on the bench next to him and stretched out my legs.

"There's coffee in the kitchen. May I bring you a cup?"

"Please." After he headed toward the kitchen, I thought how lovely it was to be considered and to be served—a kindness, indeed.

He returned with a cup of coffee and a warm muffin. "There's more food in the kitchen for us, but this might tide you over."

"Thanks, this will be fine." I set the cup on the wide railing and nibbled at the muffin.

"I wanted to talk to you about what happened at the bus station."

I kept my eyes on the garden in front of us. "As a Quaker, I know you disapprove of what I did, smashing a chair over that man."

"As a Quaker, I abhor using violence to solve conflicts, but I acknowledge if you hadn't done that, I would have been even more severely beaten, or, more likely, killed. And the same thing could have happened to you."

"I don't think I was making any conscious decision. Until I swung the chair, I don't think I knew I was holding it."

"You didn't realize you'd picked it up?"

"No, and I don't know how I found it in the dark. Suddenly, it was in my hands; I lifted it over my head, jumped, and brought it down as hard as I could. Who was he?"

"Perhaps a bounty hunter. He may have been the person at one of those restaurants or at the customs checkpoint. It was too dark in there to see him."

"What could Felipe and his family be involved in that would make someone pay a bounty hunter to kill him, as well as us?"

"I don't know. His being a witness to the El Mozote massacre would be enough by itself if they thought he could have identified them. And our connection is that Felipe would have had American power behind him." He sipped his coffee and finished his muffin before asking, "What went through your mind? What gave you the strength to do what you did? Given your injuries, I wouldn't have thought you'd be able to raise a chair with a solid iron frame over your head."

When I'd first heard Paul fall to the floor, had one of those Quaker phrases given me strength, like the time when the car ran me off the road? In a flash, I remembered, and for a split second I felt dizzy. "I prayed. I asked God for help." For the first time in days I saw light come back in his eyes. "The last time I prayed and asked for help, I didn't receive it."

"At the time of the accident?"

I nodded.

"Oh, Kate," he sighed. "Is it possible you did? You survived, against all odds."

I allowed this idea to find a home and settle; I felt an easing, a loosening. "I need to say that I shouldn't have come. If I'd been able to remember what the man in the shack had said, or even which direction his car had turned; if I hadn't gotten lost on my walk; if I could have figured out the noise above us in the church in time . . ."

"Stop. I have my own list. If I had asked more people in town; if I'd kept looking around the church earlier when you heard that sound; if I had turned left, instead of right. The 'what-ifs' don't help, won't erase what happened. Anyway, I'm not convinced the person in the church tower was Felipe. I'm not sure the timing works out. I am sure they were intent on killing him, and they would have killed us to get to him. This isn't about us. I'm not saying this to assuage your guilt or mine. This isn't about us. It never was."

We finished our coffee. "Have you called home?"

"Yes. I spoke to Will and asked him to tell the Delgados and to inform the Meeting."

"I don't envy him that hard task."

"I know. I feel bad that I won't be there, but it wouldn't be right to withhold the news."

In the courtyard the following morning, Mother Clare approached me. I felt a sense of disquiet shrouding sound and motion. I don't think anyone can give me a warm coat for this, I thought. I had the feeling something else was wrong in addition to Felipe's death, but I couldn't place it. Perhaps I simply needed to go home. While Paul put our belongings in the trunk, Mother Clare gave me a hug. "My prayer for you, Katherine, is that you'll find forgiveness in your heart and your mind. There are abundant promises for you to claim if you do. God be with you."

# Chapter 39

WE LEFT CORPUS CHRISTI and drove to Greenwood, Louisiana. "We're not going to stay with the Seales again?"

"No. I called a couple I met at a Quaker conference a few years ago, Quinton and Leah Hulbert. You'll like them. They're about our age, very active in peace and justice concerns."

Late that afternoon, we turned onto the long drive leading to the Hulberts' farmhouse. They met us on the front porch and ushered us into their home. I felt fragmented, my sorrow over the past few days trembling inside me. Leah, tall, slender, and dressed in purple overalls, reached out and held me. "Shhh," she consoled, hugging me and rubbing my back. "You will get through this," she whispered. Nodding, I stepped back. In a brisk tone, Leah declared, "Food first." Within minutes, she'd set dinner on the oak table in their kitchen. They reached for my hands for grace. After dinner, Quinton and Leah invited us onto their back porch. Quinton turned to us. "Would you like to hold Meeting?" Paul nodded.

After arranging some chairs into a semicircle, we settled into the silence. I felt heavy with unexpressed anguish. Looking out over their large field, I willed myself to focus on its serene beauty until its peace folded over me and smoothed the rough edges. It struck me that the silence, which continued until the sunset's streaks of pink and purple faded, felt like coming home. The Hulberts ended the Meeting, rising and embracing us once more.

The closer we got to Drake's Springs, the more anxious I felt. "One more day of driving," Paul said. "We should get home at seven or so tomorrow evening." Tonight we were staying with the Elkinses, but when we arrived, we discovered they'd unexpectedly been called out of town. A neighbor let us in. We found a note in the kitchen, welcoming us and encouraging us to make ourselves at home.

After a quick shower to rinse off, I dumped a handful of bath crystals into the tub and sank into the hot, frothy water. Sliding the soap down my arms, I knocked the shampoo off the tub's side. Had I washed my hair when I took the shower? I'd meant to. Holding the shampoo bottle, I tried to remember.

Feeling my annoyance grow, I stopped myself, recalling where I was. Leaning back in the tub, I admitted I was always going to forget if I'd washed my hair, forget to write notes, get lost on a simple walk, and end up flat on my face in mud and gravel. No matter how short the time between thinking of something and doing it, I sometimes was going to forget it. I was going to lose track of belongings, lose track of conversations underway, forget what I did last year, last month, last week, yesterday, three minutes ago. And, most of the time, it wouldn't matter. It was something I could manage.

I was not going to be a research scientist; I was not going to regain what I'd lost. On any given day, I would struggle with my memory. I was going to have to sign a final treaty because I could not live with this anger and hatred. I would end up hating myself. I thought of who I used to be and what I used to be. I catalogued the losses: my profession, David, the research contributions I would not make again. I thought of my parents' fear, my constant frustration, the people in the rehab center. In my mind, I pictured the Delgado family, including Felipe. Standing up, I watched in the mirror as the water slid off my body, my scarred, patched-together, Humpty-Dumpty body. This was who and what I was. So be it.

Mitchell McLaren, I cannot forgive you yet. But I cannot, will not, curse you anymore. What you did to me was a defining moment in my life, but it will not be the singular one.

"Are we going to the Meetinghouse first?"

"Yes. I called this morning to let them know approximately what time we'd arrive, but I can drop you off at your cabin if you'd like."

"No, I need to be there." I counted off the landmarks as we passed them—the road leading to town, the bridge, the turnoff to the preserve, the sign advertising the general store, and my cabin's lane.

So many times during this trip I'd been conscious of occasions and scenes that had become still photographs: driving away from my cabin with Eleanor and Virgil waving from my porch; Nick holding the gun, trembling from a fear of shooting it and from a fear of not having the nerve to do so;

holding Meeting with Felipe in the field; the bounty hunter attacking Paul in the bus station; Mother Clare talking to me in the gazebo. In between the mental photographs, I saw flashes of the Quakers waiting for our return. I thought back to my first Meeting, with the startling silence folding inward and downward like a bird tucking its wings. I wanted to be in that silence, immersed beyond thought.

Turning onto the lane leading to the Meetinghouse, Paul slowed down. The building loomed in front of us, looking like a paper cutout pasted against the dark night. We stood a moment in the light by the door, and I felt a sense of foreboding. What was it? I dreaded entering the building and stepped back from the door. I couldn't shake the tissued sadness skimming over me.

"What's wrong?"

"I don't know."

"They don't blame us, Kate."

"I blame myself."

"Let it go. It was right for you to take this journey, and I ask your forgiveness for not trusting you. I may be the Quaker, but you were the one who followed the leading of the Holy Spirit." Leaning down, he kissed me. "It will be all right, Katherine Solterra, whatever it is. You can face it."

"You cannot face what you cannot name." He looked puzzled. "Something I learned up on the mountain." Paul held my hand and we entered the Meetinghouse together.

After embracing Felipe's brothers, Magdalena, and Graciela, we sat next to Will on the facing bench. I'd have to tell him I'd been practicing accepting the warm coat. I saw the Mackenzies, Ruth and Adam, and Josiah. I looked for the Schoenfelds but didn't see them, and no children were present. I felt my energy flow out, leaving me weightless, suspended. Trying to allow the quiet to subdue my mystifying fear, I questioned myself. Did I find what I was searching for? Examples of faith and courage had been plentiful, but were they mine to claim? Mother Clare had said something about abundant promises.

The silence ended. Will welcomed us home; others came up and hugged us, but of course there was not the unrestrained joy as there had been when Magdalena and Emilio arrived. The Delgados approached us. Magdalena, looking pale, held on to Tomás, who said, "We know how hard you tried. We are grateful. It comforts us that Felipe knew he had not been forgotten."

After everyone else had left, Will made sure the front doors were closed while we started for the side door. He called us back. "I know you both want to get home, but I need to tell you something." We sat down on the facing bench. I could hear the clock ticking and the last few cars leaving. "Terrible news, I'm afraid."

"INS?" Paul asked.

"No. There's no easy way to tell you this. It's about Virgil. He had another stroke last week." Paul drew in his breath. Another? But of course. The halting speech. The strange gait. Of all people, I should have recognized the signs, since there had been many stroke patients at the rehab center.

"It was a massive stroke, and he lived for three days afterward. Had he survived, his condition would have been devastating, for him and for Eleanor. I am so very sorry." Paul stared straight ahead, not moving. "Eleanor asked that we not notify you because she didn't want the trip to be any harder than it was. The burial was two days ago, but the Memorial Meeting will be tomorrow afternoon. She wanted it to be held immediately after you arrived. After the service, she'll be leaving to stay with her sister for a week or so." Will put his arm around Paul's shoulders. "If you're up to it, members of Ministry and Worship would like you to preside over the service, and Eleanor said she'd be grateful if you would."

A barely perceptible nod from Paul, and Will said nothing more. We sat in the empty Meetinghouse and shared a silence of ineffable grief. I reached out for Paul's hand. Was this somehow connected to my earlier feelings of sadness? I'd assumed they were about Felipe, but Virgil had seemed so present on our journey that perhaps on some level I'd sensed his death.

After several minutes, Paul broke the silence. "Will, would you take Kate home for me, please? I want to sit here for a while."

"Let me stay with you."

"No, but thank you," he responded, and I didn't want to press him.

Outside, I asked, "Will he be all right alone?"

"After I take you home I'll check back here. The Memorial Meeting is at two. We wanted to give you time to rest and to deal with the shock."

When we got to my cabin, Will asked, "Are you sure you want to be alone tonight? Sharon said she'd come stay with you, or you could come stay with us."

"No, I'll be fine."

Closing the door, I turned and faced the living room. I was aware of my breathing, my fingers tingling in my fatigue. I smelled furniture wax and saw that the kitchen's floor shone. Graciela. On the kitchen table, the pepper shaker held down a note from Maggie, telling me dinner was in the refrigerator, but I knew I couldn't eat.

I called my parents. My father answered and my mother picked up the extension. She spoke first. "Are you back in Drake's Springs? Are you all right?" she asked, her voice caught between concern and coldness.

"Yes. No."

"No? What happened?" my father asked.

"Right after Felipe got across the border he was caught; they murdered him. And when we got here tonight, we found out Virgil Schoenfeld died of a stroke last week. The Memorial Meeting will be tomorrow afternoon."

"Oh, Katie. I'm so sorry," my mother said, her tone immediately changing, "about both Felipe and Virgil. I know how much you liked Virgil and respected him." We talked for a few minutes, lingering tension preventing us from having a long conversation.

My father asked, "Are you coming home soon?"

"Yes, though I'm not sure when." I recalled what Mother Clare had said about forgiveness. "I know you're still angry with me, but please don't shut me out. I want to do a better job of explaining why I felt I had to do this. I want to tell you what I've learned from it."

My mother responded, "We've been upset and confused about your decision, Kate, but we would never shut you out. Never." I promised I'd call again in a day or two for a longer conversation.

I filled the morning hours with routine household chores and unpacking. Calling Maggie a little before Virgil's service was to begin, I asked, "What is a Quaker memorial like?"

"They're simple, of course. Like any Meeting for Worship, the Memorial Meetings are conducted in silence, with Friends and attenders speaking if they feel moved to do so. I think this service will have many people sharing messages."

"I'll see you at the Meetinghouse."

# Chapter 40

SLIPPING INTO MY USUAL place, I saw Paul and the Camerons on the facing bench. I made myself look at the bench where Eleanor and Virgil usually sat, and yes, Eleanor was there, with two men I didn't recognize, one on either side of her. The benches had been placed closer to the center of the room to allow for folding chairs to be set up behind them. Through the window, I saw a van with "Mount Gilead AME Church" painted on the side. The van doors opened, and several people got out and entered the Meetinghouse together.

A little after two o'clock, people stopped entering. After a short period of silence, Paul stood and began speaking, his words unhurried. "We are here to give thanks for, and celebrate the life of, Virgil Morgan Schoenfeld." He explained for those not accustomed to the Quaker form of worship what was involved in a service conducted "in the manner of Friends," and then he introduced one of the women who had come in the van. "We'd like to welcome Miriam Showalter, the director of the choir at Mount Gilead Church in Lovingston."

A tiny woman in a simple black dress and hat walked to the center of the room. "My dear Friends," she began, "since August 1969, we have considered Virgil Schoenfeld to be our brother."

I heard a man behind me murmur, "Amen."

Miriam continued. "Virgil came over to Nelson County for months on end after Hurricane Camille, as did so many others. He helped us bury our dead. He spent so many hours cleaning out wreckage that he had to lie down on the ground and sleep until he had the energy to drive home. He prayed with us. He made us believe in hope again. He and Eleanor often came to worship with us, even when we stood in a circle in the mud before the church was rebuilt. He fell in love with our music. One morning, when the work crews gathered for their assignments that day, he asked me if I would sing a hymn. And then he asked if I would sing at the end of the day. Before long, it became a tradition. We all sang together. I brought some of my choir with me today, and Sister Eleanor, with your permission, my dear, sweet lady, we'd like to sing one of Virgil's favorites." I saw Eleanor nod and smile at Miriam. The choir members came to the front. "This hymn is from Zimbabwe, and it is called 'Uyai Mose,' which means, 'Come, All You People.'"

Their rich, resonant voices filled the small sanctuary until the room, so often quiet, was awash in glorious sound. At the end of the song, when the choir members slipped back to their seats, one of the men next to Eleanor stood and offered his place to Miriam. She accepted, putting her arm around Eleanor and drawing her close.

Soon thereafter, a man Virgil's age stood. "Virgil and I were college roommates. The Second World War interrupted our education, but we kept in touch and when we returned home, Virgil and I got together. He was disturbed by what he'd seen during the war, the destruction of so many lives, of so much promise. Since then, we've written back and forth, with his letters recording his despair and disillusionment concerning the goodness of people. After a long period of questioning and agonizing, he arrived at a more hopeful stage based on his faith. In this Meetinghouse I have felt the source of the strength Virgil drew on for his life's journey."

It was difficult to imagine Virgil ever having a time of intense doubting. He'd seemed so sure, despite what he'd said to me about wandering in a dark house with stairs. But wasn't it Virgil who had said something about my doubts being my contribution to Meeting? Now I would never get to share with him my experiences on the trip. I had counted on discussing what I'd felt and observed, on having his wisdom distill what was essential for me to learn.

Three more people from Meeting and one person who was not a Quaker stood and spoke, commenting on what part Virgil had played in their lives. I couldn't focus on their reminiscences, their voices drifting above my head. In the pauses, I chanted to myself: don't think, don't feel, don't cry.

Silence—restless, uneasy.

Calming me down after I killed the snake. Cleaning around the shed for me. His pleasure at the loaf of bread, my offering of thanks. The ride in his sleigh at Christmas. His acceptance of who I was in the present, as well as who I might become in the future. Now I understood that although

I'd missed the signs of a stroke in him, he had perceived the signs of brain damage in me.

The man sitting next to Eleanor rose. "Most of you probably don't recognize me because it's been so many years since I was here. I am Jacob McDonough." Several Friends raised their heads and turned toward him. "The last time I was here, Scott Stillman," he gestured to the other man who had been sitting with Eleanor, "Morgan, Virgil and Eleanor's son, and I lost our appeals to be conscientious objectors during Vietnam. Scott went to Canada, and Morgan and I went to Vietnam. Virgil stood by all three of us, believing we each had to follow our convictions. All these years, Virgil regularly wrote and called Scott and me. His compassionate support helped me to relinquish my bitterness and anger." He gazed down at Eleanor. "Even when I was despondent and railed against his help, Virgil refused to let me go. I owe him my life."

Silence—fragile, tentative.

Holding my hand during those Quaker graces in their home, his grasp warm and comforting. Keeping the conversation going when my parents came to visit. Teaching me how to walk in snowshoes. Our long talk by the fire in the preserve's shelter, his ability to be both forthright and kind. Camping out in my lane to make sure no one hurt me.

Silence—deep, inward.

Offering to take my place and go with Paul if I wanted to back out. Telling me I had a "courageous spirit" and to trust it and to trust the divine spark within me. Virgil, Virgil. If there is not an ultimate peace, there is no point to such pain.

After a long silence which had felt like a prelude to the Rise of Meeting, Paul stood and instead began speaking of Virgil, his voice attenuated at first, then growing stronger. "It was such a humbling honor when Virgil and Eleanor deeded their son's land to me. I felt their gift was overwhelmingly generous but highly impractical. I didn't know anything about running a farm, and at the time, didn't want to learn. Virgil knew I wasn't a replacement for Morgan, and I knew he wasn't a substitute for my father; no one person replaces another. But we planted and harvested, weathered droughts, and watched growing things blossom. We both began to heal. Virgil, always through example, guided me into manhood.

"Some of you here worked alongside Virgil to clean up and rebuild after Hurricane Camille." Paul nodded to Miriam. "Most of you have witnessed

Virgil's unceasing efforts for peace and social justice. You've pounded nails with him on a Habitat house; you've gone on one of his legendary camping trips with inner city youths where he, as the most unlikely to do so, would pull one practical joke after another; or you've watched as he relentlessly questioned a particular state senator." Paul gestured to a gentleman near him, and I recognized the retired legislator who chuckled and nodded to Paul. People around the room smiled.

"The image with me this afternoon, though, is of Virgil with a doll. Friends will remember that several years ago one of the Young Friends died after a sudden illness." I closed my eyes, feeling as though I'd been punched. Did I know the family who had gone through such unspeakable sorrow? "The Meeting felt a heartrending anguish, unlike anything we'd experienced before or since. In getting the sanctuary ready for the Memorial Meeting, we gathered a few favorite toys of this child and placed them on the facing bench. One of the toys was a doll this child had treasured, and it showed the signs of wear resulting from being taken everywhere. Her doll was a faithful member of Meeting and had attended many a Shared Meal. Virgil took this cherished doll home on the evening before the service. He washed the doll and washed and pressed her clothes. With his large hands that had designed and built bridges and buildings, he fixed one of her tiny shoes. He combed her long hair, braided it, and tied fresh, new ribbons into bows." Paul stopped and took a deep breath. "He knew, with unerring insight, that she would have wanted her baby doll looking her best. With that one compassionate act, he showed me he was the strongest of men because he was also the gentlest."

Silence—pure, radiant, Light-filled.

# Chapter 41

DIANE AND I HAD a series of marathon phone calls. "This entire stay in Drake's Springs has changed you, hasn't it? The Quakers, getting involved with the sanctuary movement, breaking up with David, resigning your job, Paul—oh, my stars and garters, Kate."

"Please tell me that expression doesn't come from your students."

"Grandma Marie, though its origins go back to the eighteen hundreds."

"You're right that this time here has changed me, the people and the place. And to throw a mountain saying your way, 'I can't keep a bird from flying over my head, but I can keep it from building a nest in my hair.' I'm trying to give things I cannot change less power over me."

"I love it! Those long-ago Scotch-Irish and Welsh settlers had such rich descriptions."

"I have an even better one: 'I don't care if it harelips granny.'"

She started laughing. "I don't care if it *what*?"

"'If it harelips granny.' It means you don't care about the consequences."

"I'm writing it down, and I'll actively look for an opportunity to use it. In fact, I'll *create* the opportunity."

"When I leave here, I'd like to come see you. Would that be all right?"

She hesitated. "It's hard right now."

"I know. That's why I'm coming. I am indebted to you for so much, Diane. Please allow me this privilege."

Maggie had promised to teach me how to make an apple pie. We sat at my kitchen table and peeled the apples. "Have you seen Eleanor?" she asked.

"Not since the Memorial Meeting, and I didn't get to speak to her then. There were so many visitors who wanted to talk to her. I left a note in her mailbox, and as soon as she returns from her sister's, I'll go see her." I started telling Maggie about the trip.

"What happened to Felipe?"

"I'm not sure, and Paul won't tell me the specifics of what he saw. We got so close. We'd had him with us for a time, and he'd gotten over the border." I told her about Paul being attacked. "It was truly awful."

We stopped talking for a moment, and then she asked, "How was the traveling with Paul? Did he argue well?"

"How do you know we argued?"

"A man and a woman spend several weeks in a car doing something illegal, and they don't argue? Come on. Surely you had at least one disagreement over directions."

"You're right, of course. We had some conflicts, but we know each other better now."

"What did you learn from him?"

I rolled out the dough for the piecrust while I thought about her question. "The importance of forgiveness. To be more accepting of what is and move on. Not to get stuck where I am."

"What did he learn from you?"

"That question never would have occurred to me. I don't know what to answer."

"Do you love him?"

"You come right to the point, don't you?"

"Being cautious can shield you from the joyful things in life, not just the painful ones. Keep in mind a fainthearted woman never caught a good man. So yes, I do come right to the point. Can you come right to the answer? Be your heart a-quiverin'?"

"Oh, Maggie, what a perfect description. Yes. I know we haven't known each other long, but yes, I love him. Without doubt, without reservation. And he knows I do. We need to get to know each other better, so that's the next step."

"Hallelujah, amen! You've come to your senses at last."

I thought of something my mother had said that day on her porch swing. I could put a name to the foreign feeling inside me, after all: I felt giddy.

As soon as she opened the door, my rehearsed speech of condolence left me. "Eleanor." Standing in the doorway, we held each other. She felt frail but her arms held me tightly.

"Come in, child. It is good to have thee back."

Please, Eleanor, I thought, don't use Quaker speech. Heaven knows I
don't need to cry anymore. She led me out to the sunroom where she'd set
the table. "Let's have tea," she said in a brisk tone, having recovered from the
moment.

From a cloth-covered basket, she withdrew hot muffins. "People have
brought more food than a body can eat, and I've put most of it in the freezer.
I like storing up kindness, being able to bring it out when I need it." She
served my tea. "How was the journey?"

"Painfully sad. And exceptional. Humbling. I wrote in the journal,
mostly impressions of the people we met and how I felt. It was the best idea,
thank you. I'd like to share it with you one day." I started describing our
hosts and the mission.

She stopped me. "Tell me, what happened?"

"Do you really want to know?"

"Yes. Virgil would have asked. I don't need to be coddled, Katherine.
Being a witness for peace often means being a witness to the horrors we
commit as humans."

I told her everything: the people who helped us along the way, the
numbing fear, being hunted down, the poverty, the attack on Paul, our desperate search for Felipe, his body in the ditch. I stopped and we both waited,
letting the images and the events I'd experienced settle into the leveling
quiet.

"And what about you and your time in Drake's Springs?" she asked.

"I'm not sure I found what I was searching for." I sipped the hot tea and
took a bite of the muffin.

"Do you know now what it was?"

"Not fully, no."

"Maybe it's not necessary to come to a full understanding. It might be
one of those mysteries that gets unfolded over time."

"That's what Virgil would say."

"You brought him such joy. We had long discussions about you, especially right after you left. He admired your determination to fashion a new
life."

"It was from necessity. This searching for a new life is painstaking
work. I hadn't known about his previous stroke, but it explains, in part, the
connection I felt with him. He knew what it was like to reconstruct one's life,
didn't he? It was an honor to have known him, even for such a short time."

"What now for you?"

"I still don't know what I'll do." I started to evade, to say I'd be making
some changes, but finished with the truth. "However, I'll be coming back
here."

"What about Paul?"

"Am I that transparent, or has the Quaker grapevine been working overtime?"

"Dear child, we've known all along; we were waiting for the two of you to realize it. Sometimes it happens this way. And when something is right and joyful, why would you want to keep it a secret? Don't be afraid to embrace it, Katherine; such a love is rare and sustaining."

When we'd finished the tea, she picked up a box from beside her chair and handed it to me. "This is for you."

Inside was an afghan knitted in shades of plum, blue, and cream. "How beautiful!"

"It was the perfect distraction for me when Virgil and Paul were away, and I finished it during those terrible days and nights by Virgil's side after his stroke. I don't know what I would have done with myself otherwise."

"Thank you, Eleanor, I'll treasure it."

She came outside with me. "How much longer do you think you'll be here?"

"Another week, maybe. I have finished my work for the most part."

"I had hoped you would stay through the summer." She stooped to pull weeds from a flowerbed.

I asked her, "You'll call me if you need anything?" It struck me how often I'd been the recipient of that offer and how, in a sense, it epitomized what it meant to be part of a community.

She nodded and added in such a low voice that I leaned over to hear her, "I miss him with such an aching sharpness, but I know it will soften. Because of Morgan, I know that someone you've loved so completely never truly leaves you."

# Chapter 42

MY LAST MEETING HAPPENED to be the final one for the Salvadoran refugees as well. Jacob McDonough and Scott Stillman had volunteered to take them to a Canadian Meeting that would help them get settled. The Drake's Springs Meeting had become increasingly concerned for their safety.

Paul and I sat with the Delgado family, and Magdalena held my hand. I thought about having to start over and about the months spent here. I had made progress in coming to terms with what I couldn't do. I'd gone caving and camping. Learned to make bread. Tried belly dancing. Faced my nightmares. Asked myself hard questions and found some answers. Made good friends. Took a large risk for a principle. Searched for faith and adventure. Discovered the values and layers of silence. A few times I accepted a warm coat. I confronted what I had finally named. And I fell in love—this time for real, for good, for deep, as Maggie would say. This was the best list I'd ever made.

Magdalena stood, and Tomás translated for her. "'My eyes, they are full of tears at leaving, but my heart is full as well because you have brought me to my family. We are thankful for everything and for everyone here.'" She tried to say more but shook her head and sat down.

At the Rise of Meeting, Sharon called for announcements. After the usual notices of committee meetings and coming events, I stood, trying to remember what I'd wanted to say. I looked at the Friends assembled in the Meetinghouse, searching out those I knew best: Paul. Eleanor. Maggie, Cooper, and Abby. Ruth and Adam. Will and Sharon. Graciela, Tomás, and their children. Emilio and Magdalena. The light coming in from the windows skimmed over their heads and brightened their faces.

"Though at some point I'm planning to return, I will be leaving tomorrow. Like Magdalena said, my heart is full." I tried to steady my voice. "The Delgado family came here seeking safety and sanctuary. I came searching for a haven as well, a place to finish recovering. Most of you don't know I was injured by a drunk driver. Not wanting to continue being his victim, I kept it a secret and tried to reinvent my life here. I thought my anger and bitterness had consumed me, but you taught me about courage and faith." I looked at Paul, and the last of my composure started to splinter. "You taught me about love and forgiveness. I am grateful beyond measure."

The Meeting enfolded me in a last blessing of silence—healing, accepting, loving.

After we had lunch together, we congregated in the yard to say goodbye to the Salvadoran family. On the front steps of the Meetinghouse, Eleanor talked to Jacob while everyone in the Delgado family hugged and kissed me. Graciela pressed something into my hand. I held it while they climbed into a van and drove down the lane. When I opened my hand, I saw she had given me her wooden rosary, the one Felipe and his brothers had carved for her, one of her few personal possessions from home. I recalled how she'd wound it around her fingers when the Meeting discussed offering sanctuary to her mother and Emilio. I clutched it and closed my eyes. With wordless, profound dignity, she was telling me that she felt I'd done everything I could.

Maggie came up to me and I held up my hand. "No long goodbyes, Maggie, I'll be back."

"You'd better, or I'll hunt you down and twirl you dizzy. Leaving early tomorrow?"

"Yes. I'm going home for a few days, then flying to Vermont to be with a good friend of mine for a couple of weeks."

She hugged me hard. "You take care now, pioneer woman."

I went back into the Meetinghouse for one last look. Paul rose from the facing bench, met me in the middle of the room, and wrapped me in his arms. "I'll call you," he promised. "Hurry back. Drake's Springs needs its resident pool shark."

Waking before the sunrise, I ate breakfast on the back porch. After checking all the rooms, appliances, and windows at least three times, I picked up the remaining items and looked back at the living room. I would miss this cabin in the mountains. Opening the front door, I almost ran into a box. Stepping around it to put my things in the car, I returned to close and lock the door and open the box. Nestled securely inside was a vase containing beautiful cream roses, tinged with pink. The card read, "Way will open. Keeping thee in the Light. Love, Paul."

I drove to the main road, stopping to get my basket from the tree. Every night I'd placed it there with sandwiches and treats for those watching over me. The note inside read, "We will miss you, Katherine Solterra." All my protectors, except for Virgil, of course, had signed their names, including Grady Mulroney. I had no idea he'd been part of the group, assuming they all had been members of the Meeting. There were a few other names I didn't recognize.

Approaching the preserve, I decided to walk around one last time. Though I knew the Friends would make sure it was maintained, who could take care of it with the same love and attention as Virgil? I scooped birdseed from one of the bins and refilled a couple of the feeding stations. This place had given me such solace. "Virgil, I will miss thee." Driving away, I heard the words, "Courage. Faith," in Virgil's voice.

The End

# Acknowledgments

D. M. Hanzlik has been my cheerleader, not just with this book, but for most of my life. In junior high school, when I spilled chocolate milk on the white dress she had just finished making, she calmly smiled and said the stain would wash out. I knew then she would always be my loyal, kind, loving friend.

Bobby Kemp, my high school English teacher, encouraged me to write, and in his classroom he provided a safe haven for me as a fledgling writer.

Professor Lynne Scott Constantine compelled me to look critically at every word and fostered a love for the structure of literary works. Her expectations for her students provided the standard for me when I began teaching.

Martina Eason, my friend and former colleague, showered me with encouragement, blessed me with her wise counsel, and stayed faithfully by my side when I needed her the most. She always held me "in the Light."

Rosa Margarita Gaído, my friend and former colleague, corrected my Spanish (any errors are mine!) and gave invaluable advice on linguistic and cultural nuances. Every day, she brings flair, passion, and grace to her classroom.

Steve Patti, OFM, answered my questions concerning Catholic practices and beliefs, and he generously forgave me when I lied to him—twice—after he asked if I were writing a book. I couldn't admit to such an outlandish undertaking. He loves books and reading as much as I do.

Laura Shaughnessy, PhD, lost me about four words into her first sentence when she explained the nature of her work as a neurobiologist. She helped me to shape the way Kate walked in the world as a scientist.

Shanna Holden's friendship has been like the lone blossom in the desert for me. She slogged through the manuscript twice, gave insightful comments, and suggested the belly dancing scene. She and her mother, Tammy, gave the discussion questions a trial run and provided excellent feedback.

As a former attender primarily at Richmond Friends Meeting and Augusta Friends Worship Group, I found a home in the healing layers of silence; these Friends enriched my life and gave me solace.

And for Richard, for being my Valentine.

# Discussion Questions

1. On a daily basis, Kate curses the drunk driver who hurt her. What enables Kate to reach the point where she calls the driver by name for the first time and pledges to stop cursing him, even though she's not yet ready to forgive him? Have you ever been wronged and had a difficult time forgiving the other person? Have you experienced forgiveness not being extended to you?

2. The Religious Society of Friends, the Quakers, may not be very familiar to many people. Known for their efforts to promote peace and social justice around the world, two Quaker service organizations received the Nobel Peace Prize in 1947 for their relief work. Did anything about their method of worship or their beliefs as portrayed in the novel resonate with you?

3. The sanctuary movement was as controversial during the Salvadoran Civil War (1980–1992) as it is today. This is not a novel about politics or policies, however, but about responding to doubt with faith, to fear with courage, and to anger with forgiveness. It is also about "welcoming the stranger" in our midst, which includes Kate as well as the refugees. The Quakers are not naive about the strong opinions the issue evokes, but their decisions emanate from the biblical injunction to treat the stranger with kindness and compassion. Does having this perspective make dealing with such a divisive issue easier? Is it a countercultural view?

4. Kate explains to the Meeting that her strong connection to the Delgado family results from the shared experience of being forced to start over. What else, however, might be driving this connection?

5. Concerning the men at her store objecting to the Quakers' involvement with the refugees, Maggie says, "It sometimes seems like the most intolerant people are the same ones who thump the Bible the loudest." Do you think there is any truth to her statement? Is she being overly cynical? How might her experiences affect this belief?

6. When Maggie tells Kate about her abusive marriage, she says, "Like so many women, I saw the warning signals but ignored them, starved for attention and thirsty for affection, for someone who thought I was special." Do some women ignore warning signals in navigating relationships? If so, why do you think they do?

7. Kate, Eleanor, and Maggie all have dealt with profound anger. What do you think enables each woman to move from the anger toward a greater peace?

8. Kate's mother questions why she has continued her relationship with David when they never had seemed to be right for each other. Why has Kate continued her involvement with David? Why, when he treats her with dismissiveness, does she try so hard to keep the relationship going after the accident?

9. Paul treats Kate with more compassion and respect than David does; however, what qualities of his might prove to be problematic if their relationship moves forward? Does Paul seem too good to be true? Do you feel Kate has made too hasty a decision concerning a relationship with Paul?

10. Paul tells Kate that although putting forgiveness into action is difficult, the choice of forgiving instead of harboring anger is an easy one to make. Do you agree? Do you think Kate will be able to forgive herself for the possibility that she jeopardized Felipe's rescue?

11. Several Quakers, and Kate herself, state that it is highly unlikely they'd allow a new attender to join Paul on the journey. Why do you think they do? Do you feel she should have been allowed to go?

12. Even before her accident, Kate experienced a loss of faith, despite having grown up in the church. What events in the book do you feel have pulled Kate closer to regaining her faith? Have you ever had times when you doubted your faith? Or, if you are not a believer, have you had times when you wished you did have faith?

13. Kate struggles with the aftermath of her accident, and she constantly laments not being able to move forward. Is there anything that would have helped her to do so sooner than she does?

14. Given the fact that Kate, by her own admission, follows the rules and maintains "a life as precise as a porcupine's quills," does it seem too "out of character" for her to plan a permanent move to Drake's Springs?

15. Maggie's grandmother says, "Truth will stand when the world's on fire." What truths has Kate learned about herself during the course of her time in Drake's Springs? What experiences have you had that taught you truths about yourself?

www.ingramcontent.com/pod-product-compliance
Lightning Source LLC
Chambersburg PA
CBHW051147030726
47504CB00004B/1084